Bitten by Frost

A Dystopian Shifter Romance

Romance

Jemma Weir

Jemma Weir

ALSO BY

HIGHLAND RIFT PACK

Buried by Earth

Bitten by Frost

Battered by Storms

ERNIE SMITH

Finding Death's Scythe

In the Cards

The Life and Chaos of a Retired Old God – Short Story
Collection

STANDALONE

Wishing For Truths – Short Story

Contents

CHAPTER ONE

MITCHEL STEPPED OFF THE train into a flurry of snow. It drifted lazily around him, not quite thick enough to hide the 'Welcome to Huntly' sign, but it was only a matter of time, going by the look of the clouds. The snow was set to fall for at least the next few days. Or until the weather warden got it under control.

He pulled in a breath, enjoying the crisp air, clean despite the hint of diesel and hot metal from the train. It was a nice change from the heavy pollution-layered air that made up Glasgow.

Someone had cleared the platform's edge, so dragging his suitcase under the station's limited shelter was easy. The building had a wide awning, large windows that showed hard plastic seats, and a very bored-looking ticket seller behind a Perspex screen.

A quick scan showed several cars in the car park, but they were all covered with thick snow, and no one got out. Mitchel's lift wasn't here yet. But to be fair, he was late, and he'd only been able to get a text through less than ten minutes ago. He could wait.

Behind him, the train chuffed and ticked as the hot metal cooled, but it didn't continue onto its next stop. It wasn't going to for some time if the weather forecast was accurate.

'We can't stay here,' a voice to Mitchel's left said. A young man huddled in his wool coat, shivering as he grabbed the train conductor's arm. 'Do you know how close the Rift Scar is?'

The Highland Rift Scar was over fifteen miles from Huntly, but Mitchel didn't correct him. It probably wouldn't help the nervous man feel any better.

Huntly had been one of the first towns to be reclaimed after the Fae War had ended over a hundred years ago. The Scottish weren't about to let a little thing like a corrupted beast-infested wasteland stop them from taking back their hometown.

The conductor was a squat man with a round waist that wasn't entirely hidden by his yellow hi-vis jacket. He kept his smile as he spoke to the young man who'd grabbed him. 'The weather ahead has blocked the line, as I've already said. You need to wait until it's cleared.' The conductor avoided responding to the Rift Scar comment altogether.

Not that it helped calm the man down. 'You're welcome to wait on the train or at the station.'

The conductor indicated to the small station building, then frowned at Mitchel, looking him up and down. Considering that Mitchel was the only one not arguing, he didn't know what he'd done to deserve that look.

'We can't stay here,' the man said again, looking back at the small group still on the train. 'It's not safe. What if something escapes the Rift?'

'I can assure you that Huntly hasn't seen a Rift creature in decades. The local rift rangers do an excellent job keeping us safe.' The conductor's voice was growing cooler by the moment. Mitchel wondered how often he'd had to deal with this kind of mentality. He was certainly more patient than Mitchel would have been.

'Great,' the man said, curling his lips. 'I feel so much safer knowing Mutts and Sparkles protect me.'

Mitchel tightened his grip on his suitcase handle, feeling the cold seep into his skin. He hadn't heard that slur to describe Shifters and Elementals in a long time, and he was no happier to hear it here. It didn't matter what they did or how long it had been; some people would never accept anything from the Rift Bloodlines.

He stepped towards the confrontation, then jumped as a hand fell on his shoulder. Mitchel turned to see a familiar man had moved up beside him. Oliver was tall, with broad shoulders, brown hair, and a wicked sense of humour. Today, he was dressed in a thick grey waterproof coat that was closed up tightly and dark blue jeans. He'd bulked up in the six months since Mitchel had seen him, not that he'd been small before.

'Don't give him the satisfaction of engaging,' Oliver said as he watched the group on the train with a flash of yellow in his eyes. There was no anger in the look, just disappointment. 'Someone like him isn't worth the breath needed to argue.'

Mitchel wished he could have been as quick to disregard the comment, even if he knew Oliver was right. 'After all these years, you'd think they'd appreciate the work the rangers do. They wouldn't be impressed if the Rift creatures started raiding again,' Mitchel said, turning away from the group as snow flurried into his face.

'They don't have that kind of foresight,' Oliver said, then he gave Mitchel a lopsided grin, which turned serious. 'You going to be okay with the weather?'

At the reminder of the weather, the air stirred, the cold pressing into Mitchel, trying to worm its way under his skin. It took effort not to allow it in. It always took effort.

'I'll be fine,' Mitchel said, trying to sound confident. He'd rarely spent time in places that were this cold, but he'd learned a long time ago how to hide that he was a Frost Elemental. A little snow wasn't going to change that.

Not that being a Frost Elemental was a problem in itself, even if it was pretty rare. But when neither of his parents were Frost, it was a secret that could ruin his family's position. God forbid he ruin his mother's lifestyle.

Mitchel bit down on the bitter thought before it could bring down his mood further. The decision to pretend he was a Water Elemental had been his, even if he'd been too young at fourteen to understand what it would mean. Now, he was stuck with the lie that he was so weak in Water Magic that he could barely raise a bead of water. He'd keep that secret even out here in the middle of nowhere, which meant suppressing the need to let the frost in.

Oliver gave him a look like he wasn't convinced Mitchel's fast answer was true. Oliver was one of only a handful of people who knew the truth. 'And that's why you're not wearing a jacket?'

Mitchel bit back a curse. He hadn't remembered to put on his jacket over his short-sleeved T-shirt. It wasn't that he couldn't feel the cold, he could. Every inch of snow around him pounded his senses, trying to pull him to connect. But it didn't chill his skin. If anything, it did the opposite.

'Thank you,' Mitchel said as he pulled his jacket out of the backpack and put it on. If not for Oliver, Mitchel wasn't sure he'd have made it past that first year after he'd come into his power and it had still been a secret.

The conductor blew his whistle, drawing Mitchel's focus again.

'The roads are still clear, so unless you want to hire a car and drive, you'll be staying here,' the conductor said to the broader group, his tone now far from polite. It looked like he'd had enough.

Mitchel shook his head at the shocked sounds from the passengers. He'd initially been scheduled to get a later train, but when the weather changed, he hadn't wanted to risk getting left out. He'd switched his tickets, which had been a good decision by the looks of it.

'Come on, let's get you to the hotel,' Oliver said, turning towards the car park behind them. A single car free of snow was now parked there. 'Then we can make the most of the free afternoon.'

'Has anyone else arrived yet?' Mitchel asked as he threw his bag over his shoulder again, trying to tramp down on his excitement as he thought about why he was there. To find out how the Rift Scar had shrunk. He let his magic seep into the ice and snow under him, stopping it from melting into his jeans.

The Rift Scars in the UK had been monitored ever since the Rifts had closed. In the last hundred years, there hadn't been any changes in size. Until two weeks ago, when the local rift surveyor had submitted a report that no one had expected to see. A change. New grass was growing where the Rift Scar had been.

Every scientist Mitchel knew had been discussing this trip north to discover how they could replicate what had happened in the Highland Rift Scar.

'No idea. But your boss is supposed to be sending the list of who's coming to Hale. No mention yet on how or when they're getting here,' Oliver said, glancing back at him as they arrived at his car. 'Did they not tell you?'

'No. But that's not unusual. The Institute of Rift Studies and Defence isn't exactly great at communication,' Mitchel said, shaking his head. That was putting it mildly. Someone in the IRS&D had put together this research trip a little too quickly, and apart from a letter with instructions on where to be and when, he'd had little else. 'Who's on the list?'

'I don't know,' Oliver said, eyes flashing to amber. This time, there was heat there as he looked around.

'Is everything okay?' Mitchel asked. Wolves tended towards territorial, but Oliver was usually a lot more laid back. Maybe working in the Rift Scar had changed some of those instincts.

'You know how us wolves get when too many strangers come into our space,' Oliver said, avoiding Mitchel's eyes. 'But enough of that. I've the perfect place to show you. You'll love it. It's got the best whisky.'

That Oliver wanted to go for drinks wasn't a surprise. He liked to party and wasn't wearing his rift ranger uniform. But it was evident that he was trying to avoid the topic of the scientists arriving.

'No one is coming to cause problems. We just want to know what happened to the Rift Scar,' Mitchel said, keeping his voice soft, but Oliver's shoulders tightened further. 'Maybe with that knowledge, we can get rid of the Rift Scars once and for all.'

'I believe you want that, yes,' Oliver said, giving a short huff of breath as they reached his car, and he took Mitchel's bag to put it in the boot. After closing it firmly, he turned to look back at the train. 'But apparently everyone but you is a Shifter. It feels a little like we're being invaded.'

'All of them?' Mitchel asked. Having an entire group of Shifter scientists was unusual. Shifters tended towards more physical jobs, and there weren't many who'd trained to be scientists. At least, not that Mitchel knew.

'That's what Hale thinks, though we can't be sure without the list,' Oliver said. Hale was the local alpha and the rift warden. There was a level of respect when Oliver spoke about him that Mitchel hadn't heard before. Though to be fair, he'd met Oliver's old alpha and father, and he wasn't someone to inspire anything but fear. 'But enough of business. We have all of tonight before work tomorrow. I want to hear about everything I've missed.'

Mitchel wanted to press, but there were things that happened in the pack that Oliver couldn't talk about. It made Mitchel glad Elementals didn't have a pack-like structure or connection. Having someone who had sway over what you could do and say sounded like a shit way to live.

The thought settled, then twisted as Mitchel realised his life was no less restricted. It was just his mum's guilt trip that bound him, not an alpha.

He got in the passenger seat as Oliver slid into the front.

'They sent us on a crash course on how to deal with the Rift Scar,' Mitchel said as he clicked in his seat belt.

The tension dropped out of Oliver's shoulders, and he smiled. 'A crash course? Did they walk you through a PowerPoint?' he said, smiling as he looked over his shoulder to reverse.

'No. It was an entire half-day of field training. I got to fire a gun,' Mitchel said, smiling despite the strange tension with the pack.

Oliver laughed. 'Did anyone shoot themselves?'

'Well, not exactly,' Mitchel said, wincing at the memory. It had been a hard lesson, mainly on the group's pride. Then a lot of frustration as none of them got picked to come north.

He relaxed further into the chair, telling Oliver the story in all its ridiculous detail. Maybe if the rest of the scientists were due to get the next train, Mitchel might have a few days to hang out with Oliver before they arrived. He'd not realised how much he'd missed his friend and being around someone who knew his secret until now.

THE ARMOURY WAS SILENT except for the hum of the air filtration system and the click as Amelia slotted the last piece into her rifle. It hadn't been fired during her patrol, but the damned snow had been nonstop, and the gun had got damp and needed to be oiled.

Between the training in London and her three months working in the Rift Scar, dismantling the SA80 A2 was nearly second nature now. But Amelia was still slower than the rest of her patrol, who'd already cleaned and returned their weapons to the armourer.

Bored, Luna, her wolf said, chuffing a breath. *Claws quicker to clean.*

I'm almost done, Amelia said, pushing down a sigh, patience thinning. This was the fourth time her wolf had complained in nearly as many minutes. *We're on patrol again tomorrow. We could offer to be wolf scouts? Then we won't have to clean weapons when we get back.*

Not like Rift Scar, Luna said, turning her back with a huff of air that sounded more human than wolf. The snark had, as always, gone over her wolf's rather literal head. *Smells bad. Not good hunting.*

Amelia shook her head. She needed to remember that for the next time. If her wolf stayed quiet.

The room had four metal tables in the middle for cleaning weapons, a worktop that split off the armoury from the store, and a door that led out into the main building.

She picked up her rifle and put it on the worktop divider. The armourer nodded, motioning he'd be a minute. He was a quiet man, human, short, medium build, and uninterested in talking except where he had to. She nodded at him and turned back to clean up the table she'd used.

The paper she'd put down was damp with no signs of Rift dust, but she folded it up anyway and put it in the biohazard bin. Anything originating from the Rift Scar could make humans sick, so there were special procedures to dispose of the waste.

The scent of rotten meat left to go putrid in the sun rose around her as she closed the lid to the bin. There really was nothing quite like the stench of the Rift Scar. Even with the snow, the smell clung to everything that went near the place.

Run in forest. Clean nose, Luna said, sending Amelia images of doing just that.

Not tonight. Remember, I'm going out, Amelia said, though she felt the pull as well. The freedom of it. Especially since Sam had changed the land agreement. They could shift and hunt any time they wanted.

Not want drink, Luna said sulkily. *Want hunt.*

You had last night. Tonight, it's my turn to have fun, Amelia said, turning back as the armourer called her name.

'Thanks,' Amelia said as she signed the log for the weapon he'd given her. He grunted, took her rifle and log back towards its designated cage, and locked it up.

Armour man could have cleaned it, Luna said with a huff, still unhappy.

It's not his job, Amelia said. Though there wasn't exactly much else for him to do between patrol shifts coming and going.

The door at the opposite end of the room opened, and Kenneth walked in. He was taller than her at six-one, but only just. Dark shoulder-length hair covered his dirt-coloured eyes. His smile when he saw her was too broad, almost predatory, as he stalked in her direction.

'Baby, are you still cleaning? I'd have helped if I'd known,' Kenneth said, drawing out the word baby. His scent said he wanted to help with something else altogether.

Not need help, Luna said, showing teeth, though Kenneth wouldn't see it. Neither of them was a fan, but Kenneth hadn't been on her patrol.

'What do you want?' she asked, not bothering to engage with him or the look he gave her. Her anger grew sharper, deeper. She pushed down on it, fighting the snarl that rose and loosening her cramped fingers, not realising she'd closed her fist.

Luna pushed so close that Amelia could almost feel her fur. *Calm. Not hunt pack. Even stupid pack.*

I know, I know, Amelia said, forcing her anger back a little further. She'd not lose her temper.

'You have to ask?' Kenneth said, either ignoring her anger or deliberately trying to push her buttons. With Kenneth, it was impossible to tell.

'Not interested,' she said, tone moderately polite.

Kenneth smiled like he didn't believe her. 'Next time then, baby.' He turned away, heading towards the patrol rota that had been put up, claiming his section. They were assigned shifts already, so it was just a case of picking an area to patrol.

The armourer gave her a brief look that implied she was the one being unreasonable. Maybe she was. But she didn't want Kenneth.

We find better, Luna said, pulling back. *Not need weak mate.*

Amelia turned and left but didn't answer her wolf. They didn't need any mate. She was happy by herself.

Outside in the hallway, she dragged in a breath to clear the lingering smells of Rift Scar and Kenneth. Old sweat, leather, and pack filled her nose, all familiar. But other scents mixed in were less familiar—hopefully temporary. Chemicals, hot metal, and brick dust. She let out the breath and headed towards the combined stink.

The building was an ugly brown-brick three-storey rectangular box that sat slightly apart from the rest of the industrial estate. Years ago, Hale had converted one half of it from an old gym into the rangers' base of operations.

The ground floor had been converted into the armoury, storage for their gear, and a kitchen. But the upper floors still held parts of the original gym for training, showers, a small space converted to allow those on rapid response to sleep and a studio apartment at the top.

Hale had negotiated with the owners earlier this month to let them use the second half of the building for Sam's rift surveyor machines. Since no one had wanted to rent the building next to the rangers' headquarters, it had been an easy win all round.

Over the past month, Hale had been helping Sam move all her monitoring and analytical machines here, letting her separate work from home. In reality, the IRS&D should have done it years ago, but not having to pay rent had been too much of an appeal for them to bother.

Amelia paused at the entrance to the new section. The door was still missing, and the walls were unfinished, but most of the machines that had once lived in Sam's garage now sat in the room.

'Come on, you can do it,' Sam whispered to a large machine with green writing on the screen. It beeped quietly. She was a petite woman, barely over five feet, with thick blond curls and green eyes.

Watching Sam work helped loosen some of the anger. It felt familiar, routine. Which, considering the short time they'd known each other, said a lot. Nothing had entirely turned out the way Amelia had expected when she'd come here.

'Does talking to it help?' Amelia asked, making Sam jump.

Sam gave Amelia a lopsided grin. 'Rarely. But it was my last resort since hitting it didn't work.'

'Did it get damaged in the move?' Amelia asked, moving closer. All the machines looked as old as this one, and Amelia had no clue what they did.

'No, I think it's just bitter we dared to move it at all,' Sam said, sighing. 'I don't know why I'm worried. If they see it broken in person, maybe IRS&D will replace it.'

'But you want it to be perfect for your boss coming?' Amelia guessed. They hadn't known each other long, barely a month, but had become fast friends, even if it was still new to both of them. In that time, she'd learned a lot about Sam.

'Part of me wishes I'd just left them where they were. But I know Hale was right. It was just another reason to have people on my land who didn't need to be there,' Sam said. 'Especially with all the scientists coming tomorrow.'

Protect pack's second home, Luna insisted, pressing for more control.

Be calm, Amelia said, her turn to soothe her wolf as her anger sharpened again. *No enemies here.*

Yet, Luna said darkly. Not fighting with the pack was one thing, but invaders deserved anger as far as Luna was concerned. *Danger come soon.*

These people aren't our enemies, Amelia said again. Her wolf huffed a breath and backed off a bit. The small group of scientists coming were unwanted rather than uninvited. However, it was hard for her wolf to make that distinction.

The IRS&D just wanted to know how the Rift Scar had shrunk for the first time in a hundred years. And they weren't alone in that desire. Even now, two weeks since they'd first confirmed the discovery, Amelia couldn't believe it, and she'd been down there and seen the fresh grass for herself.

'Any idea who's coming?'

'No,' Sam said, turning serious again. 'They are going to be sending the list through to Hale today. He's going to email it to me. Because, clearly, I'm not important enough for the IRS&D to tell me directly they're even coming.'

Frustration and fear burrowed through Sam's scent, making Amelia's nose itch. The IRS&D didn't know that Hale and Sam were together, and they should have been telling both of them that they were coming. These people were coming to check Sam's findings. She should have been told.

'It's going to be okay,' Amelia said. 'They don't know anything. They can't.'

'I know,' Sam said, biting her lip. 'I just wish ...'

She didn't need to finish. They'd spoken extensively about it over the past two weeks. It was too dangerous to tell anyone she was an Earth Elemental when Sam could lose everything. Even if she wanted to take a chance, Hale wouldn't do anything to endanger his mate. Not even to heal the land. Amelia didn't blame him one bit.

'Come on, let's get changed and get out of here. This is as good as you're getting until the workmen come to finish the walls.'

'You're going to shower first, right?' Sam said, wrinkling her nose as she pulled in a breath. She didn't quite make it all the way through the inhale before her grin broke through.

'Thanks,' Amelia said, wincing as she caught a whiff of it from her own hair. She must have become more nose blind to it than she'd realised if Sam was picking it up that clearly. She only had a human nose. 'I'd have thought the cold weather would have stopped the stench clinging to me. Clearly not.'

'There are a bunch of papers with theories on how and why the scent buries into everything if you want me to read to you while you shower?' Sam said as she stripped off her lab coat and grabbed a bag she'd hung in a small metal storage locker by the doorway.

'Ask me if I ever get insomnia,' Amelia said, snorting, feeling the calm finally replace the anger.

'I feel very underappreciated,' Sam said, laughing. 'I'm looking forward to meeting Oliver's scientist friend, especially after he's spent the past week hyping the man up. If Mitchel is dull, I'm going to be very disappointed.'

Amelia laughed. She doubted any friend of Oliver's could be dull. But she suspected that Oliver had invited them in the first place so Sam could talk science with someone who understood it for a change.

They headed upstairs towards the showers and changing rooms. A shower was definitely in order.

CHAPTER TWO

Mitchel followed Oliver as he led the way from the hotel to the closest pub. It was still pretty early in the evening, but it looked later as the snow-laden clouds stole most of the light, making it feel like dusk.

Huntly was a small town, but it was old. Narrow, tar-macked roads with one or no pavements wove through the buildings that still had worn-looking sash windows. Mitchel didn't know much about architecture, but there were still parts of Glasgow that had the same look as this. Most had been ripped out and replaced with larger flats to fit as many people as possible in a small space.

Despite the weather, a few people were out walking with scarves wrapped tightly around their necks and thick jackets zipped up. They nodded and offered a smile to Oliver as they passed, giving Mitchel a curious look. It was a very different feeling than the general ignorance of the city. There, no one acknowledged anyone.

'You get used to it,' Oliver said, giving Mitchel a grin as they turned a corner and saw a sign for a bar.

'The Dead Imp?' Mitchel asked as he stared at the sign where a wolf was ripping out an imp's throat.

'You're going to love it,' Oliver said.

A bouncer stood outside, wrapped up against the weather. He nodded at Mitchel, a tiny flash of yellow in his eyes showing the man was a wolf as he nodded at them. 'Oliver.'

'Kenneth,' Oliver said, tone neutral as he returned the nod, then he pushed open the door.

Oliver was usually friends with everyone, so Kenneth must have done something pretty bad to get the cold shoulder. Mitchel gave a nod as he passed, but the man had already turned away and didn't even acknowledge him.

The Dead Imp wasn't exactly what Mitchel had expected, especially after the tartan carpet, curtains, and stag heads at the hotel. The floor was a scarred wood, with a dozen tables scattered over it and booths at the back. Against one wall was an industrial-style bar, with metal wire crawling up the sides and a wooden top. Pictures in black and white lined the walls, showing whisky barrels being moved or large warehouses stacked full of them.

The bar was half full, with a mix of people, many looking like they'd come from work. Some in suits, some in painters' or builders' gear. Oliver headed past all of them towards a booth in the corner.

There were two menus on the table. One with more whisky options than Mitchel ever knew existed, and another for food. Even though the pub might have looked modern, the menu was proper Scottish. Haggis, neeps, and tatties were at the top of the list, followed by a steak and ale pie and other pub classics.

'What's good?' Mitchel asked, ignoring the whisky for now, as his stomach growled. The train had been nearly five hours, and he hadn't had anything but crisps and chocolate, which, while always good, didn't keep you full for long.

'Steak and ale pie's excellent, but all of it's good,' Oliver said, not even bothering to look at the menu. Oliver hadn't been much of a cook before he'd left. Living up north clearly hadn't changed that.

'Pie it is, then.'

'Pie and beer, check,' Oliver said, getting up with a grin before Mitchel could argue with him. 'This one's on me, next one's on you.'

As Oliver wandered up to order, Mitchel checked his phone. The signal was spotty, with the occasional hint that data might be possible. But he'd known that coming here.

A young couple entered the bar, holding hands, ignoring everything as they moved to a small table. Mitchel felt a twinge in his chest as he watched the way they barely seemed to see anything else but each other.

Mitchel shook his head, reminding himself again that he couldn't lose something that had never been real. It did little to make him feel better. Clara had been gone from his life for over a year, yet it still hurt to think about her. He both missed her and hated her. Hated how it ended and what she'd done. All of it twisting in his head and mixing like toxic sewage.

To top it off, he'd been taken for a fool. Clara never wanted more from Mitchel than access to his family connections. Something he should have figured out far sooner. After all, that's exactly what his mum had done, even if it had been by mutual agreement with his dad. A deal the two had made together. Whereas Mitchel had just been manipulated.

Stupid, twisted emotions. After nearly a year, Mitchel wished he could settle into feeling nothing or hate. Missing Clara made him feel raw and vulnerable, especially after what she'd done.

A beer bottle appeared before him as Oliver took his seat. 'It's a local brew and not half bad.'

'Thanks,' Mitchel said, taking a swig as he tried to shake off the residual memory of the pain. Oliver knew how things had gone with Clara, but there was no need to drag down the mood.

The beer was sweet and bitter, giving him more cider vibes. It wasn't the best beer he'd had, but Oliver was right. It wasn't half bad, and he said as much.

'I invited Sam and another friend out to have drinks with us tonight,' Oliver said, taking a pull of his own beer as he scanned the room, a flash of amber showing. His wolf was clearly not happy still.

Mitchel paused mid-swig, nearly spilling the beer down his face. 'Sam?' She was the local rift surveyor who'd discovered the change in the Rift Scar. He should have realised that Oliver would know her since she'd need ranger protection to do her job.

'I thought you might appreciate someone who understood what you were saying,' Oliver said, a smile playing on his lips. 'But I'd be careful how much you fangirl over her. She's dating the alpha.'

'I don't fangirl,' Mitchel said, even though that's probably what he'd have done. He'd pulled nearly every report she'd done in the past six months, poring over them for signs that something had been changing. Something that might have been missed. 'She's studied the Rift Scar changes.'

'I've seen the changes to the land on the border,' Oliver said, barking out a laugh. 'You didn't react like this when I told you that.'

Mitchel waved the beer at him. 'You're not a scientist. All you saw was grass. She's seen the *changes*.' He paused, realising what he'd said, and stopped. He hoped he'd have something intelligible to say when Sam arrived.

'So, scientist's eyes are now better than everyone else's?' Oliver said, still laughing. Mitchel fought to hold on to his amusement and failed. Oliver didn't miss the change. 'I don't like that look?'

Mitchel considered what he wanted to say carefully. There had been mixed reactions to the changes. 'Not everyone believes the data,' Mitchel said, twirling his beer. 'Some claim it's the result of a broken machine or mistakes. Or that a hundred years ago, when the border was measured, someone messed up.'

'That's ridiculous. I've been here six months. There wasn't grass there before. I've seen it,' Oliver said, then grew still, eyes flashing to amber. 'They're accusing Sam of lying?'

It wasn't often Mitchel saw Oliver angry, let alone his wolf. But if Sam was the alpha's girlfriend, that would change everything. 'I don't believe she's lying,' Mitchel said, not looking Oliver entirely in the eye but equally careful not to back down so his wolf knew he meant it.

Oliver blinked, eyes flashing back and forth. 'Sorry. Sam is like pack now.'

'It's okay. I don't think people are saying she's lying. I think they just can't believe the change. You know how we scientists like to argue and debate, especially regarding the Rift Scar.' Mitchel sighed and took another pull of his beer, realising he'd already finished it. He hated work politics at the best of times, but this had become very divisive, often at the expense of logic. 'It's not about Sam; it's about fear. Change, even something good like the Rift Scar shrinking, is scary.'

'Is that why it's been kept secret from the media?' Oliver asked.

'I had to sign an NDA before I could come up here. Not wanting to get people's hopes up was their reasoning.' Even the people who weren't coming had been asked to sign it, but he didn't bother mentioning that. Nor was he worried about talking about the Rift Scar changes since Oliver already knew.

Oliver cursed as his eyes settled into solid amber and didn't change back. 'Do you think that the others coming will think she's lying? Or say she is?'

'Without knowing who's coming, I can't say.'

Oliver's jaw muscle twitched.

'I'm sorry,' Mitchel said, not knowing what else to say.

'This isn't your fault,' Oliver said, eyes still not changing back. He sighed. 'I'm going to go to the toilet. I'll be back in a minute.'

Mitchel nodded but didn't say anything as Oliver got up and left. If this was how he reacted to a perceived accusation, Mitchel didn't want to see what the alpha would do against a direct one. Mitchel suspected the trip to the toilet was likely a chance to warn his alpha about the possibility. That and to get his wolf under control.

'This weather is wild,' a woman to his left said. He turned so quickly he felt his neck crack.

He froze as Clara brushed snow off her long blond hair, then stripped out of her jacket. She was petite, both in height and build, but she'd curves in all the places that mattered. Her face was heart-shaped, making her look more innocent than she was, especially when she made full use of her large hazel eyes.

She looked exactly as he remembered her. She was even wearing the same pale jeans and red strappy top she'd worn when he'd walked out of their shared apartment with only the clothes on his back and his phone.

He pressed his fingers into the leather of the booth, heart beating too fast. He tried to calm himself; his discomfort would only make this more fun for her. She smiled as she walked closer, pulling in a breath. She'd know exactly how he felt from that little inhale, yet she didn't stop.

'You must be in your element. You always did like the snow,' Clara said, smiling, clearly enjoying catching him off guard.

Her words finally snapped him out of his shock, but she didn't know his secret. Though that had been a close thing. She took Oliver's seat, those tendrils of fear and the need to run changing to anger. He very nearly got up to leave, but Oliver was still in the toilet, and he didn't want his friend to worry.

'What are you doing here?' Mitchel asked, shivering as her eyes travelled down his chest. As much as he was angry with her, maybe even hated her for what she'd done, he couldn't stop his body from remembering how good it had been between them.

'I've missed you, Mitchel,' Clara said, leaning forward, ignoring his question. Her vest top, which was far too thin for the cold weather, strained against her breasts as she moved. He wished he could say he didn't look, but Clara had always been very good at knowing how to draw the eye of anyone she wanted. 'We always had the best of times together. Late nights, later mornings. The fire going as it cast the only light in the room.'

He remembered. That and so much more. Like how many times he thought Clara was going out to work or study, then finding out later all the people she'd also been seeing. If not for Oliver, he might still have been blindly oblivious to what she was doing.

Then, the last time he'd seen her—the morning after the full moon. He suppressed a shudder, not willing to show her any weakness. He was done, even if she clearly hadn't got the message that it was over. He'd spent the last year avoiding her, which hadn't been easy when they both worked at IRS&D. At least they weren't in the same department.

'I told you I wanted nothing more to do with you,' he said firmly, looking away from Clara, eyes falling onto the cute couple again. Had he and Clara ever been like that? Had she ever taken him out in public? He didn't remember. Apart from the fact they lived together, would anyone have known they'd been a couple? Again, it was a stupid thought considering how it ended, yet the feeling of hurt was still deep in his chest. 'You're not worth it.'

'Well, you'd better figure out a way to deal with it,' Clara said, crossing her arms. 'We're both here for the same reason.'

Mitchel blinked, stomach sinking as he put together what she meant. She was here to study why the Rift Scar was shrinking. But how? She wasn't exactly the type to want to volunteer to go into the Rift Scar. Nor was she a scientist; she was just a data analyst. So, what the hell was she doing here?

'What poor fool are you chasing this time to bring you all the way out here?' Mitchel said, hating the pain that rose in his chest. He'd been that fool once.

Clara lifted her chin. 'Why I make my choices is none of your business.'

'It is if you're putting this job at risk. Finding out how the Rift Scar border changed is my number one priority. I'm not going to let your games interfere with that.'

'Well, it's good to know some things never change,' Clara said, curling her lip.

'What the hell is that supposed to mean?' Mitchel said, narrowing his eyes.

'You were always more interested in the science than anything else. Maybe if you'd been less busy proving yourself to fucking everyone, then I wouldn't have had to entertain myself elsewhere,' Clara said, shaking her head.

This time, Mitchel did stand up. Anywhere was better than being here, dealing with this woman. She still didn't get she'd done anything wrong. Any of it. 'I was done with your games a year ago. If you think I'll play them again with you now, you're very much mistaken.'

'It's not up to you what I do, Mitchel. You're not in charge,' Clara said, not bothering to look at him. 'Something else that's just like old times.'

Mitchel gritted his teeth as he fought against replying. A few people in the pub had turned towards them, listening to them argue.

'Mitchel.' Oliver's voice made Clara jump, then she turned to glare at him. 'They really are just letting anyone in, aren't they?'

OLIVER STOMPED DOWN ON his anger as Clara jumped up from the booth to glare at him. He'd caught her scent as soon as he'd re-entered the room. Cheap perfume, overripe apples, and recent sex, though her partner's scent was lost beneath a heavy floral perfume.

'Well, look what the cat dragged in,' Clara said as she looked Oliver up and down like it was him who was the intruder.

Cat not drag me, Thor, Oliver's wolf said. *Bigger than cat. Better than cat.*

Oliver tried to ignore his wolf and Thor's indignation as he moved between her and Mitchel. Dealing with Clara was never easy, but doing so with anger usually gave her the upper hand. It let her fall back on being an omega. It told all wolves that she was weak and needed protecting.

If Oliver hadn't just spoken to Hale about what Mitchel had said, it might have been easier to manage the anger. Part of Oliver was glad it had been over the phone. The pack bonds had vibrated with Hale's fury, even at a distance.

Mitchel stood from the booth without a word and stalked away, heading in the direction Oliver had just come from. Not that he thought that his friend was going to the bathroom for any other reason than to get away from Clara. It was probably just as well; the temperature had noticeably dropped a few degrees.

'Rude,' Clara said, moving as if she was going to follow Mitchel. As usual, she seemed oblivious to his anger. Oliver genuinely couldn't tell if she cared for Mitchel or just begrudged that he'd ended things instead of her. Either way, she eyed Mitchel hungrily, like he was a piece of meat.

'Leave him,' Oliver said, moving to block her. If Mitchel needed space, then he was going to get it. Any interaction with Clara was its own kind of toxic.

Toxic, Thor said, rolling the word around in his mind. *Accurate. Clara toxic.*

'You know how to spoil a girl's fun, Oliver,' Clara said, pouting, eyes changing from a glare to something more carnal. But she'd not followed Mitchel, and that had been the goal. Now, he just had to get rid of her before Mitchel returned. 'But maybe there's a reason for that?'

'No,' he said, backing up as she stepped closer. There wasn't much room left to move unless he wanted to step into the open space and draw more attention to them than he already had.

'Since when have you been so discerning about who you spend the night with?' Clara said, putting her hand on the tanned leather of the back of the bench, running her fingers back and forth. She smiled, more predatory than amused.

'I have taste,' he said, watching her hands carefully. Clara had been known to claw people who weren't watching her.

Her face twisted to anger. 'You think you're so damned special? You're nothing. Your own father sent you here because you're weak. Because you can't control yourself. You should be grateful anyone wants you.'

Not weak, Thor said. He would have snarled at another wolf for suggesting even half of what she'd implied. But he knew better than to show Clara that kind of anger, not when she was an omega.

'And yet, here you are, in the middle of nowhere as well. Who did you piss off to be assigned here, Clara?' Oliver said coldly. The surrounding bar had grown quieter, some of the people closer to him realising something was happening, though neither of their voices had raised. Yet.

'Which just goes to show how little you understand of how the world works,' she said, smile returning as her fingers stilled. 'I was chosen to come here. Gifted with the chance to change everything.'

'Last I heard, you were data entry,' Oliver said. Of all the people the IRS&D could have sent, Clara had been so far down on Oliver's list that he wouldn't have even thought to check for her. 'What makes your skills worthy of being "gifted"?'

'I've the same qualifications as Mitchel,' Clara said, scowling at Oliver. But he knew exactly how she'd got those grades, and it hadn't been hard work. She let the scowl drop and leaned forward like she was sharing a secret.

Ignoring the nearly silent restaurant goers, he went to look for Mitchel just in case he'd decided to get out of dodge altogether.

AMELIA TUCKED HER SCARF into her thick wool jacket as she stepped out the back door of the old gym into the cold wind. The whole back section was used for the rangers' cars.

In front of her was an eight-foot wall that marked the border of Huntly, with only a few cracks showing in the old cement. It wasn't the original wall. That had been moved, and then moved again, years previous.

The wind picked up, sending loose snow around her in a flurry as she stepped onto the cleared path. The weather hadn't worsened while she'd been inside, except for the expected temperature drop.

Fur better. Keep us warmer, Luna said, tone still impatient as she sent Amelia images of them running in the snow-covered woods.

It would be freezing even with fur, Amelia said, then ignored her wolf as she sent her more images.

'I hope the weather warden gets back soon,' Sam said, breath misting out in front of her as she checked the door was locked. 'I heard they hired someone to help?'

'They did,' Amelia said, wishing the council had done it much sooner. 'He isn't due to arrive for a few weeks, though, and Staci is out of town until the end of the week.'

'How's her mum?'

'The same,' Amelia said, wincing. From what she'd heard, Staci's mum was quickly slipping into dementia. The young weather warden had been having to go to hospital in Inverness with her frequently. Which was why the weather kept going wild. Or wilder than usual.

Sam's phone dinged, and she peeled off thick gloves as they headed towards her car. It needed to be cleared of snow, but if they were lucky, there wouldn't be ice underneath.

'Looks like Hale finally got the full list of who's coming,' Sam said, eyes scanning the screen after she unlocked it. 'I'm not recognising anyone on the list, though you might.'

'I doubt that. I don't know any scientists other than you.' Amelia's hometown hadn't precisely been large as packs went, despite the fact a prime alpha was in charge of her pack.

'It says they're from your hometown, Ivybridge? Right?' Sam said, scrolling some more, then she looked up. 'Just the one. Someone called Dylan?'

Amelia's heart stuttered, and the snowy road in front of her blurred. 'Dylan?' she asked, words trying to stick in her throat.

'You know him?' Sam asked, still looking at her phone.

Amelia couldn't breathe. Couldn't think. He couldn't be coming here. He wasn't a scientist. Memories of the last full moon with him rose. He stood in front of her naked, pulling on the familiar feel of lust between them. Tugging on her wolf, trying to force her to change her mind and have sex with him. She hadn't wanted him, but her body betrayed her. The Full Moon Fever showing her every other time they'd had sex, making it hard to think.

She'd fought the feeling, searching for something to break the pull. Anything that would let her funnel the energy somewhere else. Anywhere else. She'd found it, but it hadn't been the save she'd been looking for.

Something inside her had snapped. That lust had twisted into rage, and she'd lost control.

Protected self, Luna whispered at the edge of her mind as that same rage built now, coiling inside like a snake waiting to strike. Her wolf was trying to send her calm thoughts. But it wasn't working. *Dylan not here.*

But the rage wasn't listening. It coiled tighter in Amelia's gut. She couldn't let it. Couldn't lose control. The pack put down Shifters who couldn't control themselves. Or, if the government found them first, locked in cages.

Safe. Not let them put us in cage, Luna said, voice still too quiet. Too far away.

'Amelia,' Sam said, lightly touching her arm. The sense of the pack grew stronger. Safety, protection, and the feel of home. 'It's okay. You're safe.'

Her wolf leaned into the feeling, accepting it. The rage dimmed, leaving Amelia shaking and breathless. It was almost like she could feel Sam in the same way she felt Hale. Something that shouldn't have been possible.

Alpha's mate, Luna said. *Strong. Powerful.*

It shouldn't matter. Sam isn't a wolf, Amelia said. She pulled in a breath, the scent of home so strong she could almost smell the forest of pine trees. Layered through it all was the aroma of honeysuckle and dirt that was Sam.

Her wolf made a noise that might have been a laugh if she had been human. *True mate. Magic not matter. Connected.*

She didn't know how to argue with that or why her wolf was so sure. With a slow breath, Amelia put her hand on top of Sam's, feeling the freezing wall of the gym against her back. She didn't remember moving.

'I'm okay,' Amelia said, though she still felt shaky.

'What happened?' Her voice was careful, like Amelia was a wounded animal she was afraid of scaring off. Which wasn't that far from the truth. 'Who's Dylan?'

Amelia wanted to brush off the question, but Sam's concern was genuine. She might not be a Shifter, but her sense of protectiveness was just as strong as Hale's.

'Dylan is the reason I'm here,' Amelia said, letting her head drop back against the wall despite the cold. Her heart still pounded in her chest, but it slowed a little further with every breath. The rage retreated into its cage.

'Did something happen before you left?' Sam asked. There was no demand, no pressure. Just a question. But there was a new layer of steel in her voice as anger trickled into her scent.

'I attacked him.' Amelia let out a slow breath as the rage tried to grow despite Sam's touch. Dylan had broken every rule and instinct they had as wolves when he'd tried to force her to mate with him. No meant no. The wolves respected that. Except Dylan hadn't been interested in what Amelia wanted.

'I might not have known you long, but somehow, I doubt you did it without good reason,' Sam said.

Amelia hesitated. The truth didn't matter, but no one had ever asked her side of what had happened before.

'Dylan used to be my lover, but I broke it off with him when he became possessive. He chased away others who I'd been intimate with, threatening them.' Each one had backed off, not wanting to deal with the alpha's son, until he was the only one left. 'When the full moon came, I left to run somewhere else, somewhere far away from him. That way, I wouldn't be tempted to change my mind.'

'The Moon Fever?' Sam asked. Only Shifters felt the core deep need, but Sam had been with Hale through two full moons now, so she'd been on the other side of the excess energy that left the body wire tight.

Amelia nodded. 'The body remembers how good it feels. Sometimes, it's easy to fall back into old habits. He found me that morning and kept pushing, trying to use the Moon Fever to sway me. But I didn't want him. We didn't want him.' She paused, letting out a shaky breath; she could still remember how he'd watched her, ignoring her words like she hadn't even spoken. 'I chose violence, funnelled everything I felt into it until there was only rage.'

'That sounds like you defended yourself against an attempted assault,' Sam said, not understanding. Most didn't. Most assumed that Moon Fever was sex. But sex was just one way of releasing energy. There were other options.

'It doesn't matter. I lost control. I became the very thing humans fear. Wild. Dangerous. Savage.' Amelia cut off, tears threatening. 'I let the rage control me.'

Not savage, Luna snarled at her, breaking through the memory. *Just hurt Dylan. Not all. Not everyone.*

You don't know that we would've stopped hurting him, Amelia said, knowing it was an argument she couldn't win. Her wolf didn't believe they'd lost control, not really. She really thought they'd just been protecting themselves. Regardless of the rage that still sat low in their gut anytime someone tried to push them into doing something they didn't want.

The alpha hadn't believed she was in control, either. He'd sent her away. Sending her where any issues of control could be dealt with. Where she could just disappear into the Rift Scar without anyone noticing.

Not lost control, Luna said, showing image after image of the past few months. Training in London, then more training here. The fight with Lacy to protect Sam. All were times when tensions had been high, and Shifters had been afraid. *Not savage. Not broken.*

And with Kenneth earlier? Amelia said. The rage had been there, too.

Her wolf growled low. *Was in control. Not savage. Stupid pup still live.*

'Dylan survived, so I assume you didn't hurt him that badly?' Sam asked, anger filling her scent. 'I can't imagine I'd have left him standing in one piece after that.'

Good alpha's mate, Luna said, pleased as she let the feel of that shared anger sink in.

Amelia smiled despite herself. 'I only broke his arm before the alpha stopped me.' The humour left her at that memory. She would have done much worse. Dylan hadn't even had a chance to defend himself. 'If not for the alpha, I don't know that I would've stopped.'

'I think you're underestimating yourself,' Sam said.

Amelia turned away, not able to find the words. Not even knowing where to start. Dylan was here. Or at least on his way. She wasn't just worried about losing control. She was terrified. She'd finally found somewhere she felt like she belonged and didn't want to lose it.

Pack strong here, Luna said, like it would help. Like it would matter. *Protect us.*

Alaric should have protected us, Amelia said, her fear twisting into something new. Something more dangerous. She tried to shove it down, stamping on the feeling.

Alaric not good alpha, Luna said, huffing a breath. *Good alpha here.*

Amelia shivered. They hadn't all been good. She still had nightmares of Shane taking control of her, forcing her to stand in that clearing with a gun. Even her rage had been suppressed, smothered.

Better now. Alpha woken. Smarter. Learned, Luna said, sending Amelia images of Hale leading the pack in the full moon hunt a few days ago.

'You should tell Hale that you know Dylan. I doubt he'd be happy to let someone like that anywhere near the pack,' Sam said, her scent shifting to anger, so sharp that it nearly cut into Amelia's nose.

'No!' Amelia said, chest growing tight again.

Yes! Luna countered, pressing for control to speak. *Pack protect.*

'If he knows, he can keep him out of your way. Or send him home.'

'Or send me away,' Amelia said, though her wolf snarled at her for being stupid. But the reality was no pack would want someone with control issues.

Sam gave her a look that again echoed her wolf's. 'I've seen what Hale will do to protect the pack. You, Amelia, are pack.'

But would he still think that way if he found out she couldn't control herself? If he didn't know already. No one had ever said what information had passed between the alphas.

'I'll think about it,' Amelia said.

Sam was quiet for a moment. 'Are you worried about losing control?' Sam asked, voice soft.

'I've been able to control the rage since I left Ivybridge,' Amelia said slowly. She'd been watchful. Careful. Like with Kenneth.

'Are you worried about losing control around Dylan?' Sam asked. Amelia's rage bubbled at the idea of Dylan touching her. Sam pulled her hand back and rubbed her fingertips together. 'I'll take that as a yes.'

'I never meant to lose control the first time. I just let go,' Amelia said, looking away. She'd had a lot of time to think about everything that had happened. 'I know better now. Know what letting go means. I can control it. But I've not seen Dylan since then.'

Sam watched her. For once, her scent didn't give away anything about what she felt. 'I'll not tell Hale if you promise that if Dylan tries anything, you'll tell Hale yourself?'

Amelia wanted to say no, but her wolf rose around her. 'Yes. Promise.'

Sure, take control. Because that will convince Sam I'm safe, Amelia said.

Stronger if I promise. Not break promise to alpha's mate. Her wolf was right. The words had felt different. Stronger. Binding. It didn't make Amelia feel any better.

She'd never felt anything like this in her previous pack. It made her wonder if it was just Hale who was a better alpha. Or if Alaric had been a terrible one.

'Seems like your wolf is on board, and you, Amelia?' Sam asked, not showing any concern over seeing Amelia's wolf.

'I promise I'll tell him if I need help,' Amelia said. That same tingle flowed over her skin as the words held power they shouldn't have. She would have to speak to Sam about it but now wasn't the time.

Sam nodded, pulling her jacket tighter like she'd just remembered where they were. 'Do you still want to go out?'

Amelia considered it, then nodded slowly. 'I could use a night out. Something to make me forget for a bit.'

'Good. Because I'm freezing. Let's get out of this weather,' Sam said, rubbing her hands together.

Amelia shivered, though it was less from the cold than the residual feel of the magic between them. She might have been sent here as punishment, but the longer she stayed, the more like home the Highland Rift Pack was starting to feel.

They cleared Sam's car together; the movements helped push away most of the anger and fear, making her feel closer to normal again.

CHAPTER THREE

MITCHEL SPLASHED WATER ON his face, then huffed a breath as the water froze and fell into the sink to smash.

'She's gone,' Oliver said, making Mitchel jump. Oliver didn't comment on the broken ice, though his avoidance of mentioning it spoke louder than any words.

'Maybe this is why my dad agreed to send me so quickly. Maybe he thought it would be funny to torture me,' Mitchel said, trying to grab another handful of water, being more careful this time as he splashed his face. The cool water did little to calm his temper.

'That would require your father to know who she was and how she affected you. Both of which I doubt. You were picked to come because you're good at what you do.'

'With the bar set at Clara's level, it doesn't seem like it's hard to meet that,' Mitchel said, grabbing a towel from the dispenser to wipe his face.

'If everyone they sent is at Clara's level, I'm going to have other questions,' Oliver said darkly. 'But enough of that. Let's go back and get our drinks and dinner.'

For a men's toilet, the small room was better than most bars he'd been to. There were two cubicles, one urinal, and two sinks. For the most part, it was clean. But regardless, it wasn't exactly the ideal place for a conversation, even about his ex.

'I'm not sure I'm hungry anymore,' Mitchel said, considering returning to his hotel room. Except he'd just have to deal with Clara tomorrow. And the day after. So, it wasn't like he could escape. Even if he was willing to go home, the trains weren't moving.

Oliver snorted. 'Sure, I believe that.'

Mitchel smiled as he followed Oliver back into the main bar. The server brought the food out as they returned to their table. It smelled amazing, and Mitchel's hunger jumped back into focus, stomach growling. Oliver laughed but didn't comment as he took a bite.

The pie was as good as it smelled, especially with the mint and butter tatties, though he could have done without the peas. They ate in silence, letting the festering anger dissipate. He'd need to find a way to deal with that before he saw Clara tomorrow.

'Oliver!'

Mitchel looked around to find the source of the voice. A petite woman waved at them as she headed in their direction. She had pale blond curls and green eyes. Mitchel recognised Sam from her photos. She stripped off her jacket as she reached their table, dusting the floor with snow.

'Amelia managed to drag you away from your work, I see,' Oliver said, smiling at her. Sam gave him a mock scowl and turned to Mitchel.

'I'm Sam,' she said, offering him her hand. 'You must be Mitchel. Oliver's told me all about you.'

'Good things, I hope,' Mitchel said, shaking her hand. Sam's grip was firm, confident.

'Mostly that you're familiar with the struggles of the IRS&D,' Sam said, hooking her jacket on a well-placed peg between the high-backed booths. 'Did you come up with any of the other scientists?'

'Not that I saw. I was the only one who seemed to want to get off the train when it arrived.' Mitchel shrugged, debating about mentioning Clara, but decided against it. There was no point in spoiling his mood again. 'But maybe they were supposed to get the later one. I moved mine earlier when I saw the weather.'

Sam laughed. 'Wouldn't that be funny after their rush to get up here?' She turned as another woman appeared at her shoulder with drinks, passing one to Sam. 'Me and Amelia were just laughing about the same idea.'

Amelia smiled as she turned towards Mitchel. His heart skipped a beat as he felt a tug towards her deep in his gut. She had straight honey-blond hair, pale blue eyes, and a slim runner's build.

As her eyes met his, that tug grew sharper. He had to fight to keep himself seated. Reaching out and caressing a stranger's hair would undoubtedly get him punched in the face. Something Amelia looked more than capable of doing as her eyes swirled from a pale blue to a lighter shade that was nearly white. She was a wolf.

'Mitchel,' he said slowly, putting his hand out. Amelia took his hand. Heat tingled down through his arm like an electric shock. He searched for something to say. Anything.

'Amelia,' she said, not letting go of his hand. Her voice was light, almost musical. He wanted her to say more.

'Was the pie good today?' Sam asked, voice distant, as Mitchel tried to tell his hand to let go.

'Isn't it always good?' Oliver said.

The front door banged open. Amelia released Mitchel's hand and spun round. Mitchel's breath left him in a rush as the connection dropped away. He shuddered, both wanting to feel it again—feel Amelia again—and wanting to run.

He'd never felt anything like it before.

'Can you believe they wouldn't let us have the car?' a male voice said. It was familiar, the man from the train. 'I'll be raising a complaint as soon as I get a signal.'

Mitchel forced himself to focus again. Oliver was on his feet, a step in front of Sam, Amelia at his side.

'You've known Oliver for years, right?' Sam said as she looked at Mitchel, a smile playing on her lips. 'Tell me, have you found a way to make him stop doing that?'

Mitchel laughed, still struggling against the residual tingles in his hand. 'Not yet, but if you find a way, let me know.'

Sam smiled as Oliver gave her an embarrassed look. Amelia didn't look embarrassed at all. She just continued with a slow scan over the room.

Mitchel shuffled further down the booth as Oliver moved out of the way to let Sam go in first on his side. She sat opposite Mitchel, leaving a space beside him for Amelia.

His skin prickled at the idea of her sitting next to him. Which was stupid. She'd shown no interest in him at all. Besides, she was a wolf. He knew better than to get involved with another one after Clara. Even if his body disagreed with him.

'I'm going to grab us some food,' Amelia said, not quite looking at him. 'I'll be back in a second.'

AMELIA RUBBED HER FINGERTIPS together, trying to erase the tingling as she ordered food. It was like she could still feel Mitchel.

Like. Touch again, Luna said, nudging her to go back to the table.

No. Bad idea, Amelia said. She ignored her wolf's yip of annoyance as she gave her order to the server behind the bar. But the need grew stronger, like a knot in her gut that kept coiling tighter. In more ways than one.

She glanced back at him. He was just about her height but lanky, like he'd been stretched too thin. His face was long, with high cheekbones and delicate features.

He was so far from what typically drew her eye that it was hard not to stare in order to find out what it was that pulled at her.

Smells good, Luna whispered as if to help find the source of the attraction, nudging her to take another deep breath.

The scent of morning frost, crisp and clean, filled her lungs even through the chaos of smells that filled the room. She wanted to hold her breath, keep that tiny part of Mitchel inside her, which was ridiculous.

It would have been easy to blame the Full Moon Fever for playing with her body, making her desire sharper. Except the full moon was days past, and this didn't feel exactly the same. It was deeper than just desire; she wanted to touch him and lean into his warmth.

Not knowing where the feelings were coming from made her nervous, especially with Dylan potentially being in town.

Mitchel not Dylan, Luna said, tone emphatic. *Not feel same. Not angry.*

I know, she said. But the knowledge didn't help the fear of the rage. How did she know this new pull wouldn't be just as dangerous?

Not dangerous, Luna said, urging her to go back to Mitchel again. *Feels good.*

Amelia couldn't argue with that, despite the underlying fear.

Oliver's scent tickled her nose as he approached. She was surprised he'd left Sam alone, given his reaction to the loud idiot earlier. Not that she'd reacted any better, and she was very sure Sam would have something to say about it later. But Amelia couldn't shake the remaining edge after hearing about Dylan.

'Do you need more beer?' Amelia asked. The alcohol wasn't strong enough to last long against their wolf metabolism, so she wasn't worried about being hungover tomorrow.

'Two, please,' Oliver said, nodding to the server who turned around to rake in the fridge, familiar enough with Oliver's regular drinks that he didn't even need to ask. 'I want to tell you something, but I don't want you to freak out.'

Amelia stiffened, the comment a little too close to her own worries that she had to stamp down her earlier fear. Oliver didn't know about Dylan, and she wasn't about to tell him. Not unless she wanted Dylan going home in a bag. Appealing as that was, it wasn't a good idea. Her old alpha, Alaric, might be aware of Dylan's issues, but she doubted he'd take kindly to the death of his son, regardless of the reason. Though why he'd been sent north at all escaped her.

'I'm listening,' Amelia said when it became clear that Oliver was waiting for something from her. The bar was loud enough that their conversation wouldn't carry unless there were other wolves here, and she didn't smell any except the two of them. Kenneth had been outside working as a bouncer but he wouldn't be able to hear them over the noise. Especially not the way he'd been sucking the face off the girl at the far end of the building.

'Some of the IRS&D think that the reports of changes to the Rift Scar are a mistake,' Oliver said, taking a slow breath as his eyes flashed to amber. She could feel his wolf spread out, energy trying to fill the room even as Oliver tried to pull it back.

Think Sam is liar, his wolf said, words a growl as he closed his eyes, clearly fighting for control. Something she'd never seen him struggle with before.

But if anything would cause it, the accusation that their alpha's mate was a liar would be high up there. Especially when they'd seen the change to the Rift themselves. Amelia's own wolf rose, anger sharp and wild. This anger was more familiar than the rage, easier to control.

Protect Sam, Luna said, though whether she understood what they were protecting Sam from, Amelia wasn't sure. *Invaders. Told you. Dangerous.*

Great, just what she needed, more reasons for her wolf to not like the visitors. Amelia pushed her wolf back with effort. *Calm. They're not going to hurt Sam.*

Shane hurt Sam. Lacey hurt us. Not think could before, Luna said, anger still needle sharp. That was something Amelia couldn't argue with at all.

'Sorry,' Oliver said, voice tight. 'I didn't mean for you to get the backlash of that. We're angry.'

But he wasn't sharing this just because he was angry. There was more. 'Have you told Hale?'

Oliver shivered. 'Yes. It went about as well as could be expected.' He paused, looking back at the table. 'Sam's done good work here with the Rift Scar. She's changed everything by becoming Hale's mate. I don't want anything to hurt her. I imagine others will feel the same way.'

Amelia wished she could tell him just how much more Sam had done for them and how the pack lands had been created. But as much as she trusted Oliver, it wasn't her secret to share. Not with Oliver or any of the pack. 'What does Hale want to do?'

'For now, nothing.' Oliver's wolf was still pulsing out from him, anger strong as he clearly didn't like the idea of sitting on their hands. 'I wish I knew more about who all was coming.'

'We'll find out soon enough tomorrow,' Amelia said, again biting down on the need to mention Dylan. That wasn't Oliver's problem.

'Well, at least we know one of them,' Oliver said, glancing back at Mitchel as a grin appeared. 'Maybe you can get to know Mitchel a bit more.'

Amelia's face heated, and she looked back at Mitchel without meaning to. He was listening to something Sam was saying, nodding, an easy smile on his lips.

The server coughed politely, making her turn back to him. He was clearly waiting for her to pay. Amelia offered him a weak smile and paid for everything before Oliver could jump in.

'I'm sure Mitchel is very nice, but I'm not looking for anything right now. Especially not with our uninvited guests.' Amelia scowled as Oliver made a noise in his throat that implied he didn't believe her one bit. Damned Shifter sense of smell.

'I'm not suggesting you marry him,' Oliver said, taking the beers from the bar. 'But I'm sure the two of you could use a bit of fun on what I imagine will be a dull trip.'

She didn't bother answering him as the idea pulled at her, tempting her. Oliver smiled again and returned to sit beside Sam, offering Mitchel a beer. The only seat left was beside Mitchel, which she suspected was deliberate.

As she sat down next to him, that tug pulled her towards him again, tempting her to slide closer to him than needed. To let his leg press against hers, to share in his warmth.

Instinct good, Luna said, clearly amused when Amelia didn't move closer. *Hunt better when slow. But too slow and lose prey.*

She ignored her wolf. The last thing she needed right now, with Dylan and a bunch of other unfamiliar wolves coming into town, was to be distracted by a new lover.

Even if she could smell Mitchel's desire as it echoed her own.

MITCHEL FOCUSED ON KEEPING himself on his side of the bench as Amelia's warmth seeped into him. It was harder than it should have been. Especially as they moved from beer to whisky, as Oliver challenged him to work his way through all the drinks on the menu. Not in one day, thankfully, or Mitchel may have given himself alcohol poisoning.

Amelia and Sam bowed out from that challenge, sticking to beer and coke. Mitchel probably should have, but with the prospect of seeing Clara tomorrow on the horizon, he decided a little indulgence was justified.

They talked about nothing in particular, letting the conversation drift and flow naturally. Mitchel felt comfortable, even if he really wanted to ask about the changes to the Rift Scar, but that would come tomorrow.

'What's the worst creature you've seen in a Rift Scar?' Mitchel asked, sipping his whisky—this one had a peaty base with a smooth burn as it went down—as the conversation drifted over to what the rangers did daily.

'I saw a wyvern once,' Oliver said, knocking back another shot. He paused to enjoy the surprised silence.

A wyvern was one of the largest creatures in the Rift Scars. Thankfully, the sheer size meant that most Rifts Scars couldn't give them enough food to survive.

'There aren't any wyverns here,' Sam said, snorting.

'I didn't say I saw it here,' Oliver said, smiling, though some of his humour had dropped off like he'd regretted speaking. 'London's Rift has them. I think they leave them alone because they help control the population of other Rift creatures. That and they're very hard to kill.'

'Are they as big as they say?' Mitchel asked, trying to imagine being in Oliver's place. What would he do? Probably crap himself.

Oliver nodded. 'This one was as big as a rhino, with wings connected to its front legs like a bat, a long-barbed tail, and grey scales. The smell was like nothing I've ever scented before; I don't even have words for it.'

He trailed off, mood shifting as the memories got the better of him. Oliver wasn't one to let memories drag him down. Whatever he'd seen must have been bad.

'So, nothing like your room tomorrow after you've drained this bar of whisky, then?' Mitchel said, smiling wide as he tried to draw Oliver's attention. Pulling him out of the memory and back into humour.

Oliver laughed, some of the tension leaving him. 'I'll have you know that whisky is never the cause of any such problems.'

'You're probably right, as long as they don't serve wolfbite here,' Mitchel said. Wolfbite was a super-strength alcohol designed for Shifters. Most places didn't serve it because it would give humans alcohol poisoning with just one glass.

Oliver's smile grew even wider, and he leaned back to wave at the server, making a symbol with his hand. The server nodded and pulled a key from around his neck to open a cupboard under the counter.

'And on that note, I'm afraid I'm about done for the night,' Amelia said, taking the last pull of her beer. 'We all have to be up early tomorrow.'

Mitchel wanted to ask her to stay so he could hold on to her warmth. But he'd never been one to press someone to continue to drink when they were done.

'We have to be there for nine. That's hardly early,' Oliver said, but he also didn't try to pressure her to stay.

'Unfortunately, not all of us have your constitution,' Sam said, smiling, nudging Oliver to let her out. 'But this is a good time for me to bow out, too. It's been great meeting you, Mitchel. I'm looking forward to tomorrow.'

'Me too,' Mitchel said, offering them both a smile, but his gaze focused on Amelia. That tug grew tighter, wanting him to follow her. He shoved it down, though with the alcohol glow, it was harder to remember why.

'I'll see you all tomorrow,' Amelia said, standing and grabbing her jacket.

Mitchel couldn't look away as she walked away with Sam. Amelia looked back once as she reached the door, looking at him, face showing nothing of what she thought, then she turned and was gone. He shivered, skin feeling too tight as that tug towards her stretched thin. It wasn't the only place that was tight. It was stupid to react like this when she'd shown no interest.

Oliver clicked his fingers in front of Mitchel's face, making him finally turn away from the door with a flush.

'What?' Mitchel asked. Part of him wanted to get up and follow Amelia, make sure she made it home safely, maybe ask her to invite him inside. But those thoughts felt awfully like he was turning into a stalker, so he shoved them aside.

'I asked you what you thought of Amelia?'

He fingered the whisky glass, face heating further. 'She seems nice.'

Oliver laughed, the sound bursting out of him almost like a bark. 'Nice? That's what you're going with.'

'She's not interested in me,' Mitchel said, but he didn't deny his interest. His desire would have been in his scent. Something, even as drunk as he was, he should have remembered sooner. His blush was so hot that he thought his face might melt off.

'You'd be surprised,' Oliver said, tapping his nose.

Mitchel hesitated. That scent worked both ways. But whether or not he was interested, there were other reasons why it was a bad idea.

'I think I've learned my lesson after Clara. No women. No Shifters,' Mitchel said, then belatedly added. 'No offence.'

'None taken, though you're really not quite my type. Maybe if you grew your hair out a bit?' Oliver said.

Mitchel snorted as his friend took the hint and dropped the topic. He almost wished Oliver hadn't. Almost. Probably due to the alcohol.

He knocked back the last of the whisky in his hand. Even with the women gone, he still wasn't quite ready to return to his rather dull hotel room. Even if it was just for a few hours.

'Another round before we turn in?' Mitchel said, raising his bottle.

'Only if it's your round,' Oliver said, emptying his glass and offering it to Mitchel.

Mitchel grinned and wobbled to his feet before he took the glass. Just one more.

Or two.

AMELIA PULLED HER JACKET closer as she stepped outside The Dead Imp. The slow fall of snow had stopped at last, though it had been enough to cover everything in a fresh white layer while she'd been inside. Kenneth looked to be gone, though she doubted that his shift was over yet. The owners wouldn't be happy with that.

'Mitchel was nice,' Sam said, checking her phone, putting it in her pocket, and grabbing her gloves.

Amelia made a non-committal noise in her throat. The tug in her gut was growing tighter, pulling thin with every step. She tried to ignore it as they headed back towards Sam's car. She hadn't had alcohol, so she'd be fine to drive home, and Amelia's metabolism was fast enough that what little she'd drunk was already done and gone.

Should have stayed, Luna said, annoyed. *Want fun.*

Next time, Amelia said, though they both knew she was lying.

Sam gave Amelia a sly grin and said, 'If the rest of the scientists don't make it through the snow, maybe you two could go have some fun.'

'I don't know what you're talking about,' Amelia said, but Sam snorted.

'He certainly seemed to like you,' Sam continued as if Amelia hadn't spoken. 'I don't think I saw him look away from you even once.'

'I'm not interested in starting something,' Amelia said as they reached Sam's car. There was a layer of ice this time as she swept the snow off the windscreen.

'I said the same thing,' Sam said, unlocking the car to climb in and start the engine. Once the heaters were on full blast, she handed Amelia a scraper. 'Then I ended up with Hale.'

'Mitchel isn't my mate,' Amelia said. But even as she said it, she couldn't help but think about the tug towards him. The strange feeling of it, and how it felt different. But it wasn't possible. 'Mates are so rare that they're something you see a handful of times in a generation. You're the only mate I've ever heard of.'

'We aren't in some fairy tale, Amelia. Fate isn't dragging us around by our ear, forcing us towards our mates, and not giving us a choice. I ignored what I felt about Hale for literally years. Don't repeat my mistake.'

Amelia sighed and started to scrape the ice of the windscreen. Just because Sam had found her mate, it didn't mean that Mitchel was Amelia's.

Would make good mate, Luna said.

You don't know anything about him, Amelia said. *He could be a serial killer, for all you know.*

Not killer of cereal. Cereal already dead, Luna said, like Amelia was being stupid. She ignored her wolf.

'Besides, I'm not saying he's your mate. All I'm saying is you clearly both like each other. I've never seen you look at anyone with that intensity, let alone act on it in the last month,' Sam said, taking the scraper back as Amelia finished, trying to hold her gaze. 'I want you to be happy, even if it's just for a little while.'

It had been a lot longer than a month, but Amelia didn't say that. It wouldn't help her case.

'I am happy,' Amelia said, glancing at a young couple leaving the pub. Their arms were looped together as they helped each other balance even though the snow hadn't frozen yet. 'Even if I wasn't, a lot is happening now. I don't want to make things more complicated right now.'

Finding mate not complicated, Luna said, nudging her. *Is easy. Just accept.*

I don't want a mate, Amelia said, harsher than she intended. Her wolf whined. *Sorry. I like being free.*

Mate not cage, Luna said, but she backed away at the words, not wanting to argue more. Great, now she'd upset her wolf.

'You know you can talk to me, too,' Sam said as Amelia sat in the front passenger seat. 'I'm a good listener.'

That Sam had noticed she'd been talking to her wolf at all said a lot about how observant the woman was becoming. 'I know, it's just hard.'

Amelia debated what she wanted to say as Sam headed back to the rangers' base, where Amelia had left her car.'

'I've been by myself for so long now I don't know how to let someone in,' Amelia said, trying her best not to sound whiny. 'Dylan alienated me from everyone a piece at a time. I didn't know it was happening at first, and then when I did, it didn't matter. Everyone was afraid of him. Hell, even my own mother wanted me to mate with him.'

Amelia stopped, stamping down on her anger. There were reasons for her mother's actions. Good ones, even if Amelia disagreed with them. Her mother had believed that by mating Dylan, no one would have sent Amelia away if she lost control. Because Amelia wasn't the only one in her family who had. Her father, who she'd thought had been a hero, dying in the Rift Scar, had been sent there because he'd not been able to keep his wolf under control.

That was what Hale could do to her if she went the same way.

Not lose control, Luna said, pressing close, offering comfort this time.

Amelia didn't argue and tried to push the thoughts away. None of them were helpful right now.

'No one here will be scared away by Dylan,' Sam said, fingers tightening on the steering wheel, scent heavy with her anger. 'You're pack, and Hale would send Dylan home in a box before he could hurt anyone here.'

Amelia smiled, throat closing at the words. But it wasn't that easy. 'Dylan is Alaric's son. I doubt Hale would want to challenge the prime alpha.'

'Do you think the prime alphas are happy with anything Hale has done recently?' Sam said, slowing as they hit the last roundabout to the industrial estate. 'Everything he's done has been a challenge. The new pack lands, the change to the rules. Not letting them come and scoop up the pack bonds until the wolves have all healed. Don't discount what Hale will do for this pack.'

Amelia put her hand on Sam's as she pulled in behind the old gym. She could smell the fear under the anger, fear for Hale. 'We'll keep him safe, too,' she said.

Sam nodded once, a hint of tears in the shimmer of her eyes. 'Good. Now, let's get out of the cold and home.

I'm looking forward to curling up in a warm bed with a warmer body against me.'

Amelia let go of Sam and ignored her not-so-subtle reminder about Mitchel as she got out of the car. The wind changed direction as she closed the door, bringing her a familiar scent. She froze, her heart hammering in her chest.

'Amelia,' Dylan said, getting out of a brand-new car that looked out of place among the rest of the beaten-up old Land Rovers. She'd not even seen it as they drove up.

His brown eyes were on Amelia, travelling up and down her body like he was trying to memorise her. He'd cut his brown hair short since she'd last seen him, but that was all that had changed. His jacket was open, showing off his broad shoulders and muscular body. Most wolves had muscle; they were naturally built that way, but getting to this level of definition took work. In Dylan's case, it was to look better rather than to be stronger.

Rage rose in her gut, hot and sharp like someone had shoved a hot poker through her. Dylan had no right to look at her like that; she wasn't his.

She fought to shove the rage down, to suppress it. But every time she made progress, it slipped through her fingers, rising further. This wasn't her wolf trying to make her fight. This was all her own anger at how he'd looked at her that night. How he'd not listened to her.

Not want Dylan, Luna said. *Found mate.*

The rage shrivelled in the wake of her wolf's announcement.

What? Amelia asked, panicked. She didn't want a mate. But her wolf didn't answer. *Mitchel isn't my mate.* But her wolf just shook her coat and sat beside her, watching Dylan.

'... Dylan Evans,' Dylan said, voice breaking through her thoughts. She'd missed his introduction. Sam stood slightly in front of Amelia, back stiff like she could stop Dylan. Or maybe stop Amelia.

'Amelia's mentioned you,' Sam said, voice colder than the snow around them. If Dylan noticed, he didn't acknowledge it as he turned back to Amelia.

'You're not a scientist,' Amelia said, clinging to that detail like it would help keep her balanced. It helped a little. 'Why are you here?'

Dylan smiled, showing all his teeth. 'The prime alphas thought it was important that they send a representative who can help manage all the Shifters coming.'

Amelia bit down on a growl at the accusation that Hale couldn't do his job. It did nothing to help the rage rising as her shock dissipated, and her wolf debated if she wanted to attack him. But even Luna hesitated, unsure if they'd be able to stop once they started.

'Do you have a problem with how Hale runs the pack?' Sam said. If it was possible, her voice was even colder than before.

This time, when Dylan turned to Sam, Amelia saw the condescension. 'This isn't your business,' he said. 'Whoever you are.'

'That would be my mate,' Hale said. He stood in the doorway to the main building, nearly as short as Sam, with black cropped hair and glowing gold eyes. After a heartbeat, they slipped back to their usual brown.

His alpha energy was muted, and the link between them was barely open, which meant he was likely furious. But she couldn't blame him when Dylan had basically insulted his mate.

The rage at seeing Dylan dropped further away, though she wasn't sure whether that was Hale's presence or Dylan being put in his place.

Dylan's wolf rose like a cloud around them as he stiffened and turned so he could see Hale. 'I wasn't aware you'd taken a mate.'

Hale didn't bother with a response.

'Your father failed to notify me personally that you were coming, Dylan,' Hale said, voice soft and even. Dylan flinched back like Hale had done more than speak. 'I'm very disappointed.'

Amelia frowned, not liking that Hale recognised Dylan. As far as she knew, Hale had never been to her pack's home, nor had Dylan been near his. But there was familiarity there, at least on Hale's side. If not for the fact that Sam had never been out of Amelia's sight, she might have suspected that the woman had said something to him.

'I don't need your permission to come here. David agreed to it, and since he's the prime alpha over Scotland, what happens here is his decision,' Dylan said, but when Hale didn't react to the rising wolf energy, he seemed to lose some of his confidence.

Hale smiled slowly, a trickle of energy rising. 'He's not the rift warden,' Hale said, letting the smile drop as his eyes shifted to gold. 'This is my territory, and while you're here, you'll do as I tell you.'

Behind Hale, Lance stepped outside and leaned against the wall, watching everyone. He was over six-six, with broad shoulders and bronze skin. He was wearing a long-sleeved T-shirt and a black glove on one hand.

He was the only wolf other than Hale who'd stayed longer than their one-year term at the Rift Scar. While he didn't interact much with the rest of the pack, today, he stood behind Hale like he was an alpha in his own right. The feel of the pack and home increased, surrounding them.

Dylan curled his lip and moved to argue, but the pressure of Hale's wolf increased. Amelia's wolf revelled in the power and strength of it, though she was careful to keep her side of the link locked down in case that rage came back.

'You should probably head back to your hotel. It's getting late. Tomorrow is going to be a busy day,' Hale said.

Dylan's jaw muscle twitched like he wanted to argue. But he looked between Hale and Lance, then stepped back, backing down. Dylan gave her one long glance, a promise that this wasn't over that nearly made her rage spill out. Then he turned and stalked back to his car. It wasn't designed for snow, but he pulled out and drove away without hitting anything.

'Make sure he goes to the hotel,' Hale said once Dylan was out of sight, glancing at Lance. 'I don't want any trouble tonight.'

Lance nodded, saying nothing as he pulled keys out of his pocket and headed towards a car further down the car park. Her fear eased a little more, though the rage still rolled deep in her gut.

'You two okay?' Hale asked, pulling in a breath.

His gaze lingered on Amelia. Between her scent and the link between them, he'd know she was angry and afraid, though not why. The pack's connection to the alpha was unfairly skewed in Hale's favour. He could sense what the pack felt, but she could sense nothing of him unless he chose to share it. Or maybe he just had better control than her.

'He was just rude,' Sam said, not looking at Amelia. Sam was leaving the choice to tell Hale the details up to her.

'Bad memories of similar fights,' Amelia said when Hale focused just on her, technically not lying. She'd plenty of those, even if that wasn't where the fear and rage had come from today.

'How does his father expect him to lead his pack if this is how he acts in another alpha's territory?' Hale said, shaking his head.

Amelia didn't say anything; she suspected it wasn't a question he expected an answer to.

'I hope this isn't a sign of what the rest of them will be like,' Hale said. Sam moved closer to him, wrapping an arm around his waist.

'We'll find out tomorrow,' Sam said, then a smile tugged at her lips as she turned back to Amelia. 'At least Mitchel is nice.'

Amelia tried not to scowl, but going by Sam's growing grin, she doubted she was successful.

'I'm going to head out. I'll see you both at the town hall tomorrow,' Amelia said, though the feel of Hale's wolf was still around her, and that comfort made her want to linger.

'Be careful,' Hale said, watching her like he knew she was hiding something. But he didn't press, didn't command her to tell him. That freedom made her feel strangely light.

'You too,' Amelia said as she went to her car. Sam's words about telling Hale rose again. But Amelia had seen Dylan, and she'd not attacked him. She'd kept her cool, even if only because her wolf had shocked her.

She hoped that if she'd done it once, she could keep doing it. It was only a few days, and then they'd be gone. She could do this.

CHAPTER FOUR

Mitchel slumped in his chair, feeling sick. The meeting room in the town hall was too warm and smelled stale, like it had been years since the place had been aired. His unsettled stomach twisted as the heater fan clicked on again, pushing out more heat.

He was never drinking again.

'Here,' Oliver said, offering him a glass of what looked like water. But Mitchel knew Oliver's method of dealing with a hangover well enough to be suspicious. Oliver must have seen the look because he gave a lopsided smile and added, 'It's water. Promise.'

Mitchel took the glass gingerly, the army of minions in his head picking up speed. He sniffed it and decided that he was probably safe enough. It was cool and didn't immediately make his stomach want to rebel, so he took that as a win.

'Thanks,' Mitchel said, putting the glass on the table. They were early because after ten shots of wolfbite, even

Oliver hadn't wanted to drive, and he'd slept on Mitchel's hotel room floor. Of course, that had meant when his friend had needed to be up early, Mitchel had been dragged along for the ride.

'Can't do much about the heat, though, I'm afraid,' Oliver said, sitting next to Mitchel, looking at the fan heater. 'Try not to chill out too much.'

The phrasing was odd, but Mitchel got the meaning. His magic was leaking. With a sigh, Mitchel concentrated on pulling his magic back. 'Sorry,' Mitchel said quietly, reaching for another sip of water.

A series of mismatched tables were set up in the middle of the room, with various chairs around the edges. There was a large flip chart at the head of the table. With no screen or projector, it seemed this would be a low-tech meeting.

Sam was also early, her wild curls tamed into a ponytail, making her look younger. She was playing with a stack of paper, looking around the empty seats in the room as she chewed on her lower lip. If he hadn't been hungover, he would've tried to speak to her, but right now, he wasn't sure he'd be able to form a coherent sentence.

Everyone else was due to arrive in about half an hour, and he'd get his first look at the scientists and the rest of Oliver's rangers. Hopefully, that would include Amelia.

Which was a stupid thing to want. But the desire was still there, regardless.

'That's Hale,' Oliver said as the door opened and a man entered, going straight to Sam. He was only slightly taller than her and looked more like a university student than an alpha and warden. Mitchel wasn't a Shifter to feel his power, but it was hard to imagine this small unobtrusive man had the power to lead the pack.

Sam turned to him, eyes following his movements like she was mesmerised. Hale's smile widened.

Mitchel's mind went to Amelia, but he wasn't so deluded to think she'd stand there and watch him walk the same way, even if she was interested. Not with his skinny, awkward build. He'd likely face-plant halfway to her.

Nor did he want that; he was done with women. Done with Shifters. He was going to focus on work and the Rift Scar changes. Even if he scanned the room every few seconds to see if Amelia had arrived while he'd not been watching.

The next person to enter wasn't Amelia, but she was familiar. Madeline was a wiry woman in her sixties. With wild white hair, a wrinkled face, and a long white winter coat, she could have passed as a mad scientist.

She had been his professor at university and one of the reasons he'd specialised in the Rift Scar. Most of her experience was academic since she was human, so it was a surprise to see her, even if she was the UK's leading expert.

'Madeline,' Sam said, sounding equally surprised to see the woman. Clearly, she'd not been on the list. 'They aren't expecting you to go into the Rift Scar, are they?'

'Even the head of the IRS&D doesn't have the power to force me to do that, child,' Madeline said, though Sam was clearly at least in her mid-twenties. 'But I've never had the pleasure of coming this far north before. I thought it was time I remedy that.'

'Is that why you weren't on the list that was sent only yesterday?' Hale said. Though his voice was mild, Oliver shuffled in his seat like he wanted to be standing.

'I wasn't aware I needed to provide notice to visit my staff and do my job?' Madeline said, raising an eyebrow.

Sam blinked in surprise, looking over at Mitchel. He offered her a shrug, sending the men in his head into a frenzy. He'd not heard that she'd changed positions either; last he'd heard, she was still working in education.

'I wasn't aware that the head of surveyors position had become available,' Sam said, voice neutral.

'My predecessor decided to retire early, and I needed a break from education. I've been asked to step in to deal with this situation,' Madeline said, glancing at Hale. 'But, as I'm sure you can understand, there's pressure to keep what happened a secret, so I didn't advertise my visit. No one wants to bring hope where there might not be any.'

Sam stiffened but didn't argue with Madeline over her word choice. Mitchel expected a reaction from Hale or Oliver, but neither said anything. Maybe yesterday's warning had helped prepare them for this.

'Although, since the prime alphas provided most of the resources for this trip, I'd assumed they'd notify you directly,' Madeline said, pulling off her coat and throwing it over one of the chairs. 'They've had the full list for weeks, including myself.'

Hale's eyes narrowed, and his body language changed. He was no longer someone you could pass on the street and not notice. Instead, Mitchel saw the alpha, someone who was powerful and dangerous. He couldn't pinpoint what had changed. Then, between one blink and the next, Hale slipped back into that unassuming persona.

Shivering, Mitchel glanced at Oliver. He looked as unhappy as Hale. Clearly, something was going on between the packs, some politics Mitchel wasn't privy to.

'I wasn't aware that the prime alphas had taken such an interest in the Rift Scar changes,' Hale said.

'I'm not sure there would be any other reason every scientist would be a Shifter,' Madeline said, raising her eyebrow. A hint of annoyance that was so familiar from his university days slipped into her voice.

Hale turned to Mitchel. The little hangover army in his head took offence at the look and pounded harder. Madeline followed Hale's gaze, eyebrows rising even further. She'd clearly not noticed him when she'd first come in.

'I hadn't thought you'd made it through the snow,' she said. Her tone was neutral, carefully so.

'I took an earlier train,' Mitchel said. He stomped down on his anger as the condensation on the glass started to freeze.

'How many others didn't make it through the weather?' Hale asked, turning back to Madeline.

'None.' Her lips thinned as she turned back to Hale. 'All the rest came through yesterday morning, early.'

Hale didn't say anything as Madeline's words settled over them. That was why they'd waited until the last minute to give Mitchel the late train tickets. They were relying on the weather to stop him from getting through. They'd not wanted him here.

Mitchel felt the bile rise in his throat. His father had said he'd recommended Mitchel for the position. But it was evident that his father must have done more than that, even if it hadn't been enough for them to want to bring him.

Oliver shifted his foot, touching Mitchel with a light tap. He took a breath, looking away from Madeline. But it didn't matter. He knew the truth now. He'd not been picked to come; he was something they'd not been able to get rid of.

The door opened again, and Clara entered, hesitating in the doorway as everyone turned to her. She'd dressed in a cut-off jumper, a vest top underneath, and a pair of low-rise jeans. Neither were appropriate for the weather. Kenneth entered behind her, nudging his way past her to lean against a wall at the back. He wore grey combat trousers and T-shirt.

They'd picked Clara to come here. The woman had done the bare minimum her whole life. They'd sent Madeline, who had no experience in practical work. He'd been so stupid, so optimistic. But he should have known better the moment he'd seen Clara. This wasn't an investigation; this was some kind of political game.

Oliver kicked Mitchel again, less gently, making him look up at him. There was sympathy there and shared anger. It helped ease some of the knots growing in Mitchel's stomach. These political games weren't just going to affect him. Someone was trying to hurt Oliver's pack.

Taking a breath, Mitchel took the glass of water in hand, pulling the cold back in, melting the layer of ice on top before anyone noticed. He could be bitter and angry later, but for now, he was here, and he was damned well going to make the most of it.

'Why don't we discuss this later,' Madeline said, nodding at Hale, drawing the focus back to her.

Clara relaxed, looked towards Mitchel, and stepped like she intended to sit beside him. He stiffened, straightening despite the headache and churning gut. He wasn't in the mood to fight with her, nor was this the place to do it when she could manipulate Shifters.

But Clara didn't get far as Madeline continued, 'Clara, why don't you sit with me? You can take notes of anything we must do before you go out into the field.'

Clara flinched, but there was no chance to argue as Madeline sat near the head of the table. Mitchel relaxed a fraction as Clara changed direction and did as Madeline asked.

More people arrived after that. It was easy to separate the local rangers from the visitors because the former was dressed in the same gear as Kenneth, and they all took positions against the walls. There were rounds of general introductions, though most of the names escaped Mitchel.

He didn't know or recognise any of the names of the other scientists that arrived.

When Amelia appeared, she moved to lean against the wall behind Hale. She reminded him of a warrior standing guard. It wasn't even that she was physically imposing, but he could feel a wildness in the way she watched the room.

Most wolves had it, and it had been part of what had attracted him to Clara. She'd burned him too badly for it to be enough on its own anymore. But there was more than just wildness there. There was a feeling of protectiveness to the watching that had never been something Clara had shown.

Part of him wanted to get up and go to Amelia. Even if it was just to say 'hi'. Though she hadn't even looked in his direction that he'd noticed yet.

Oliver tapped Mitchel's foot again, but there was no ice in his glass this time. The move might have been accidental, but Oliver was very aware of his size and rarely did anything by accident. Mitchel watched Oliver as he tapped his nose, a tiny grin appearing before it disappeared, and he went back to watching the new people.

Heat warmed Mitchel's cheeks. It was easy to forget how good a Shifter's sense of smell was. Though after an entire relationship with Clara mocking him about his scent, he was surprised he ever forgot.

He tried to avoid looking at Amelia. It wasn't easy. His eyes kept going back to her as if drawn by a magnet. It was so strong that he'd almost forgotten Clara was in the room, something he'd never have imagined possible before.

'This looks to be everyone,' Madeline said as the door closed behind two men, one in a leather jacket and another tall bronze-skinned man with a glove on one hand and the standard grey ranger uniform. The latter leaned against the wall, and the former sat beside Clara. There were about a dozen scientists in all. They'd sat together on the opposite side of the table, looking very uncomfortable for the most part. 'Let's get through the safety part so the team can get on with their jobs.'

Mitchel sat up further in his seat. Some of the hangover had eased, though not by much, but he wouldn't be accused of slacking, especially when it was obvious they'd not wanted him.

Amelia pulled in a breath, letting the scents fill her nose, trying to sort them. Dirt, grass, wildflowers, peat, old books, spices. Layers and layers of different wolves' scents, familiar and unfamiliar, combined into one massive nose-searing stench.

Among it all, she picked up their fear and excitement as well as other emotions, like curiosity and anger. The latter probably came from Shifters who had to let a group of strange wolves into their home.

Buried underneath it all, she caught Mitchel's scent. Morning frost and a hint of last night's whisky. She wanted to let go of all the rest and pull in his, but that wasn't possible.

He'd spent most of the time since she'd arrived watching her. She'd felt his eyes. Felt the heat of them on her skin. It had taken every inch of her self-control to not return the stare.

Not need to pretend, Luna said, nudging her to look. To let him see they were looking. *Our mate.*

We're not going to start something with him, Amelia said, refusing to even acknowledge the word mate. *He's here to do a job, nothing more.*

Her wolf huffed a breath of amusement but let her focus on the crowd again. Mostly because Dylan had looked around at her. He'd entered last and taken a seat near Madeline. It put him with his back to her, at least, and that was easier.

The rage was still there, but Hale's presence helped keep it at bay. Helped to keep her calm.

Hale did some introductions, then debriefed the scientists on the status of the Highland Rift Scar. Most of what he said was standard. Imps and scorpions were everywhere. A few more dangerous creatures were situated further into the Scar, but they wouldn't get anywhere near them today. That might change, though, because they wouldn't know how deep they'd need to go later without understanding what had changed to make the Scar shrink.

'The weather warden arrived back in town last night and is doing her best to divert the storm. That will give us a break from fresh snow, if not the cold,' Hale said, looking around the table. 'The one benefit of the cold, however, is that the worst of the Rift Scar residents will be hibernating.

'Many of you have been through a short course, though some have been through something a bit longer. Regardless of your experience, you won't be given weapons during this trip.' There was a muttering through the group, and Hale raised his voice. 'To make sure everyone is secure, you'll be broken up into groups and assigned rift ranger guards.'

Dylan made a noise in his throat and leaned forward. 'If you let us have weapons, we wouldn't need the rangers to protect us.'

Hale looked at Dylan, tilting his head. 'How much experience do you have working inside the Rift Scar?'

'How much experience could you possibly need? Point and shoot, and then it's dead,' Dylan said. A few rangers rolled their eyes. 'If my father was here, we'd already be in the field.'

'Your father isn't here. How we go into the Rift Scar is my decision.' Hale's voice was calm and careful, but his energy was starting to leak, and his scent was overpowering everything else in the room.

Dylan stood, half growling. 'My fath—'

'Careful, Dylan,' Hale said, letting more of his power into his voice. 'You're a guest. One who I can have removed if you cannot follow orders. Sit down.'

The word 'guest' might as well have been substituted with 'intruder'; it would have fit the tone better. The wolves around the table grew still as they waited for Dylan's answer.

Hale had given Dylan a clear order. One that, if he didn't follow, could mean Dylan could be sent packing. But he wasn't backing down. Her earlier rage was back with this new fuel, pressing at her to attack, and this time, it wasn't alone.

Fight, Luna growled. *Protect pack.*

Her wolf wasn't the only one reacting. Shifter energy writhed against her skin. There was going to be a fight. All because of Dylan. Because he couldn't back down.

'Has the border changed any more since it was first reported?' Mitchel asked, voice slicing through the tension and drawing every eye to him. Amelia stepped towards him, the need to protect him as deep and sharp as her rage had been moments before.

Oliver saved her the need as he shifted in his seat, reminding the room of his presence, though the weight of his wolf was hard to pick out against the feel of Hale's.

'No,' Hale said, energy peeling back a few levels. His eyes never left Dylan. 'Just the previously receded half a mile. Sam has been forwarding everything daily.'

'Like a human is going to know anything useful about the Rift Scar,' Dylan said, clearly not done trying to make a scene. He curled his lip and added, 'She's probably so terrified of being stung or bitten that she got the recordings wrong. I wouldn't be surprised if we were here for nothing.'

The room froze. The scientists' eyes went to Madeline, and the packs' went to Hale. Thankfully, Mitchel didn't try to break the tension this time.

Amelia imagined what might have happened if Hale hadn't been expecting something precisely like this statement on top of the earlier challenge. Dylan might not have survived that reaction. As it was, Hale's knuckles were white, and his scent was thick with his anger. But his energy was even.

Dylan frowned at the silent group. He'd clearly expected some kind of support or a different reaction. Was he deliberately trying to get Hale to attack him?

'I can assure you that I'm very capable of doing my job,' Sam said, looking straight at Dylan. 'But if you have any doubts, you'll see for yourself soon enough.'

'Oh, I'm sure he will. Especially since us humans cannot enter the Rift Scar, there will be plenty for him to do,' Madeline said, emphasis on 'us humans' strong enough that Dylan twitched. He'd forgotten what Madeline was. 'Why don't you continue with your overview, Hale? Hopefully, we can make it through the rest without any more interruption.'

This time, Dylan stayed quiet as he took his seat. He smelled of frustration, like he'd wanted more of a reaction. But why was he trying to provoke Hale at all? If he wanted to fight Hale, why not issue a challenge?

Hale good alpha, Luna said, lying down as she watched through Amelia's eyes. *Not challenge good alpha.*

I suppose that's possible, Amelia said. If Dylan challenged Hale without a good reason or extenuating circumstances, the prime alphas could punish Dylan for the challenge. But if Hale lost control and attacked, and Dylan just defended, then it would be a different case.

Kill Dylan if challenge Hale, Luna said, pressing close. *Not let him be alpha.*

Amelia suppressed a shiver at the idea of Dylan as alpha and silently agreed with her wolf. If it came to it, she'd rather let the rage out and remove Dylan than give him power over her. Even if it would mean her own death.

Hale continued with his briefing, but his eyes rarely left Dylan's.

'How big a group are we going out in?' Mitchel's voice drew her eyes back to him. He was the only one in the room asking questions. The rest just looked nervous as they looked between Hale and Dylan.

'I'll go with Amelia,' Dylan said, turning around to watch her, making her skin crawl and rage rise.

'No.' Hale's voice held an edge of power this time, making Dylan stiffen. 'You're not a scientist.'

'My f—'

'Since you seem unable to follow a simple order without arguing, you can join me or stay here,' Hale said. The excuse was a good one, but it was apparent from the way Hale watched Dylan that he'd never let the other man out of his sight if he could avoid it. 'I'm sure you'll enjoy seeing the Rift Scar for the first time while the scientists do their job.'

Hale drew on the pack bonds for power. A warmth bloomed in the centre of Amelia's chest, and the feeling of the pack grew so strong it was almost like all the wolves stood together under the full moon. It flowed into the room, taking a small piece of her with it.

Dylan's eyes widened a fraction, breathing ragged. Hale was letting all of the outsiders see the power he could call. It couldn't control Dylan like it did Amelia or the rest of the pack, but she couldn't help but revel in his shocked expression.

Then, just like Hale had flicked a switch, he pulled it all back, and Dylan sagged forward. Hale closed the pack bonds again, gently letting go of the link. Amelia took a slow breath, touching her chest, missing the warmth. That hadn't been an attack against Dylan. That had been a show of strength. But she'd never felt anything like it. Anytime her alpha had called on the pack strength before, it had always hurt. Especially Shane.

'Let's take a break while Madeline and I assign you into groups,' Hale said, standing, nodding at the wolf closest to the door. 'There's coffee and tea set up down the hall. Kenneth will lead the way.'

Kenneth seemed startled to be given the job but pushed away from the wall. After that little demonstration, everyone wanted out of there, so it didn't take much work to get everyone moving. Even Mitchel, despite his earlier confidence asking questions, followed Kenneth eagerly. Dylan didn't wait for anyone else as he stalked out of the room.

Amelia didn't join the crowd, though both the scientists and the rangers were leaving. Instead, she moved over to join Hale, who still stood by his seat. The anger in his scent was obvious, even if she couldn't feel it crawling over her skin. Lance stayed by the door, head tilted as if listening to the outside.

'Tell me, Madeline,' Hale said as the door closed, 'when Dylan has no scientific experience, what exactly do you want him to do?'

Madeline looked over her shoulder, face tight. 'Nothing. You can do whatever you want with him.'

The unspoken words that she hadn't invited him couldn't have been any louder. Hale let out a slow breath. 'And the rest, do you have a preference for how and who you want out there? If I'd known what they'd be doing, I'd have been able to organise something in advance.'

Madeline pulled out a piece of paper from her pocket and handed it over. Names were printed on it, dividing the team into four, with a few other details about their jobs. But there was a name that was missing.

'Mitchel isn't on this list?' Amelia said, looking up at Madeline. Sam took the page from Hale and scanned it.

'He wasn't supposed to make it through,' Madeline said, seemingly unconcerned at admitting that they'd deliberately tried to block him. If Amelia was Mitchel, she'd be furious. 'I'm sure you can find an area to send him to.'

Not add him to one of the teams. Send him on his own.

The way Madeline said it made her wolf's hackles rise, but Amelia saw something else. Something about the way she'd dismissed him was too intense. Like she was trying to send a message.

'You could send him round the outer edge and have him double-check my work,' Sam said, waving the page. 'You don't need a whole team to do that.'

Madeline smiled fleetingly before her face became serious again. 'That seems logical to me. He can bring the readings back to your lab for me to evaluate. I'd rather not go out in this cold if I don't have to, and it does seem wasteful to send a whole group to do it.'

Sam's smile grew strained at the mention of her lab, but she gave Hale a slight nod. This was an excellent way to avoid sending strange wolves into the pack lands. The only chance they'd get.

'Amelia, you take Mitchel and Oliver to the area in question,' Hale said. 'I'll open the pack bonds a fraction since so many of us are in the field.'

That made sense, and as long as there was a Shifter in each group, it would let Hale know if they were in danger and needed help, if not much else. It was better than nothing, with the comms being so spotty. Unfortunately, it would also open her up so Hale could feel her conflicted emotions. She'd need to be extra careful to keep her rage in check.

With a nod, she turned away to go give Mitchel the news he'd be riding with her. As she did, the link between her and Hale opened that tiny fraction, and she felt a layer of his worry for a moment. Most would assume it was either the outsider wolves or taking untrained people into the field. But she knew the actual source. Sam.

They'd tested everything they could think of to make sure Sam's magic wasn't visible in some way. But as much testing as they'd done, it had all been between Amelia and Hale. They couldn't be one hundred per cent sure what an Elemental like Mitchel might sense.

'As to the rest, four groups, it will mean that we have to use the rapid response unit as well, though, with the cold weather, I expect that there won't be much need for the team,' Hale said as Amelia left, clearly unhappy with the idea.

Lance nodded at her as she passed him. The quiet Shifter felt even more distant than usual, clearly not liking all these strangers any more than she did. None of the pack did.

Amelia closed the door silently behind her, cutting off the rest of Hale's discussion. She'd barely made it down the first hallway when she almost walked into Dylan as he came around the corner.

She backed up before he could reach out and try to touch her. Or she tried to do something to him she might regret. She also did her best to lock down her end of the pack bonds, which wasn't the easiest thing to do.

Not regret hitting him, Luna growled as he looked her up and down. The rage Hale's presence had been smothering was trying to claw its way up her chest.

Hitting him landed us here, Amelia said, trying to get a hold of the anger. Her wolf pressed closer.

Would not have found mate if not here, Luna said, as she helped lend her focus to stop the rage.

'Amelia,' Dylan said, smiling like they were two friends meeting. Did he not have any idea how much she hated him? 'Looks like the Rift Scar is working for you.'

'I don't have time to talk to you just now,' Amelia said, digging her nails into her palm, trying to distract herself from the anger. 'I have work to do.'

'Look, I wanted you to know I had nothing to do with you being sent here. My father overreacted,' Dylan said, moving closer to her. 'You know I'd never hurt you.'

That he still didn't get that she wasn't interested shouldn't have surprised her. Nor did the fact he seemed to be ignoring the anger that must have laced her scent.

'I don't care,' Amelia said.

Dylan laughed. 'Of course you care. That's why you've been ignoring my calls. I'm not stupid, Amelia. How could you not be mad? I'm just telling you I don't blame you. It's not your fault for thinking that I abandoned you. But I'm going to make it right. Then, things can go back to how they were. You can come home.'

Amelia stared at him, then snapped her jaw shut when she realised it was hanging open. He looked so confident. That this was why she was mad at him. Even the rage abandoned her as she grasped the depth of Dylan's self-delusion.

'Amelia?' Oliver said, appearing behind Dylan.

Dylan scowled at Oliver and tried to reach for Amelia, but she stepped back. Dylan didn't follow, thankfully.

'Just think about what I said. I can find a way to make it right.'

Amelia didn't get a chance to answer as Dylan spun and shoved his way past Oliver. Oliver raised an eyebrow at Amelia, but she shook her head.

'Don't ask,' Amelia said. The last thing she needed was Oliver being her white knight. Besides, with the assignments, she wouldn't have to deal with Dylan for the rest of the day. 'Hale said for you and me to take Mitchel up to the border where the changes started so he can take readings.'

Oliver exhaled, smelling of relief as he nodded. He might not have known the whole truth, but he wouldn't have wanted strange Shifters on the pack lands any more than Hale or Amelia did. 'I left him with the coffee.'

'Maybe if you two hadn't drunk so much last night, he wouldn't be in such desperate need of it,' Amelia said, somewhat harsher than she intended as she headed towards where Mitchel would be.

'But it was worth it,' Oliver said, grinning as he spun to walk next to her. 'You should have stayed. Got to know Mitchel a bit more.'

Amelia scowled at him, but he just grinned wider.

Not wrong, Luna said, joining in.

Amelia ignored both of them. She didn't want Mitchel. Even if she could feel that tug grow stronger, leading her straight to where he was leaning against the hallway corridor, plastic coffee cup in his hands.

He looked a little pale as he hunched over his coffee. His scent hinted of pain and last night's whisky still. It took far too much effort not to reach out and touch him. To not brush back his hair where it had fallen forward into his eye.

Between the rage and her desire, she just had to hope Hale hadn't picked her emotions out of the rest of the pack. That wasn't a conversation she wanted to have with anyone, let alone Hale.

CHAPTER FIVE

MITCHEL SAT IN THE back of Amelia's Land Rover, try-ing his best to stop the contents of his twisting stomach from coming up. He never got car sick, but between the rough roads and the hangover, it was bad enough that he almost wished he'd missed the train.

Almost. The chance to see the part of the Rift Scar border that had changed was too good to pass up, even if it meant he felt a little unwell. Or he had to wade through whatever politics was going on behind the scenes.

He doubted anyone would be happy that Mitchel had been assigned to scan the changed area. Not that anyone had been friendly or approachable so far. When they'd been dismissed for coffee, the scientists had clustered together in a little clique, avoiding everyone, including Mitchel.

They hit a pothole hard enough that his teeth clicked together, and his stomach tried to complete an evac.

'You doing okay back there?' Oliver asked, looking over his shoulder from where he sat in the front passenger seat. He looked at Mitchel like he'd sensed the near miss on seeing last night's whisky.

They'd stopped by ranger headquarters, and Oliver was now wearing grey combat trousers and a Kevlar vest over a long-sleeved grey T-shirt. He and Amelia had also collected weapons and some other gear that they'd locked in the boot.

'I'm fantastic,' Mitchel said, swallowing hard. That was the last time he ever drank with Oliver. Or at least until all the work was done.

Oliver squinted at him, giving him a once-over. 'We can stop for a minute if you need,' he said, glancing at Amelia.

Mitchel followed his gaze. She'd also put on a Kevlar vest when they'd stopped. Knowing she had that extra protection made him feel better, which was stupid. He'd not thought that about Oliver or the body armour that Madeline had given him. It sat on the seat next to him, and he wasn't looking forward to putting on the extra bulk.

'I'd rather stop than have you throw up in my new car,' Amelia said, not taking her eyes off the road. It was the first time she'd spoken to him today other than to tell him of the assignment. Somehow, he suspected she disapproved of the hangover. To be fair, if he was in her shoes, he'd probably feel the same.

'Or on the Corruption Detection Scanner,' Oliver said, a smirk rising. 'Sam might skin you if you mess it up.'

Mitchel glanced at the black case in the back footwell. Before he'd left, Madeline had also given him the newest Corruption Detection Scanner, or CDS for short. Once the investigation was over, it was going to Sam.

It wasn't all that different from the old CDS machine. It was still a small rectangular box with an extendable reader that could detect the Rift Scar corruption. Except now they could upload the readings through the network. If they had a stable connection, which, out here, was unlikely. He'd not had a solid signal all morning.

'I'll not make a mess, promise,' Mitchel said, swallowing again as the nausea eased.

Amelia slowed and turned off the two-way road onto a single track with a warning sign. A plough had been through recently, and the road was clear of snow, if not ice. Mitchel's magic helped the tyres stick almost automatically, though Amelia's car was doing pretty well on its own.

The silence fell over them again, and Mitchel turned to watch the trees as they thinned out on his left. Their road was raised, and the Scar was clearly visible down a slight drop. This section was a large wasteland, the scarred and broken earth evident even with the snow covering it.

He'd been so excited to come here. Now, Madeline's words had soured everything.

'Welcome to the Highland Rift Scar,' Oliver said, glancing back at him like he'd sensed the direction of Mitchel's thoughts.

In the distance, he could see the crumbling ruin of an old stone building. Before the Rifts had opened, this area had been farming land. Families had lived here. Now, nothing grew except what came from the Rift.

Ahead of them, another car appeared. It was too far away to see much more than the blue colour.

'Idiot,' Amelia muttered, scowling as she looked left and right, clearly trying to find somewhere to let the car pass. The piled snow from the plough wasn't leaving them with many options. 'No one is supposed to be using this road.'

Oliver sighed. 'Someone always thinks they know better than the signs. The council should just rip up the turning. It's not like we ever go that far south.'

Mitchel didn't comment as his stomach twisted. The car was going fast. The straight road clearly gave the driver a false sense of security as it barrelled closer. But instead of slowing gradually, he saw the flash of red against snow. Brake lights.

He'd always been told accidents happened in slow motion, but in the few times he'd ever had the misfortune of being in one, that had never been the case. Watching this little car fight for traction, however, he could see every step of where it went wrong. Steering away from the spin, it hit the bank, bounced and spun faster. Brake lights flared brightly on the snowbanks.

He tried to reach out with his magic. To grab the ice under the car and force it to stick. But they were too far away, and he didn't have that kind of control.

The front wheel went over the edge of the short cliff. For a heartbeat, he thought it might beach itself there. But it didn't.

The car was just going too fast.

The other wheels slipped over, and the car roared into the Rift Scar, where it smashed into a pile of snow, stopping hard.

Amelia cursed and exchanged a look with Oliver. 'Do you have a signal?'

'No signal,' Oliver said, already putting his phone away as Mitchel turned back to him.

'We have to help them,' Mitchel said. Whether they were Rift Bloodline or human in the car didn't matter. Out here in the middle of nowhere, with the temperature this cold, the weather would easily kill them. Unless something else in the Rift got to them first.

'If we go down there alone, Hale is going to be pissed,' Oliver said, ignoring Mitchel as he looked at Amelia.

Amelia's mouth thinned into a white line. 'Do you want to leave them, then?'

'Hell no,' Oliver said. His eyes were amber, his wolf shining through. 'I'm just giving you all advanced notice.'

'Good,' Amelia said, urging the Land Rover to go a little faster, but not enough that they'd be joining the car in another accident. The car disappeared as they entered a section where the mountain rose higher.

Mitchel swallowed hard; his hangover, nearly forgotten in the adrenaline spike, returned. He was never drinking again.

AMELIA TOOK THE LAND Rover as close as she dared to where the car had gone off the road. As much as she wanted to help whoever was inside, there was no point in risking themselves. Even if, despite the other car going over, hers seemed to grip well. But all it took was one wrong move to lose control.

She searched the area before she got out of the Land Rover. This part of the Rift was mostly barren, with a low fence and a four-foot drop to get in. They'd stopped maybe a hundred metres back from where the car had gone over. Though the drop had been lower there, she didn't want to risk the road.

The car's engine screamed. Maybe the accelerator was stuck on, or something else broken? She didn't know enough about cars to be sure. But going by the fact it wasn't moving, it must have hit something solid that she couldn't see. There was no smoke, but fire was a real risk despite the snow. If the car caught fire, there wouldn't be much they could do to help the people inside.

The scent of rubber and fuel scored her nose as she exited the Land Rover. She couldn't hear any voices over the top of the noise. No one calling for help. Unconscious or confused, then. Or dead.

Amelia thrust that thought aside and moved to the boot to grab her weapon. She'd assume they were alive unless there was proof otherwise. Car injuries like this could go a lot of different ways, and she wouldn't know how bad it was until she got there. If she'd been able to finish her medical degree, she'd have been better equipped to deal with it. Of course, if she'd finished the degree, she'd likely not be here at all.

'Just take the small gun,' Oliver said as he joined her at the back of the car, grabbing his rifle. 'You'll need your hands free to deal with whoever is in the car. With us being close to the edge and the cold weather, we shouldn't be too likely to run into anything that dangerous.'

Amelia nodded. She was no longer the green recruit she'd been, but Oliver had more experience in the field than she did, so she was happy to follow his lead. She grabbed the chest harness designed to go over the Kevlar and took the smaller handgun from the metal lock box. She felt naked without her rifle, which wasn't something she'd imagined she'd feel when she'd first arrived.

'What do you need me to do?' Mitchel asked as he joined them at the back of the car. He'd put on the armour vest and glanced at the weapons like he hoped she'd give him something. She closed the lock box before he got any ideas.

Oliver moved quickly to the cliff's edge, sliding more than walking over the road. On the other side, he planted his feet more solidly on the piled snow and leaned against the low fence, bracing the rifle on his shoulder. He'd warn them if he saw anything out there. That left her to answer Mitchel.

His scent made her skin tingle. She wanted to force him back into the car so nothing could hurt him. He didn't belong in the Rift Scar. He needed to be somewhere safe and far away from danger.

Not a pup, Luna said to her, clearly thinking she was being foolish. Even though she'd been protesting about helping him with his hangover the whole way. Luna growled at her. *Not same.*

Unfortunately, it didn't matter what either of them wanted. If there was more than one person in the car, she'd need the help. Oliver would be tied up watching for anything trying to attack them. She just hoped Mitchel could keep his head in a crisis. She grabbed her large medical bag from the back of the car and handed it to him to carry so she'd have both hands if she needed to react.

'Stay close, and help me if I need it,' Amelia said, resisting the urge to take another pull of his scent. She needed to focus. As it was, the entire car journey had been an exercise in self-restraint. 'We've no idea who's in the car or their condition.'

The pack bonds flared in Amelia's head as Hale reacted to her worry. She wished she could send something more than just emotion back to him. But that wasn't how the magic worked. Even if it did, they'd be an hour away at least by now, and there was no way they could wait that long.

Oliver glanced at her, obviously feeling the same thing. She shrugged. There wasn't much they could do about it now. They needed to focus on what they could do.

She stepped onto the road carefully, and her feet immediately slid. Mitchel reached out and took her arm, helping her keep her balance. She felt her connection to him sharpen, and his scent filled her nose, making her want to lean into him more. She didn't. But it was a close thing.

With his hand on her arm, they had no issues keeping their balance as they crossed the road. He let go once they reached the crunchy snow, and part of her wished he hadn't.

Amelia drew her gun to cover Oliver as he secured his rifle and climbed over the low fence. He stepped over the edge without a word, dropping four feet to land in a snowdrift that came up to his knees. He moved out of the way, pulling his gun up and motioning for them to join him.

She looked at Mitchel. Going into the Rift Scar would make most people hesitate, but he didn't pause as he stepped off the edge, holding the medical bag to his chest. He landed with less grace than Oliver, but he kept his feet.

See. Not pup. Strong, Luna said, urging her forward to join them.

He's inexperienced and has no training, Amelia said, but she knew she was fighting a losing battle with her wolf when Luna just turned her back on her.

She put her gun back in the holster while she jumped. The snow was softer than she'd expected, and she sank to her knees. Her combats helped protect her from some of the cold, but they weren't designed for this kind of weather. As soon as the snow melted, she'd be wet and miserable. They'd also foolishly left their thick jackets behind in the rush.

Oliver waited for her to wade out of the snow and re-draw her weapon, holding it with two hands and pointing it at the ground. She nodded at Oliver, and he stalked ahead of her, head swivelling as he scanned the area. She motioned Mitchel to go ahead and took up the rear.

Her movements were now so familiar they were automatic, even with Mitchel in front of her. Being part of a team felt good in a way that she'd not expected when she'd first come here.

The engine's sound grew louder, still hiding any sounds from inside. She kept expecting it to cut off or something worse, but it stayed the same.

They were ten metres away when the wind changed direction. Oliver froze, gun coming up as he scanned the ground.

Amelia caught the scent at the same time. 'Scorpion,' Amelia said for Mitchel's benefit.

Mitchel cursed, going still as he scanned the area. Even with the snow, they should have been easy to spot. They were dark grey and grew up to two feet long. But she couldn't see anything.

Despite their size, they wouldn't have been that dangerous except for the Rift venom they carried. Unfortunately, the venom was nearly always fatal to humans, with the few who survived becoming Elementals. Those who were already Elementals lost access to their magic, and Shifters got stuck in the form they were in. Wolf or human.

Hate scorpion, Luna said, pressing on her to shift. They both hated being trapped like that, unable to make the choice. All Shifters did. But if her wolf had to choose, she wanted to be in their animal form.

We'll be fine, Amelia said. *We're still fast and strong as a human, and the guns are a safer weapon today.*

Her wolf didn't entirely believe her, but she did back off on the pressure.

'How many?' Mitchel asked, his voice tight. His scent grew thick in her nose, almost drowning everything else out. It was peppered with fear and desire. The latter was fading the closer they got to the car.

Oliver winced. 'More than one.' There was a lot more than one going by the strength of the scent. 'Maybe the snow is keeping them down,' Oliver said, shifting his grip on his gun.

It was possible but unlikely. Scorpions were aggressive at the best of times, but when someone intruded on their territory, they were even worse.

'We don't have much choice but to keep going,' she said, looking down at her feet buried in the snow up to her ankles. It would be too easy to miss standing on one if it was under the snow. But if that was the case, maybe it had already frozen to death.

However, she also doubted the scent would be that strong if that was true.

She moved to take another step closer to Oliver, but Mitchel grabbed her arm, pulling her back. She stumbled at the unexpected change in balance, growling at Mitchel. The last thing she needed was to babysit a frightened civilian, regardless of how she felt about him.

Mitchel didn't react to the growl. He just pointed at the ground. A few inches in front of her was a hole, almost invisible in the snow. If she'd taken that step, her foot would have gone in, and the best-case scenario was she might have twisted her ankle.

Amelia swallowed the urge to apologise to Mitchel. He still shouldn't have grabbed her.

'Please tell me that's not a scorpion nest?' Oliver said, but he stopped moving. How many more holes were hidden from their sight?

'How the hell are they this close to the border?' Amelia asked though she didn't expect her question to be answered any more than Oliver's. Scorpions liked to be much deeper into the Rift Scar usually.

'The hole is deep. There are several of them around us,' Mitchel said, looking at Oliver.

She'd never heard of an Elemental being able to sense nests like that before. But Oliver nodded, accepting his words without question.

'How do you know for sure?' Amelia asked. Part of her might like Mitchel, but he'd never been in the field before. Never had the pressure or the fear. Not everyone dealt with it the same way.

Her wolf made a huffing noise in her mind. *Our mate smarter. Stronger.*

She ignored her wolf.

'The water,' Oliver said, answering for Mitchel so fast that it felt like it was something he'd done before, but why? She pulled in a breath to catch Oliver's scent, but it was lost under Mitchel's. 'All this ice is just water, basically. It flows down into the holes and makes it possible to see them.'

Which made sense, she supposed, but if he could sense them, maybe he could do something about them too? 'Could you drown them?' Amelia asked. 'Flood them with water?'

'Wouldn't that just bring them all out here with us?' Mitchel said carefully, like he didn't want to offend anyone.

Told you. Smart, Luna said, chuffing out a breath like she was laughing at Amelia.

'You could use the water to seal the entrance, though? Right?' Oliver said, looking at Mitchel. There was an odd emphasis on the suggestion, making Amelia feel like she was missing part of the conversation. She was going to have words with Oliver later.

Mitchel frowned, then nodded slowly, still looking at the ground. 'I could do that.'

'What happens if they're already out here? If we block their only escape, won't they just come for us instead?' Amelia said, looking at the car. She skirted saying what she really meant. If the car had hit the nest, there were likely scorpions in it. They were going to rescue the people inside either way.

'Leave one hole open?' Oliver said. 'It gives us one point to guard for as well. Then maybe we can scare them into their hole if we need to.'

That might work, though Amelia didn't like the looseness of scaring the scorpions. Fire was about all that frightened them. Well, that and the larger Rift creatures.

'Flares?' Amelia said, looking at the medical bag. It was one of the items packed inside. Though not usually used in this way.

Oliver nodded, taking the bag from Mitchel to fish for the narrow tubes. There were only two, so he handed one to Amelia and kept the other for himself. She wished there was more time, but they'd already taken too long. The fact that they hadn't seen any scorpions yet made her stomach tight. Where were they?

'Let's do it,' she said, nodding at the two men.

Mitchel's scent grew stronger again until she could nearly taste it. The feel of it made her skin prickle warmly, tugging at her desire like the morning after a full moon. She shuddered at the pleasure of it, trying to fight the distraction. Right now, she needed to focus.

'Show me where the holes are. We can choose one to leave open,' Oliver said. He seemed unaffected by the burst of power, but he avoided looking Amelia in the eye. Her scent would tell him exactly how it had affected her—if he could smell her past Mitchel. This little display wouldn't help her convince Oliver she wasn't interested in Mitchel.

Mitchel looked around and started moving over to the left. There was a calm surety in his movements. Even though this had to be stressful. That steadiness hadn't been something she'd looked for before in a partner, but now, seeing it in Mitchel, she had to wonder why.

Not that she wanted Mitchel as her partner. Her wolf laughed at her.

MITCHEL REVELLED IN THE feeling of ice and snow all around him, letting his magic spread out for a dozen metres. The natural cold made the process easier. He wasn't cooling anything down, just connecting to what was there.

His hangover dropped away like it had never existed, though he suspected it might not stay that way when he was no longer using the magic.

The area sprung up in his mind as clearly as if he was seeing what was under the snow. He could see the outline of the rock that the car had hit. Snow had piled inside the car, and he could feel it touching something warm. A person. He could only feel one, but that didn't mean there wasn't more outside of where the snow had reached, and they were still too far back to get a good view inside the car.

Some patches were less clear. Strange spots of darkness where he couldn't feel what was touching the snow, something he hadn't experienced before. But he had used this magic so rarely that he shouldn't be surprised. There was a lot he didn't know.

Taking a shuddering breath, Mitchel pulled back from the car and focused on the ground around their feet. He couldn't do anything to help the person in the car, but the half a dozen holes were something he could fix.

It was impossible to see how deep the nests went because only the top layer of soil was frozen under the ice, but he could see where they emerged in the snow well enough. There was no sign of any Rift scorpions, but he trusted Oliver's nose.

Now Mitchel had found the holes, he walked carefully forward, pointing them out to Oliver. After they'd inspected them all, Oliver chose one that was out of the way of the path back to Amelia's Land Rover and not too close to the car.

'This one,' Oliver said, using his foot to carefully clear the snow. His shoes were thick, but a two-foot scorpion's stinger would rip right through them if one attacked.

'Careful, doing this could set them off,' Amelia said, eyes scanning the snow.

Mitchel shivered as the reality of what he was doing registered. He'd never seen a Rift scorpion. What if his magic wasn't enough? What if he couldn't create a thick enough barrier? What if he burned himself out?

'You got this,' Oliver said, voice low enough that Amelia probably wouldn't have heard over the background noise of the screaming engine. 'Just like you practised.'

Mitchel took a slow breath, remembering how his previous practice had gone. 'From what I remember, most of that practice didn't go the way I'd planned.'

'I can't see that working against us,' Oliver said, giving him a grin. Trust him to think that freezing an entire room was a plus.

Mitchel tried to push aside his worry and focus on the task at hand. In science, ice was just another form of water. But in terms of magic, it was very different.

He could still call to water, but as he did, his magic changed it, freezing it. He spent all his time blocking the freeze effect to hide his magic, and the effort of doing that would typically burn him out. But he didn't have to worry about masking what he was today.

Calling the water from the snow, he let it freeze even as it moved to his will, defying the laws of physics as it settled over the holes in the ground, sealing them. Then, slowly, to ensure there were no gaps or thin sections, he built up the ice until it was two inches thick.

He did it to each hole in turn. It seemed to take ages, but in reality, it was a mere few minutes. It felt good to be working with his magic. Better than good. It had been so long since he'd been able to use his full magic that he didn't want to let it go. He wanted to hold on and sink into the welcoming feel of it. To let his senses spread further, to see and feel everything the snow had to offer. But he couldn't afford the distraction with lives at risk ahead of them. He pushed the magic away, feeling oddly colder as it faded.

The little army in his head that had moved in with the hangover returned, pounding away, but his stomach felt better. More settled.

Mitchel nodded to Oliver. 'It's done.'

Oliver shivered, breath misting far worse than it had been moments ago. But he didn't complain as he watched the last open nest. They waited for a few long moments, but nothing happened.

'I don't like this. They should be reacting to us,' Oliver said, looking at the car. 'Where are they?'

'The cold could be keeping them down,' Amelia said, but she didn't look like she believed it. 'Either way, we have to check the car. We have already lost enough time.

Mitchel can help me get anyone out of the car while you cover us, Oliver.'

'Works for me.' Oliver nodded. 'Be careful.'

'What do you need me to do?' Mitchel asked, moving closer to Amelia as she put away her handgun. He couldn't see the people in the car from here. One side was pressed against the snowbank, and most of the front was hidden by more snow.

'It's too dangerous here to hang about, so we just need to get into the car and get the people out,' Amelia said, glancing at the medical bag that was still on the ground behind them. 'Don't worry about injuries. If we stay here, they're dead either way.'

He could almost feel the frustration and anger coming out of her as she set out the plan. Even Mitchel knew that wasn't how people were typically taken away from accidents. But he knew she was right. The risk of staying was worse.

'And if a Rift scorpion has stung them?' Mitchel said, voice soft.

Amelia's mouth thinned. 'Then we take them out, anyway. No one deserves to be Rift Scar food.'

Mitchel didn't reply to that grim statement. They all knew the survival chance if exposed to Rift venom.

Amelia reached into one of her many pockets and pulled out two knives, handing one to Mitchel. 'For the seat belt,' she said, giving him a once-over. 'Don't stab yourself.'

Mitchel took the knife, wishing he could find a witty reply, but his fear had frozen his tongue. He started forward with Amelia.

The smell of fuel clogged his nose as he approached the car. The snow piled on the front was starting to melt with the heat from the engine still running. The front driver's door was crumpled, and the front windscreen had shattered, letting the snow in.

Everything was exactly how it had felt when he'd reached out with his magic. But even knowing what he would see next, his breath caught as he saw a woman with grey hair slumped forward in the driver's seat. She didn't appear to be moving, and there was no sign of any airbags having deployed to break the crash's impact.

Initially, Mitchel didn't think anyone else was in the car, but then he realised the flash of red on the back window on the driver's side was hair. Curly and long, it hid the face of whoever was in the back. Again, she wasn't moving.

'Two people,' Amelia said, looking at Mitchel. 'You get the girl in the back. That door looks like it should open. I can't see any scorpions, but there's snow on the woman, which could be hiding them.'

Mitchel nodded and reached for the door handle at the same time as Amelia reached for hers. It was tempting to tell her he'd not sensed any with his magic before, but not only would that be impossible to explain, but it could have changed since then. And reconnecting now wasn't an option. He needed to focus.

He let Amelia work on her door first. Initially, it didn't look like it would open because it was so damaged, but Amelia gave it a hard yank, making the door squeal and open a half inch. She braced to pull it again.

His door wasn't as twisted, but he needed to be careful with the girl leaning against it. He pulled the handle, happy to hear the catch click as it started to open.

'Shit.' Amelia's curse brought his head around in time to see a scorpion fall out, landing at Amelia's feet. It was two feet long and dark grey, the tip of its tail tinged red with blood.

Amelia stabbed the knife almost faster than Mitchel could follow, but it wasn't fast enough. Just as the blade connected, the creature twisted, swiping the tail out and straight into Amelia's calf.

She grunted, stumbling back a step as the scorpion made a high-pitched chittering noise and struggled against the knife. Mitchel moved to grab her, but she waved him back.

Out of pure instinct, he reached out to the surrounding snow, pulling the feel of it into his lungs. But he fought the urge to do more. Closing a bunch of holes was one thing, but he couldn't freeze the car with people still in it. Not unless he wanted them to die of hypothermia.

'Amelia!' Oliver said, half a step towards them before he stopped himself, head swivelling between the nest and the car. 'Are you okay?'

'Yes,' Amelia said, voice a low growl as she forced herself to straighten. 'Watch the nest. I'll be fine.'

The scorpion stopped making that awful chittering noise as it fell still.

'More will come; you need to move fast,' Oliver said, but Amelia was already headed back towards the car.

The door was wide open now, and the woman still slumped on the wheel. He couldn't tell if she was alive, but seeing the scorpion was putting the odds very low.

'I don't see any more in the front. But be careful, get the girl, get out,' Amelia said through gritted teeth, glancing at Mitchel.

He hated that look of pain on her face, but she was right; they had to move fast. The pressure of the cold weighed down on him, making it hard to breathe fully. But he was too afraid to let the magic go.

Turning back to the girl, he opened the door carefully. He watched Amelia from the corner of his eye, bringing out another knife and cutting the seat belt.

The girl in the back started to tip towards him, and he grabbed her as carefully as he could, half expecting another scorpion to fall out. But there was nothing. It did little to ease his too-fast heartbeat.

Gunfire came in a sharp burst that made Mitchel jump, heart leaping up to his throat, suffocating him. He spun to stare at Oliver.

'Hurry up, they've found the last exit,' Oliver shouted before another burst of gunfire blinded Mitchel.

Mitchel turned back to the girl. Glass and blood spotted her, including the side of her head, where it looked like she must have hit the window. He couldn't tell if any of the wounds were due to being stung.

He moved the girl to lean against his shoulder so he could free up his hands to work on the seat belt.

More gunfire came from behind him. He could see Amelia lifting the woman over her shoulder in a fireman's carry. Sweat covered Amelia's brow, and she grunted as she put weight on her leg.

His knife made it through the seat belt, and the woman slid more heavily against him. He reached round to grab and lift her like Amelia had done.

A raspy breath burst from her lips as he tried to grip her. He almost let go as the fear sharped.

'You're okay,' he whispered, hoping it wasn't a lie as he pulled her towards him. A black shadow moved against the seat.

Mitchel froze, staring at the scorpion. It had been hidden under the girl, but now it was free. The red-topped tail twitched, swaying slowly.

Amelia called for him to hurry, but he was afraid to answer. If he moved, it would attack, and there was no way to move the girl in time. Shouting would result in the same.

The cold pressed in on him as his fear grew. He had to do something. The girl was alive. If she hadn't been stung, this would kill her for sure.

The swaying stopped, and the tail moved back, bracing.

Mitchel threw himself backwards with the girl. Hoping he could move faster than the scorpion. They hit the snow awkwardly, the girl landing on him, stealing what little breath he had.

The Rift scorpion was coming towards him fast. He wasn't going to be able to move in time.

The girl was going to die because of him.

Except there was something he could do as the pressure in his body grew, the feel of the cold seeping deep until he was warm when he knew he should have been freezing.

He let the magic loose without any real thought, and it exploded from him towards the car.

Pain burned up Amelia's leg as she carried the woman away from the car. She listened for something that might indicate the woman was still alive. She was too still, her chest not moving against Amelia's shoulder. Even with the car engine noise, she should have been able to hear a heartbeat. But there was nothing.

Fire seared her leg, and it nearly gave out as she reached where she'd left the medical bag. She put the woman down as carefully as she could, leg shaking. There was no way Amelia would make it to her Land Rover with the extra weight. But she didn't want to leave the woman for scavengers, either.

Frustrated, Amelia reached for her gun in case anything else came out of the car.

Want change, Luna snarled in her head, anger, fear, and pain all mixing together as she raged against being trapped as a human. *Claws safer.*

It's going to be okay, Amelia said, trying to send calming thoughts to her wolf. *We have been through this before.*

In a controlled environment, with teachers watching her and guiding her. Not in the field. Not with enemies in their territory. Her wolf just snarled and mentally swiped at her, too angry to care that it was only temporary.

Emotional pain battled against the physical pain for her attention. Every breath hurt like knives being dragged through her veins.

The pack bonds flared in her mind in response to her fear and panic. Hale reaching out. But he was too far to be anything but a fleck in her peripheral vision. Again, she wished the bond would do more than send emotion.

'It's going to be okay,' Oliver said, echoing her words so precisely that she shivered as he released another quick fire of bullets into the nest. Funny, she didn't believe him any more than her wolf believed her.

The smell of phosphorus stung her nose as Oliver lit a flare, placing it onto the nest's exit. While giving the scorpions somewhere to flee was a great plan, if they couldn't stop the flow, it wouldn't matter.

They needed to get out of there. What was taking Mitchel so long?

'Mitchel!' Oliver's shout made Amelia spin.

Mitchel had fallen backwards into the snow, the redhead from the back seat on top of him. A Rift scorpion stood at the edge of the seat, ready to launch itself at them. She pulled up her gun, getting ready to take a shot, knowing she'd be too slow. But she never got the chance.

The air filled with Mitchel's scent as it grew heavy with a sudden drop in temperature.

All at once, the car turned white as frost covered it. Then the sound of the engine cut off abruptly, and the side windows cracked, then shattered. But the glass shards didn't fall like they should have; instead, they froze in place.

Amelia wasn't sweating anymore as the cold seeped into her body so fast she didn't even have a chance to shiver. Oliver fell to his knees, his breath a freezing mist in front of him.

'Mitchel,' Oliver shouted. Mitchel didn't react.

Amelia had never felt this kind of cold before. Not the depth nor the suddenness of it. It had to be coming from Mitchel, but somehow, she doubted this was the effect he'd been aiming for. He wasn't trained for this. She should never have let him help. This was her fault.

She had to get him to stop. Drawing a breath, she tried calling to him again, chest burning from the effort. She coughed, choking, as she tried to force the words out.

'Mitchel, stop!' Amelia shouted. But there was no reaction from him. She fell to her knees in the snow. It wasn't soft anymore. She had to get through to him.

The air changed direction, bringing Mitchel's scent of winter's morning to her nose a thousand times stronger than it had been. There was nothing else in the air, no scorpions, no fuel. Just Mitchel's scent.

Pull him, Luna said, calmer now that they'd something to focus on, something other than their pain.

Pull what? Amelia asked, but even as she did, her wolf wrapped herself around that odd feeling that tugged her towards Mitchel. It thrummed in her mind, having become background noise when she'd seen the crash. But it was pulling her towards him, not the other way around.

Like pack, but not, Luna said, but she didn't sound sure.

The pack bonds to Hale didn't feel like this. But her wolf was right. There was a similarity to it, a sense of being connected. Hale could open and close that link, so maybe she could do the same to whatever this was with Mitchel?

'Mitchel,' she croaked, wrapping her mind around that invisible link with her wolf, then pulling on it. She felt the change, like a bell ringing in her mind.

Mitchel turned his head. But those clear blue eyes looked through her like he wasn't seeing anything. Everything around him was misty and white, losing colour. He was the exception with the girl in his arms, a vibrant splash of colour.

'Stop,' Amelia said, pulling harder on the link.

Mitchel blinked, finally seeming to focus on her. His eyes widened, and he turned back to the car, the scent flickering as his fear broke through the frost.

Suddenly, the pressure holding her down lifted, and she slumped forward, head spinning. Oliver coughed, visibly shuddering. She followed suit as the cold registered. Her fingers and toes were so numb that it hurt to move.

The wind rose, stirring the mist, drawing it away until they could see the car. Or what the car had become. A ragged-edged chunk of ice sat around the car, crystal clear despite the deformed edges. It was unnatural and yet somehow beautiful.

Amelia hadn't even known that a Water Elemental could do this. This was more than freezing water. The car hadn't been in a pool. Mitchel had not only moved the water into place but also frozen it and sealed the car and any Rift scorpions inside.

Mate powerful, Luna said, pleased despite how afraid they'd just been. *Magic claws sharp.*

Since he'd almost killed them doing whatever he'd done, Amelia wasn't sure it was all that useful as a weapon.

Saved girl. Protected us, Luna said, giving her a sharp mental nudge like it was obvious.

Amelia didn't bother arguing with her wolf this time. But it did help cement her decision to avoid anything to do with Mitchel. She had enough of her own control worries, especially with Dylan nearby. She didn't need someone who had similar issues.

Stupid pup, Luna said, turning her back as she settled into a sulk.

CHAPTER SIX

Mitchel stared at the car. He could see the scorpion that had been coming after him. It was mid-jump, encased in the ice, frozen and very dead. Any other scorpions still in the car would be the same.

Shuddering, Mitchel turned to Amelia and Oliver. They were both pale, lips tinged blue, with ice in their hair. How close had they come to dying, too? Too close.

He hadn't meant to lower the temperature so far, or at all, really. Yet, it had been terrifyingly easy, like letting out a breath. He'd felt like he was part of the ice, connected to it all. He'd let himself be lost in it.

At least until Amelia had called out to him. He could still feel her pulling at him. It had been the only thing that had broken him out of the connection. Her fear. Letting him see what was happening.

He didn't know what might have happened if she hadn't been here.

Mitchel gently rolled the girl on to the snow beside him. It didn't sink as her weight settled. The previously fresh snow they'd been wading through was now frozen solid.

Shaking his head, he checked her before he stood. She was in her early twenties, wearing a thick jumper and light-coloured jeans marked with blood and spots of black. There was a wound on the side of her head, blood matting in her hair.

She was warm, unaffected by the freezing ice around him. That part hadn't been intentional either. How had she been unaffected? Shaking his head again, he tried to focus. That answer didn't matter just now; making sure she was okay did.

She hadn't reacted to being moved, but he could see her chest flutter erratically, but it was movement. He looked again at those black and red stains. How many times had she been stung?

'Are you okay?' Amelia asked, making him look around again. She moved slowly, flexing her hands, limping heavily.

He nodded, though his headache was settling into a new level of fierceness, and his body ached like he was coming down with the flu. He'd used too much magic, but he wasn't about to complain about his own hurts when he'd nearly killed everyone. Especially not when there were others far worse off.

Amelia frowned like she didn't believe him but didn't argue as she knelt beside him. Her breath came out in a hiss. He wanted to do something, anything, to help her. He could feel the cold still deep inside her because of him. It was hurting her more than her leg.

He reached out and carefully rested a hand on her shoulder to pull back all the cold still inside her. Unlike the active power he'd used to freeze the car, this one was something he had a lot of practice using.

Amelia exhaled sharply, breath misting in front of her. The blue tinge from her lips faded, and her face flushed with colour.

'I'm sorry,' Mitchel said as he pulled back, though he wanted to linger, soak in the feel of her.

'Thank you,' she said, but she watched him with a caution that had been missing before. Like she thought he might be dangerous. She wasn't wrong.

Mitchel turned towards Oliver and the older woman Amelia had rescued. The woman lay on the ground, painfully still, with a layer of frost over her clothes.

'She's gone,' Amelia said quietly, voice tight. Mitchel's stomach dropped. Had his power killed more than the scorpions after all? But before he could berate himself more, Amelia added, 'She was gone before I got her out of the car.'

Some of the tightness eased, but not much. Even if Mitchel hadn't killed the woman, she was still dead. There was nothing to celebrate here.

'Is the girl alive?' Oliver asked. He was still kneeling next to the scorpion nest, lips just as blue as Amelia's, though he was still trying to cover the nest exit.

Amelia turned to the girl, her hand moving to the woman's neck. 'She's alive,' Amelia said, then she carefully ran her hand down the girl's body, avoiding the black patches. She was gentle and careful. 'But she's definitely been stung. We need to get her to a hospital.'

Oliver breathed out a curse. They all knew that just because she was alive now didn't mean she'd stay that way. Not all deaths were instant. Even the hospital would only be able to do so much.

'Go help Oliver,' Amelia said, nodding, as she leaned over the girl again, this time doing a slower check.

Mitchel nodded and struggled to his feet. A wave of tiredness seeped into him. This part was familiar. Not burned out, but close enough that he knew he'd feel this for the rest of the day.

'You did good,' Oliver whispered, shivering as he opened and closed one hand at a time, trying to warm them up. His gun was loose in his grip, and his dead flare sat above the nest's exit. 'You saved us.'

'Funny, I wasn't aware that nearly killing your friends was classed as helping,' Mitchel said, voice sharper than he'd intended as he put his hand on Oliver's shoulder. He groaned as he thawed out.

'You're too hard on yourself. There were a lot of scorpions in that nest. More than we could have outrun,' Oliver said as he repositioned the gun, moving to point it at the hole in the ground. The movement looked so natural on him that Mitchel had a moment of pause. He'd never seen his friend quite so focused before.

'It's closed now too,' Mitchel said, and Oliver let out a relieved sigh, then shivered as Mitchel let go of his shoulder.

'Good, because I think my finger might fall off if I bend it too far,' Oliver said, a smile playing on his lips. Mitchel flinched, which made Oliver sigh.

'Too soon,' Mitchel said as he helped Oliver to his feet. Though helping might have been stretching it somewhat.

'It's my finger. You don't get to decide if it's too soon,' Oliver said. 'You did the best you could with the tools you had. Most people would have frozen and done nothing.'

Mitchel shook his head but didn't get a chance to answer as a soft groan came from the red-haired woman. They spun round to stare at her. It was weak, but it was definitely a sound.

'Is she awake?' Mitchel asked.

'No, thankfully,' Amelia said, looking around, shaking her head. For humans, the pain from the venom was like having acid poured into your veins as it tried to change your body at its core. 'Once we get her to the hospital, I think they can help keep her under.'

It was about all they could do. Even the best-equipped hospital couldn't help much. People survived the initial infection. Or they didn't. Sometimes, it was instant, like the older woman. Sometimes, it was slow and painful. Then, very rarely, they survived and became an Elemental.

'We need to get you both to the hospital,' Oliver said, crouching beside Amelia.

'I'm fine,' Amelia said, lifting her chin, though sweat had covered her forehead, and she was breathing hard just from trying to help the girl.

'I'll carry her,' Oliver said, ignoring Amelia's annoyance, as he handed her his rifle. 'You can provide cover. Then I'll drive us to the hospital where you can both get treatment.'

Mitchel was sure Amelia would argue, even though she was obviously struggling. Her eyes became a brighter blue, the change so subtle that he would've missed it if he hadn't been watching. Oliver's turned amber. Amelia looked away first, taking the gun from Oliver.

Just like that, it was over. Mitchel let out a breath. Wolves' dominance was a strange thing. There always had to be structure. Someone in charge. Oliver usually hated it when it was him, but his protective streak was a mile wide, and when he needed to, he would press his power.

'Can you take a photo of the licence plate, Mitchel? Someone in town should be able to figure out who these two are,' Oliver said, eyes still amber.

Mitchel suppressed the apology that rose as he did as Oliver asked. Another 'I'm sorry' really wasn't going to cut it when he'd almost frozen everyone to death.

Oliver reached down and scooped up the woman. 'Damn, she's warm,' he said as he settled her weight.

'Her body is fighting the infection,' Amelia said, standing as she pointed the gun at the ground. 'It's a good sign.'

Mitchel hoped she was right, though she didn't sound confident.

As they passed the older woman, Mitchel struggled to put her into a fireman's carry, not wanting to leave her behind. His nausea had returned by the time they got back to the car. It didn't help that they had no choice but to put the old woman in the Land Rover's boot.

Oliver helped Amelia and the redhead into the back seat, then got into the driver's seat while Mitchel slipped into the passenger side. Nothing else attacked them, for which he was grateful. He wasn't sure he had anymore fight in him.

After a slow turn, they headed back the way they had come. So far, he wasn't much liking his first visit to the Highland Rift Scar, and he doubted the day would get much better.

AMELIA SHIFTED THE POSITION of her leg in the back seat of the Land Rover. It did nothing to ease the pain in her calf. It throbbed with each beat of her heart, sending tendrils of fire up her leg. The ache would last a few days at least, but the poison would work out of her system by tomorrow.

Then, she'd be able to shift again.

With everything that had happened after she'd been stung, it seemed like the smaller of her worries. But the longer the silence in the car held, the more her thoughts circled. Surprisingly, her wolf was being quiet on the matter.

Though she wasn't being quiet about everything.

Stupid like pup, Luna said again. *Mate not hurt us.*

Amelia sighed and glanced at the source of their argument. Mitchel was in the front seat, head resting against the window, eyes closed. A small patch of frost had spread out from where he touched the glass.

She'd moved to wake him when she'd noticed, which was when her wolf had taken to arguing with her. Ultimately, she'd let him sleep because the frost hadn't spread further.

He need sleep. Magic hard, Luna said, though there was no way she could know that for sure. *Warm us. Warm girl. Magic good.*

That part was right, she supposed. She felt warmer now than she had all day. Some of that was the venom. But the rest ...

She wanted to touch him again, to feel the smoothness of his skin. Bury her hand in his hair and pull in his scent.

Which was stupid. Amelia couldn't afford to let herself be tempted. Dylan had taught her better than that.

Dylan problem. Not ours, Luna said, digging in her claws. *We want what we want.*

The Land Rover hit a rut, making her hiss as her leg jarred. Though they were both belted in, she tightened her grip on the girl. Amelia rechecked the woman's pulse. It was weak and erratic. Which was the same as every other time she'd taken it.

Oliver glanced at her in his rearview mirror. 'How is she?'

'The same,' Amelia said, brushing the woman's hair back. She'd not made a sound since they'd settled her in the car, and the heat coming from her felt like a mini furnace. Amelia hated there was nothing she could do.

She'd found more than one sting from the scorpion along the girl's leg, but other than that, all she could see was that nothing looked broken. Once they got to the hospital, they could do more tests to check for further damage the car crash might have caused. If the woman lived that long.

Letting her hand drop back into her lap, Amelia shifted in her seat again. At least the girl was alive now. That meant there was hope.

'And what about you?' Oliver said quietly, eyes flashing to amber as his wolf rose to check on her.

'I'm peachy,' Amelia said, keeping her voice low to not wake Mitchel. She was lying through her teeth, and they both knew it. It would be days before she resembled any-thing remotely good.

She could feel and smell Oliver's dissatisfaction. He hat-ed pulling rank. Hated being at odds with anyone. She shouldn't have pushed him earlier, especially since she'd known he was right.

'I'll be okay,' Amelia said, letting part of her wolf shine through in her voice.

Some of the tension in his shoulders eased. 'Did Hale reply to your message yet?' he asked, though he'd have heard the phone go if one had come in.

'Not yet,' Amelia said, checking her phone anyway. 'He knows something is wrong. I felt him reach out through the pack bonds when I got stung. It's only a matter of time before he gets into range or comes to us directly.'

It wasn't the only time Hale had reached out. He'd been doing it steadily every few minutes since they'd left the Rift Scar border. He was as protective as Oliver, and nothing, not even this expedition, would stop him from discovering what had happened.

'Me too,' Oliver said as he slowed the car as they neared another junction. The trees were thick here, crowding in on either side of them. Despite the condition, he'd been driving relatively fast, but the car had been holding solid. The snow tyres she'd put on the old beast had been worth it.

Thinking of the snow again drew her eye to the frost on the window. Mitchel was still sleeping. She could hear his breath coming in slow, steady draws.

'Can I ask you a favour?' Oliver asked, voice low and hesitant.

'Of course,' Amelia said automatically. She had a suspicion of what the request was going to be.

'Please don't tell anyone what Mitchel did to the car,' Oliver said, shifting his hands on the steering wheel.

And there it was. Oliver protecting his friend.

'How long have you known that Mitchel can't control his power?' Amelia asked, turning back to Oliver to see his reaction. 'How many times have you protected him?'

His jaw muscle twitched. 'It's complicated.'

Which didn't answer the question at all. 'Oliver—'

'Please, Amelia. I don't care if you tell them he lost control, but just don't tell anyone about the ice. Please,' Oliver said, interrupting her. 'It's important.'

'I don't understand,' Amelia said, looking again at Mitchel. Losing control was the worst thing an Elemental or Shifter could be accused of. There was some leeway as a child, but as an adult, there were a lot fewer chances given.

'It's not my secret to share, but please. They can't know he used ice.' Oliver looked at her in the rearview mirror again. His scent hinted at fear, but not for himself, she was sure. 'He won't ask you, and you know I wouldn't ask if it wasn't important.'

'Okay,' Amelia said slowly but raised her hand as the scent of his relief filled the car. 'But if something like this happens again, I won't keep silent. I'll not keep a secret at the cost of others' lives.'

Oliver gave her a weak smile. 'Thank you.'

MITCHEL WOKE WITH A start as a lorry rumbled past them. The low sunlight blinded him as he struggled to place where he was.

In a car. In Amelia's Land Rover.

He looked behind him, finding Amelia sitting in the back, one leg extended as far as the car allowed and the girl's head in her lap. She looked up, meeting his eye, making his heart rate jump a notch despite the wariness now in that look.

'How you feeling?' Oliver asked, drawing Mitchel's focus away from the back seat. Oliver made a slight motion with his head towards Mitchel.

Mitchel turned towards the window, biting down on a curse. The window was frosted over, though it was already melting now that he was no longer leaning against it.

It had been years since something like that had happened when he'd been asleep. He reached out to the frost and pulled the cold back towards him. The last of it turned to water and dripped down the window. Fatigue washed through him in a wave. He might have slept, but it clearly hadn't been enough.

'I'm fine,' Mitchel lied, suppressing a wince as he rolled his neck. His head ached, though he suspected it was no longer due to the hangover but instead the overuse of his power. 'How long was I asleep?'

'Long enough that we're almost at Huntly,' Oliver said, giving him another look before he turned back to the road. 'You're sure you're okay?'

Mitchel glanced back at Amelia, debating how much he wanted to say. No matter how much he was pulled towards her, he didn't know her. He'd been burned before, thinking he knew Clara before Oliver had shown him the truth.

'I used too much magic, I think,' Mitchel said at last. 'It's been so long since I—' Mitchel broke off, unsure how to say what he wanted without telling the truth. It had been too long since he'd used Frost Magic at all.

'When we get to the hospital, they can check you out too,' Oliver said, eyes flashing amber. The set of his face warned against arguing with him. So, Mitchel changed the subject instead.

'How's the girl?' Mitchel asked.

'The same,' Amelia said, voice soft like she feared waking the woman. 'It will be a couple of days before there are any changes.'

'Does this happen here often?' Mitchel asked, looking between Amelia and Oliver. 'People finding their way into the Rift Scar?'

'From what I've been told, someone usually wanders in a few times a year. Mostly, it's stupid kids doing a stupid dare. Normally, the Rift creatures are far enough away from the border because of the patrols,' Amelia said, hands moving to the girl's throat, checking her pulse. 'But every few years, we'll be too slow. Or there will be an accident like this.'

'What happens to those who survive?' Mitchel asked, looking back at the girl again. It was strange that he'd never once thought to ask in all the years he'd been studying the Rift Scar.

'I've only ever heard about three people surviving all the way through,' Oliver said when Amelia was silent. 'None of them made the news. The media doesn't like to report on it, in case it encourages people to take the risk.'

Which made sense, he supposed. In the early days of the war, people wanting to fight had taken that risk, along with those who wanted power. A lot of people had died. History never said how many exactly had survived.

'What happened to those three you heard about?' Amelia asked, gently pushing back a strand of red hair from the woman's face.

'They were paired off with an Elemental with the same ability to train them,' Oliver said. 'A mentor. They had to stay with them until they learned control.'

Elemental magic wasn't exactly an easy skill to learn. It wasn't tough to imagine that getting it as an adult was even more challenging. Of course, maybe Mitchel wasn't a good judge, considering he'd never learned to use his.

The car slowed as they reached a junction. Oliver took the turning that followed a rusted sign that told him they were approaching Huntly. A few moments later, the town walls came into view. Made from old stone, they rose six feet and stretched into the distance, presumably around the town, most of which was hidden by trees.

He'd seen the wall when they'd left but assumed it had been from the war and kept out of habit or respect for the past. Now, he had to wonder if it was something more.

'I've never heard of a Rift creature making it this far out, and it's never happened while I've been here,' Oliver said, proving once again he was paying far too much attention.

'Then why keep the walls?' Mitchel asked. The old walls in Glasgow had been torn down in most places so the residents could build new houses. What had survived had been turned into a monument to those who had died in the Fae War.

'Because it could happen,' Oliver said. 'If we fail. If we don't do our job right, this town is the closest to the Rift Scar.'

'So, what you're telling me is that the locals don't trust the rangers to keep them safe?'

Oliver smiled. 'No. I'm telling you they've survived having the town taken from them once, and they aren't going to let it happen again.'

'That's because you Scottish are too hard-headed to know better,' Amelia said, her own amusement telling Mitchel that this was an argument they'd had before. Likely often. 'But it won't happen. Even the farmers who are two miles out with their cattle don't get bothered by Rift creatures as long as we keep on top of the patrols.'

Oliver slowed as they reached the entrance to Huntly. Heavy metal gates on each side of the road were propped open. Like the walls, they looked in good condition and could be closed if needed.

There were a bunch of turns through the town, too many for Mitchel to follow, before Oliver pulled into the A & E parking. This hospital was a long, squat two-storey building. It looked like it had seen better days.

'We phoned ahead while you slept,' Oliver said as they caught sight of a small team of four waiting at the door. They had two wheelchairs and a trolley.

'I'm fine,' Mitchel said, scowling.

'Well, it's a good thing we have a medical team to confirm your theory, isn't it?' Oliver said as he stopped the car.

A tall man with dark skin and heavy-lidded, tired hazel eyes led the group into the cold, pushing one of the wheelchairs. They moved quickly despite the sleety snow around the entrance.

Mitchel got out of the car and opened Amelia's door for her. With the girl on her lap, there wasn't much she'd be able to do. She offered him a nod as he backed away.

'How bad?' the lead doctor asked Amelia as he looked over the red-haired girl.

'Multiple stings,' Amelia said, giving a detailed breakdown of stats and times.

The doctor nodded as she talked and signalled to two of the people behind him to come forward. With a lot of work, careful movement, and securing a brace around her neck, they got the girl out of the car and onto the trolley. She made no sound through the entire process, making it look like they were moving a rag doll around. When they were done, they wheeled her towards the hospital, talking in low voices about what came next.

The lead doctor crouched beside Amelia as she swung her legs out of the car. He put a hand on her knee, stopping her from rising.

Mitchel shoved down a spark of jealousy at the familiarity of the touch. Amelia wasn't Mitchel's. Hell, as far as he could tell, she barely tolerated him.

'And what about you?' the doctor said, eyes on the ragged hole in her combats.

'It was just one sting, Pascal,' she said, pushing him back so she could stand. More colour drained from her face as she gave him a strained smile.

Mitchel reached out to catch her shoulder and wrist as she wavered. Their connection sent pins and needles up his arm like an electric shock. That tug grew tight as she turned to him. He saw more than caution in that look for the first time as her eyes dipped to his lips.

'Careful,' Mitchel said hoarsely as she regained her balance.

Amelia let out a slow breath and pulled away from him to lean on the car. 'I'll be fine.'

Pascal snorted and shook his head, clearly not believing her any more than Mitchel did.

'Your chariot awaits,' Pascal said, indicating to the wheelchair. 'Once we wash your wound off, I can tell you how bad it is while you rest in a hospital bed. Maybe, by then, your common sense will have returned.'

Amelia scowled, eyes growing a brighter blue, but she did as he asked. Her gaze flickered to Mitchel's, wolf still in her eyes. Then she was turned around, and one of the nurses pushed her towards the main building.

Mitchel made himself stay where he was as the pull between them grew tight. It would be so easy to follow her, to see if that look had meant what it had felt like.

Oliver had been hovering out of the way near the front of the car. He moved closer as Amelia was pushed through the hospital doors. 'I told you so,' he said.

Mitchel flushed, giving Oliver a disgusted look even as his stomach did a back flip. 'I don't know what you're talking about.'

'Which one of you two is also hurt?' Pascal asked, not commenting on the exchange.

'Mitchel overused his power,' Oliver said, too fast for Mitchel to argue. 'He's as stubborn as a Shifter but with only a quarter of the bad humour.'

Pascal smiled and nodded towards the second wheel-chair. 'Grab a seat, and we can get this show on the road. Unless you want us to wait for exhaustion to overwhelm you so we can roll you in after you pass out.'

Mitchel sighed, feeling the tiredness dragging him down. Oliver was right. Though, it wasn't like the hospital could do much other than give him fluids and let him sleep. Both of which he could technically do at the hotel. Though at the hotel, he wouldn't get to see Amelia.

The last part was what had him sitting in the seat in the end.

'I'm going to wait for them to take away the other woman, then park up and watch for Hale,' Oliver said. Mitchel shivered at the reminder of the dead woman in the back of the Land Rover. Logically, he knew there had been no other choice, but it still felt wrong how she'd been shoved in the back like that.

Oliver lowered his voice so only Mitchel would hear and added, 'I asked Amelia not to mention the ice.'

Mitchel's stomach dropped, but he couldn't ask any more questions as Oliver pulled away. What did that mean, exactly? How much had he told her?

'Call me if you need anything,' Oliver said as another trolley came out of the hospital, a black bag draped over the top.

Pascal pushed the wheelchair, discussing the weather as they passed through A & E's doors. The heat hit him almost immediately, making him shiver as sweat beaded down his spine. He fought to keep his magic inside.

This was one of the reasons he hated hospitals. But he consoled himself with the thought that he was at least closer to Amelia here.

CHAPTER SEVEN

'Stop fidgeting, Amelia, you're only going to make it worse,' Pascal said as he gently held her leg still, trying to see what he could through the trousers.

Pain spiralled out, sharp and deep. What she wouldn't give for painkillers to work on Shifters right now. The pack bonds flared in response to her pain, but she focused on being calm and sending it back to Hale. It must have worked because he eased off the link.

Amelia sighed. She felt useless sitting on the bed. She wanted to be helping. Wanted to be near Mitchel, even if that was stupid. 'I'm sorry.'

It was just the two of them in the small room. The door was closed, but Pascal had opened the window despite the cold to help pull out the stink of the Rift Scar that clung to her.

'The rest of the staff are well trained. They'll take care of your friend and the woman,' Pascal said, pulling back from her leg.

He wasn't much older than her, and despite being a Water Elemental, he'd made it through his medical degree, unlike her. But sabotaging Shifters by putting the exams after a full moon was easier. Elementals weren't bound by the lunar cycle.

Though going by the fact he was working in the middle of nowhere, maybe they'd found other ways to make his life hard. Or maybe she was just unjustly paranoid. She'd never been brave enough to ask.

'I know they will,' Amelia said. The staff here had always been excellent for the most part, though a few were prejudiced. But they usually just avoided treating any of the Rift Bloodlines.

'Well, I've got some good news and bad news,' Pascal said, glancing at her as he moved to the medical trolley and unwrapped scissors. 'I'm going to have to trash your lovely combats, but that means you'll need some new ones.'

Amelia laughed softly despite the pain. It was an old joke she'd heard him use before, and not really funny. But it helped ease some of her tension as he cut away her trouser leg. He put the blood-soaked material into a bag so it could be burned later.

As he turned away, she got her first look at the injury. A ragged hole oozed blood and black liquid on her lower calf, and dark red lines spread from the wound upwards. She looked away as her wolf whined.

'So, are you going to tell me about your friend?' Pascal said, giving her a little smirk. It didn't take much to guess who he meant. Oliver wasn't new.

'He's a Water Elemental,' Amelia said. The comment got the look it deserved, and she rolled her eyes, giving him more. 'He's a scientist they sent to look at the Scar.'

'He's cute,' Pascal said as he prodded the wound. She stiffened as the pain spiked.

Mine, Luna said. Jealousy left a bitter taste in their mouth.

I told you. Mitchel isn't mine. He isn't anyone's, Amelia said, but her wolf sent her images of him lying back in the snow, arms wrapped around the girl to protect her, the car a solid block beyond him.

Strong. Protect. Luna huffed. Sending her more images. This time, it was Mitchel's hand on her wrist by the car. The look in his eyes. The hunger. His scent on the air, desire thick and clear. *Want us.*

'Ah, so your wolf noticed that too?' Pascal asked, a smirk playing on his lips as he recognised the sign a Shifter was arguing with themselves and returned to her leg.

'Don't you start too. Mitchel is just visiting,' Amelia said. Pascal just continued to grin. 'I'm serious. He's not mine.'

'Sure he's not,' Pascal said, pressing down on her wound. She didn't have the air to reply as he started to clean the deep hole, drawing out as much venom as possible. His timing was deliberate.

It felt like it took hours as her leg burned from the inside out, though it was likely only minutes. The pack bonds flared wide as Hale's presence pressed into her mind, trying to take some of her pain. It helped enough that she could take a full breath again.

Pascal pulled back, letting her catch her breath. She was shaking, sweat pooling down her spine. He didn't comment, nor did he stop. It was up to her to tell him she needed a break, and she stayed silent. The quicker he treated the wound, the quicker she'd heal.

Her wolf wasn't feeling quite so polite about the process, and even less so when he grabbed the antiseptic from his kit.

Not want smelly liquid on leg, Luna snarled. *Better to lick clean.*

It will make it heal faster, Amelia said, trying to show images of a festered wound versus a clean one. But her wolf didn't believe her.

'More good news. There's no sign of a stinger in the wound,' he said. It was rare, but sometimes the tip could break off and cause more damage. Something she should have checked herself if she'd been thinking. He opened the bottle of antiseptic wash. Amelia let out a hissing breath in anticipation of the pain coming. 'Bad news is I think you have denialitis. It's rather serious if untreated. Especially since I didn't say Mitchel was yours.'

Amelia gave him a dark look. 'He's only going to be here a few days.'

'I didn't say to marry him, girl,' Pascal said, that wicked grin back. 'Just make the best use of your recuperation time.'

'You need to find a new boyfriend, Pascal. Your fantasies are spilling into my reality,' Amelia said, shaking her head. But he'd inspired an unexpected thrill at the idea of spending the next few days with Mitchel. Not that she had any intention of following Pascal's advice.

'I'm serious. Your friend nearly burned himself out. There's no way Hale will let him anywhere near the Rift Scar until he's back to one hundred per cent, you either. Make the most of the time you have,' Pascal said, moving her leg so he could run the wash over it. 'Though I'm not surprised he hurt himself. Trying to use Water Magic when it's that cold outside is always a bad idea.'

'What do you mean?' Amelia asked, remembering the way Mitchel had lost control. If it wasn't his fault, why wouldn't Oliver have just said so?

'Well, when it's this cold, all the water is frozen. There's very little we can do at that point,' Pascal said, setting up the rest of the tools for the wash. He was a Water Elemental, so he'd know how it worked. 'He probably burned a load of energy doing something that was normally easy.'

She hoped that what Mitchel did wasn't usually easier. Oliver's words flashed through her head. *Don't tell anyone about the ice.* 'Isn't ice just another form of water?'

Pascal laughed and shook his head. 'God, no. It's a whole other section of magic. Frost Magic,' Pascal said, bringing the trolley closer. 'Temperatures like this only increase their power. The results can be pretty incredible.'

If Mitchel's Element really was Frost, then incredible was right. What he'd done to the car had been something she would've thought impossible had she not seen it. Mitchel had said he was a Water Elemental, but if Pascal was right, that was a lie.

'I've never heard of Frost being its own element,' Amelia said.

'There aren't many who can do it. Frost is its own bloodline, but there haven't been many of them in the UK. Their magic is very powerful, but things must be cold, which isn't normal for our weather. They can cool things down if they have to, just like I could melt ice, but it takes energy,' Pascal said, shrugging.

'But they're not restricted, then?' Amelia asked, making sure to meet Pascal's eyes as she continued. 'Like Earth Elementals.'

Pascal's smile slipped. No one wanted to think about how easy it was for the government to control the Earth Elementals. 'No. Just rare. Why? Did something happen out there with Mitchel?'

'No,' Amelia answered, trying to keep her voice even as she lied. 'I just don't understand why I've never heard about them before.'

Unfortunately, Pascal's explanation didn't help her understand why Oliver was hiding what Mitchel really was. It didn't make sense.

'Well, it's not like they teach the history of magic to us in school. There's probably a lot we don't know or has been lost over the years,' Pascal said.

Like how the pack lands had been made. Or how Hale managed to bring Sam into the pack. But she didn't say either of those out loud.

Pascal shook his head and gave her a smile, though it was more strained this time. 'Right, here comes the hard part. Are you ready?'

Amelia glanced at the wash in his hands. No. She wasn't ready. But there wasn't really a choice. Her wolf snarled and tried to get them to pull their leg away. Amelia held her down.

It'll just be a minute of pain, Amelia said, then nodded her head sharply, gritting her teeth.

As Pascal poured the first few drops, she nearly screamed. Once again, only Hale's presence let her breathe as her entire leg felt like it had caught fire.

MITCHEL TRIED TO SIT still as the nurse took his blood pressure. She was an older woman with grey hair and a severe expression. It was the third time in the last hour since he'd arrived that someone had taken it.

They were in a single-person room, done in white and grey. Everything in the hospital had been done that way. White walls, a grey floor, and fewer people than he'd have expected to keep the place running. Like all hospitals, it felt sterile and unpleasant. He'd visited enough of them as he attempted to pretend he could only use Water Magic and had burned himself out.

The machine beeped and flashed up its readings. The nurse turned it off and then moved to take his temperature with an ear thermometer.

'Your temperature is still lower than I'd like,' she said as the little machine beeped too. She picked up the clipboard at the end of the bed and scribbled some notes. 'But the rest of your readings look okay. Or at least within what I'd expect for someone in your condition.'

The phrasing felt odd but familiar. No one said the words 'because you almost burned yourself out'. Especially not in a public hospital where other patients might overhear. Though why, he wasn't sure. Being burned out, or nearly being burned out, meant that there was less, or no, magic for him to use. But prejudice didn't always follow logic. He was just glad the nurse seemed not to care.

'Thank you,' Mitchel said, rolling his sleeve back down.

'I'm going to get you another blanket. See if we can get your temperature up a bit,' the nurse said, pulling her cardigan tighter. 'You rest.'

Mitchel winced and pulled back on his magic. He hadn't meant for it to leak out, but it was so damned warm it was hard. He'd not had this many issues controlling his passive powers in years. First, the car, and now this. If he didn't get himself under control, there was no way he'd be able to continue hiding what he was.

His thoughts circled back to Amelia. Oliver had said he'd told her not to talk about the ice. But what did that mean? After so many years of hiding what he was, having someone else know the truth was tantalising. But also terrifying.

'Rest? I don't think he knows how,' Clara said from the doorway.

The nurse turned to her, lips thinning. 'You were told to stay in the waiting area.'

Clara gave an easy smile, shrugging. 'They said he was doing better. I thought that meant I could come through.'

Mitchel recognised that look from Clara. He'd been round her often enough to know it meant trouble.

He put his hand on the nurse's arm. 'It's okay.' She gave him a searching look, then sighed.

'Very well, but visitors are only allowed to stay for ten minutes,' the nurse said, brow wrinkling. 'When I return with the blanket, I can escort you out.'

Clara offered a neutral smile to the nurse as she unlocked the wheels on the cart that held all her tools to push it out of the room.

'What do you want?' he said to Clara as the nurse disappeared.

'What's wrong? Am I not allowed to care what happens to you anymore?' Clara said, moving closer and reaching out to touch him. He leaned back.

'We're not together anymore, Clara,' Mitchel said, wishing he had the space to get out of the bed and away from her.

'You say that like it's that simple. I care for you. I can't just turn it off like a switch.' Her voice held a tone that implied that was precisely what he'd done. He wished it was that easy.

'You were the one who cheated, Clara. You were the one who didn't accept no as an answer.' It was stupid that even now, it hurt. How much he'd trusted her and how wrong he'd been. 'Maybe you should have thought about how much you supposedly cared for me then.'

'And you think Amelia will be faithful to you?' Clara said, raising a slim eyebrow.

He tried not to react, but he couldn't help the spike of jealousy that rose. Clara's nostrils flared, and she crossed her arms, leaving no doubt she'd caught it in his scent.

'I barely know Amelia,' Mitchel said tightly. The last thing he needed was for Clara to focus on Amelia.

Clara leaned into the bed, stealing his personal space. 'She's a wolf as well, you know. When the full moon comes, do you think she will wait until she returns to your bed before she satisfies that itch?'

'You don't know anything about her,' Mitchel said, trying to push away the doubt that Clara was stirring, which was hard since he didn't really know Amelia well. Worse, his scent was certainly giving away how much he cared as Clara took a deep breath.

Clara barked out a laugh. 'But don't worry, you won't get to keep her, anyway. She's already spoken for.'

'Amelia is free to make her own choices,' Mitchel said, struggling to keep his voice even. He'd about as much success dealing with the doubt as he did the Frost.

'Her and Dylan make a cute couple, and in less than a year, she will be back home with him,' Clara said, giving him a smile that was all teeth. 'You think she will pick you when she can have the alpha's son?'

The thought of that arrogant wolf from the meeting touching Amelia made his gut twist. Was he really Amelia's ex? It seemed unlikely from what Mitchel had seen of her so far. But what did he really know about Amelia?

'You'd be better off with me,' Clara said, leaning forward that last inch until she touched him, one hand over his wrist, pinning him. He had nowhere to go. Panic tingled along his skin. 'Don't you remember how it used to be?

Just the two of us. Alone in that small bedroom. You inside me. Nothing but us and the moment.'

Old memories rose in his head. The history she was painting was through a skewed lens. The sex had been good, but not enough that she'd only wanted him. He wanted more than that. More than the cheating. More than the lies.

'So good that you needed to bring other men into our home?' Mitchel said quietly. 'In our bed? Our shower?'

Clara leaned back like he'd slapped her, face going blank. Relief filled him as she released his wrist. He pulled his hand into his lap, not wanting to be trapped again.

'You and me, we were good together,' Clara said. The words were cold, like he was the one to blame. But that was how she always dealt with the truth, pretending it didn't exist.

'There was never any *we*.' Mitchel paused, trying not to hold on to the old anger and pain. Trying his best not to give her that power over him. 'You always wanted more than I could give. And when I was done giving, you tried to take it anyway.'

'You think you'll be enough for *her*?' Clara said, spitting the last word. She stomped towards the door, turning at the last moment. 'You're not a wolf, Mitchel. You'll never be enough for her. I'm the only one who wants you.'

'You don't want me,' Mitchel said carefully. 'You wanted to control me. It's not the same.'

The nurse appeared behind Clara at that comment, and she growled, then lifted her chin and turned to stalk out, nearly slamming into the nurse's shoulder. The woman shook her head but followed Clara like she didn't trust the woman to leave.

He took a slow breath, trying to slow his heart rate. But even with Clara gone, her words wormed their way under his skin like maggots on dead flesh. He wanted to remind himself it didn't matter. Amelia wasn't his, and she didn't want him. There was no need for doubts because there was nothing there.

Except for that pull that kept tugging him towards Amelia, urging him to go to her, make sure she was alright. More than just desire.

But he wasn't a wolf—would never be a wolf or pack member. Why would Amelia choose him when she could have both back home?

Why did he want her too?

Stupid thoughts ran through his too-tired brain. This wasn't why he was here.

He closed his eyes, pressing his fingers to his forehead in an attempt to push back the throbbing there. All of this was a problem for later. Right now, he had to convince the nurse he was fine. Then he could go.

Maybe check on Amelia.

He sighed. Stupid, tired brain.

OLIVER SHIVERED, RUBBING HIS hands together as he shuffled to his other leg. He should have waited for Hale inside the car or in the hospital. But both smelled like pain and fear. And in the case of the car, death.

They had taken the woman's body away. She'd be fingerprinted so they could scan the police database and see if she was in the system. Between that and the car plates Mitchel had forwarded him, they might have a good chance of figuring out who she was so they could call her family.

If the young redhead survived, she would need a hell of a support system. If she didn't, he imagined her family would want to be with her as things deteriorated. But every hour she survived, her chances got better.

The wind changed, bringing the smell of the hospital close, antiseptic and people in pain. Oliver shivered again, trying to convince himself that it wasn't cold. After how cold Mitchel had made the accident site, this was nothing.

His friend had always feared his power; this wouldn't help. If Mitchel's mother hadn't been such a crazy bitch, then maybe he'd have got the chance to train.

Family important, Thor said reproachfully.

He sighed but didn't argue with his wolf. Thor wasn't wrong. But Mitchel's family had taken all and given nothing. Especially his mother.

The pack bonds flared in his mind as Hale reached out. He was close now, using the link to find Oliver rather than calling. It was strange to feel Hale, to feel the strength of the connection after six months of near silence. It was hard to imagine finding your mate would change so much.

Better this way, Thor said, enjoying the feel of the strength that came with Hale. The power of the alpha.

It was very different from his dad's power. That had been cloying and oppressive. Oliver had assumed that was how it had to be. The silence had been a blessing after that. This new strength of Hale's was inclusive somehow, like he was sharing what he was with the pack.

The only problem was that it made Oliver's wolf want to show himself even more.

Not mean to, Thor said, pulling back.

It's not your fault, Oliver said, soothing his wolf. Both of them had learned long and hard at his father's hand that showing your wolf was an intolerable weakness.

Make strange wolves leave. Will feel better, Thor said, showing his teeth. *Or kill leader. Scare rest away.*

Oliver didn't entirely disagree with his wolf. Dylan had been the only one who was causing problems. Both with his near challenge to Hale this morning and how Amelia reacted to having him around. That wariness and anger was so unlike her that it set Oliver's teeth on edge.

We fight. We win. Others leave, Thor said, rising so close to the surface that the surrounding scents grew sharper. *We be alpha again.*

Calm, Oliver said, old fear rising with his wolf. But this time, his wolf ignored him. *We aren't alpha here.*

Hale would not be mad. Not like Father, Thor said, showing them the images of Hale staring Dylan down at the conference this morning.

Dylan is a prime alpha's son. Killing him could mean war, Oliver said, showing his wolf many of their pack dead. His wolf disagreed, changing the image to many of their enemies dead.

Oliver gave up arguing, letting his wolf settle close under his skin. He'd never been good at keeping the two of them separate like his father wanted. Oliver's wolf was part of him, part of his soul. Unless someone tried to hurt them or their pack, they worked together. When under attack, his wolf was much more bloodthirsty than Oliver. But they balanced each other.

The wind changed direction, bringing a familiar scent to his nose. His wolf retreated in his mind, leaving him cold again, but their eyes would no longer be amber. No one would see Thor close to the surface.

Hale had parked at the other end of the car park and was walking towards Oliver, Dylan close behind. Oliver let out a sharp breath as he saw Hale's wolf so close to the surface that his power spread out around him in a haze. His annoyance was sharp enough that Oliver's skin tingled. Clearly, Dylan had not been behaving himself for Hale to be showing this much of his wolf.

Oliver's wolf pressed close to the surface again, wanting to protect Hale. So much for showing control. Thor was only slightly apologetic. Not enough that he backed away.

'Are they okay?' Hale asked as he drew level.

There was no reprimand to Oliver for not controlling his wolf, though he should have known that by now. In the six months Oliver had been here, Hale had never once beat him down for it.

'They're both going to be fine. The doc is cleaning Amelia's wound just now, and Mitchel is just exhausted from overusing magic,' Oliver said.

'And yet you sit here completely fine? Are you so weak that you let your women go in and get hurt while you stand back safe?' Dylan said, pushing forward.

Oliver growled, anger so strong it was all he could do to stay where he was leaning against the car. His wolf wanted to launch forward and put Dylan in his place. His comment not only disrespected Oliver's wolf but Amelia as well.

Dylan's wolf rose in response, filling the air around him. It was an unnecessary show and a waste of energy. Unlike Hale, Dylan was forcing the spread. Hale just leaked power around him.

'Amelia is trained and bloody good at her job,' Oliver said, watching Dylan closely to see if he would do more than puff his chest out. 'These are the risks we face every day when we go into the Rift Scar.'

'She shouldn't be anywhere near the field,' Dylan said, looking at Hale now. 'You already lost two wolves recently. I'll not let Amelia be next.'

This time, Oliver's wolf didn't get a chance to react as Hale's unfolded around them, filling the car park. Dylan stumbled back a step at the weight of the power.

'Those wolves died because they were careless,' Hale said, every word a hammer.

It was technically accurate; they'd been careless. They'd thought they were stronger than Hale and could take the pack from him. They'd both been killed in the attempt. But to the world, Lacey and Shane had died in the Rift Scar. That was what the prime alphas wanted people to think because anything else might lead to other Shifters thinking they could do the same.

'I allowed you to come this far so you could hear she was fine for yourself,' Hale said, letting the power curl back inside him. This wasn't a loss of control; this had been a show, and the way Hale pulled the power back couldn't have made it clearer. 'Now that you have, Lance will happily return you to your hotel.'

Lance, who had managed to keep his scent out of the wind, stepped forward. Oliver shivered. The man was just a little too good at sneaking for someone bigger than Oliver.

'I want to see Amelia for myself,' Dylan said, turning towards the hospital. There was definitely no way he was getting in to see Amelia with that attitude.

'No,' Hale said, voice low, nearly a growl. Dylan stopped in his tracks, back stiff. This wasn't pack magic stopping him—Dylan wasn't connected to Hale. This was just the power of Hale's wolf. Dylan turned slowly like he wanted to argue but kept his mouth shut. 'Amelia isn't going to be able to receive visitors today. The hospital is very strict. I'm sure she can reach out if she wishes to let you know how she's doing.'

Dylan made a noise in his throat that might have been a growl, but he looked at Oliver, then Lance, and seemed to think better of it. Without a word, he turned and stalked back the way he'd come. Oliver took more satisfaction in that than he probably should have. Lance followed, taking his time, which only annoyed Dylan more as he reached the car first and found it wasn't open.

Hale waited until Dylan and Lance got into the car and left before he spoke again. 'If I kill Dylan, do you think his father would be upset?' His tone was just on the edge of casual, making Oliver unsure if he meant it.

'There are some who would think you're doing him a favour,' Oliver said. Everyone knew that Prime Alpha Alaric spoiled his son. Rarely calling him to account. 'How did he do out in the field?'

Hale scowled. 'Let's just say we'd have been here sooner if not for him and leave it at that.' He paused and added, 'If you're around him, watch him. I don't like that he's here. He doesn't fit with the rest.'

Oliver nodded, wanting to ask specifics, but he held his tongue. He'd have a better chance of finding out more if he asked the rest of the patrol that had gone with them.

Hale let out a breath. 'What happened? Amelia's message was light on detail.'

Oliver talked Hale through the car accident and the rescue, missing out Mitchel's show of power. He'd been serious when he'd said to Amelia it wasn't his secret to share. If Mitchel wanted to, that was his choice, and it didn't change the events.

'That close to the border?' Hale said, frowning. 'They had to have been there before the weather changed to be able to make the nest.'

Oliver blinked; he hadn't even considered that. How had the patrols missed it? 'The scent wasn't strong until we walked over the nest, but that was the cold likely suppressing it,' Oliver said. Without the cold, it should have been obvious.

Hale looked at the hospital, a sharp edge on his energy. 'Tomorrow, I want you to check the rota. Find out who was on patrol down there the last few weeks before the weather changed,' he said.

'You think someone didn't do their job?' Oliver asked, feeling uncomfortable at the idea. The rangers relied on each other. If someone wasn't pulling their weight, then it risked all of them. His wolf preened at the trust that Hale was putting in them.

'I don't know, but I don't like it. Not after last month,' Hale said, looking back at Oliver.

'I can go now,' Oliver said, looking at Amelia's car. He really didn't want to use it, but his was at the town hall. Though it wasn't really that long a walk despite the cold.

Walk, Thor agreed.

'No. Tomorrow is soon enough. You might not be in the hospital, but it's been a stressful enough day. Look tomorrow when everyone is out in the field,' Hale said. 'Even if we find something wrong, there's little we can do about it until after our guests are gone and the weather has changed. I'll have the mayor close the road with barriers and warn all the patrols to steer clear until we can get a full unit down there to clear it.'

Oliver nodded, hearing what he hadn't said. Hale didn't want anyone to know that he was checking the records. Oliver didn't mention that the entire area was frozen solid. Mitchel might have killed the whole nest, but they'd need to check either way.

'I'll go check on Amelia,' Hale said, a trickle of his wolf coming out with a scent of worry.

'I don't think she'll be able to drive, but here are her keys,' Oliver said, handing Amelia's car keys to Hale. 'Even if she could, with the scent of death and blood clinging to it, I doubt she'll want to drive it. But at least she'll have the option.'

Hale winced in sympathy. 'I'll make sure she gets them. Maybe Mitchel can drive her home.'

Oliver grinned. Clearly, he hadn't been the only one who'd noticed the pairs' interest in each other during the meeting earlier.

He headed in the direction of home. He'd shower the stink of the Rift Scar off, then grab dinner from The Dead Imp. Maybe he'd convince one of Hale's patrol to give him more details about what had happened today. If he couldn't start work until tomorrow, the least he could do was learn more about Dylan.

AMELIA STUFFED THE REST of her ruined clothes into the hazardous waste disposal bag that Pascal had given her and sealed it, then stepped under the hot shower. The heat seeped into her immediately, even though the pressure was terrible.

She didn't want to use the seat, but within less than a minute, the throbbing in her calf got so bad that her head started spinning. Sitting helped.

Heal faster if shifted, Luna said morosely.

Amelia didn't bother answering. There was no point. They both knew it wouldn't be possible for some time yet. Even if she wasn't happy, Luna was still calmer than Amelia had expected.

Avoiding her plastic-wrapped calf, Amelia scrubbed the sweat, blood, and stink of the Rift Scar off her body. When she was done, it took her another minute to convince herself to get out of the chair to get dried and dressed.

She pulled on the stupid hospital gown since there was nothing else to wear. What hadn't been cut off had been covered in the woman's blood, and she'd put all of it in the hazard bag.

Mostly covered, she sat on the dry toilet seat to peel the plastic off the bandage and dumped it in the bin. The bandage underneath was dry and clean still, which was good. Pascal would have made her change it again if it got wet. It had hurt enough the first time.

'Amelia?' Hale said from the other side of the bathroom door.

She hesitated to reply. As stupid as it was, she didn't want him to see her weak.

Not weak, Luna said, shaking her head.

Hale repeated her name, a sense of worry spilling through his energy. She shook her head, trying to let her wolf's encouragement fill her. It wasn't easy when she had to limp to the door.

'I'm okay,' she said as she opened the door.

Hale's scent hit her full-on—pine trees and honeysuckle. The last part was new, appearing after he'd become mates with Sam. Most people had assumed it was just because they were practically living together. Over it all was the Rift Scar and old sweat. But even with the less pleasant smells in the mix, she immediately felt better.

It was stupid that a scent could do that. More stupid that she kept forgetting.

'Sam wanted to be here,' Hale said quietly, looking at the wound on her leg. She could feel his own remembered pain through the pack bonds before he locked them down tightly. He was clearly remembering how Sam had healed him.

It was the only one of Sam's abilities they hadn't been able to test. Healing. They still didn't know if it was just Hale or if she could heal others. But with Amelia being in the hospital, that meant everyone would know about the injury. Healing it now would risk Sam's secret. Amelia and her wolf understood that, though she suspected Sam might not be taking it so well if Hale's expression was anything to go by.

'I understand,' Amelia said, letting the truth in her scent speak for her. 'I'll be fine.'

Hale let out a breath, his wolf flashing in his eyes. It seemed Sam wasn't the only one who wanted to do more. He offered her his arm, helping her back onto the bed. He was alone, she noticed, and her fear eased further.

The realisation that she'd been afraid Dylan was with him was a bitter pill to swallow as she settled back on the bed. She never wanted to let Dylan have that kind of control over her, even in her own head.

Safe, Luna said, sending her comfort. *Protected.*

But Amelia didn't want to be protected. She wanted to be able to defend herself. But she did appreciate that Hale hadn't let Dylan come. She didn't doubt that he would've tried to insist on coming from what she'd seen of him earlier.

'Oliver told me what happened,' Hale said. 'I'll save my breath on the safety lecture and just tell you what you did was reckless.'

'You'd have done the same,' Amelia said, not quite meeting Hale's eyes as she challenged him on it. She pulled the thin sheets over her legs, though she wasn't cold.

'Yes, but that doesn't make it right. But it's why I'm not wasting my breath lecturing you,' Hale said, tone firmer this time.

'Have you heard anything about how the woman is do-ing?'

'About as well as can be expected.' Hale shook his head. Which meant she was still alive. 'How long are they going to keep you?' Hale asked, switching topics.

'They're letting me go soon. Pascal thinks there is no benefit in keeping me overnight,' Amelia said, keeping her leg as still as possible so her pain wasn't obvious. 'I still want to help.'

'You can help by resting and getting better,' Hale said, raising his hand to forestall any argument. 'Three days off minimum after being stung. There are rules for a reason.'

'We don't normally have strange wolves in our home,' Amelia said, pushing, though she already knew the an-swer. Again, her wolf was surprisingly quiet on the re-turn-to-work front. Usually, she wanted to be out there.

Sore, Luna said like it was that simple. *Not help. Be like a pup learning to walk. Useless to hunt.*

'We have all the rangers involved, and we are increasing the size of the groups just in case,' Hale said. 'I'm not risking yours or anyone else's life just because you want to be involved.'

Amelia knew her wolf, and Hale was right. Even if the snow hadn't been a foot deep everywhere, she was a liability out in the field. But surely there was something she could do.

'I can't sit and do nothing,' Amelia said, feeling the whine in her voice and hating it.

'You're not doing nothing; you're resting,' Hale said, finality to his tone this time. He switched legs where he leaned against the wall and hesitated before adding, 'How's Oliver doing?'

She raised her eyebrow at the question and the abrupt switch of topics. There was a hint of something more there, especially since Hale had spoken to Oliver. 'He's doing good. Why?'

'I felt the shift in the pack bonds,' Hale said, hesitating. 'If that's the right word.'

'He was right to challenge me. I was being stupid,' Amelia said, forcing herself further upright as she watched Hale fidget again.

'But he immediately backed down after,' Hale said, looking past her out the window. Pascal had closed it when she'd gone for a shower, and it mostly just gave the view of the side of the car park. 'I keep thinking he's going to figure it out. But there's always that backwards motion.'

There was impatience in his tone that surprised her. Not that she'd expected concern—Oliver wasn't strong enough to challenge Hale; no one in the pack was. But the impatience implied that Hale wanted Oliver to become an alpha.

Typically, only prime alphas were allowed to have other alphas under them. But Hale was more than powerful enough, even if he didn't have the title.

'He doesn't want to be in charge,' Amelia said. However, she agreed it was only a matter of time before something came up that pushed Oliver past the point of no return. From what little he'd said about why he was here, she suspected it had already happened, and his dad hadn't taken to it kindly.

'Sometimes we don't always get to make that choice,' Hale said, offering her a smile. 'Oliver has the potential to be a powerful alpha. He just needs to accept who he is. Or his wolf will choose for him.'

'He's going to have to, eventually. He's his father's firstborn,' Amelia said. Strength wasn't always genetic, but Oliver was more than strong enough to take over from his prime alpha father once he figured it out.

Anger flashed over Hale's face for a heartbeat, and then it was gone.

Amelia leaned forward. 'What aren't you saying?' That wasn't just a passing thought, not if it broke through Hale's normally ridged control. She replayed the conversation again, feeling like she'd missed something.

'It doesn't matter,' Hale said, pushing away from the wall.

Mitchel appeared in the doorway before she could form another argument. Desire slithered through her as his scent registered. Clean of any hint of the Rift Scar, it seeped into her like a balm, even though he brought a wave of chilled air. He hesitated when he saw Hale.

'Good timing,' Hale said, giving Mitchel a smile. There was no way Hale had missed the smell of desire in her scent. 'I was hoping you'd do me a favour?'

Mitchel blinked at Hale, glancing at Amelia like he thought she might provide him with an answer. But she didn't know what Hale was doing.

'Sure?' Mitchel said cautiously.

'Everyone is being sent home or to a hotel for the night. We can continue the work in the Rift Scar tomorrow,' Hale said, pulling out a set of keys from his pocket. Her keys. 'I have to organise the rest of the pack, and Amelia isn't being released yet. She won't be allowed to drive when she is, so I was hoping you'd be willing to give her a lift home.'

Good idea, Luna said, suddenly paying full attention. *Good alpha.*

Amelia was becoming suspicious about why her wolf was so calm about not being included.

I'm not going to spend more time with Mitchel, Amelia said.

Foolish pup, Luna said, shaking her head, but she didn't back down, just sat close to the surface.

Hale handed Mitchel the car keys.

'Go home, rest,' Hale said, nodding at Amelia. He gave Mitchel a brief look. 'Both of you. Madeline has taken you off the rotation for tomorrow to give you a chance to recover.'

Mitchel opened his mouth like he intended to argue as well. The childish part of Amelia hoped he had as much success as she had. But Hale didn't even give him a chance to speak.

'It's not up for debate. Overuse of power is not a small thing. I'll not be responsible for you burning yourself out because you pushed yourself too hard,' Hale said.

Mitchel nodded slowly, but Hale was already leaving, expecting that would be the end of the argument.

'He's a bit intense,' Mitchel said quietly as he looked down at the keys in his hand. He was wearing some ill-fitting scrubs. His clothes had probably been burned, too.

Amelia wasn't quite sure how to answer that, so she shook her head. Her fingertips burned with the need to reach out and touch him.

Pascal knocked and entered. 'They're finally ready to release you if you're ready to go.' He gave Mitchel a quick once-over. 'Both of you.'

Amelia sighed, nodding. 'Do you have anything I can wear?'

Pascal smiled and held up a bag with a set of scrubs similar to Mitchel's. 'It might not be the most attractive, but it covers all the important bits.'

Amelia sighed again and put her hand out for the bag. Being home was going to be better than being here. But she would send Mitchel away as soon as she was there.

Then maybe try to figure out what Hale had meant about Oliver.

CHAPTER EIGHT

Mitchel gave Amelia privacy while she got dressed. Unlike him, she looked cute when she came out in the scrubs, even if they held no real shape. Then they both did their release paperwork, which, for Amelia, involved a long lecture about taking care of her leg. By the time that was done, at least another hour had passed.

It was a relief to step outside into the cool, fresh air. Amelia had reluctantly let him push her out in a wheelchair, though probably only because Pascal had been watching.

She sat in the chair long enough to reach her car, then got out of the seat and limped towards the driver's door. Before he could say anything, she paused, looked back at him, sighed, and went to the other side.

He unlocked it for her, made sure she got in okay, then dumped the wheelchair in the lobby and got back to the car in record time. For all of it, she was quiet, watching him with the occasional flash of a brighter blue. He felt a little like he was prey, and it wasn't an entirely unpleasant experience.

Reversing her Land Rover out of the car park felt like he was about to rip his arm from his shoulder. He understood why they used cheap old cars when they went near the Rift Scar. The dust did a lot of damage over time. But really, did they need to have cars without power steering?

'Have you always been able to do that? With the ice?' Amelia asked before they'd even left the car park. She'd pushed her seat as far back as possible to stretch her leg out and watched him full-on.

Mitchel hesitated, debating about what he wanted to say. He should have expected the question, especially after what Oliver had said.

'I have always been able to control ice,' Mitchel said slowly. Not everyone would know what that meant. 'When my power came in, it was the first thing I could control.'

'So, you're not a Water Elemental like you said then?' Her voice held a note of accusation. Clearly, she knew enough.

He stamped down on the old fear and pain that had followed him ever since discovering the truth about where his magic came from. It had changed everything. But Amelia wasn't one of his family or their circle to care about the truth. Yet, he didn't know what would happen if he told her. What would that mean? Who else she might tell? Oliver clearly thought she was worth trusting, or he wouldn't have asked her not to mention the frost to anyone else like he had.

'My mother is an Air Elemental, and my father a Water Elemental. No one was happy that they had a baby together, and even less so when they found out I barely have any magic,' Mitchel said, feeling like he was repeating an old, worn-out tale. The lie was so damned easy.

'So, Water and Air make Frost?' Amelia asked, frowning. 'I thought it was one or the other?'

'It is,' Mitchel said, tightening his grip on the steering wheel. Telling the truth was more challenging than he'd expected. 'My parents lied. My father isn't my father. I don't have any Water Elemental blood in me.'

Amelia stared at him for a minute, clearly thinking it through. 'Your mum cheated?'

'Not exactly,' Mitchel said, taking a turn that Amelia pointed to. 'My father always knew I wasn't his. But my mum had told him the father was a Water Elemental, the same as him. He claims he agreed so his family wouldn't pressure him to marry someone he didn't even like. My mum did it because she wanted to hide the embarrassment of having a baby out of wedlock.'

'They're aware it's not the nineteen hundreds, right?' Amelia said, but her voice was soft. 'We no longer shun people for having a sex life before marriage.'

'When you have as much money as my family does, it's almost like we go back to the old-fashioned ways,' Mitchel said. He'd not really appreciated how different life had been until he'd gone to university on a scholarship when he'd walked away from his family. 'Old money, old blood-line. High expectations.'

'So, you're telling me you're from a family of rich snobs?' Amelia said. 'I don't understand what effect that has on you telling everyone you're something different than you are?'

'Because if anyone found out I could control Frost, they'd know that there was no way that Howard Hill was my father, and my mother would lose all her status.' Mitchel paused, that anger rising like a weight in his gut. Even years later, he kept the secret so she could have the life she wanted.

'You're a Hill?' Amelia said, eyebrows rising. Everyone knew the name. Even in the human world, the Hill name was pretty powerful. 'Funny, Oliver failed to mention that.'

'I asked him not to tell people,' Mitchel said, fidgeting in the chair. 'I cut as many ties as I could when I left.'

'But you're here. The only one not a Shifter,' Amelia said, wincing. 'Sorry, I didn't mean it to come out like that.'

'No, it's okay,' Mitchel said. 'This is why I don't like people knowing the truth. They assume the worst.'

'So, you didn't ask your father to arrange for you to join this trip?' Amelia asked, pointing to another street for him to take.

'Are you kidding? For a chance to come here and study the change in the Rift Scar, I'd have begged at the devil's feet if I had to,' Mitchel said, offering her a smile to tell her he was only partly serious. 'I worked hard to get where I am and rarely ask for favours. But this? This was something I wasn't going to pass up for pride.'

Not that it had helped. Mitchel kept that part to himself, though he doubted she hadn't already figured it out since she knew he was the only one not a Shifter.

Amelia smiled, face lighting up with it. 'So, to summarise. You're really a Frost Elemental, and you don't tell anyone so your mother gets to go to fancy parties?'

'When you say it like that,' Mitchel said, drawing a breath, 'it sounds perfectly reasonable.'

'It seems like family drama is the reason most of us end up here,' Amelia said, losing some of her humour. She gave him another turn and pointed to a small detached house at the end of the street.

'Is that how you ended up here?' Mitchel asked, pulling up in front of the house. There was no driveway, but the road barely had anyone parked on it.

'I decided I wanted to make my own decisions,' Amelia said, voice holding enough heat that he turned to her. She sighed. 'I made the opposite choice from you. I chose my future over what my family wanted me to do.'

'Maybe you need to give me some pointers on how you did it,' Mitchel said, trying to hold on to the light mood.

'I'm here,' Amelia said, turning towards the passenger door to open it. 'That should tell you all you need to know about how it worked out for me.'

'Careful,' he said, undoing his seat belt, but Amelia wasn't interested in waiting. 'Let me help you.'

'I'm fine.' Amelia opened the door and slid out of the seat. As soon as she put weight on her leg, she hissed and grabbed the door with a white-knuckle grip.

Mitchel got out and went round the car, hating the sound of pain that escaped her.

'I just need a second. I'm just stiff from staying still.' Her face had gone white, and her chin was lifted.

'Please let me help you,' Mitchel said. She wasn't the only one who was frustrated. He could see how much pain she was in; it practically radiated from her. But he could also see how much she wanted to do this herself. 'I won't tell anyone. Hell, I'll tell them you pirouetted inside if you want. Just let me help you.'

Amelia barked out a strained laugh. 'I doubt they'd believe that.' She ran her hand through her hair. It was starting to dry, the lighter blond coming back. She nodded slowly and put her hand out to him.

Relief filled him as he carefully put his arm around her waist, pulling her towards him so she could use him like a crutch. The connection between them pulled tight, sending his thoughts down an inappropriate path. He tried to ignore it.

They limped to her front door so she could unlock it and help her inside. Her hallway was long and narrow, with the stairs pressed against the wall, the kitchen directly in front, and the living room to the right. There was a lot of white from the glimpses of the rooms he could see.

He sighed in relief as he helped her lean against the wall; it might not have been far, but clearly, she wasn't the only one at the end of their reserves. 'Wait here while I lock up the car.'

Amelia smiled at him. 'We're in Huntly, not Glasgow. No one is going to steal that car. Hell, I'm not even sure someone in Glasgow would steal it.'

Mitchel smiled. 'Old habits.'

He locked up the car in record time and was back at Amelia's side before she could try to move more than a single step. After a short debate, she agreed to let him help her upstairs to her bedroom.

Every step hurt her, and they were both sweating by the time they reached the top. The pull he usually felt when he was this close to her felt muted through the discomfort.

Amelia's room had a large bed against the back wall, with a deep purple throw. She'd draped purple silky material over the walls in places, adding colour without having to paint. On his right was a large armchair, a purple blanket over one arm, and a stack of books on the side. Small knick-knacks and photos covered various surfaces, but despite looking cluttered, it felt welcoming.

'Put me on the bed,' Amelia said, making him flush as he realised he'd stopped to stare.

He helped her cross the room, but thankfully, the bed was low enough that it was only a small shuffle to help her sit after she'd pulled back the throw and covers. More purple.

There was an audible sigh of relief as she sat. She lowered her head, her hair slipping forward. He reached over without thinking and brushed the strand of hair back from her face. There was so much heat coming from her he wanted to lie next to her and never leave. It was the opposite of what he usually felt when it came to touching people.

Amelia's breath caught, her eyes coming up to lock on his. The connection pulled at him, making him feel he was in free fall towards her. Even though neither of them was moving.

They were both tired. Amelia was clearly in pain. The timing couldn't have been worse. Yet, he wanted to lean in and kiss her more than he'd wanted anything in a very long time.

'I should go,' Mitchel said, shivering, but he didn't move; he wasn't sure he even remembered how. 'Do you need anything first?'

'You look as tired as I feel,' Amelia said, eyes dipping to his lips. She tried to sit up, a squeak of pain escaping her.

He pulled back, though every part of him wanted to do the opposite. 'I'll be fine after a sleep. Using that much magic just took it out of me.'

'You can sleep here. If you want,' Amelia said, not looking away. 'It's a long walk back to the hotel.'

He should have said no, left, and not looked back. But that wasn't what came out of his mouth. 'Are you sure?'

Amelia smiled, her wolf showing in her eyes for a moment. 'Yes. Stay.' She flushed, eyes fading back to their darker blue as she looked away. 'Sorry.'

He'd seen that same look from Oliver before, fear over being judged on how they let their wolves show.

'I grew up with Shifters,' Mitchel said, sitting on the edge of the bed, wishing he didn't feel so weary. 'You'll have to do much worse than that to worry me.'

Her surprise was frustrating. Shifters had to follow so many damned rules to soothe humans who feared the change of colour. It wasn't about losing control; it was about sharing it. So few understood what that really meant, even Shifters themselves.

He wanted more for her—more for all Shifters. But for now, he could give her his trust, and hopefully, that would be enough.

AMELIA DIDN'T KNOW WHAT to say to Mitchel as she could damned near feel the confidence of his words spread through her. The acceptance.

Make good mate, Luna said, nudging her to move closer.

Amelia wasn't sure she believed he was her mate, but after everything he'd said in the car, she understood him a lot more. Understood why he hid the truth, and so did her wolf.

'Stay here with me,' Amelia said, leaning into Mitchel. Having him here with her was almost like having the pack close, but better. Closer and more intimate somehow.

'I don't know if that's a good idea,' Mitchel said, voice tight as he looked down at her leg. He couldn't see the bandage under the scratchy scrubs. 'I don't want to hurt you.'

She pulled in a deep breath. Their mixed desire filled her lungs. But so did his exhaustion. 'Right now, I'm not sure either of us has the energy to do more than fall asleep,' she said, shuffling back a few inches, trying to hide the pain. 'Stay, keep me warm.'

While Shifters didn't take on all the aspects of the wolves, the need to have the pack close was true. Touching and sharing a bed could be just as much about connection as it was about sex. It had been a long time since she'd felt connected with any of the pack. Even before she'd come here.

Some of that had been her fear of losing control. She'd mostly been afraid to allow herself to be connected. This pack and job were temporary. But she was tired of keeping her distance.

His eyes widened at the offer, and his scent shifted through a rainbow of emotions so fast she couldn't catch them all until it settled into a mix of desire and peace.

Clearly, he'd spent enough time around Shifters to know what her offer meant.

'You're sure?' he said, and she felt a thrill at his need to check with her. There was no pressure.

'As long as you don't kick me in your sleep, then you're going to be fine,' Amelia said, fighting a smile as she saw him consider whether that was a risk.

His shoulders relaxed, and he nodded. The connection between them rippled, making her shiver. God, she wished she was fit to do more than sleep.

Will be stronger later, Luna said. She hadn't considered that option, or maybe she had. There was a spare room in the house. *Silly pup.*

Her wolf withdrew from her on that comment, not giving her a chance to argue as she settled into her own sleep. Amelia silently cursed the scorpion. But in fairness, without it, she didn't see how they ended up here at all.

She should have changed out of the scrubs, but at this point, she was just too tired. Besides, she usually slept naked, which might have been stretching their self-control even as tired as they were.

Mitchel backed off the bed to flick the light switch, then turned back to her. There was enough light coming in through the closed curtains that she could just make him out. She carefully moved further into the centre of the bed, pushing down the top blanket. It was too hot in the room for anything else. Or maybe that was just her.

As he knelt on the edge of the bed, she turned on her side, being careful with her calf, then held the blanket up so he could slip in behind her. She expected him to be cold because of the frost, but he was fiery hot.

At first, he was hesitant, but when she placed her arm over his, he settled more firmly against her. It was impossible to miss his attraction as it pressed into her back, but again, she thought about waking later. It was still mid-afternoon, after all. They wouldn't need to sleep all day and night.

Part of her had expected that the desire would make it hard to sleep, despite her earlier comment on how tired they were, but it didn't. Having him wrapped around her made her feel safer than she'd felt since Hale had rescued her from Shane.

THE DREAM CAME SLOWLY. Amelia was in her wolf's body, running through the familiar hills back home. The moon was full above her, so bright and bloated it looked like it was daylight, except without the colours. Her leg didn't hurt at all, and she felt free.

Beside her was another wolf with brown fur and blue eyes, frost forming with every step as it ran.

The dream wavered. Wolves couldn't use magic.

Dream makes magic possible, Luna said, slowing them to a half-run. *Mate keep up here.*

Mitchel in a wolf's body, because that was who it had to be, slowed with her. He was panting, watching her. At the same time, she could feel him pressed against her back. The frost spread out further.

It wasn't possible.

The dream shifted, and they stood under an old tree. Sam's yew tree. Tiny buds of leaves fought to survive the cold, trying to recover from last month's damage. Moonlight flickered through the branches over Mitchel, who was human now, dressed in the jeans and T-shirt he'd worn the first night she'd met him. She was human, too, wearing a long blue summer dress.

'Where are we?' Mitchel asked, voice soft in the quiet clearing. Tiny tendrils of frost spread out under his feet to the grass, growing, stretching, then disappearing and starting again. His magic searching, something she couldn't see when she was awake.

'Part of Sam's home,' Amelia said, taking another look around. She mainly had bad memories of this place, so it was interesting that this was where her mind had gone.

Running was better, Luna said, brushing against her leg.

Amelia looked down at her wolf in surprise. Her fur was a pale blond, so light she almost looked white. She had blue eyes, lighter than Amelia's. This was the first time she'd seen her wolf like this.

Her wolf stretched, preening under Amelia's attention before she turned to stare at Mitchel. Amelia expected to smell fear from him, but there was nothing but curiosity.

'I was running with you,' Mitchel said to Luna. 'Like I was a wolf.'

Amelia shivered, trying to understand what was happening. This place, Mitchel, her wolf, it all felt real, vivid. Like it was more than a dream.

'Is this your dream?' Mitchel asked, looking up at her.

She couldn't tell if he'd sensed her thought or if he'd just come to the same conclusion. 'I don't know.'

The dream wavered, the tree disappearing and a lake appearing. It wasn't familiar, nowhere she'd been. Moonlight shone down on them, halfway to full, reflecting in the clear water.

Mitchel inhaled sharply beside her.

'Your dream?' Amelia asked, looking back at him. He'd paled, staring out at the water. Her wolf pressed into his legs, sensing his fear. He looked down and saw the white tendrils coming from his feet.

Mitchel tried to back away, but her wolf didn't let him retreat as she shoved him towards Amelia, magic and all. She expected it to feel cold, like the frost, but it was the opposite. Warmth filled her like a fire had been lit deep in her gut.

'I'm sorry, I didn't mean to,' Mitchel said, fear closing in around them both as he tried to pull away. Tried to pull the magic back.

She changed her grip, wrapping it around his waist, pulling in his scent. Frost. Clean and fresh in her lungs. 'I'm okay,' Amelia said as his fear grew. 'You're not hurting me.'

Mitchel stilled, looking up at her. 'How?'

'I don't know, but it feels'—she paused, breath hitching as the magic moved higher—'good.'

His eyes widened, and he stopped struggling to push away from her. Instead, he leaned in so they were pressed more firmly against each other until she could feel his arousal against her hip. But his fear was still there at the edges—fear of this place. She didn't want him to be afraid.

She thought about the mountains of her home again, the grassy hills and broken rocks where she had run most of her life. Unlike Sam's land, there were only small patches of scraggly trees among the rocks. The world shifted and changed again, and they stood in the spot she'd imagined.

She'd had vivid dreams before, but this was something different.

Mitchel shuddered and pulled in a deep breath as he looked around. Dawn had risen, casting a pale red and gold glow over a thin layer of snow that hit the grass. A winter breeze brushed against her skin. Again, it wasn't cold, though she knew it should have been.

'This place is beautiful,' Mitchel said, heart rate slowing as his scent changed, blending into the mountains. 'Where are we now?'

'Home,' Amelia said, looking at the tree behind her. She expected to feel longing, the pull, and go back like she had in the beginning. But there was nothing more than a flicker. This wasn't her home anymore.

'This is the strangest dream I've ever had,' Mitchel said, lowering his hands so they were clasped behind her. 'It feels so real, so detailed.'

'I'm not sure it's a dream,' Amelia said, remembering what Sam had said about her experience with Hale. But it wasn't possible. Neither Amelia nor Mitchel was near death. Nor did she really believe that they were mates, despite her wolf's words to the contrary.

'What else could it be? You're healed and here with me,' Mitchel said, looking around at the patchy grass on the surrounding hills. 'We were in a forest, then on the lake, now here. It has to be a dream.'

'Why are you so sure I wouldn't be here if this wasn't a dream?' Amelia asked, catching the start of his sentence. The certainty of it. Part of her could still feel him in the bed behind her, a distant feeling like it was the dream, and this was the reality.

He looked back at her again, the red of the frozen sunrise highlighting the brown in his hair, making it look auburn. 'I saw Dylan. I'm not exactly on his level.'

The images around them flickered, showing the same clearing on a different day. The alpha on the hill. Dylan on the ground, holding a broken arm. Her rage like a snake inside her stomach, wanting to get out and strike.

She shoved the images away before Mitchel could see them. But when she blinked, she was no longer in his arms. She was standing two feet away, shaking, alone and stinking of her own fear.

Her wolf sat at her feet, hackles up, and turned towards where the images had appeared. They didn't want Dylan. Didn't want anyone like him.

'I want nothing to do with Dylan.' She spoke quietly, trying to lock down her anger. It wasn't aimed at Mitchel.

He frowned, looking around, unsure. He'd sensed something had happened, but not what. Amelia wanted to keep it that way. She tried to let go of the rage and focus on Mitchel. On what it had felt like to have him pressed against her.

'I make my own choices,' Amelia said, stepping back towards him. There were so many reasons she should step away. The timing was terrible. But she was tired of being sensible. Tired of holding back. She wanted Mitchel. Wanted him more than she'd ever wanted anyone.

His breath caught, and surprise flitted through him. Real surprise. He really didn't think she wanted him. Even though she'd invited him into her bed. Did he not know how good it felt to have him close?

'This feels so real,' he whispered as she closed the gap, leaning closer to capture his mouth with hers. He tasted like the mountains around her. Of fresh water from a frozen stream. Of snowflakes.

He deepened the kiss, his teeth scraping over her lip. Tongue dipping into her mouth. The dual feel of him was back, in front, and behind. But she wanted more. More than a dream.

She pulled back, heart pounding as she fought to catch her breath. She leaned closer to his ear and whispered, 'Wake up.'

MITCHEL WOKE WITH A shudder. His lips tingled like Amelia's mouth was still on his. His erection pulsed like it had been connected to electricity, pressed so tightly against Amelia's back that he feared he might come just from the contact.

The dream was vivid in his mind. Kissing Amelia. Being accepted by her. He suspected that when she'd invited him to sleep next to her, this hadn't been what she'd had in mind.

But she'd scented his arousal. She'd known how he'd felt and invited him to bed, anyway. But that didn't mean she wanted to be accosted in her sleep while he had a wet dream.

Enough time had passed that night had crept in, and it was now dark outside. There was little light coming into the room, just a hint of an orange street light casting shadows. He couldn't see anything but the outline of her shoulder.

Unable to stand being pressed against her, he started to move away, carefully unwrapping his arms that had woven themselves tightly around her. Amelia moved before he could let go, rolling over to face him, inhaling sharply.

He froze, trying to make out her features. His desire was evident in more ways than one, and he was about to tell her he would leave when she spoke.

'I make my own choices,' Amelia said, leaning into him to press her lips against his. Just like the dream. Except it was somehow better. He groaned, pulling her tighter against him, the scrubs they'd been wearing scratching against his skin.

When she pulled back, he heaved in a gulp of air. Trying to get his brain to work. The dream. Except it hadn't just been a dream. It can't have been. What the hell had happened?

'Do you believe me now?' Amelia said, voice low and breathy as she pressed closer to him. His body arched almost of its own accord.

'I don't understand what happened,' he said, the scientist in him wanting to figure it out, but the man in him couldn't care less as his body ached to get closer to Amelia. 'But I believe you.'

He felt rather than saw Amelia smile as he leaned forward, lips hovering over hers. Then he closed the gap, kissing her gently. It didn't stay gentle for long as she moved her hip, rubbing against him.

Pushing her onto her back, he ran kisses down her neck, moving slowly, enjoying the smooth, silky skin. She tasted earthy, with a hint of salt from the sweat.

She clawed at his back, grabbing the scrubs, pulling them up and over his head in one quick movement, forcing him to break contact. His leg moved, brushing hers. She hissed, and he froze, pulling further back, heart pounding in his chest. Clearly, Amelia wasn't healed like she'd been in the dream. He should have thought about that sooner, should have known.

'Don't stop,' she said. His eyes adjusted to the limited light, and he could make out her face in the shadows. Her eyes were bright, and a smile played on her lips. 'I'll tell you if it hurts more than it feels good.'

'Are you sure?' Mitchel asked, still hesitating.

Amelia nodded, putting her hands around his waist, under the scrub bottoms where she could just brush the top of his arse. 'Shifter healing is a wonderful thing,' she said, though he had heard her pain before. 'Now strip.'

The command was half growl. Mitchel shivered as it rumbled through him. He held himself still for a moment longer, watching her, checking if she was sure. When she didn't waver, he reached around her back and pulled at her scrubs. 'You first,' he said lightly, smiling.

They stripped off the rest of the clothes, which wasn't quite as smooth as he would've liked, as he helped support her weight so she could wiggle out of the bottoms. When they were done, she threw their clothes across her room as if they'd offended her.

Then she turned to him. He could just about make out her slim muscular frame, the soft swell of her breasts and the smile on her lips as she returned the look.

This wasn't how he'd seen his day going. Any of his days. Yet being here with her felt right all the way down to the pit of his stomach. The strength of it should have scared him, but his erection was throbbing far too much for that to worry him right now. Especially as Amelia lay back on the bed, blond hair fanning out around her.

AMELIA WATCHED MITCHEL IN the dim light. Despite his lanky frame, he had a six-pack and muscle definition that she'd never have guessed at. His skin was the flawless pale white of a man who had spent most of his time in-doors.

She let him look at her, eyes skimming her body like a touch. She didn't know how well he could see in the light, but clearly, it was enough as the smell of his arousal grew sharper.

With his scent in her nose, she felt good. She'd have felt better without the stabbing pain in her leg, but she'd been truthful earlier. It wasn't enough to stop the pleasure she felt. But she wanted more. Wanted to feel him inside her.

She'd been through Moon Fever before, been lost in wave after wave of pleasure until there was nothing but the feel of skin and the sound of her heart beating. But this was more than that. Sharper. Stronger. She wasn't lost. She felt like she was home. As much as that thought should have scared her, it didn't.

He lowered himself slowly, being careful of her leg as he moved. Part of her had expected he'd be a cold balm to that heat, but he was just as hot as she was. Just like in the dream.

She could feel his erection against her stomach. The solid pressure belonged somewhere else. Foreplay was all well and good, but she already knew what she wanted and was more than ready to take it.

'More,' she hissed, lifting her leg, tightening her grip around him, dragging her teeth over his lip.

Amelia trembled as Mitchel ran his hands down her body, brushing her core as he kissed her. A finger slid inside her, making her cry out and arch towards him. He moved slowly, finger sliding over her sex, then back inside her again, teasing her.

She felt like she was on fire. Every nerve in her body was alive until the pain in her leg was a distant memory. One she was going to regret abusing later, she suspected.

Arching into him, she clawed at the back of his neck. She wanted him inside her. All of him. 'No more games.'

Mitchel chuckled, vibrations sliding through her, tightening her core right to the very edge. He kissed her and pulled back, making her hiss for a different reason this time. He repositioned himself until he was against her, so close but still not entirely inside. Each breath felt like torture as he hovered at the edge of entering her. She squirmed, but he held himself there, one hand on her hip.

She half expected that he would continue with the slow torture, but he moved with one thrust, sheathing himself in a single motion that sent her over the edge.

She screamed, arching up as her climax seared her. Mitchel moved inside her, each movement sending another wave crashing into her. Just as she was sure she was coming down, he sent her over another edge.

Then he finally followed her over, body spasming against her as he came. It was almost like she could feel him. Feel his pleasure as he came too. Feel the friction. The joy.

The absolute certainty that this was where she belonged.

CHAPTER NINE

MITCHEL RAN HIS FINGERS over Amelia's hip, enjoying the softness of her skin. She lay on her side facing him, her head on his arm and her injured leg on top of his. Her fingers trailed down his hip in a mirror of his motion. His hips bucked forward, making her inhale sharply.

'What happened to resting?' he whispered against her lips. He felt a hundred times better than yesterday, though he knew from experience it would be a few days before he was back to normal. He'd happily spend all of that time in this bed with Amelia.

'Resting was your idea,' she said, but she stilled her fingers, giving him a sly smile as her eyes slipped closed despite her previous words. 'Besides, I'm too warm to sleep.'

He looked at her in surprise. Warm?

The sheets lay on the floor beside the bed, but as he looked around, he saw a thin layer of frost crawling down the mirror. Why wasn't Amelia feeling the cold? She should have been freezing. But maybe this was another part of his magic he didn't understand.

He pulled back on the frost the best he could. She might not be cold now, but he still needed to get his magic under control. Once the ice had melted, he went back to running his fingers lightly across her arm.

Last night, he'd felt connected to her like she was part of him. Then there had been the dream. The changing landscape, her wolf.

It wasn't a Shifter thing because it had never felt like this with Clara. Not even after the full moon. Sex with her had always been fast and hard. Then, after they were done, she'd shower and curl up on the far side of the bed, usually only after he'd fallen asleep.

It always amazed him how much he should have noticed back then. How things were never more than just physical. They were never really a couple, just two people who happened to live together and have sex. None of it had been obvious at the time.

He shook the thoughts off, not liking thinking about Clara when he was lying next to Amelia. He wanted to be here with her, not dwelling on the past.

His stomach growled quietly, reminding him there was more to regaining his energy than resting. He started to ask Amelia if she was hungry, but she was so still that he stopped himself. She'd fallen asleep.

He smiled, stilling his hand so he didn't wake her. It would be so easy to stay here. But his stomach rumbled again. With a sigh, he untangled himself from Amelia carefully so he didn't wake her. With her injury, she'd likely be starving when she woke again. Especially since neither of them had eaten dinner. He'd see if he could find enough food for the both of them.

She shivered as soon as he let go of her, so he grabbed the sheets from the floor and wrapped them around her. He waited to see if she woke, but she sighed and settled into the purple material.

As quietly as he could, he put on the trousers from the hospital but couldn't see his top, so he left it and headed downstairs.

The morning sun lit up her kitchen in a soft glow. It was small but modern, done in red and grey, with a glass door leading into the back garden. He searched for food and found that either Amelia didn't like cooking or she couldn't. There was little more than bacon, burgers, and some frozen meals in her freezer.

He wished Huntly was big enough for an early morning takeout. What he wouldn't give for an Uber eats with a few bagels and coffee from Starbucks. With some hunting, he managed to get enough food together. A fry-up with bacon, probably okay mushrooms, a burger instead of a sausage, and some eggs.

The burgers were almost done when Mitchel heard a knock at the door. He turned to look in that direction. Amelia needed to sleep, but answering her door was weird.

When the knock came again, more insistent this time, he sighed and turned off the heat on everything in the kitchen. The door was unlocked, making him silently curse himself. He should have remembered to do that last night. Shaking his head, he opened the door.

'Who the hell are you?' Dylan's voice was a low growl as he stood in the doorway. He pulled in a deep breath, eyes flashing to yellow, and that growl came again, on its own this time.

Mitchel didn't need to be a wolf to smell the jealousy or anger. Clara's words came back to him about how Dylan was Amelia's mate. That she'd go back to him.

Amelia had said last night that she hadn't wanted Dylan. Yet here he was.

'Invited,' Mitchel said, not as confident as he would've liked.

'She's mine,' Dylan said, taking a step forward. He was a big guy who filled the doorway, forcing Mitchel back into the hallway.

He instinctively reached for his magic, but this room wasn't cold. There was no icy chill to pull towards him and defend himself. He didn't let go of the power only because he didn't know what else to do.

'Amelia doesn't belong to you,' Mitchel said, wishing he could say it with more confidence.

Clearly, Mitchel's words struck a chord because Dylan snarled and stiffened, pulling his fist back. Mitchel braced, but the blow never connected.

'Stop,' Amelia said, making Dylan look past Mitchel to the stairs. Mitchel turned just enough to see her standing halfway down. She'd pulled on an oversized T-shirt. Her eyes were bright blue, her wolf evident as she focused entirely on Dylan. 'What are you doing here?'

'I came to check on you,' Dylan said, looking back at Mitchel. 'To make sure you were alright. I found this stranger in your house. I wasn't aware you were giving out charity now.'

The insult barely registered with Mitchel; he'd been called worse by people he valued more highly than this arrogant sod.

'You've checked, and I'm fine. You can leave,' Amelia said, coming down the stairs to stop a step in front of Mitchel. The bandage was a bright white slash on her leg, but it didn't slow her down.

'I want a word, in private,' Dylan said. Not 'can I' or 'do you have a minute'. 'I want'.

Amelia's eyes narrowed, but she nodded slowly. 'Outside,' Amelia said, not looking away from Dylan.

Dylan looked like he would argue and tell her Mitchel was the one who should leave. But he didn't. Without a word, he turned and stalked out onto the snow-dusted path.

Amelia took a slow breath and finally looked at Mitchel. 'Stay here,' she said, then looked at the wall behind him. 'Don't freeze the house.' Then she turned and followed Dylan out, slamming the front door behind her.

Mitchel shivered as he let his magic slip from him. Slowly, he turned to look at the spot she'd turned to. Frost had spread out on the wall, creating a white pattern. He'd not meant to freeze anything.

Was that why she'd taken Dylan outside? Or did she want to be alone with him?

Mitchel hated that he cared so much about the answer. He'd been through hell with Clara; he didn't want to do it again. But in less than two days, somehow Amelia had become so much more than Clara ever had been to him.

He didn't even know if Amelia wanted more than a passing good time from him. What happened after his job was over? Or hers?

Mitchel shook his head and turned back to the kitchen. He couldn't control what was going on with Amelia or what the future would hold, but he could make them some breakfast. If Amelia still wanted it after speaking to Dylan.

AMELIA STEPPED OUTSIDE, SHIVERING as the chilly breeze hit her. She'd thrown on an old T-shirt when she heard Dylan's voice downstairs, and she wished she'd taken the time to put on more.

Make leave, Luna said, furious for Dylan invading her territory. *Not welcome. Not want.*

Patience, no fighting in the street, Amelia said, which was part of the reason she'd sent Dylan outside, along with wanting him out of her house. Her control would be easier with the street watching. She hoped.

So far, it was working, but not for long. The rage was simmering just under the surface, but it was hard to push it away when Luna was livid about the invasion of her home. Dylan knew better than to enter any wolf's home without permission. But just like everything else about Dylan, he didn't even seem to realise he was doing anything wrong.

Broken, Luna said, pressing at her to move Dylan further away from the house. *Not let hurt mate.*

I won't let him hurt anyone, Amelia said, not bothering to argue with her wolf about Mitchel being her mate. She didn't think Luna would hear her. Seeing Mitchel cornered like that had nearly made her attack Dylan outright.

'It's fucking freezing in your house,' Dylan said, shoving his hands in his pockets. 'It's damned near warmer outside. Does that ridiculous alpha of yours not pay you enough to put your heating on?'

'What are you doing here?' Amelia asked, careful to keep her anger in check as she stayed on her doorstep.

'That's it? You're in there whoring it up with a complete stranger, and you want to know why I'm here?' Dylan said, looking her up and down, lip curling like he didn't like what he saw. 'You're lucky that I don't go in there and tear him apart for daring to touch my mate.'

She clamped down on her wolf as she snarled in her head. Being called a whore was bad enough. But having him call her his mate just about sent her wolf into a frenzy.

'What I choose to do in my own time is none of your business. You and I aren't mates.'

He took a step towards her, eyes flaring yellow. The energy of his wolf lashed out at her like a wave of heat, scalding her skin. Fear trickled through her at the feel of it. That fear fed the rage.

Her wolf snarled and backed off from the pressure to attack, sensing the fear. But she didn't slip away; instead, she settled more firmly in Amelia's mind until it was like they stood side by side, no longer looking to attack but rather to defend.

Unlike last time, when rage had been the only option, there was something else. Another choice. They knew what they wanted now. There was no indecision or lingering lust in their body for this man they had to battle. All they felt was anger and disgust.

His energy that once would have soaked in and buried her washed over her like it couldn't touch her. The rage flickered in her mind, the need for its protection wavering. Dylan didn't control her anymore.

When she didn't react, Dylan didn't take a second step. But it was obvious he hadn't given up. Even though when he'd pulled in a breath, he wouldn't have scented even a tiny piece of desire on her.

'You're mine. I won't let some weak little water boy take you from me,' Dylan said. But the energy had dropped away. It was just him this time, no wolf behind it.

His wolf knows the truth, Luna said.

'What I do is none of your business. You're no longer my pack. Your actions made sure of that,' Amelia said. Her wolf pulled on the connection to Hale in a way she had never done before, like she was wrapping the feel of the pack around them. It soaked into her, giving her extra strength.

Dylan curled his lip, a hint of his wolf coming through. 'Hale can't have you. You're part of my pack.'

She laughed. 'It's not your pack,' she said, shaking her head. 'And it's not your decision to make.'

'You think my father can't make Hale give you back? Do you think he will protect you when he knows you're my mate? That you were sent away because you couldn't control yourself,' Dylan said, his anger thick in his scent. 'You need me. You need my protection.'

Dylan was lying. He had to be. She felt bile rise in her throat at the idea of returning to that life. She wasn't his mate, had never been, regardless of what he thought. When she'd left, his father had said she should look at where she wanted her future to be. The intent had been clear: don't come back. He couldn't or wouldn't protect her from his son. But he had set her free to protect herself.

'That foolish little water boy is only here because his father's family funds half the IRS&D's projects. He has no experience, no specialisation. He's the extra wheel,' Dylan said when he didn't get a reaction from her, fists at his side, white-knuckled.

Her wolf stepped forward in her mind before Amelia could stop her. Dylan wasn't pack, he wasn't their mate, and she was tired of being pushed around.

'Mitchel Mine,' her wolf said with her lips. A growl followed.

Dylan's eyes widened, and he stepped back, his own wolf retreating from his eyes entirely until he stood alone in front of her again.

She let her wolf step them forward, not bothering to spread their weight. Pain sliced through their leg. But they wouldn't show weakness to this coward. 'You. Not pack. Not mate.'

Dylan shuddered as her wolf found her voice. A voice that Dylan had tried to steal from them when they were in his father's pack. They weren't going to let him do it again.

'Everything alright here?' Oliver said, voice sharp.

Dylan flinched, turning to Oliver, but he didn't say anything, didn't do anything like they'd expected except turn and stalk towards his car, shoving Oliver when he didn't move out of the driveway fast enough. Oliver stiffened but didn't follow him.

Her wolf wanted to chase after Dylan and hurt him for hurting their friend. They took half a step towards him. She tried to pull back control, to stop her wolf, but it was hard when she couldn't think of a single reason not to.

Oliver stepped in front of her. 'Amelia? As much as I'd love to see that fight, I think your neighbours would disapprove.'

Her wolf didn't want to let go. She wanted to protect her mate. Oliver's wolf rose beside her. Not pressing on her, not trying to force her to do anything, just there, watching.

It was enough to break through the rage. Her wolf turned to him. 'Protect pack,' Luna said.

Oliver nodded, wolf in his eyes too. 'Protect pack,' he agreed.

Her wolf let go, leaving her shaking as she breathed, the air so cold her chest nearly ached. She'd forgotten it was cold. Dylan's fancy car started down the street, pulling away loudly.

'I'm sorry,' Amelia said, looking away from Oliver as she felt his wolf retreat. She shuddered as she tried to rebalance herself. The rage that had controlled her back when she'd first attacked Dylan was strangely silent, leaving just the familiar feel of her wolf's anger and her own.

Sorry, too, Luna whispered.

'After spending less than five minutes with the man, I'm not sure I'd blame you for ripping him apart. But if it comes to that, let's find somewhere private, then we can bury him right there,' Oliver said, not sounding like he was joking exactly. Though she was pretty sure she knew him well enough that he wasn't being serious either.

'I'm fine,' Amelia said, answering the question he hadn't asked.

'I'm serious about no one blaming you,' Oliver said, wolf flickering in his eyes. 'Kenneth ranted at me for a full hour last night about being assigned to the same team as the guy. But it would be easier on Hale if you could avoid doing anything permanent to Dylan.'

'I'm sorry,' Amelia said again, forcing a smile she didn't quite feel yet.

'Don't apologise. All of us have moments or people who push our limits,' Oliver said, looking down at her short T-shirt. 'Why don't we go inside before you freeze? Or the neighbours decide to come see what we are doing.'

'I dunno, inside was pretty frozen too,' Amelia said, giving Oliver a look as she remembered the frost on the wall. 'Mitchel told me about his mum.'

Oliver let out a huff of breath, relief trickling into his scent. 'Smells like you found a way to keep warm,' he said, grinning. 'Not that I'm one to say I told you so or anything.'

Amelia snorted and turned away from him. Feeling lighter, she led Oliver inside. Dylan was still going to be a problem, but it wasn't something she had to deal with right now.

OLIVER WATCHED AMELIA LIMP inside. The scent of her anger still filled the morning air. He'd never seen her that angry at anyone. It had taken all his willpower not to follow Dylan and join her in whatever vengeance her wolf had planned.

Should have, Thor said, huffing. *Deserved it.*

It's not our place, Oliver said, though he knew that wasn't entirely why he'd hesitated. If he challenged Dylan like that, there would be no going back. There would be a fight. He'd have to accept being an alpha for real.

Would win, Thor said. *Would make good alpha. Protect pack.*

But it didn't matter if they won or not. Oliver knew his father would hit the roof at him challenging another prime alpha's son. It wouldn't matter the reason.

'Why are you here?' Amelia asked as they went inside the house.

'Ah, I was just checking in with you, making sure you were fine,' Oliver said. He'd started at the hotel with

Mitchel, but when he'd seen his friend wasn't there, he'd hoped they'd ended up at Amelia's.

He shivered as he stepped through the threshold. The house stank of Mitchel's anger and magic. Dylan had made an impression on him, too, it seemed. But it was receding as Mitchel regained control. Underneath was the scent of their sex, clinging to them both despite the anger.

Oliver had hoped that encouraging Mitchel and Amelia to get together would help them move on, especially since they were attracted to each other. But the longer Mitchel was here, the worse his control seemed to get. Though, that might have been more to do with the weather than anything else.

'Oliver?' Mitchel's voice came from the kitchen. The smell of cooking food made Oliver's stomach growl. Burgers, bacon, and more. Amelia gave him a look and shook her head.

'Mitchel, please tell me you have extra food,' Oliver shouted, moving into the living room. It was the biggest room in the house, with a pair of dark green sofas, a TV, and little else.

He heard the sigh from Mitchel, exaggerated as it was. He guessed the answer was yes as he heard more rattling as Mitchel worked to add more food. That would keep him busy for a few minutes. And it would mean Oliver would be able to have a second breakfast.

'I didn't say you could stay,' Amelia said, smiling. She hadn't said he couldn't either. 'Besides, do you not have to be at the town hall for the briefing?'

Oliver looked at his watch. It was nearly nine, and the rest of the team would already be there getting organised for the day. Part of him wished he was there. Hell, most of him wished he was there. But Hale had asked for his help.

'Not today,' Oliver said. 'Hale has asked for me to help out with something else.'

Oliver still didn't want to believe Hale was right, that someone could have been deliberately slacking to cause a problem. But even if it was someone simply being lazy, they needed to find out how it was possible the nest of scorpions was missed.

Amelia was careful of her leg as she settled on the edge of her sofa's arm. She was better but nowhere near healed.

'I'm surprised he wants anyone to do anything else with so many strange wolves in town,' Amelia said, raising her eyebrow.

Oliver debated about telling her. Out of all the rangers, she was someone he was least worried about being the problem. She was still too new, and he'd been on most of her patrols. 'Hale asked me to check the patrol records.'

'I can help if you need it?' she said, perking up.

'No. Hale was very clear. You're benched. Take the time to chill,' Oliver said, nodding towards the kitchen. He kept his voice low and added, 'Besides, you clearly have better things to do.'

Amelia looked down, anger and frustration slashing through her scent, along with a flicker of desire.

'Don't think I don't know why you need to check the records,' Amelia said, looking back at him. He shouldn't have been surprised she'd be able to figure out the truth.

'Then you understand it's ranger business,' Oliver said, glancing at the kitchen again. There was already enough going on without dragging Mitchel into this.

'Call me if you need me,' Amelia said, shaking her head. 'Almost everyone will be out in the field today, so it's a good time to look. Though I expect Sam will be there with Madeline. I doubt Hale will let her pick up the work we had planned to do yesterday.'

Oliver winced, imagining that argument between the pair. Hale did not take danger to Sam lightly. 'I'll call if I need you,' Oliver said, though they both knew he wouldn't.

Amelia let out a breath, fingering her bandage. He could damn near feel her frustration at the restriction of it. Injuries were always hard when you needed to be active, but it was even harder with all the strange wolves in town.

'Do you think Mitchel intends for us to starve?' Oliver said, pitching his voice louder as he heard Mitchel approach, the smell of bacon growing stronger.

'Well, you're going to have to wait a bit,' Mitchel said. He was dressed in ugly trousers, with no shirt, Amelia's scent on his skin. In his hands was a single plate stacked high with food. He handed it to Amelia.

Her gaze followed him, lingering on his chest, wolf flashing in her eyes. The intensity was a surprise, especially when the full moon was long past. Oliver couldn't help his smile as she accepted the plate but never looked away from Mitchel.

'I found some more bacon and eggs for Oliver. I hope that's okay?' Mitchel said.

'I suppose we should probably feed him,' Amelia said, moving to sit in the chair instead of on the arm, balancing the plate on her knee. 'I wouldn't want Hale to accuse me of starving Oliver to death.'

'I'm sure that would be terrible for you,' Oliver said, sitting on the opposite sofa.

The next half hour passed too quickly as they all got food. They avoided talking about Dylan, the Rift, or anything serious. If only all his mornings could be so easy.

When he finally left, it was with a measure of sadness. Those patrol logs were going to bring more strife and pain. It was just a matter of who was involved and why.

CHAPTER TEN

MITCHEL WATCHED AMELIA AS she limped towards the kitchen, stubbornly refusing to let him tidy the plates after Oliver had left. The breakfast had been cobbled together, but it had been good, and the company had been better. Though one less might have made for something a little more intimate. Not that he'd hold it against Oliver.

'I want to go and check on the woman in ICU,' Amelia said, returning to the living room doorway. 'You're welcome to stay here if you want.'

Her words were hesitant like that wasn't exactly what she wanted to say. Her gaze lingered on his chest before rising to his eyes again.

'No offence, but I can see you limping. Your car isn't exactly set up for comfortable driving,' Mitchel said, avoiding outright saying he didn't think she could drive. 'I can drive you there if you want. I'd like to see if she's okay too.'

Amelia shifted the weight onto her hurt leg like she wanted to prove he was wrong. After a second, she changed back with a hiss. 'Fine,' she said begrudgingly, 'but if you go dressed like that, they'll have questions.'

Mitchel looked down at his bare chest and dark blue scrub bottoms. 'I don't know, I think it could be a new fashion trend?'

Amelia laughed and shook her head. 'Give me a minute to get dressed, then we can swing past your hotel,' she said and turned towards the stairs.

It was tempting to follow her up, but he hesitated. Dylan's arrival earlier still bubbled at the back of his mind. Then there was Oliver, who'd never said why he was there. Casual atmosphere aside, Mitchel felt like he was being excluded from something. Pack business.

He was still debating about going up by the time Amelia came down. She was dressed in black leggings and a long-sleeved jumper that hung about mid-thigh. Her hair had been pulled back into a ponytail.

All he wanted to do was pull Amelia towards him, press her against the wall and forget about going anywhere for a long time. But he stayed where he was. Last night had been much simpler, with his arms wrapped around her and her heat soaking into him.

'I thought you might appreciate something a little more comfortable until we get to your hotel.' She handed him a

T-shirt, not the hospital scrubs. He took the T-shirt that was still warm from when Amelia had been wearing it.

The oversized T-shirt was still big on him, though slightly less so than it had been on Amelia. It felt good to have it on in a way that had nothing to do with warmth. He could smell Amelia all around him, cedarwood and spice that made his skin tingle.

'Thank you,' Mitchel said, wishing he had something a little sturdier than the thin hospital trousers to hide his reaction. Not that it would have mattered. He was sure his scent told her all about his arousal.

Amelia's eyes flashed to that bright blue again, then she blinked and stepped away. 'We should go.'

Mitchel forced himself to his feet and out to the car. He started defrosting it while Amelia locked up the house. She sighed as she sat in the passenger seat, showing the strain on her leg. The tight set of her jaw told him he was probably safer not to mention it.

Once the car was defrosted, he pulled out and followed Amelia's directions to the hotel. There was parking to the side of the hotel's main building. Mitchel manoeuvred the car into a spot and pulled on the handbrake. 'You have to get a car with power steering,' Mitchel said, rolling his shoulders.

Amelia exhaled. 'I think a new car is going to be necessary,' she said, though there was an undercurrent that didn't match his humour. He glanced in the back, catching a flash of red, and realised he'd missed the obvious. Everything from last night would be etched on the car: blood, pain, and death.

He wanted to say or do something to offer comfort. Or help. But they didn't have another car or another option to get to the hospital. He wished he had pressed for them to stay at her home, but it was too late for that.

Unable to do anything else but hurry up and get moving, he opened the door. 'I'll just be a minute,' Mitchel said, then he slipped out into the chilly morning.

Salt had been put down on the car park and path to the hotel, but whoever had laid it had done so unevenly, so there were icy patches everywhere.

His magic surged in the back of his mind, wanting him to reach out and connect with the ice. The need was so strong that he had to pause. Something about this place just wanted to tear at his control. If he didn't figure out how to rein it in, Amelia would be the first of many who figured out the truth of his magic.

Trying to shake off the feeling, he headed into the hotel. He waved neutrally to the receptionist, trying not to blush as she frowned at his odd dress. His room was set on the opposite side of the building to the car park.

A man slightly older than him passed by, looking as dishevelled as Mitchel. The man blushed and kept walking, trying to pretend Mitchel didn't exist. He smiled, taking the old-fashioned room key out of his pocket, and opened the door. Who was he to judge someone else?

His room was in a mess from the night before. He vaguely remembered arriving back, though mostly he remembered Oliver forcing him out of bed yesterday morning. It felt like a lifetime ago.

Hunting through the mess, he found the jeans he'd travelled in. He'd one more set of clean clothes in his bag, but if this trip went on much longer, he'd have to buy or wash something. He didn't bother looking for another T-shirt, deciding to wear the one Amelia had given him, not wanting to let go of her scent.

The door to his room clicked and swung open. The image of Amelia rose in his mind as he turned. But it wasn't her.

Clara stood in the doorway, nose flaring wide and eyes flashing to her wolf's amber. 'You stink of that bitch.'

'Get out,' Mitchel said, not even arguing with her.

She did the opposite, entering his room and closing the door behind her. 'The least you could have done is shower. There's no need to rub it in my face.'

'What I do is no longer any of your concern,' Mitchel said, holding the jeans tightly, fingers aching. 'Nor are my actions anything to do with you and what you prefer.'

Clara smiled, giving a little chuckle as she walked closer. 'You say that, but we both know you don't really believe it. I know why you're playing with Amelia. It's a brilliant way of getting back at Dylan for how the prime alphas tried to sabotage you making it here. They're furious, you know?'

Mitchel froze. Suspecting it was pack politics that had caused someone to stop him coming was one thing. Having it confirmed was something else altogether. He pushed the knowledge away. It had nothing to do with the problem of Clara in front of him right now.

'I'm not playing games with you, or her, or anyone, Clara. Why can't you understand that no one else is playing those games but you?'

She didn't react to his words as she moved closer, going around the bed, until she stood in front of him. His heart rate jumped as she closed in on him. He didn't want her here. What did he have to do to convince her he meant it?

'Except here you are in this little town with me?' Clara said. 'I know you. I know how you work. What you want.'

She closed the gap before he could stop her, pushing him backwards into the wall hard and pressing herself flush against him. He tried to push her away, but she wasn't giving in that easily as she pressed her hand low into his pants. 'You remember how it used to be? How it felt to take me from behind, to fuck me until we were both sweaty and couldn't catch our breaths?'

Mitchel couldn't stop his hips jerking as she wrapped her hands around his half-deflated erection. All the attraction from being so close to Amelia still burned through him, body looking for what his head knew wasn't right.

Clara leaned forward, licking his neck, stroking him, pressing him into the wall hard so he couldn't move. He didn't want her touching him. Bile burned his throat, and he felt his magic spill from him. But in the warm hotel room, there was nothing it could do again.

'It feels so good, doesn't it?' Clara said, tightening her grip. 'Like old times.'

Mitchel didn't want old times. He didn't want any time with Clara.

He wanted Amelia.

Mitchel twisted in her grip, shoving her again, this time without any worry if he hurt her. She fell away from him, nails scraping down the length of his sex, making him hiss in pain. She landed in a sprawl on the bed. Because, of course, the room was too small for her to end up anywhere else.

His breath came in a ragged gasp as he fixed his trousers, feeling sick.

'You like it rough now, Mitchel?' Clara said, running her hand down her chest, stomach, and lower. 'You know how I like variety.'

'Yes, I do know,' Mitchel said, spitting out the words. 'A variety of lovers. Which no longer includes me. Not now, not ever.'

Clara shivered, slowly sitting up. 'I'm the best you'll ever get. Do you think Amelia can give you better? That she really wants you? You're just a distraction to make Dylan jealous. If you believe anything else, you're lying to yourself.'

'You don't get it, Clara,' Mitchel said, closing his hand into a fist, not trusting himself to step towards her. He didn't trust that he wouldn't do something he'd regret later. Especially as her words cut deeper than he wanted to admit. 'This isn't about Amelia. This isn't about anyone but you. Your lies. Your games. Your mistakes.'

Clara's eyes narrowed, and she moved to the edge of the bed, opening her mouth to speak. But he didn't give her the chance.

'No, you might believe that what we had was something special in your delusional little brain. But it wasn't special. It was subpar, disconnected, and toxic.' Mitchel took a breath, feeling the weight of the memories of their relationship. 'I don't want you.'

That got Clara to her feet, anger so strong that it was a wonder he couldn't feel the heat of it against his skin.

'When you realise how wrong you are, I'll make you beg to take me back,' Clara said. Then she spun away from him and stalked out of the room. Mitchel followed to lock the door behind her, hand shaking as he struggled with his anger.

He felt sick, with tiny tendrils of pain spiking through his sex from where her nails had removed a layer of skin.

And on top of it all, the door handle under his fingers was frosted over, ice so thick he couldn't even see the metal.

Cursing, he stepped back, trying to rein it in. Again.

He had to find a way to regain control. Somehow. Before he hurt someone. Because if Clara had tried this outside, he wasn't sure he wouldn't have done serious damage.

Part of him wasn't sure he cared, not after this.

THE CAR STANK OF blood and pain, making Amelia's stomach roll as she breathed it in. Mitchel's arousal and scent were a thin layer over it, but it wasn't enough to drown any of it out.

She managed about one minute in the car alone before getting out. Mitchel might have said he'd not be long, but even that was too long to be stuck with those scents around her. Her calf throbbed as she moved it, then sent shooting pains up her body as she put weight on it.

Part of her wished Mitchel had just followed her upstairs earlier. Though she knew they'd have ended up here, eventually. Probably. Or maybe she should have followed him to his room. Either would have been a good option.

Except, things had been different after Dylan. Mitchel had withdrawn, and she couldn't figure out how to bring him back.

Stupid. Is mate, Luna said, huffing a breath. *Go to him.*

You don't know that's what the connection was, Amelia said, shivering. It was stupid to make this argument with her wolf, who lived on instinct for the most part. But that didn't mean she was always right. *You're guessing.*

Felt it. Saw it. You foolish pup, Luna snarled at her, sending her images of small wolves doing things they should know better than to do and a mamma wolf correcting their behaviour.

Amelia sighed and gave up arguing with her wolf. She agreed there was something with Mitchel. But finding her own mate when Sam and Hale had just found each other seemed unlikely, considering how rare it was.

She carefully made her way around the back of the car, avoiding the icy patches that Mitchel had seemed to navigate without even noticing. It might have been easier if both her legs had been good. But no, she was stuck with a shooting tendril of fire every time she put weight on her hurt leg. Mitchel had been right. There would have been no way she'd have been able to drive like this.

The wind stirred, mixing the smell of a nearby coffee shop with the morning traffic. Under it were hints of the salt on the ground and the people who had passed by, including Mitchel.

As the breeze changed direction, she caught a new scent. A Shifter. Kenneth. Amelia frowned, searching for the person to go with the scent. Eventually, she caught sight of him walking away from her. The only place he could have come from was the hotel. Kenneth hunched his shoulders like he was trying to make himself look shorter or avoid anyone noticing him. Of course, the hunch did the opposite.

Kenneth didn't even look in her direction as he walked away fast. He must have been off rotation today if he wasn't in the field, but why was he at the hotel? His scent reached her again, this time bringing with it another layer. A female wolf whose scent was apples and slightly overripe fruit. She was familiar, probably one of the visiting wolves, but Amelia couldn't tell which one.

Finding the woman's scent in Mitchel's hotel made her hackles rise. Her wolf rose close to the surface, wanting them to mark her territory. Not that they could do that in their human form. Nor was this her territory in that sense.

All ours, Luna said, like Amelia was being stupid. She showed her images of Huntly, the surrounding woods, and, surprisingly, the Rift Scar.

Again, Amelia didn't bother arguing or shout after Kenneth to find out who the woman was. She didn't like him already, and she certainly didn't want to talk with him about another woman. He'd assume she was jealous. Besides, if he wanted to sleep with the visiting Shifters, that was his choice.

He disappeared around the corner, leaving her alone again in the cold. Bored but unwilling to follow Mitchel inside, she played with her phone, replying to a message from Sam that she'd missed. Spending the day with Madeline was apparently both exciting and frustrating.

She was so focused on her phone that she almost missed the feeling of someone coming closer. A petite, curvy woman with long blond hair stalked right up to Amelia, pressing into her personal space. A growl slipped from Amelia's lips before she could stop it. The woman rocked back a step, then scowled.

There was no sense of the woman's wolf, but her scent was the same as the one that had clung to Kenneth. Over-ripe apples.

Needs taught lesson, Luna said. *Our territory. Not welcome.*

Amelia didn't disagree. But she tried for a calmer approach. 'Who are you?' she asked, voice a low growl that wasn't calm at all.

'You know you're nothing more than a passing fancy to Mitchel, right? When he's done, he will come back to me,' the woman said, still not giving her name as she continued to try to challenge Amelia. But there was still no sense of the woman's wolf, which was strange when she was so aggressive.

Luna snarled and pressed for control. *Not let woman have Mitchel.*

No, she can't, Amelia said, pushing her wolf back, though her anger made it hard.

'Who. Are. You?' Amelia said, this time letting the feel of her wolf flood the small car park. Let's see the woman evade the question this time.

The woman's wolf finally rose, but it wasn't to fight; it was to cower. She filled the space around Amelia with fear and submissive energy. An omega. Luna backed off immediately as she was overwhelmed with the need to protect those who were weaker, even though this strange wolf wasn't pack.

Weak. Afraid of us, Luna said cautiously, forcing them to pull in another breath. That scent of apples grew until it felt like she would choke on it. *Don't understand.*

'My name is Clara.' The woman's voice was tight, but weirdly, the tone didn't match what Amelia could feel from her wolf. 'And Mitchel is mine.'

Not hers, Luna said, but she didn't go on the offensive again as she tried to figure out how to react to this woman.

Amelia didn't answer her wolf this time as her gut tightened. She didn't know anything about Mitchel's life back home. Was this woman his girlfriend or lover? He hadn't mentioned it, but it wasn't like they'd had much chance to talk about their previous lives.

'If he wanted you,' Amelia said, ignoring her conflicted thoughts, 'then he'd be with you. And he's not.'

'You don't know anything about him,' Clara said, lifting her chin. Again, that submissive energy battered against Amelia, utterly contrary to the aggression in her tone. 'Mitchel loves me.'

'Really? Then why was he with me last night?' Amelia said, this time choosing to step into Clara's personal space. The scent of Mitchel clung to Amelia, and there would be no missing it.

Her leg did not like having all her weight on it. But just because she couldn't use her wolf's presence, it didn't mean she'd show weakness if she didn't have to.

Clara stiffened but didn't back away. 'Really? Then maybe he was left unsatisfied because he certainly enjoyed my touch,' Clara said, bringing up her hand so it stirred the air. Then she licked her finger. 'I've always loved the way he tastes.'

Amelia pulled in a deep breath without consciously meaning to. Mitchel's scent was definitely on her, even if it was faint, but there was a hint of blood there, too. Amelia's wolf stepped them forward so she was almost touching Clara. 'What did you do to him?'

'Nothing he didn't enjoy,' Clara said.

Amelia growled, wanting to punch this woman in the face. But Clara's omega wolf's fear rose higher in response. Amelia's wolf stalled out painfully, fighting against her nature as she tried to attack Clara. She didn't know how to deal with the need to protect the omega wolf versus the need to put Clara down.

Usually, Amelia could push past her wolf's conflict, but it spilt into her, making it harder for her to think and react. She'd met omegas before, but none of them had ever felt like this.

Clara smiled, clearly knowing the pain she was causing. Then she backed off a step, her wolf smelling like she was about to wet herself. 'No matter what you do, he will come back to me. He's mine, now and always.'

Not like, Luna said, whining, pressing close against Amelia as she fought against the pain.

It's okay, let her leave. She's wrong, Amelia said, wishing she sounded more confident.

Hurt mate, Luna said, shuddering as she tried to fight the feeling. *Must protect.*

Though the images weren't so much about protection, but instead to punish and make sure Clara could never lay a finger on Mitchel again. Except that every time the thought rose, the need to protect Clara grew until Amelia's head throbbed, and her body ached.

It's okay, Amelia said, though it wasn't, and her wolf was beyond listening.

Clara turned and headed towards a car a few spaces down. Only when she had driven away did the pressure on Amelia release.

Amelia collapsed back against the car, body shaking, leg throbbing. What Clara had done shouldn't have been possible. Omega's human and wolf natures were in sync; if one was afraid, both were. But Clara was using her wolf's fear as a weapon.

Clara hurting wolf, Luna said, still shivering against the residual feel of the magic. *Not like.*

Luna was right. That's exactly what it felt like. Bile burned her throat as she imagined anyone doing that to Luna, let alone herself. *I'll not let anyone hurt you like that,* Amelia said, pulling Luna closer.

Unfortunately, there was little they could do for Clara's wolf, nor was this likely the first time she'd used it as a weapon. It was too practised.

There might not be anything she could do for Clara's wolf, but she needed to check on Mitchel. She straightened, forcing her aching leg to take her weight as she headed towards the hotel.

She'd barely stepped towards the building when Mitchel came out. His hair was damp, and he wore a thin blue coat and dark jeans. As he grew closer, she could smell the soap he'd used to have a shower, but not Clara.

But that didn't mean anything Clara had said had been the truth. There were plenty of reasons why he'd have had a shower. Amelia's wolf echoed the statement with none of the hesitation that had surrounded Amelia's thoughts.

'Are you okay?' Amelia asked, pulling in a breath. There was no sign of any blood on him nor Clara's scent. But the soap was masking almost everything, including Amelia's scent from last night.

'I'm fine,' Mitchel said. He looked distracted and even more distant now than before. 'Come on, let's go to the hospital. You must be freezing.'

Amelia nodded, though she barely felt the chill in the air now he was close. But it was an excellent excuse to turn away and head towards the passenger seat. Clara's words circled in her head. She wanted to ask Mitchel about them but was afraid of the answer.

Ours, Luna said. This time, it was Luna who was trying to reassure Amelia.

But it wasn't that simple. Mitchel was his own person, able to make his own choices. Not to mention, he was only here for a week at most. Then he'd leave to go home, back to his family and life. Back to Clara, maybe. Something she'd known, even if she'd let it be buried at the back of her mind.

She and Mitchel were only ever going to be temporary. It didn't matter that a connection between them buzzed like electricity under her skin. Or how much her wolf snarled at her that she was being stupid.

Mitchel was going to leave.

CHAPTER ELEVEN

M ITCHEL STARED AT THE ICU sign in front of him. It
was in an isolated section of the hospital, with no one else
about. Not that any of the hospital had felt busy. The door
was staff only, and Amelia had called on her doctor friend
to let them in.

Amelia was strangely quiet, but faced with the sombre
tiny ICU sign, he could hardly blame her. Part of him
wanted to wrap his arm around her, pull her close, and
remind himself that she was safe.

Though after everything that had happened with Clara,
maybe it was more his need to feel better. He'd grabbed a
shower, unable to stand the idea that she'd touched him at
all.

'Are you sure they'll let us in?' Mitchel asked, looking at
Amelia. She favoured her good leg as she leaned on the wall
beside him. 'We aren't family?'

'Normally, we wouldn't,' Pascal said from behind
Mitchel, making him jump as Pascal came around to swipe

a pass against the door. 'But we don't know who her family is yet, and I'm sure she'd appreciate the company.'

Mitchel added in what Pascal had avoided saying. The chances of survival were so low that the family might not arrive in time.

'You've not had any luck tracking her family down, then?' Mitchel asked, moving to follow Pascal through the door.

Pascal shook his head. 'We're pretty confident that the woman was her mother, but other than that, nothing. She was wearing a necklace with Natalie on it, so that's what we're calling her.'

The room held three beds, all with their own monitoring systems and complicated-looking machines. Natalie was in the closest one, her red hair pleated to one side. A tangle of wires and tubes whose purpose Mitchel could only guess twisted around her, feeding into a machine that beeped quietly beside her.

Mitchel had spent years studying the Rift Scar, looking at the research, the numbers, and the stats. But he had never watched the effect before. How broken the woman looked, how fragile. A twist of fate and bad luck that the car had landed in that nest, and now a life hung in the balance. A few metres the other way, and it would have been different.

Amelia touched his wrist. That connection from last night bloomed into something more solid until it was like he could feel her. Feel her pain that echoed his. Which was probably just him being overly dramatic. But with Clara's words like poison in his head, the link helped him feel grounded again.

'She's doing good. She's a fighter,' Amelia said.

'I wish there was something we could do for her,' he said, holding Amelia's hand in his.

'We are. We're here.'

Pascal moved forward, checking the machines. 'People don't come north when the weather is this bad for no reason. Someone will be looking for her. Until then, Amelia is right. Being here with her is the best you can do.'

Mitchel nodded, even though it didn't feel like enough. He was a scientist at heart, and science was failing them. Why did some live and some die? No one had an answer.

'Why don't they send her to one of the bigger hospitals?' Mitchel asked, looking at Pascal. 'No offence to you guys here.'

'No offence taken,' Pascal said, smiling to prove he meant it. 'This hospital is the closest to the Rift Scar. They've equipped it for these kinds of cases because of that. But there really isn't much to be done for the first few days except monitoring her vitals and providing fluids to help her body fight. If she lives past that, we'll transfer her south to the specialist unit.'

A nurse came in the door in a rush, calling to Pascal.

'There's been another attack,' the woman said, breathless, as she took in everyone. 'He's hurt, but they say he wasn't stung. He's fully awake. Do you want us to bring him in here?'

Pascal frowned, then nodded. 'Better to. Just in case.'

Amelia pulled Mitchel back towards the wall as they pushed in a trolley. It held a heavy-set middle-aged man. He wore a pair of workman pants and a heavy-knit jumper. His shoulder was twisted at an unnatural angle.

'I didn't get stung,' he said, trying to sit up, but the nurses pushed him back down. 'It didn't get anywhere near us. I just slipped on the ice.'

'I know, Max. But we need to be careful,' Pascal said.

'What happened?' Amelia asked, shouting to be heard over the noise.

'You guys have to leave,' Pascal said, looking at them like he'd just remembered they were there.

'I need to know what happened,' Amelia said, letting go of Mitchel's hand to step closer. 'If there are more people in the Rift Scar, Hale needs to know.'

'I wasn't in the Rift Scar,' Max said, groaning as the nurse pushed him down again. 'I was at the farm. But they'd already got him.'

Mitchel bit down on a curse as he realised this meant someone had been hurt, and this time, it hadn't been in the Rift Scar. Mitchel exchanged a look with Amelia. She was as pale as he felt.

A doctor in a white coat entered the room and took one look at Amelia and Mitchel. 'Get them out of here now. They're not cleared to be here for this.'

'I need to know—'

'I don't care what you need. I'm well aware that you're a ranger, but this is my hospital, not the Rift Scar. Let me do my job, and maybe you can do yours?' The doctor didn't even bother to look at them as he spoke. But his words made Amelia flinch.

Mitchel's gut tightened as more staff arrived, moving with purpose as they put on their protective gear. Even though the man seemed fine. But Mitchel understood the need for protocol.

When Amelia still didn't move, Pascal gripped her arm, gently turning her towards the exit. She let him, though Mitchel knew she was strong enough, even with her hurt leg, to refuse. He followed them.

'The nurse said his wife is outside,' Pascal said, pausing as they reached the door to look over his shoulder. 'His vitals aren't good despite it just looking like a shoulder injury. I know you want to help, but you must let us work. Go talk to his wife if you have to. Then, for god's sake, take some weight off your leg.'

Amelia looked like she wanted to argue, but she nodded and stepped through the doors. Before they'd even finished closing, she'd turned and headed deeper into the hospital. Mitchel didn't bother trying to stop her. He'd seen that look on Oliver's face often enough when he'd decided he was going to do something, no matter the cost.

AMELIA'S LEG BURNED FROM the speed she set. Her wolf paced in her head, urging her to move faster. She needed to protect the pack and hunt those who would attack what she saw as hers to keep safe. Even though she didn't know Max except in passing, he was included among them.

She had met Max and his wife maybe half a dozen times when working around the Rift Scar. Their farm had high walls and thick wire around their whole place. He'd always been a happy, welcoming man who didn't care that she was a wolf. A rarity in this area.

The reception to the hospital's A & E was small, with maybe a dozen seats and a reception desk that had a plain-looking woman working behind it.

It wasn't hard to find Max's wife. Tammy had the same large frame as her husband, broad and solid. It was more muscle than fat, though you wouldn't know it to look at her in the baggy jumper.

Tears streaked her face as she sat in a plastic waiting chair, eyes vacant.

'Tammy. Do you have a minute to answer some questions?' Amelia asked, lowering herself carefully into the plastic seat next to Tammy.

'Amelia?' Tammy said slowly, focus coming back. 'You helped Max and his dad fix the gate? You're a rift ranger, right?'

Tears stung Amelia's eyes at the memory. When the snow had first come, it caught many people off guard. Hale had sent out all the rift rangers to the local farms, offering help when it was too cold and snowy to do their regular rotation in the Rift Scar. Max's old metal gate hadn't wanted to close, the frost digging in hard. It had been more than just her who had helped.

'I helped, yes,' Amelia said, forcing the words through her tight throat.

'I told them we should sell the farm to someone else, but they wanted to keep up family tradition,' Tammy said, tears streaming down her face. 'It was too much between the weather and extra costs for the cattle. But my father-in-law wouldn't listen, and Max wouldn't leave his dad there to take care of the farm.'

Mitchel motioned to the receptionist behind the counter, and she handed him a wad of tissues. He passed them to Tammy. She started crying even harder.

The small act of kindness struck a chord deep in Amelia's chest. He didn't know Tammy. If that had been Dylan, he'd have dismissed the woman if he had bothered to talk to her at all.

Protective mate, Luna said, pleased. *Take good care of pack.*

That doesn't mean he's going to stay, Amelia said, but her wolf just huffed a breath and went back to focusing on the woman.

'Can you tell us what happened?' Mitchel said. He didn't take the seat but instead crouched between Amelia and the woman so she could see them both. He'd that look Hale sometimes got when he was dealing with people who were upset. An openness that made people want to talk.

'We'd come into town for supplies, my husband and me,' Tammy said, looking down at her hands. 'It was cold,

so we decided to stop for coffee. If we hadn't stopped—'
She cut off, gulping in a breath.

Amelia reached out, putting her hand over Tammy's, offering support. 'Don't do that to yourself. No what-ifs. You can't change the past.'

Tammy nodded, though she didn't look remotely convinced as she roughly brushed away tears. 'We came back, and the animals were making so much noise. I've never heard a noise like it before.' Tammy shuddered, swallowing hard. 'We knew something was wrong. We ran to the barn ...'

A sob escaped Tammy again as she shuddered. Amelia stayed silent this time, letting Tammy gather herself. 'Max's dad was in the barn. He was so still we thought he'd fallen at first. We went to go to him. Then I saw the scorpion.'

Until now, Tammy's eyes had been down on her hands, but she raised them, looking Amelia directly in the eye. 'I've never seen one in all my years here. And there it was, grey and ugly, standing next to my father-in-law. I panicked.' Tammy put her head in her hands, tears coming harder. 'I tried to run.'

'It's okay, Tammy. Fear is understandable,' Amelia said, wishing there was something, anything, she could do for this woman. But the guilt was too fresh.

'It's not okay. It's all my fault. I slipped. Max tried to catch me, and we fell. He landed on his shoulder, and I heard it pop. But he didn't even scream,' Tammy said between sobs. 'He grabbed me, pulling us clear. He got us back to the car, even with his shoulder barely usable.'

Amelia exchanged a glance with Mitchel. It didn't sound like he'd been close enough to be stung. A nurse standing close by, her own tears shining in her eyes, slipped away. Presumably to relay the story to the doctor.

'He did a good job,' Mitchel said, voice soft as he drew her eyes to his. 'He protected you.'

Tammy shook her head. 'My husband has a shotgun, just in case. But it was locked in the safe in the house. If I hadn't panicked, maybe he could have got it. Maybe we could have helped his dad,' she said, breaking down entirely at the last words.

'This isn't your fault,' Amelia said, but she wasn't sure Tammy could hear her.

'No, it's yours,' a woman said, bringing Amelia's head around. The speaker was a middle-aged woman in a pink skirt suit, with her pale brown hair in a tight bun. Joyce King. She was part of the town council and a known hater of anything to do with Rift Bloodlines.

Mitchel opened his mouth to speak, but Amelia grabbed his arm, squeezing hard enough to make him look at her. She shook her head. Arguing with Joyce was a waste of time, if only in part because she wasn't wrong. Scorpions shouldn't have left the Rift Scar.

'Mrs King,' Amelia said, carefully keeping her voice neutral. How the hell had Joyce found out about this already? Amelia didn't know, but she obviously was trying to make a stink. Hale was going to be pissed.

'What? Nothing to say for yourself?' Joyce said, shaking her head. 'The rift rangers are supposed to protect us from this. Where were you when these scorpions wandered out of the Rift Scar?'

Useless woman, Luna said, sending angry images of the woman being pushed out of a pack. It was a pretty bad insult from her wolf and also accurate. Joyce liked to look important, but she didn't do anything except upset people.

'Amelia was hurt yesterday, pulling a young girl out of the Rift Scar,' Mitchel said, voice somehow neutral despite the scent of his anger. 'Something I imagine you already know since they've taken the time to inform you about this incident.'

Joyce looked him up and down like he was trash left on her driveway. 'And who are you to know about what I have or haven't been told?'

'Mitchel Hill,' he said, standing. He visibly changed, body language shifting so that he looked down at her.

Joyce's eyes widened slightly, recognising the name. Or that the family was a Rift Bloodline, maybe.

She stared for a moment, then seemed to gather herself and turned to Amelia, clearly deciding that ignoring him was the best option. 'Regardless of your condition, I expect Hale to be here immediately to explain what happened and how. His job is not to be gallivanting around with a useless science team.'

'You're more than welcome to speak to him,' Amelia said, offering a thin smile. 'He's in the Rift Scar.'

Joyce paled faintly, then lifted her chin to compensate for even that show of fear. 'No wonder so many people have been injured in the past two days if that's the sort of thing you're recommending.'

'Ahh,' Mitchel said, voice cool. 'So, you were aware of all the injuries, after all?' Despite the even tone, he was practically vibrating with his anger; it was so strong she could damn near feel it as it seared her nose. She tightened her grip on his arm, trying to bury her anger.

Instead of answering, Joyce shivered and turned to the woman behind the reception desk. 'Do something about the heating already, woman; it's freezing in here. Your budget is more than enough to make sure the people here are at least warm.'

'Ahh, Mrs King, there you are. The director is free now,' a man in a slightly rumpled suit said, offering Joyce a weak smile.

'About time,' Joyce said, turning to stalk away without another word to anyone, heels clicking. The man in the suit looked at Tammy like he wanted to talk to her, but he sighed and turned to follow Joyce.

Amelia relaxed her grip on Mitchel's arm. It hadn't done much to keep him from talking, but it made her feel better. Her wolf settled, too, wanting her to lean into Mitchel.

'That woman should come face to face with a Rift scorpion and then see how she finds it,' Tammy said. Her tears had stopped now, even if her voice was raw and her eyes were red. It was amazing what anger could do. 'My husband has been hurt, and not once did she ask me how he was. And she wonders why no one votes for her to be mayor?'

Amelia offered Tammy a smile, showing she appreciated the support.

'How did she know to come here?' Amelia asked, though she didn't care about the answer. It did seem to be helping Tammy stay solid, though.

'Hospital had to call her,' Tammy said, shaking her head. 'I heard them when I was waiting.'

Amelia hated politics. But there was something Joyce had said that had made Amelia's stomach knot. 'I know this is hard, but can you remember if your father-in-law was ...' Amelia broke off, unable to say dead.

'He wasn't ...' Tammy swallowed hard, then drew in a deep breath. 'He wasn't moving. But we didn't get close enough to be sure.'

They needed to get rift rangers out there to check. Except all of them were in the field, even the rapid response. All but Amelia and Oliver, and she wasn't exactly in good condition to be doing anything. Kenneth apparently was also out there somewhere, but if he was off rotation, he wouldn't answer his phone for extra work.

She cursed silently. Why couldn't they fix the damned cell towers?

Amelia couldn't leave Tammy's father-in-law alone, maybe still alive, like the young redhead. The longer he was out there, the worse his chances would be. They couldn't wait for Hale.

She still had the weapons locked in her car's boot, probably Oliver's, too. Really, she should have dropped them off before coming here, but now she was glad she hadn't.

Scorpion not a match for us, Luna said, then she hesitated and added, *with sharp claws.*

Amelia sent her agreement as Luna sent her images of guns instead of claws. Again, she was taking not being able to shift exceptionally well.

Too busy to shift, Luna said, but Amelia got the sense that her version of busy had nothing to do with what was happening and everything to do with Mitchel.

'I'm going to go out and check if your father-in-law is okay,' Amelia said, keeping her voice low. 'If I can help him, I will.'

Tammy's relief made Amelia's heart skip a beat. The woman's tears started again, but a doctor called her name, and she stood to talk to him. That left Amelia alone with Mitchel.

Amelia pushed herself to her feet carefully to avoid sending a lightning flash of pain all the way to her hip as she changed position. She wasn't really successful, as she saw Mitchel watching her.

'Don't tell me to stay here while you go off into the farm and check the old man,' Mitchel said before she could speak. 'Not only can't you drive that far, but you also can't drive and shoot if things go wrong.'

Anger sparked through her. She wasn't some helpless pup who needed a protector. But he also wasn't wrong, which was frustrating, so she focused on him instead.

'You're not trained. You remember what happened last time we faced these things?'

'Yes. I remember you getting stung.' Mitchel let out a breath like he'd wanted to say more but held back. 'I've been working on my control. The ice block won't happen again.'

'Really? Is that why they've had to turn the heating up?' Amelia asked, raising her eyebrow.

He flushed, proving she'd been right to assume the temperature drop had been him. Though she didn't feel particularly cold. That might have been the residual venom, of course.

'Then we wait for the rest of the pack to return,' Mitchel said. 'You heard her description. The chance of a man his age still being alive and well isn't good.'

'The girl wasn't moving when you pulled her from the car,' Amelia said, pain in her leg growing stronger as she remembered the moments after they'd pulled the old woman free. She hadn't been as lucky as her daughter. 'We have to be sure.'

'Oliver wasn't going with the rest of the people this morning. We can call him, he will help?' Mitchel said.

'He can't go alone,' Amelia said.

'Then we can meet him,' Mitchel said, giving her a look that said even if Oliver turned up to collect her, Mitchel wouldn't let them go without him.

Part of her enjoyed the look of protectiveness, but most of her was annoyed. It wasn't his job to protect her. She had to wonder if he was like this with Clara. The traitorous thought crept in and wasn't helpful. The woman was a submissive wolf. Everyone would be protective of her, likely even Mitchel.

She shoved thoughts of Clara away because she had a bigger problem. There was no chance that Oliver would let her go into the farm with her injuries. But maybe she could take that choice out of his hands?

'Fine, I'll text him and tell him to meet us there,' Amelia said, stepping forward. 'You can drive, but you'll stay in the car.' Mitchel wisely kept his mouth shut.

She knew Hale would have words with her about going to the farm later. But she also knew he wouldn't have made a different choice. Her wolf echoed her. Making this decision two days in a row felt strange, like déjà vu. She just hoped this time went better.

She texted Oliver, then Hale, though she didn't expect the latter to answer for several hours. There would be less chance of the pack bonds bringing him to her this time. He'd closed it down almost to a sliver to block the pain.

As to Oliver, if she was already at the farm before he got there, then he couldn't send her away. Which was unprofessional, but she wouldn't let him go in alone.

MITCHEL TIGHTENED HIS GRIP on the steering wheel as he hit another sharp corner. He really missed power steering. Amelia was silent except for directions. He'd tried a few times to start a conversation. She was still angry with him, her face pale, eyes tight.

He couldn't help but wonder if she'd be as mad if Dylan was pushing to come instead of him. The bulky wolf looked like he could take care of himself, even if he sounded like an arrogant prick. It wasn't the only thing he wondered about regarding Dylan. God, he hated Clara and how she could make him doubt everything.

Most of the roads Amelia had directed him to use, even the single-tracked ones, had been ploughed and gritted. But he let his magic slip out anyway, just in case, checking the road, searching for any place that ice might try to spin the wheels and send the car out of control.

Amelia had unlocked the boot before they'd left and pulled out the same gun and holster she'd worn yesterday. She'd fingered the second rifle but had left it where it was.

There was no body armour today for either of them. They had left those at the hospital yesterday and were likely burned with the rest of their clothes or returned to someone to clean. Either way, they didn't have them.

Amelia directed him down a final turn to Max's farm. The snow-covered track was rutted and torn up by a car moving too fast. The couple were lucky they hadn't gone off the road. He saw the walls first; thick stone with snow drifted against it. That answered how the scorpions had got in, at least.

'Did Oliver reply?' Mitchel asked. It had taken them half an hour to get here, so they were looking at the man being alone with the scorpions for over an hour. Mitchel passed through the open gate slowly. The snow had been shovelled to leave a space big enough for cars to come in and turn.

'Nothing yet,' Amelia said, leaning forward to examine the area.

The farm comprised a series of stone buildings surrounded by a six-foot wall and barbed wire. The main house was a two-storey building that looked to be mostly original. The front yard had a few small paths that had been cleared in the two-foot snow to allow access between the buildings without having to wade through.

He turned the car in a full circle, pointing it back toward the exit, just in case, and then put the handbrake on. They were too far from the barn to see any sign of movement.

Amelia opened the door almost as soon as he stopped, letting in the crisp air. Manure and other farm scents he didn't have names for filled his nose.

Opening his door, he slid out onto the small section of clear concrete. His magic pushed out around him, letting him feel how cold it was, along with all the dips and divots in the snow and ice. None of the information was particularly helpful, of course. There was nothing about scorpions. But he'd not felt them with his magic yesterday, either.

'I told you to stay in the car if you wanted to come,' Amelia said, voice a low growl as she approached his side of the car.

'You're hurt. You can't go in there alone,' Mitchel said. He hadn't agreed precisely, but he hadn't argued with her over it either. But there was no way in hell he was letting her put herself at risk without any backup.

'Oliver will join me when he gets here,' Amelia said, lifting her chin, eyes scanning the yard.

'Then I'm happy to wait for him.'

She hesitated. He could see her thinking through her options. Oliver hadn't replied yet, hadn't even acknowledged that he'd got the text, and he would've if he'd seen it.

'I can't wait. If that man is alive, I need to help him now,' Amelia said.

'Then I'm coming,' Mitchel said, trying to sound confident as he argued with her. 'I can help. I helped last time.'

Amelia's lips thinned. 'We didn't know there were scorpions when you left the car then. We do this time. I can't let you go in there.'

'If it was Dylan here arguing with you, would you make him wait in the car?' Mitchel said, anger sharp as a blade. He clamped down his teeth to stop any more stupid words from coming out of his mouth.

Amelia growled. 'Dylan wouldn't be here to argue with me.'

'I saw how he looked at you yesterday, how you took him outside,' Mitchel said, words slipping free even though he wanted to say the opposite. Stupid brain. Stupid Clara. 'You're telling me that he wouldn't be here if he knew you were in danger?'

Amelia's face went blank, showing nothing of what she felt. He wanted her to deny it, tell him he was wrong. But he wasn't. Mitchel would never be good enough to compete with someone like Dylan.

'Maybe you're used to someone a little more obedient, but I'm not a weak omega to stand on the side-lines under the protection of anyone,' Amelia said, half the words a growl. 'I'm not Clara.'

Mitchel rocked back at Clara's name. Stupid that he hadn't considered Clara would have seen Amelia outside. Not after Clara's words to him. 'I want nothing to do with Clara,' Mitchel said.

'Really? Then why don't we discuss what happened between you and Clara at the hotel?' Amelia said, drawing in a breath.

Mitchel swallowed back bile at the memory of Clara touching him. 'Nothing happened between Clara and me.'

'Really? And that's why you had a shower after you saw her?' Amelia asked, voice a low hiss. 'Tell me, is it just you have a thing for wolves, or is it just convenience?'

Mitchel stepped away, feeling like she'd slapped him. She thought he wanted Clara? That he'd chosen her? Clara had done this. Even though she wasn't bloody there, she was shoving her filthy claws into his mind and making him doubt himself. Making Amelia think he wanted Clara.

'This is getting us nowhere,' Amelia said, turning away from him to limp towards the boot. 'Stay in the car.'

'I'm not letting you go in there alone,' Mitchel said, keeping his voice carefully neutral.

'You don't get to tell me how to do my job,' Amelia said as she opened the boot to pull out the rifle.

In the frustrated silence, Mitchel tried to think of some way to break their stalemate. Regardless of what had been said on either side, he still wouldn't let her get hurt again. He frowned, looking around. Silence? 'Didn't Tammy say there was a lot of noise?' he asked.

Amelia stilled, then turned around slowly, pulling in a breath. Nothing moved or made a noise. 'I can't smell anything past the manure and frost.'

'How many cattle did Tammy say she had?' Mitchel asked, pulling in the feel of the ice again.

'She didn't,' Amelia said, 'but I remember there being a lot of them here when I helped fix the gate.'

'How many cows do you think the scorpions would take down?'

'Not that many.' Amelia pulled in another breath. 'Get back in the car.'

Mitchel was set to argue with her again, but something in her tone made him step back towards the door. His senses showed him the snow behind him crumbling like something had taken a step. He couldn't see the source of what had caused it, just a dark spot like he'd seen in the car.

'Down!' Amelia shouted, bringing her gun up as Mitchel threw himself to the snow. Multiple gunshots ripped through his ears until all he could hear was ringing. He felt something fall to the ground into the snow. Again, it was a spot of darkness, invisible except for the impact. Until he turned to look.

The imp lay dead in the snow, face down, a mess of black blood on its back. It had grey skin, long arms, a short body, and hind legs that looked like they belonged to an animal.

Then there was an inhuman scream that he heard even through the ringing. Others echoed the wail of anger and pain that was pure animal.

Not just one imp, but multiple. All around them.

CHAPTER TWELVE

Oliver rolled his neck as he looked up from the handwritten patrol logs in front of him. The writing quality was mixed, but he was starting to get a feel for who was who based on the scrawl. Unfortunately, recognising it wasn't helping it go much faster.

He was in the small kitchen area on the ground floor. It had a table in the centre, basic worktops in laminated chipboard and a row of white cupboards. The essentials were here: a fridge, cooker, hob, and a pantry stocked with high-calorie items. He'd made good use of the food already this morning.

Not that the food was helping him focus. Clearly, working in the Rift Scar had been a good job option for him. He wasn't sure he'd have survived as a paper-pusher. After two hours of reading logs and searching for scraps of paper that no one seemed to want to keep ordered or in the same place, he was about ready to rip out his eyeballs.

Hale created the rota of who was on shift and a pool of areas that needed to be patrolled. But he left it up to those rangers on each shift to group up and pick their locations. Those who got in early got the best choice. It was a system that allowed flexibility while making sure everything was covered.

Bored, Thor said, showing him Sam's woods and them running, hunting. *Want to hunt.*

We can't leave yet. But a break sounds good, Oliver said, sighing, looking at the nearly finished stack of patrol sheets. They were all from before Shane's and Lacey's betrayal, but he'd not yet found any pattern in them. No one group favouring the area in question. But a lot could change in a month, and he needed to find the more recent records. He'd asked Sam if she'd seen them, but he'd not heard from her yet.

He stood, stretching. Going to check in with her was a good choice for a break. He wandered out into the main part of the building, brick dust tickling his nose from the ongoing construction. Sam's new area still had no door, and he could hear her and the science team leader, Madeline, talking quietly. It was the only sound in the building.

It felt empty without any of the other rangers here. Usually, a rapid response unit was hanging about, but Hale had needed the manpower. Not that there had been much use of the unit the last few months with the cell towers being down.

As he entered the room, the voices stopped. Sam had a pile of papers in her hands. He could see the familiar scrawled writing. She'd found the missing pages. But she also looked very annoyed.

'Everything okay?' he asked quietly, looking over her shoulder into the room, but Madeline had her back to him.

'Let's get something to eat,' she said, not looking back. She waited until they were back in the kitchen before she continued. 'Madeleine had taken them to use for her records. Even though they've nothing to do with her job. Or the science. Or anything she should be involved in at all.' The words were clipped, and she stopped and took a breath.

Oliver's stomach twisted. Another piece of the puzzle that didn't make sense. 'How did you find them?'

'They were just on the edge of the desk she was using,' Sam said, eyes narrowed. 'In plain sight.'

Oliver frowned. None of it made sense. Why take them, then leave them out? Shaking his head, he reached out for the files.

'Is everything okay?' Sam asked, echoing his earlier words back to him.

Oliver forced a smile. 'Of course, everything is fine. Why would you assume it's not?'

'Because you're here asking for records to see where people were over the last few weeks. Right after you and Amelia found a nest where a patrol should have passed. Would you like me to continue?'

'You have more?' Oliver asked, offering her a grin, but it didn't work to distract her.

Smart, Thor said. *Good mate to alpha.*

Oliver had to agree with his wolf, though that didn't help him figure out what to tell her.

Truth, Thor said, shaking out his coat and turning away like Oliver was being stupid.

'Hale has been on edge with all the strange Shifters in town,' Sam said. Which was an understatement. 'I know he thinks something is going on with the prime alphas, but he doesn't know what yet. I want to help. You can talk to me.'

Oliver's phone dinged in his pocket, giving him the perfect excuse to avoid the question. As much as he trusted her—which was a strange thing to admit considering she was so new to her relationship with Hale—Oliver wasn't sure that Hale wanted her to know.

He took out his phone, finding a message from Amelia. He swore as he read it. Then, he swore again when he saw the time it had been sent.

Sam's fear peppered the air at his reaction. 'What happened?'

'There was another scorpion attack,' Oliver said, typing back to Amelia to tell her to wait for him, that he was on his way. But he already knew she'd ignore it if it meant she might be able to save someone. He'd have done the same thing—most of the pack would have—but that didn't make it right.

'Hale?' Sam asked, paling.

'No,' Oliver said, reaching out to take Sam's hand as his wolf echoed her fear. 'He's fine. I'd know if he wasn't. It's a civilian.'

'Another crash?'

Oliver stood, shaking his head. He hesitated a moment before telling her, but this was no longer about something inside the Rift Scar. If Amelia's message was correct, then scorpions were outside the border. 'No, these were found outside the Rift,' he said gently.

He'd expected her reaction to be more fear. But her scent shifted to anger so strong it filled the small room, stinging his nose. If he'd had any doubts Hale had picked a good mate, this would have eased them.

'Amelia and Mitchel are going out to investigate, but she's not waiting. I have to go help her,' Oliver added, trying to remember how far away the farm she'd mentioned was.

'I'm coming with you,' Sam said, moving closer.

'There's no way in hell I'm taking you anywhere near a scorpion attack,' Oliver said, wolf rising with him. Hale would kill Oliver if he let anything happen to Sam. 'One mistake, and you're dead. That's not a risk I'm willing to take.'

'That's not your decision to make,' Sam said, chin lifted, not out of defiance but because she was too close and short to do anything else. 'If Amelia is hurt, I can help her. You can't do everything by yourself.'

Oliver growled, suspecting this was precisely the argument that Mitchel had used to end up with Amelia. 'No.'

'Take me to them, now,' Sam said, pressure rising around Oliver. The sensation was so much like a command from Hale that Oliver moved to comply before he realised Hale wasn't there.

Oliver stopped and turned back to Sam, who had paled. Humans couldn't become pack. They couldn't funnel Hale's pack magic. Hell, he didn't even think a wolf's mate could either.

Everything that had happened over the past month replayed in his head. The pack lands. Hale finding his mate. The changes in the pack. He'd never once considered Sam had anything to do with it. Clearly, he should have.

'What are you?' Oliver asked, his wolf echoing the question so strongly that it felt like they spoke together.

'I'll explain later,' Sam said. 'But first, let's help Amelia.'

That wasn't a suggestion; it was an order. Though it didn't have Hale's magic behind it, the previous echo lingered, and his wolf pulled at him to obey. 'What happens if you get stung?' Oliver asked.

'It will hurt like hell,' Sam said, giving him the answer he needed.

Sam wasn't human.

Taking a slow breath, Oliver led them out of the room, letting Sam grab her jacket and tell Madeline they were doing a quick errand. All nice and calm, like on the inside he wasn't screaming that his pack was in danger. Or that Hale was going to kill him if something happened to Sam.

AMELIA SHOT AT A second Rift imp, who appeared behind Mitchel, taking it straight through the head. The beast collapsed like a puppet whose cords had been cut.

It was a dark grey, with a short muzzle and arms long enough they scraped the ground. Its clan screamed from around her, making her flinch. But the imps backed up again, watching them cautiously.

Fear twisted her gut even though she knew it would only excite the beasts more. She should have left Mitchel at the hospital. He wasn't equipped for this. Hell, as she looked around, losing count of the imps, she realised she wasn't equipped for this either.

Fight, Luna said. This time, she did push against the barrier that stopped them from shifting. It was nearly gone, and they could almost feel their other form. Almost, but not quite.

There's not enough time to shift, Amelia said, though her wolf had already stopped pushing. *We rely on the weapons we have.*

She didn't add that she only had one load of ammunition or that her gun wasn't useful when they got close. With their razor-sharp claws and fangs, this many could take them down before she could kill them all with the gun. She just hoped it took them too long to figure it out.

The pack bonds flared in her mind with her fear. But this time, Hale was really far away. She could only just feel him, meaning it could be an hour or two before he responded.

They didn't have that kind of time.

The screaming stopped, and one imp took a step forward, braver than the others. It was too close; they'd not be able to get to the car without it attacking them. She glanced at the extra ammo, so close but not close enough.

Mitchel struggled to regain his feet, eyes wide, looking around as he backed up beside her. 'Tell me I'm hallucinating,' Mitchel said, voice holding a quiver. The car windows started to frost over, ice spreading quickly.

'No such luck,' Amelia said, repositioning her gun. The imps had mostly surrounded them, blocking the exit and the path to the car's front doors. They made a faint clicking noise as they talked to each other.

'They're blocking the exit and the car deliberately, right?' Mitchel said, seeing the same thing. 'Stopping us from leaving?'

She nodded, backing up a step and spreading her weight evenly despite the pain. Mitchel moved with her without needing to be asked. The imps had left space behind them, trying to herd them deeper into the yard where they'd have no defendable shelter. Unless they could get to the house?

She risked a glance behind her. It was still a good few metres away but was stone, with shutters over the window. It must have been built in the years after the war, designed to protect them from attacks that had been much more common back then. She just had to hope that Tammy's family had kept the maintenance up.

The imps took the moment of distraction as a chance to advance. Amelia caught the movement from the corner of her eye and brought the gun round. Two imps were close, running awkwardly over the snow, claws raised. She was never going to be able to get both of them. Let alone the others who would come behind after they got close.

Her gun barked, catching the first imp in the shoulder and slowing it. Then Mitchel's magic rose beside her, ice springing out almost like a spear in front of him. It caught the two leaping imps, freezing them in place, along with part of the car.

The imps who were following slowed, heads tilting towards their dead friends. Amelia shot a short, wide burst, chipping the ice and catching two more imps in non-lethal wounds. The imps screamed and darted back out of reach.

Cowards, Luna said, tense and ready in her mind.

The stink of fear filled the air, hers and Mitchel's. It would draw the imps back quickly, as would the need to avenge their dead clan mates. She needed to find somewhere defendable while they had the chance.

She backed up another step towards the house, being careful of her leg, trying not to let them see any sign of weakness. They'd lost four of their clan now. What had probably started as a game for them quickly shifted into something more serious.

Mitchel didn't copy her step this time as white mist rose from the ground. It was light, barely there, but if it got worse, she'd not be able to see the imp's attack.

'Mitchel,' Amelia said, but he didn't react. Didn't seem to hear her as he stared at the imps. They had pulled back to the outbuildings' edge, still stopping them from leaving, but out of range of whatever Mitchel was doing.

She shifted her grip on the gun, remembering the searing cold from yesterday. The feel of it in her bones as she slowed down. There was none of that today. But why? Unfortunately, now wasn't the time to get answers.

'Mitchel,' Amelia said again, firmer this time. He shuddered, looking around, fear growing sharper, but the mist stopped growing. 'How you doing?'

'I'm okay,' Mitchel said, but she could hear the tightness of his voice. She wanted to tell him it would be fine, but she couldn't bring herself to lie.

'We need to get to the house,' Amelia said, taking a single shot at an imp as it moved. It was going sideways too fast for her to do more than clip its shoulder. These imps had learned from their first dead clan mates not to come directly towards the guns. Great.

Mitchel nodded, moving to stand behind her, guiding her steps back so she could watch and shoot at the imps while he made sure she never slipped. It was like the ground moved around her to ensure the footing.

She tried to remember how many shots she'd fired already. How many did she have left? If Oliver had been here, he'd have known. Stupid to let fear get the better of her. She wasn't sure she'd have time to reload, even if she had more ammo.

The imps tried to creep forward on the other side, so she let off another shot towards them, sending them scuttling back a few paces. She wasn't out of bullets yet, but it wouldn't be long. She still had her Glock 17 in its holster, but that was only seventeen bullets. It wasn't going to be enough.

The imps screamed, sound coming from all around, except behind. They'd realised what Amelia had been trying to do. But they were too late; the house was too close.

She just hoped it was open. If it wasn't ...

There was no point in lingering on that question. Not when it was their only chance. She heard Mitchel try the handle behind her. The old metal creaked.

An imp pushed forward, trying their luck. Amelia shot at it. She caught it in the chest. It fell to the ground, black blood spraying out as it fell hard into the snow, screaming in agony. The imps joined its cries.

She tried another shot, aiming at one of the creatures that took a step towards her. The gun clicked empty. The imp flinched, expecting the hit. Which showed a level of intelligence that experts argued about constantly.

It lifted its head, eyes focused on her. It knew she was out, knew this was its chance. It snarled and lunged forward.

Mitchel wrapped his arm around her waist and pulled her backwards through the doorway, slamming the door closed and slipping the bolt across.

The beast slammed into the wood, hard, screaming. Frost crawled over the wood as she watched. Becoming ice.

Amelia turned in Mitchel's arms, forcing him back a step, causing his focus to shift to her. Sweat had broken out over his face. If he overdid the magic, then he was going to be defenceless. She needed to help him get it under control.

'We're safe,' Amelia said, though she wanted to check the rest of the house before she really believed it. 'Let it go.'

Mitchel didn't react immediately, so Amelia reached up to place her hand on his neck. She shivered as she felt the tug she'd ignored all day grow sharper. His fear flooded her like it was more than just a scent. It was like she could feel it. Feel him.

There was more than just the fear there. Desire. Anger. Frustration. Emotions that came too fast for her to decipher.

She let go, pulling back with a shudder. Mitchel focused on her, eyes wide.

'What was that?' he asked, voice so low it was nearly a whisper.

Mate, Luna said, pleased with herself that she had been right all along.

Amelia wanted to argue with her wolf. But it was getting harder every time she could feel Mitchel.

How could they be mates when Mitchel and Clara clearly still had something between them?

Ours, Luna snarled, voice even louder than it had been before. This time, Amelia ignored it. She didn't have time to deal with this now.

'I don't know,' Amelia said, hating that she was lying. But how did she explain this to Mitchel? She didn't even know if this was what she wanted. 'Let's check the rest of the house. Make sure it's locked up tight.'

Mitchel frowned, but the imps chose that moment to let out a cackle as they moved around the house. No matter what Amelia and Mitchel had between them, this really wasn't the time to deal with it.

Even if every part of her wanted to fall back into Mitchel's arms and touch him again. Instead, she turned away, putting the now useless rifle down near the door and pulling her handgun. The Glock 17 only made her feel a little better. She really wished she'd taken the time to pick up more ammo.

MITCHEL SHIVERED AS HE walked through the old house. Its old-fashioned set-up wouldn't have been out of place in a horror movie. Eighties wallpaper, wood panelling, and a tired-looking red carpet that seemed to have been used everywhere.

The imps circle the house, their claws scraping over the stone brick. Their high-pitched cackle made his stomach twist as they talked to each other. Or maybe they were just trying to make him more afraid. Not that they needed help with that. He wasn't sure he'd ever been this terrified in his life.

Imps. The scavengers of the Rift Scar. What the hell were they doing here?

He wanted to reach out and touch Amelia again. To bring that connection back. He'd felt Amelia. Felt her fear and pain. So much pain that she was hiding. Then, something underneath it all, another current of emotions. Her wolf.

The more he thought back, the more he realised he'd felt it that morning. When they'd been curled up together in bed, relaxed and content, he'd felt something more. An echo of his emotions. Then again in the hospital. Except they hadn't been an echo. It had been Amelia.

Going by the surprise and recognition as she'd let him go, she had felt it too, and she'd known what it was. But she was also right when she'd said they needed to ensure the house was safe. So, he let her keep her lie, at least for now. Later, he'd be having words.

Another cackle came from further around the house. The imps were moving faster than he and Amelia could, looking for a way in.

So far, all the windows were closed off with their wooden panels, and the back door was solid and locked. They moved through the house together in silence, even though splitting up probably would have been faster.

'Do you have any more ammo?' Mitchel asked as they returned to the front of the house. He'd heard her gun fail to make the last shot as he'd got the front door open. He had no idea how many shots were in the handgun, but he wasn't optimistic it would be enough to defeat all the imps. There had to be at least a dozen still out there.

Amelia shook her head. She held her handgun pointed at the floor. 'I should have grabbed more.'

If they hadn't been fighting, she would've been able to. Neither of them said it, but if he was thinking it, he was sure she was too. Then he'd frozen the car, removing any chance they'd have been able to get any.

He'd not meant to use his magic at all, he'd just reacted without any intention behind it. It had hurt, draining him with each use until his head throbbed, and he felt sick. Only Amelia's voice had broken the magic flow before he'd hurt himself. If he hadn't spent years trying to hide what he was and protect his mum, maybe now he'd be able to really help.

'We need to find a way to deal with the imps,' Amelia said, eyes following the sounds from the imps as they circled. 'If they get bored, they could head towards town.'

Easier said than done. They needed help.

'What about the pack or Oliver?' Mitchel asked, then his stomach dropped as he grabbed for his phone. No signal. 'He's coming here. He won't know.'

'He will be careful,' Amelia said, but she'd paled along with him. 'We train for this. He will see the car, see the bodies.'

'If he got your message,' Mitchel said, hoping his friend had not.

'Either way, we can't wait for him. He might not see the message for hours, depending on where he is,' Amelia said, turning back to Mitchel. 'I should have made you stay at the hospital.'

'Then you would have been here alone. Somehow I don't think that's any better,' Mitchel said.

The imps cackled again, sounding loud as they moved higher rather than around.

'Were there covers on the upstairs windows?' Amelia asked, freezing as she looked up.

Mitchel tried to remember. He was pretty sure he'd seen glass and said as much.

Amelia cursed, grabbed his sleeve, and dragged him back towards the front of the house. But there was nowhere to go, even if the door wasn't covered in ice. They were trapped.

'Do they have some kind of bolthole or panic rooms built into these houses?' Mitchel asked.

There was snuffling beyond the ice, then a high-pitched cackle. There was far too much intelligence in what the imps were doing for Mitchel's liking. It felt like they were being herded.

Amelia shook her head slowly. 'If they do, we don't have time to find it.'

There wasn't a good place in the house to defend. Glass smashed above. There was a thump and another. Then, more noise, claws against wood.

His chest grew tight as he saw the first imp at the top of the stairs. 'There here,' he said quietly.

He felt his magic spill out. But they were no longer outside in the freezing cold with ice around him. There was nothing for the magic to gather. Not yet, at least not until the house was a lot colder than it was now. His magic was working on it. He could feel the strain. But it was too slow, the heating working to counter him.

Amelia aimed the handgun. Its range would be less than the rifle and slower. He wished he had a weapon, some way to fight. Hell, at this point, he'd have jumped for the knife Amelia had handed him yesterday.

Three imps crouched at the top of the stairs, but he could hear more claws scraping on the floor above him.

'Stay close,' Amelia said, taking her first shot; the sound was so loud his ears rang, a different kind of pain than that rifle had caused.

The bullet hit true, blowing through one imp's skull, sending it backwards, making the rest scatter, moving so it wouldn't be easy for her to hit them all.

Mitchel put his hand on Amelia's back, letting her know he was there, wishing he could touch skin and bring up the connection again. But that was for his comfort, not something that was likely to help her fight.

Another imp tried to move forward. Amelia only let it take a single step as she took a shot. The imps screamed, blood spreading over its chest as it went down.

A third imp moved forward before its friend fell, and Amelia changed her aim. The shot went through its belly as it jumped over the bannister. It hit the ground hard, writhing on the floor, screaming. Amelia put another shot through its head, stilling its movements.

More imps appeared at the top of the stairs until there were six. The room still wasn't cold enough for him to be of any help.

'Be ready,' Amelia said.

Mitchel swallowed hard. There were things he wanted to say. Or do. But faced with the imminent prospect of death, he found no words, only the need to protect Amelia. Considering she was better placed to do the protecting, he doubted the instinct would be of any use.

Another imp appeared at the top of the stairs. How many of the bloody things were there? It was bigger than the others, with dark streaks covering its slick skin. It swayed, tilting its head, black saliva dripping from its muzzle as it looked down at its fallen clan.

One of the others jumped onto the bannister. Amelia shot it, knocking it back. How many more bullets did she have? It wasn't going to be enough. Ice was starting to form on the walls behind him, slowly. Too slowly.

'I'm sorry,' Amelia said, not looking away from the imps as they waited for the surge.

Mitchel moved his hand from her back to her neck, touching her skin. 'This isn't your fault,' he said, exhaling sharply as he felt her guilt and fear. He didn't know how the connection worked, but he tried to let her see he meant his words. Let her see their truth.

She inhaled sharply, eyes flaring to blue.

'Next time, let's both stay behind,' he said lightly, though they knew there was no next time.

Two imps jumped onto the bannister, making clicking sounds. Amelia couldn't shoot both before they dropped. A third joined them while the larger imp crouched at the top of the stairs, watching them. Waiting for them to make a mistake.

Mitchel flinched at the sound of rapid-fire coming from outside. An imp screamed and thumped against the door, then went silent. A second shot followed, then a third. More imps screamed.

Amelia looked at Mitchel, and he let his hand drop as his fear rose. It had to be Oliver, but that meant he was out there alone.

The larger imp froze, rocking back on its clawed feet as it stared at the door. Its clan was getting smaller. Mitchel could see the debate as it curled its muzzle, showing yellow teeth as it snarled at them. Amelia and Mitchel were no longer just two easy targets.

'Amelia?' Oliver shouted, voice rising above the ringing in Mitchel's ears. 'Mitchel?'

The larger imp hesitated. For a moment, Mitchel was sure that it would run. But it snarled and leapt forward, moving faster than the others. Amelia shot. Missed. It dodged to the left, using the wall for momentum as it flowed towards them.

She re-aimed. Shot.

Black blood hit Mitchel as the imp crashed into them, sending them backwards into a heap. Claws scraped his side, sending searing pain through him. He kicked at the creature, trying to get free without hurting Amelia, who was sandwiched between them.

Amelia twisted, shoving the creature away from them. Those claws took another slice of skin off his side, and then it was gone, sliding down the hall. Amelia pulled her gun back up and shot it twice more. It stilled.

The entire clan screamed. It was so loud that Mitchel was deafened. The imps from the stairs pulled back, leaving the dead bodies as they bolted.

'Amelia!' Oliver shouted again, closer this time, though the sound was almost lost in the residual screaming from the imps.

'We're here!' Amelia answered, still not taking her eyes off the dead imp at her feet, like she didn't trust it. Then she added to Mitchel, 'Are you okay?'

Mitchel sucked in a breath, touching his side. It was tender but not bleeding badly. 'Just a scratch,' he said, checking Amelia. She looked pale, but he couldn't see any blood.

There was a light thump against the ice behind them. 'Are you okay?' Oliver asked.

Amelia looked at Mitchel, checking him like she wanted to be sure before she answered. 'A little scratched up and bruised, but we're fine.'

Mitchel swallowed a lump in his throat as relief threatened to overwhelm him. He placed his hand on Amelia's neck, pulling her close. She put her hand on his, leaning in, letting him feel her relief.

'Mitchel, did you have to freeze the door closed?' Oliver asked, voice light.

Mitchel laughed. He couldn't help it. It was that or cry.

CHAPTER THIRTEEN

IN THE END, AMELIA had to go around to the back door and let Oliver in since the front would take hours to melt.

Sam's face appeared first, and Amelia's stomach sank even though she welcomed the hug from the woman. 'What the hell are you doing here?' Amelia said as she wrapped her arms around Sam's much shorter frame.

'I couldn't leave you alone when you might be hurt,' Sam said. 'I should have come to see you yesterday. I told Hale—'

Amelia tightened her grip, then pulled back so she could see Sam's face. 'I'm fine. I promise.' Sam didn't look like she believed Amelia, but she stopped talking.

Amelia let Sam go and stepped back into the kitchen so they could let Oliver enter. His forehead was creased in a frown as he looked at Sam. She had no idea how Sam had convinced Oliver to bring her here, but she suspected it was at the cost of her secret.

'We should leave,' Oliver said, eyes scanning her, then Mitchel. 'Before those things come back.'

'What if they head towards town?' Mitchel said, hand moving to rest on her lower back again. His heat filled her, warming her. He'd done the same thing during the fight, a single touch to steady her.

Mate. Keep, Luna said, between images of hunting down the imps and ripping them apart for daring to attack them.

Thankfully, the insistence was weak. They both knew her leg wasn't in good enough shape to hunt and track, even if she could shift.

'Hale will bring the rangers out here as soon as he gets my message,' Oliver said, eyes scanning the snow. It was clean out here at the back of the house. 'They can trace all the scents and ensure none went towards the other farms.'

'And the farmer?' Mitchel asked, uncertain as he looked behind him into the house like he could see through it to the sheds outside.

Amelia exchanged a look with Oliver. She had come here for a reason, though with the silence in the barn and the number of imps that had been out here, she had even less hope than before.

'Tammy hadn't been sure if he was still alive,' Amelia said quietly. Oliver gave her a look that said he knew what she did. Their chances were slim, but they couldn't leave without checking.

He sighed, looking at Mitchel and Sam. 'The two of you will wait in the car,' Oliver said. There was no question. It was a statement of fact. Sam didn't try to argue, though she could feel Mitchel stir behind her. Oliver added, 'Or we can all leave now.' Mitchel went still.

They went outside and piled Mitchel and Sam safely in Oliver's car, ready to drive away if they had to. Oliver then provided her with fresh ammo for her rifle.

Since her car was frozen, they couldn't get to Oliver's normal rifle, but he'd brought a spare from the armoury. He hadn't been pleased with that, nor Amelia walking on her injured leg, nor the fact she had no armour. But he kept his grumblings to a low-level muttering.

They avoided the dead bodies of the imps as they headed towards the barn, black blood melting into the snow. She didn't expect any of the clan to have lingered. Once they broke, they ran, and it would take time for them to regroup. Imps were cowards at heart. But she kept her gun up just in case.

'You managed to kill quite a lot,' Oliver said, tone pleasing.

'Snow made them slow and cautious,' Amelia said because she had no illusions that she could kill that many otherwise. The imps had thought they were getting an easy meal and had wanted to play with them.

As they got closer to the barn, they slowed. The doors were partially closed, and the inside was dim. They couldn't see much more from here than a series of bloody imp footprints.

She might have seen it sooner if she hadn't been arguing with Mitchel when they'd arrived.

She shivered as she got further from the car; the air changed from mild to freezing within a few steps. She'd not realised how much she'd got used to whatever Mitchel was doing.

'Maybe we should've had Mitchel come with,' Oliver said, rolling his shoulders. 'Then it wouldn't feel like my balls are about to shrivel up inside me.'

Amelia snorted despite the flash of fear at the idea of bringing Mitchel. She knew Oliver wasn't serious. 'You're getting soft.'

'Just because you're happy with driving that old Land Rover without any heating in it doesn't mean the rest of us are savages.' Oliver paused, glancing back over his shoulder. 'Though, I don't think any amount of heating now will save it.'

'I was going to have to get rid of it anyway,' Amelia said, wincing as she slid on a patch of ice, sending a wave of pain through her leg. Oliver caught her and helped her regain her balance. 'Thanks. There was no way I was ever getting the scent of death out of it.'

'Speaking of death,' Oliver said, face screwing up as he lifted a hand to his nose.

The wind was blowing in the other direction, so she'd not caught the strength of it before now. The combination was beyond anything she had scented before. Shit, vomit, rot, and Rift imps all mixed together. She couldn't even pick up the scent of the scorpions, even though the first thing she saw was a scorpion tail on the ground, the rest of its body missing.

Her stomach churned and threatened to revolt, which made her take another breath.

'Shallow breaths through the mouth,' Oliver said, looking paler than he had.

Amelia did as Oliver suggested. It helped a little. Oliver paused. He looked up, as well as left and right, as they reached the doorway. There was no sound in the barn beyond them, but that didn't mean there wasn't a straggler or scorpion inside. They kept their weapons ready, just in case.

They found what was left of Tammy's father-in-law first. They wouldn't be bringing his body back.

She moved further into the barn, finding some dead cattle, gore and blood sprayed everywhere. There were clusters of bodies that were partly eaten. She tried not to look too long at the pieces. The imps had killed everything, even though there was no way they'd have the time to eat it.

'Have you ever seen a clan this big?' Amelia asked.

'No,' Oliver said. 'At least not this near the edge. Deep in the London Rift Scar, they gathered in bigger groups to deal with larger predators that kept to the centre. But there isn't anything like that in the Highland Rift Scar. It's too small.'

'To have scorpions, and then Rift imps come out, something must be wrong,' Amelia said, shivering. 'Something we aren't seeing. A couple of missed patrols wouldn't have caused this amount of change. Not when it's this cold.'

Oliver's expression was grim. 'I don't know, but the IRS&D woman tried to take the patrol logs.'

Amelia exhaled sharply. 'First Lacey and Shane last month, now this? I don't like it.'

'Except this time, they aren't just setting up a couple of traps and hoping something hurts Hale,' Oliver said, shaking his head. 'This is putting all of us in danger. If people no longer think we can protect them, how long before they decide we belong in the Rift Scar too?'

'Or, more simply, if they can prove Hale can't do his job, they can force him out,' Amelia said, then cut herself off before she could say more. That wasn't her secret to share. She turned away from the broken corpses of the cows, deciding that anything lurking in the ruined bodies would have attacked by now. She couldn't hear or smell anything over the other scents.

'Why now, after letting him work for the last seven years?' Oliver said, moving over the gore to the far side of the barn, pushing open the door that was there. It opened onto a small walled-in section of grass and a large metal gate that allowed the farmer to let the cows into the field. The air blew in, clearing some of the stench, but not much. 'It's not the pack lands. Shane and Lacey were before that.'

She moved out towards the door, checking the area and searching for signs of more scorpions. But mostly, she was biting down on her tongue to stop from answering. Something must have given her away because Oliver focused on her.

'Amelia?' Oliver asked quietly. 'Is it to do with Sam? How she feels like pack?'

Her stomach twisted as she looked away. She'd made a promise. One she had to keep, even if he suspected the truth. Or at least part of it.

'Or is it because he was trying to get more time for the pack to shift in the first place?' Oliver asked, making Amelia spin back to him. He gave another grimace. 'I'm the son of a prime alpha, remember? There are things I know that I probably shouldn't.'

Oliver moved back a step into the room. 'Hale upset the apple cart, and the prime alphas are in a pissing contest with him.' Oliver's tone was harsh, but Amelia wasn't sure it was directed at Hale.

'Right now, we need to focus on what we can do,' Amelia said, looking around, eyes skirting over Tammy's father-in-law. She wished she could remember his name. 'Which isn't much here.'

Oliver gave her a long look that said this conversation wasn't over, but he didn't push. 'I really wish they'd fix the signal tower. We really need more manpower to make sure the creatures aren't going towards town.'

'With the weather this cold, they'll be looking for somewhere warm,' Amelia said, patting Oliver on the back as she passed him, leg pain spiking with each step. 'There isn't any other farm close to here.'

'Well, maybe instead of risking your life, you can finally curl back up in a soft bed with Mitchel,' Oliver said, a slight grin on his face.

Like idea, Luna said.

But Amelia wasn't so convinced. She turned away so Oliver wouldn't see her face as she remembered Clara's words. Mitchel wasn't hers.

'What happened?' Oliver asked, grabbing her arm to stop her as she started to step away from him.

'This isn't the place,' Amelia said, which was the truth. But this hadn't been the place for any of the conversations so far.

'Like hell, you guys were good this morning. What happened?' Oliver said, looking past her out the barn door, though they couldn't see the car from this angle. 'Was it Dylan again?'

'No. I've not seen him all day.'

'What else would—' Oliver cut off. 'Clara? What did she do?'

Amelia shook her arm out of his grip, taking a step away. There was nowhere to look that wasn't covered in some kind of gore, so she turned back to Oliver. That he knew who Clara was didn't surprise her. Not when she and Mitchel had clearly been a thing. 'Clara said they were together.'

Oliver barked a laugh, though it had a bitter tone to it. 'Trust me. That's something you never have to worry about.'

'Then why did he have a shower after he saw her?' Amelia said, hating how petulant she sounded. 'Yet she had his scent on her when she came out?'

Oliver's anger burst up around her, not in scent but in the energy of his wolf. The strength of it made Amelia freeze. Her wolf stared. They'd felt some of his power before. But this was different. Purer. Like he wasn't holding back. It was gone almost as soon as it had come, and Oliver's energy settled back into his normal calm flow.

'Mitchel wouldn't touch Clara,' Oliver said, voice low as he struggled to keep his tone even. 'Not after everything that happened.'

Listen, Luna said, filling her mind and stopping her from interrupting. *Important. Would not be angry over small thing.*

Amelia wasn't as convinced as her wolf. There were a lot of reasons to be angry. But she kept quiet.

'I was the one who told him what Clara was doing, how she was sleeping with everyone and anyone she could. He believed me. Though being fair, I suspect he might have known underneath it all that something was wrong.' Oliver paused, pulling in a breath, face screwing up as he got a nose full of sour rot. 'Maybe if I'd left it alone, she'd have got bored and moved on. But I had to stick my damned nose in.'

'I doubt any of this is your fault,' Amelia said when Oliver went silent.

'She tried to stop him from leaving by using her wolf against him like she does us. But it didn't work. So instead, she tried to use her strength and the full moon against him.'

Amelia felt sick as she stared at Oliver. She thought back to what Dylan had done to her. How he had tried to use the desperate need of the Full Moon Fever against her. 'You're telling me that Clara tried to assault Mitchel?'

Ours, Luna snarled, followed by a series of images of them hunting Clara that Amelia didn't bother to translate. The pull to go back to Mitchel burned through her.

'What happened?' Amelia asked.

'He was staying with me at the time, in my spare room. I'd taken a friend home for the night, and I didn't hear Clara come in for a start,' Oliver said, jaw tightening. 'I came out to find her pinning him to the wall. She was trying to kiss him, even though he was clearly trying to get away from her. It was one of the few times my wolf has ever managed to override the submissive omega bullshit she pulls.'

Oliver's eyes flashed to amber, showing his wolf. She could imagine how hard that would have been.

'Only wolves feel the need of the Full Moon Fever,' Oliver said, jaw muscle twitching. 'She's so used to getting her way that she forgot he wasn't a wolf. That everything he had felt for her had been real and a choice. Not because of what she was or how she used her wolf.'

'What happened when you reported her?' Amelia asked. Dylan had escaped because of who his father was. Few others had the same privilege, female or male.

Oliver looked away, and Amelia felt sick. Clara hadn't been stopped. That was the problem.

'Even if you reported her, her omega wolf would mean the alpha wouldn't be able to deal with her, right?' Amelia said.

Oliver nodded. 'Mitchel avoided her. Changed his job and apartment. It worked until now.'

Again, Amelia had done the same. She'd left Dylan behind, and he'd followed her.

Oliver stiffened, attention shifting away from her as he pulled in a deep breath. She shivered at the intensity of his look and tried to copy him. But she got nothing she hadn't expected and had to exhale slowly as her stomach threatened to overflow.

But Oliver had clearly scented something she hadn't because the growl that rolled out of him was feral, and he'd paled.

'Wyvern.'

MITCHEL GAVE SAM A sideways glance as she leaned forward to clear the mist off the window. It was the third time she'd done it in the past ten minutes as the car's heaters struggled to balance the temperature.

Conversation had died off after the first minute, and they'd been sitting in an awkward silence ever since. He wasn't sure if it was both their impatience to have the others back or the intensity coming from Sam that was causing the problem.

'So,' Sam said unexpectedly, turning to Mitchel. 'You and Amelia?'

Mitchel flushed, feeling uncomfortable for a whole other reason. 'There isn't any me and Amelia. Not when she has Dylan waiting for her.'

Admitting that out loud hurt something deep in his soul. No matter how good it felt to hold her or how he felt the tug pulling him in her direction, Amelia wasn't his.

'Trust me, she wants nothing to do with Dylan,' Sam said, pulling out her phone to check it. 'Dammit, still no signal.'

'You can't know that Amelia doesn't want him,' Mitchel said. This wasn't the side of the argument he wanted to be on. He hated the way it made him feel. The jealousy. The feeling that he wasn't enough. 'He's the alpha's son back where she lives. When her time here is finished, she will go back there. Go back to him.'

'She won't,' Sam said, putting her phone away again. 'She's never going back there.'

Mitchel stared at Sam. There had been absolute certainty in her voice. 'Why wouldn't she go home?'

Sam shook her head, leaning forward to clear another patch of the window before she pulled back and turned to him again. She gave him a once-over that made him feel like he was missing something. He was starting to wish they could go back to the silence again.

'Look, I don't know you. If Amelia wants to tell you about how her ex is an arsehole who can't respect boundaries, that's her choice. But don't assume because you have been here for five minutes that you know what she wants more than she does,' Sam said. 'Amelia is her own person and will make her own choices.'

Mitchel turned away as he replayed her words, his anger rising. The idea that Dylan wasn't respecting boundaries hit close to home after everything with Clara. The scratch marks along his sex still stung as he moved, and he still felt sick at the idea of Clara touching him.

He wanted to be outside the car. To bury his feet in the snow. At least then he'd feel grounded. Maybe he'd even be useful somehow, even if his power had been erratic.

They could see the spear of ice that covered Amelia's car from where they were. Maybe useful was stretching it a bit. Every time he used his power, he seemed to make things worse.

Without warning, the sickly scent of decay, rotting meat and sewage from the Rift Scar surrounded them so completely that it was difficult for Mitchel to breathe.

Sam coughed, blinking rapidly. 'Did the wind change direction? If the barn smells that bad to us, I don't know how they are coping.'

Mitchel took a shallow breath through his mouth. 'It hadn't been that bad outside,' he said, looking around. There was a flash of grey, just at the corner of his vision, like a large shadow. Mitchel moved to open the door, but before he could, something hit the car hard.

The impact threw him back against his window, head hitting hard enough to make his ears ring.

The world spun.

He couldn't tell what was moving. Him or the car. He struggled to grab something, to stabilise himself. To check if Sam was okay. But he could barely catch his breath, let alone stop the movement.

Distantly, he thought he heard something roar as the car rolled one last time and grew still. At least, he thought he was. He could feel the curve of the roof under him instead of the seats.

He struggled to take slow breaths as his body checked in. His ears were ringing. It hurt to pull in a breath. Hell, it hurt to everything.

The roar came again. It was impossible to mistake this time for anything else as the deep rumble made his bones rattle. There is no way that came from an imp. Only a few things that could live in the Rift Scar were big enough to make that sound. But the Highland one was too small for all of them.

Except clearly, it wasn't.

Sam groaned next to him. He turned to find her in a crumpled heap, blood on her face. Mitchel started to call out to her but stopped as he remembered the roar. Without knowing what it had been, he didn't know if their voices had been what had attracted it. But whatever it was, he could hear snuffling sounds and snow crunching under something heavy.

He needed to get out of the car before whatever had hit them decided to take another swipe. He tried to sit up and get a better look at his options. The glass tinkled to the car roof as he moved.

The sounds outside stopped, and Mitchel could almost feel its eyes on him. Sam let out a slow breath, eyes open now. She'd heard the change, too.

They needed to get out of the car now. He looked at his side window. It was pressed into a snowbank, blocking him from getting out there. The front of the car was at an angle into the snow, also blocked.

The driver's side window was a gaping hole, a flash of blue sky visible. That was their way out. He tried to move closer to Sam, but even that slight movement made black spots dance across his vision, nausea on its heels.

Stilling himself, he took a slow breath. The stink of the Rift Scar and spilt fuel was so strong it was like he was back at the car wreck saving the girl. But this wasn't a scorpion that could be stabbed. Or a nest that could be frozen.

He felt the vibration through the car roof as something big took a step. Before he could think better of it, he tried to reach out with his magic to see what was out there, but it just made his head spin faster. He let go before he threw up, body shaking.

He knelt there, tense, expecting the car to be hit again. Every moment that didn't happen, fresh sweat beaded down his spine. He couldn't wait for the beast to come to him. He had to do something.

Mitchel started towards Sam again. She tried to sit up, moving her leg with a hiss. He couldn't see any blood or obvious damage, so he hoped she could walk on it once they got outside.

He motioned to the window behind her; she looked at it and nodded. They tried to move quietly, but it was impossible with glass fragments everywhere.

Another footstep came, but this time, something knocked the car, making it rock back and forth. Mitchel bit back a moan as he tried not to imagine what could be that big.

A burst of gunfire battered his still-ringing ears. Another roar followed it, drowning out everything else.

Mitchel's heart pounded as he imagined Amelia and Oliver facing the creature alone. Whatever it was, it sounded big enough that a gun might only piss it off.

He needed to make the most of the time the distraction had given them. Sam clearly had the same idea as she gripped the broken edge of the window, trying to pull herself out into the snow beyond. He helped her the best he could. Once she was clear, she reached back for him.

Amelia shouted, but her words were lost to a deep, bone-jarring growl. Mitchel's stomach dropped. He needed to help her. He crawled into the driver's seat, slicing himself on the glass. Sam offered her hand, and he tried to reach out to her, but something hit the car again.

Metal crunched as the car rolled, throwing him back into the seat. He screamed as pain sliced into his side. His vision wavered, darkness crawling close as it threatened to pull him under. Part of him wanted the pain to end, but the rest of him knew if he stayed still, he'd probably not wake up.

Carefully, he looked around, trying to see where he was. The car had landed on its wheels, and he was now half in the driver's seat. He tried to push against the dash trapping him, but the pain in his side grew worse. Biting down on another scream, he stilled himself again, body shaking.

He had to get out of the car. He had to find out if Amelia was okay. If all of them were okay. Gunfire came again.

Mitchel reached out with his magic, trying to connect to the ice to feel what was happening. But it hovered just out of reach. He cursed, trying again, but every time he thought he might be able to connect, the pain would spike, and it would slip from his grasp.

Maybe if he'd spent more time learning about the magic rather than hiding it, he'd know how to push through. How many times had he thought that over the last few days? Too many.

Giving up on the magic, he grabbed the top of the car through the broken window and tried to pull himself free. His sweaty hands slid on the metal. He fell back with a grunt and tried to wipe his hands on his jeans, but it wasn't sweat. It was blood.

Trying to ignore what the blood meant, he reached up again, pulling as hard as he could. But he wasn't strong enough, even if he'd been able to handle the pain.

Cursing, he let go, breath coming in ragged gasps. He was trapped. Nothing was working.

The creature roared, thumping down on the ground heavily enough that the car rattled. Dammit, what the hell was this thing?

Oliver came into view in front of the car, still at a distance, rifle pressed into his shoulder as he backed up. A burst of gunfire flashed on the muzzle brightly. He was alone, with no sign of Amelia.

Then, what Oliver was shooting at came into view. Mitchel couldn't immediately process it. His brain refused to believe what he was seeing. Then his fear doubled as the wyvern took another step.

Mitchel had always assumed that the description of a wyvern had been an exaggeration of old myths. Seeing this beast, he knew it had been wishful thinking on his part.

The creature was bigger than the Land Rover, with a wide body, grey scales, and spiked ridges ran down its spine onto its long tail. Its muzzle was short, with teeth overlapping its lower jaw by at least an inch. It had wings, but both were tattered like mouldy cloth, the thin webbed skin flapping around it as it moved slowly towards Oliver. It stalked him on four feet with massive claws that tore up snow and ground alike with each step.

There shouldn't have been a wyvern in the Highland Rift Scar. There hadn't been in over a hundred years. But he had no doubt that was what this was.

Oliver shot at it again, making it shake its head and spray black blood onto the snow. Its eyes were a bloody mess, the damage looking fresh. But there was little sign that the guns had done any more damage than that.

The beast roared again and took another step towards Oliver.

How the hell did you fight something like that?

AMELIA'S LEG BURNED AS she limped around the edge of the barn towards Mitchel and the crushed car. Her chest was so tight it was a wonder she could get a breath. She couldn't see him from this angle, just scent hints of his blood in the air.

She'd seen Sam limping behind the house, but she'd been alone. Amelia had to hope Sam would stay there and out of the fight.

Not that it would matter if they couldn't kill this beast.

Stupid to have let them stay. Amelia should have made them drive off the minute they were in the car.

Memories later. Fight now, Luna said, huffing. She was hovering close to the surface, wanting to fight the beast with claws and teeth. But even if they had time, the venom was still there, stopping the shift. *Still strong enough to protect mate. Protect pack.*

Amelia nodded, trying to let go of everything except getting to Mitchel. Her wolf was right. She couldn't change the past, and dwelling on it wouldn't help anyone.

Oliver fired another burst of bullets at the beast's face, trying to do more damage to its eyes and draw it away from the car. The unspoken plan wasn't good, as he was dangerously close to the creature, and the barn wasn't sturdy enough to protect him for long if he went inside. But there wasn't anything else they could do until they got everyone on their feet and safe. Unfortunately, they had to get the wyvern further away from the car than its current body length to do that.

The creature spun, throwing out its tail towards Oliver. He was able to get clear before it hit him; the tip caught the hood of the car with a loud metal *ting*, but it didn't move the car. She'd not been so lucky the first time. The pain in her calf was like a fire that ran from hip to ankle, even worse than before.

Hale gave a light tug on her through the pack bonds, his fear for her clear. He'd left the link open, which he never did. He was coming. Had been coming since she'd first seen the imps. But he wasn't going to be fast enough.

Never had she both wanted and not wanted them to arrive and help at equal levels. If they came, more of the pack would get hurt. If they didn't arrive, the chances of the four of them surviving weren't good.

Pack good hunters, Luna said, but she echoed Amelia's fear for them. *We stronger together.*

Oliver took another shot at the wyvern's face as it finished its spin. It threw its head back and roared. Its grey scales were battle-scarred, and its wings tattered. At least that meant it would be stuck on ground level, though it wasn't helping them all that much. The wyvern's hide was too thick for the bullets to do more than bruise. They'd managed to take out its eyes, but the beast had no problem tracking them by sound.

Turning away from the fight, Amelia searched for Mitchel's scent. It was hard to get anything past the stench of the wyvern. It was worse than sickly rot. More than noxious sewage. It was like it made the air heavier and thicker. It made her chest ache. But under it all, she could just smell Mitchel's blood. Unfortunately, it didn't help her know what condition he was in.

She took another step towards the car as Oliver drew the wyvern further away. She had to get Mitchel out before the beast decided to hit it again. If he was okay. He had to be okay. She half expected to see ice around the car, but there was just a dusting of disturbed snow from the roll.

Our mate okay, Luna said with a pulse of confidence. *But needs our help.*

Amelia didn't ask how her wolf knew as she held onto her words. The car's side was crushed where the tail had swiped it and forced it to spin out of control. It was back on its wheels now, half buried in snow, the black blood of the wyvern spotting the ground.

The beast took another step towards Oliver. Its tail was finally out of range. Moving closer to the car, she heard glass crunching beneath her feet in the snow. The beast swivelled its head around, searching.

She tried to slow her breath and remember what kind of hunter these things were, sound or scent. It seemed to be using a combination of both, nostrils flaring and head swivelling and tilting like it was listening. When Oliver wasn't shooting at it, at least.

Oliver looked at her, motioning to the car, then held up three fingers. A countdown. He'd distract it, and she'd run to the car and get Mitchel clear.

Though what happened after that, she didn't know. The bullets weren't making any difference.

Amelia braced to sprint across the gap to the car as Oliver lowered a finger. The pain in her leg flared, but she tried to ignore it as a second finger went down, and he moved his hand back to brace the gun.

As Oliver's last finger dropped, Amelia pushed off, moving as fast as she could. The wyvern's head tilted towards her, hearing the movement. But Oliver fired, the sound making it rear its head again, screaming.

She stomped the glass deeper into the snow, searching for which side of the car Mitchel was on. He was in the driver's seat, twisted at an odd angle. She ran around the back of the car, making the most of the beast's scream. It stopped as she reached Mitchel's window. She stilled, trying to smooth out her breathing and keep herself quiet.

Inside the car, she could see the steering wheel was trapping Mitchel's leg, and she could smell the rich scent of his blood, though she couldn't see where it was coming from.

His skin was clammy, and he was breathing too fast, but he was awake and watching her silently, clearly aware that any noise was bad. That was a good sign. She wanted to tell him it would be okay anyway, but she kept silent.

She looked at the twisted metal around his leg, reaching in carefully to try to move it. Glass tinkled to the floor of the car.

The wyvern turned back, muzzle twitching. Amelia froze.

Oliver raised one hand, warning her to stop. He took aim, sending another burst towards the wyvern, turning it back. It roared again and took another step towards him. Oliver was running out of places to go, his back getting close to the end of the barn. Beyond that was the wall.

They couldn't keep this up for much longer, she realised as the wyvern snarled. It was choosing its direction carefully, taking single steps on purpose. It was a smart move. Too smart to give her much hope they could hide or run from this thing. Not to mention, Oliver would run out of bullets very soon.

Wolf stronger. Wolf faster. Wolf better, Luna snarled, swiping at Amelia to the point of near pain. *We fight. We win.*

Oliver met her eyes across the distance and motioned to the car again. Telling her to hurry, like he could also sense her fear and doubt. Neither of which she had time for here.

She turned back to the car, letting her wolf rise closer to the surface. Holding onto Luna's confidence. There was no way she would be able to free Mitchel quietly. As soon as she started trying to pull the metal, it would draw the wyvern.

Amelia motioned to Oliver as she grabbed the handle inside the roof and lifted herself into the empty window frame. She braced her good leg on the steering wheel and her back on the inside of the door. It hurt and was awkward as the metal dug into her, but if she could get enough leverage, she could free him.

Warmth spread through her as Mitchel touched her. She hadn't realised how cold she had been until he did. He shook his head, motioning for her to leave. She mimicked his head shake, then awkwardly leaned further into the car and pressed her lips against his. The contact flared up the link between them.

She felt his pain. His fear. His frustration. His magic as it flowed around her. She tried to send him a sense of safety. A promise that she was going to help him. As she pulled back, enjoying the taste of him on her lips, she wished she had time to do more.

But time was something none of them had. She shifted position, gripping the top of the car's twisted metal and leaning into the window frame. Her leg throbbed even though she wasn't using it against the steering wheel. She showed Mitchel three fingers and slowly counted down, checking Oliver. He was past the edge of the barn now, nearly out of sight.

She lowered her second finger, wishing she could give Oliver more warning. More glass skittered to the car floor, loud in the silence.

The beast swivelled towards her, breath coming out in a sharp huff. Oliver took another shot, but it had turned its head already, and bullets just bounced off its scales. It didn't turn back. Oliver tried to move and get into a place where he could shoot. Blood spurted, thick and dark, out of the creature's neck as bullets hit a patch of scarred scales. The beast screamed, twisting and writhing.

Oliver tried to back away, but he'd let the wyvern get too close. In a motion that felt too slow and fast simultaneously, the wyvern spun, and its tail swiped Oliver, hitting him in the side and sending him out of sight towards the wall.

Amelia screamed and pushed. Metal screeched with her.

MITCHEL'S BREATH CAUGHT AS Amelia pushed against the steering wheel. The pain was immediate, and he couldn't help his scream as the metal screeched but didn't break.

The wyvern was spinning around, clawing at the back of its neck. Mitchel couldn't see Oliver.

Amelia sagged back, leg shaking, as she looked at him. He tried to move, but his leg was still caught. He was still trapped.

'No, dammit, no,' Amelia shouted at the car, moving to try again, eyes moving between the twisted plastic and the wyvern. It wouldn't stay distracted forever.

'Stop,' Mitchel said, grabbing Amelia's wrist. He wouldn't be responsible for Amelia dying in a vain effort to save him. 'You still have time. Go help Oliver and Sam. Go.'

'I'm not leaving you,' she said, shifting her feet, this time bracing both. Every part of Mitchel wanted to shove her away, scream at her to run. But he could feel her pain through his touch, feel how much her leg hurt; he didn't want to hurt her more.

Which was stupid, considering what was about to happen when the beast remembered about them. Amelia pushed again, screaming as her pain spiked to a new level along with his. Metal screeched again. He felt the pressure ease, and then suddenly, it was gone. He was sure he must have screamed, but his vision wavered, and all he could hear was a white noise in his ears as his stomach threatened a mass evacuation.

'Please go,' Mitchel said when he could get a full breath. Even though he was free now, he wasn't going anywhere fast enough. She had to know that.

She ignored him, wrapping her arms around his shoulder to drag him out of the seat. He screamed again as something pulled along his side, bringing more pain.

The wyvern echoed his scream, but this time, it was an angry sound, and it had stopped spinning, now just shaking its head. It wouldn't be long before the beast refocused on them. If the guns hadn't worked. He didn't know that they had enough to kill it.

Amelia continued to drag him out of the car. The window was small and awkward with both of them wounded and in pain, but eventually, they stumbled onto the hard-packed snow. His magic flared to life immediately. Information exploded around him.

He could feel the gouges in the snow from the wyvern. Feel the broken glass and twisted tyres where it lay twisted at the wrong angle. Fuel spilling into the snow. Old footsteps and blood splattered over the frozen ground. And Amelia. She pressed close to him, wrapping her arms around him. She'd landed with her leg twisted under her in the snow. He could feel her through the bond, through the ice, and through his own body. The triple feed made his already aching head spin, so he pulled away, searching.

Further out, Oliver lay still, the snow melting into his warm clothes. Sam was behind the house, crouched, probably in sight of Oliver.

Amelia wrapped an arm under his shoulder, forcing him upright and away from the car. He bit back a scream at the pain in his side, and Amelia stopped after they'd moved a few feet from the car. But it wasn't far enough. Her frustration and fear were so intense it was almost like it was part of him.

All around them, silence fell. He couldn't see past her, towards the beast. He couldn't feel it in the snow.

'Run,' he whispered, chest so tight that even that single word hurt.

Amelia shook her head. 'I'm not leaving you.'

His magic sang to him, pressing on him. But every time he'd used it, he'd hurt someone. He couldn't live with himself if he used it now and hurt Amelia.

'Go, I'll use Frost on it, but I don't want to hurt you again,' he said carefully, flinching as he felt the snow dip. He couldn't feel what was touching it, but it wasn't hard to guess the wyvern was creeping towards them cautiously, head swivelling, nose flaring.

'I'm not leaving you,' Amelia said, grip tightening on him.

'You have to. I almost killed you last time,' Mitchel said, shaking his head, remembering seeing how blue her lips had been. 'You need to run. That way, you have a chance. All of you will be able to get away.'

'You didn't hurt the girl,' Amelia said, warmth soaking into him where she was pressed against him. The connection between them sent him the feel of her confidence. 'You were holding her. She wasn't affected. I was beside you today and didn't feel the cold.'

'I don't know how I did that,' Mitchel said, fear twisting in his gut as he realised what she wanted of him. 'I don't know how to protect you.'

'You're doing it already. Right now, I'm not cold,' Amelia said. 'Every time you've used magic today, I've not felt the cold.'

Mitchel shook his head. 'It's too dangerous.'

The wyvern reached the car, roaring when it bumped into it. It struck out with claws, swiping at the metal with an awful screech, tearing a long gash down the passenger side. Amelia tried to drag them back another few steps.

'More dangerous than facing off against a wyvern?' Amelia said, tilting her head towards the beast. It was making too much noise, attacking the car, ignoring them. 'Of trying to run with a leg that can barely take my weight?'

His stomach twisted like she'd speared him with a knife. He wasn't the only one who was hurt. They all were. Even Sam had hurt her leg. They'd never outrun the wyvern. 'What if I hurt you? What if I hurt them?'

Amelia's eyes flared blue. 'I trust you.'

For years, Mitchel taught himself how not to use his magic. How to stop it spilling out. Was Amelia right? Was he unconsciously protecting her from the effects of the magic? But what if she was wrong?

'I trust you,' Amelia said again.

Mitchel shuddered as he tried to clear his head. To think. The pain made it hard. He ached everywhere. There was so much of it that he couldn't be sure where it was coming from.

His magic was there, too. Ready to spread out from him, react to what he wanted. But if he let it loose and Amelia was wrong? He could kill her. If she hadn't pulled him back yesterday, what would have happened?

'What if I get lost?' Mitchel said, feeling the magic spread now he was thinking about it. 'What if I hurt the others?' He wasn't sure he could forgive himself if that happened.

'I'll bring you back,' Amelia said, touching his face. 'Both are further away than we were yesterday. Further away than where the ice had been frozen solid.'

He hadn't noticed that. Hadn't even looked. But now Amelia was relying on him to protect them both. She trusted him. Even though he'd done nothing to deserve that trust and confidence.

The memory of the first time he'd used magic rose in his mind. He'd been a teenager, upset at his parents. He'd let go then, too. Frozen pieces of a lake. He'd done the same yesterday out of fear.

But today, he let go deliberately. Letting the magic free, leaning into Amelia, wrapping his arms tightly around her as he focused on the wyvern. Sending all his magic, all his cold, straight towards it.

The wyvern screamed, then stopped, turning back to them like it had sensed something. There was nothing between them and the beast now.

He forced his mind to picture the beast, and it only. Trying to keep the frost away from the warm patches in the snow where he could feel Sam and Oliver. But above all, he pushed it away from Amelia, not letting it touch her.

CHAPTER FOURTEEN

AMELIA HELD ON TO Mitchel as the mist rose around them. The savaged car disappeared from sight. She fought the image of Mitchel still stuck inside. His broken body twisted. She'd got him out. He was safe, at least for now.

The wyvern stepped towards them, head moving left and right, searching for them in the silence, nose flaring. For a moment, she thought they were too late.

She should have told him she trusted him sooner. That his magic had been protecting her. But then, between one blink and the next, the mist was so thick that everything disappeared.

The scent of morning frost came with it, pure and clean, as it erased the smell of rot. She could feel it in her lungs like he was inside her. Part of her.

There was something familiar about the magic. Almost like her links to the pack, but not quite. It was singular. Quieter. She let it sing through her.

Her wolf howled at the joy she felt. This was their mate. *Powerful.*

They held onto Mitchel, letting him feel her, feel that she was there with him. She could hear the cold moving around them. The ground cracked. She wished she could see Oliver and Sam to know they were okay. She'd been truthful when she'd said they were out of range of what he'd done yesterday, but that didn't mean she wouldn't have felt better seeing them.

The wyvern didn't come through the mist. Didn't take another step. Did that mean it had worked?

Mitchel's face was still, eyes closed, almost like he was asleep. But sweat was beading on his forehead, and his eyes flickered under his eyelids. He didn't look at peace. She put a hand on his face, shivering at the wild mix of emotions coming from him.

'Mitchel?' Amelia said, voice low as she called to him. There was no response.

Then she felt the pull she'd felt so often from him since she'd first met him. Yesterday, she had given that link a slight tug to bring him back to her.

But she hesitated. Had it been long enough? With the mist all around, she couldn't tell except that the wyvern hadn't broken through. She hadn't heard anything from it.

Did she dare to pull him back? Mitchel let out a small sound, like a whimper. He was so pale it looked like he was already half dead.

Cursing, she pushed aside her doubt and tightened her grip on his arm. Without any effort at all, she pulled on the link between them, just as she'd seen her wolf do. Except she didn't wake Mitchel.

A storm of energy, power, and emotion flooded her, and she fell into darkness.

AMELIA BLINKED AS EVERYTHING around her wavered, then settled into a familiar scene.

Moonlight glinted off a large lake. It was big enough that most of it was lost in a pale mist. Someone had strung lights around the bank, and she could see them disappear into the distant mist. Mitchel's dream from last night.

She could recall it vividly now. She'd not even realised she'd lost the certainty of this place when she'd been awake. But now she was here, she remembered Mitchel's fear as she'd held him. His pain.

She turned, looking behind her, but there was only more mist this time, no Mitchel. Looking at the mist left her faintly dizzy, so she turned back to the lake.

Find mate, Luna said, voice feeling different.

Amelia looked down. Her wolf's pale gold fur rippled in the breeze as she watched her with blue eyes similar to her own. Luna cocked her head like Amelia was the anomaly and this strange place was normal. Like it all made sense. Except none of it did.

Think too much, Luna said, jaws opening so her tongue lolled out. It distinctly felt like her wolf was making fun of her.

Sam had told Amelia about what it had felt like with Hale. How she had been inside his memories, though she'd been unwilling to say what she'd seen there. But Amelia had expected it to be more … metaphorical. Not literally walking through a memory despite what had clearly been a shared dream last night with Mitchel.

If she hadn't been so adamant that Mitchel wasn't her mate, she would've realised what last night's dream had meant a lot sooner.

Shaking her head, she looked around again. If this was Mitchel's dream, then where was he? She didn't like the way he'd been afraid here last time.

A teenager was sitting further down the bank with his feet in the lake. His brown hair was long enough to hang in his eyes, and he wore an overly large suit.

Part of her wanted to shout at him to get away from the water. It was too dark despite the bright moon above. It would be too easy for something to go wrong. But it was a silly instinct because none of this was real.

Despite the mild weather, ice appeared around the boy's ankles. He yelped, jumping back, frowning as the water melted. The familiar scent of morning frost touched her nose. Mitchel. A young Mitchel.

Carefully, he put his foot back on the lake, and the ice spread out under him. Amelia's heart was in her throat as she watched him step fully onto the ice. He laughed, and the ice spread. He moved with it, walking, then running. After a moment, he moved from running to gliding, sliding over the ice like he had ice skates on.

He was so excited and happy that she could feel it from here, like a warmth in her chest. Except it wasn't coming from the young Mitchel, she realised as she turned to find her Mitchel standing beside her. This was a different feeling than he'd had the last time they'd been here.

'It's funny the things that stick with us. This is the first time I used my magic,' Mitchel said, watching his younger self. 'I remember the lake so clearly, but my grandfather's house on the cliff above is a blur. I wasn't welcome back after this day.'

'It's a beautiful place,' Amelia said, moving to take his hand, wanting to feel him. The connection between them flared brightly, letting her feel the sorrow and fear that mirrored his joy at seeing his younger self.

She tried to move them like she had done in the last dream. Take them somewhere different. Somewhere that wouldn't hurt. Except she couldn't. Nothing happened. It was like nothing else existed in this place. She shuddered, her wolf moving to brush her fur against her legs.

'Mitchel!' an older man shouted. 'Get back here now!'

Mitchel's joy drained from him in a rush as the teenager stopped playing. The older man was at the edge of the lake where Mitchel had started. The boy turned, smile wide, clearly happy. Mist had risen with the ice all around them, and it was getting harder to see them now.

Young Mitchel laughed. 'I finally found my magic, Father.'

'Get back here now!' the older man said.

Young Mitchel lost his smile as he watched his father on the shore. Amelia heard the ice crack. She took a step towards the teenage Mitchel, heart in her throat. Mitchel tightened his grip on her arm, holding her still.

'It's okay,' Mitchel said, but he wasn't watching his younger self.

Help, Luna said, whining, taking the step Amelia couldn't.

Mitchel shook his head, putting his hand on her wolf's fur. Amelia could feel the warmth of the touch even though he wasn't touching her directly. It was a strange feeling.

'This is just a memory,' Mitchel said, but he looked like he was holding himself back, too, as his younger self fell through the ice.

Then the world went misty, hiding everything around them. It cleared almost as soon as it had come, but they had moved, now standing on the bank with Mitchel's dad leaning over young Mitchel. The pair were soaking wet.

'What happened?' young Mitchel asked, body shaking as he struggled against the cold.

'I burned my magic out,' her Mitchel said, squeezing her hand like he'd heard her thought. 'Without the magic, the cold affects me just like everyone else.'

Amelia leaned into Mitchel, wishing she could do something more to comfort him as he focused on his dad.

'You almost drowned,' his dad said, voice quiet as water dripped off his face. Amelia could hear the anger in his voice, and it was obvious that teenage Mitchel could feel it too because he looked devastated.

She expected Mitchel to be angry in return, but he was just sad. 'I didn't know why he was angry then. That he wasn't angry with me,' Mitchel said slowly. 'Finding out he wasn't really my father broke something between us. We were never close after that. A formal relationship that existed because we had to keep up the pretence for the outside world.'

Amelia couldn't even imagine what that would have been like. When her father died, her mother had always been there, even if she was trying to make Amelia be something she wasn't.

'Rest. You lost control and burned out,' Mitchel's father said, head turning as another voice called out. 'We'll talk about this later.'

Teenage Mitchel's eyes drifted closed like he couldn't keep them open anymore. Just as she thought he'd fallen asleep, he spoke. 'I found my magic.'

'You found something,' his dad said, voice barely audible as the pair faded from the bank. The memory falling apart.

'I'm sorry,' Amelia said, tightening her grip on his hand until he looked away from where the pair had been.

Her wolf bumped into their legs, sitting between them so she could touch both of them.

'How are you here?' Mitchel said, looking at her wolf, then back at her. There was something in his eyes like he knew she'd been holding something back. 'How were you here last night?'

Protect, Luna whispered, making Mitchel frown. *Mate.*

Mitchel stared at her wolf for a heartbeat, then refocused on Amelia. She fought a blush that rose.

'I'm here to bring you back,' Amelia said, trying to ignore the question in that glance. 'You stopped the wyvern. You did it.'

Mitchel frowned, and then his eyes widened. 'My magic. Is that how you're here? I hurt you?'

'You didn't hurt anyone,' Amelia said, shaking her head as she pulled Mitchel closer, letting him feel the certainty of her words.

'So, we're here because we're mates?' Mitchel said, fear shifting into something else as he circled back to her wolf's words. Her wolf leaned into Mitchel harder.

Yes, Luna said.

'No,' Amelia said.

Mitchel smiled at her.

Human wrong, Luna said, giving Amelia a shove before she could argue again.

Amelia glared at her wolf, who just pretended Amelia didn't exist. 'It's not that simple.'

'Mates are part of the wolf pack history from the closing of the Rifts. A connection between two people that goes so deep that they can feel each other when they touch,' Mitchel said, tilting his head. 'Which, in hindsight, I suppose, should have been obvious much sooner. But in my defence, I'd thought it could only happen between wolves.'

Amelia stared at him, then closed her mouth. 'You've spent too much time with Oliver.'

Mitchel laughed, pulling her closer so that he could kiss her. The connection flared like lightning around them: pleasure, joy. On its heels, a tiredness that she felt bone deep.

'Are you okay?' Amelia asked breathlessly as she pulled back. She hadn't liked that feeling of tiredness.

'So, is this something all the pack can do, or unique to mates?' Mitchel asked, avoiding the question as he nodded at the lake when he said mates. Clearly pleased with the word.

She let him change the subject for now and shook her head. 'In the pack, we can sense each other, scent, and sometimes feel emotion, but we can't interact like this. Not even with the link to our alpha.'

'I'm sure there are far more interesting memories we could relive,' Mitchel said, shivering as the memory wavered and reset. His younger self sat at the edge of the water again.

Adult Mitchel frowned, sweat beading on his brow as he pulled away from her to stare at his younger self. That sense of tiredness came back. Something was wrong. Something she couldn't see.

'We can't stay here,' she said, touching Mitchel's shoulder. 'You need to wake up.'

'I'm so tired,' Mitchel said, letting go of her to step back. Blood spotted his side. It hadn't been there before. The car. He was still hurt. Mitchel looked down, surprised at the wound on his side.

'Let me help you,' Amelia said, reaching out.

'No,' Mitchel said, his image wavering and moving so they were no longer standing together. 'You should go. It's not safe here.'

'I'm safe with you,' Amelia said, trying to reach out to him again, but it felt like he was slipping away from her. Amelia's wolf whined and tried to move closer to Mitchel to grab him.

'I hurt you yesterday,' Mitchel said. The mist was growing thicker around him. The temperature was dropping, and without him touching her, she could feel it. 'I don't want to hurt you again.'

'No, you didn't hurt me,' Amelia said, but she couldn't reach him. It was like he was blocking her. Stopping her from taking a step. 'Dammit, Mitchel. Look at me.'

'I'm just so tired,' Mitchel said, turning back to the lake to watch the boy fall through the ice again.

'No,' Amelia shouted. 'Mitchel, don't you dare let go.'

Mitchel didn't seem to hear her as he started to fall.

The image of the lake shattered like the ice had. Breaking apart and spinning too fast for her to catch hold of.

But she refused to give up. If she did, she wasn't sure she'd ever be able to find him again.

OLIVER WANTED TO PACE. But he'd tried that already, and pacing over slippery ice wasn't any fun. Less so with his broken ribs. He needed to stay close to where Amelia and Mitchel were huddled on the ground together as Sam tried to do something for their wounds.

After the mist had cleared, it had taken every piece of the wyvern's scent, leaving only the smell of Amelia and Mitchel's blood. It was so strong that he knew that something needed to be done. But Sam had ordered him to back off. But unless she planned on ordering them to get better, he couldn't see what she was going to be able to do.

Even unconscious, Amelia had curled her hand around Mitchel's wounded side. Sam had pulled her hand back only long enough to see a ragged wound before she let Amelia's arm slip back into place. Blood slipped between her fingers too fast, and they had no medical equipment to help them.

Amelia looked no worse than before, but nothing he'd done had been able to wake her. Not his wolf or physically shaking her. Oliver didn't like it.

'I'm trying my best,' Sam said, giving him a look. The feel of the pack danced around him wildly. Her fear and his mixing until he had to look away from her.

'I'm not doubting you're trying,' Oliver said, fighting against his wolf as he scolded him for talking back to Sam at all. 'They need the hospital.'

'Mitchel won't make it to a hospital,' Sam said. Her voice was soft. 'And Amelia ... I don't know what's wrong with her.'

A different kind of pain sliced through Oliver. He couldn't lose his friend. Either of them.

Oliver growled and wished again he could move. Could do something. Anything. Both cars were trashed. His ribs ached. They had been attacked by imps and a wyvern already, so leaving the relative safety of the farmyard wasn't wise.

His eyes went to the frozen wyvern. It was entirely encased in ice, much like the car had been yesterday. Mitchel had saved them again.

And he was going to pay for it with his life.

'There has to be a way to help them,' Oliver said, shivering as the feel of the pack ebbed and flowed around him. Amelia's fear and Mitchel's blood filled his nose.

'What do you think I'm doing over here?' Sam said, brushing back a strand of Amelia's hair. She didn't react.

'Which takes us back to the conversation we didn't have earlier,' Oliver said, knowing he sounded cold. 'What are you?' Again, his wolf swiped at him for being rude.

Sam took a breath, let it out slowly, and finally looked at him. 'I'm an Earth Elemental.'

Oliver opened his mouth, then snapped it shut. The pack lands. The dead tree where Shane's body had been. Oliver cursed; it was so damned obvious that he'd overlooked it all.

Earth Elementals were persecuted by the government. Picked, seemingly arbitrarily, over a hundred years ago so the humans could feel proud that they had prevented one of the Rift Bloodlines from spreading. Or at least that's how Oliver saw it. He could see no other reason why Earth Magic would be singled out as more dangerous. Especially considering what the other elements could do.

That an Earth Elemental had managed to slip through the net and was living outside the government's radar didn't surprise him. Nor was Hale protecting the secret.

'You made it so the pack lands are aware?' Oliver asked, moving forward carefully over the ice, ribs pulsing painfully. He knelt next to Amelia and Mitchel.

'We don't know,' Sam said. 'It's not like we can ask someone. I saved Hale from dying, and then he saved me. Whatever we did changed everything.'

'You healed Hale?' Oliver asked, focusing on the crucial part of what she'd said, though he had every intention of finding out the rest of the details later. He shivered, remembering the pain of that day, of feeling Hale slip away from them. 'I felt him die.'

'He didn't die,' Sam said quickly, her own pain stinging his nose. 'But he was hurt much worse than he said. I was able to use my magic to heal him. Earth Magic.'

Hope rose, but it felt weak. But he also knew that if it was that simple, she'd have done it already. 'You can heal them, then?'

'I'm not on my land. I don't have the power to do it here,' Sam said. Her frustration was obvious. 'I barely had the power to do it back then. Hale had to accept my help.'

Oliver stared at Amelia, her eyelids flickering as she was lost in whatever had pulled her under. Going by how tightly she held Mitchel, he didn't doubt she was still try-ing to protect him.

'You're part of the pack now,' Oliver said. He'd felt that familiar tingle of the pack more than once from Sam. But it moved without guidance. It was just filling the space. He raised his hand as she moved to say something. 'I can feel you, feel Hale's magic.'

Sam watched him, a sheen of tears threatening to fall. 'I can feel it, but I can't use it. I've been trying.' She shuddered and looked at Amelia's arms wrapped around Mitchel. He was so pale now that he damned near blended into the snow. 'Hale is too far away. He isn't going to make it in time.'

Oliver's heart stuttered. Mitchel was slipping away with every breath. He had to do something.

'What if I tried to help?' Oliver said, pushing down the pain of the last time he'd been able to use the pack bonds. Of the temporary and small pack he'd created. 'I could guide you, direct the magic to you.'

Sam's head shot around to his. 'You can do that?'

'Yes,' Thor said through him before he could answer. 'Protect pack.'

Sam frowned at him, but if she was concerned that his wolf was showing, she didn't smell afraid. 'I think it's im-portant she accepts as well. Can you tell her to let me in?'

Oliver's wolf considered it, looking at Amelia, then nodded.

'Do both of you agree?' Sam asked, showing she had at least noticed his wolf.

'Yes,' Oliver said, pulling back control. 'But last time I did this, it created a new pack.'

Sam's eyes widened a fraction. Clearly, Hale had been telling her a lot about how the pack and Shifters worked for her to understand the significance of that. 'I'll deal with Hale,' she said, looking down at Amelia, then back at him. 'He'll understand.'

He might not. Taking wolves away from an alpha was one of the biggest insults there was. If Oliver did this wrong, he could be taking Amelia from Hale.

'We still have a problem with the plan, though. Mitchel isn't part of the pack,' Sam said. 'Even if I could use the magic with your help, how does that help Mitchel? All I'd be able to do is heal Amelia, who isn't critical.'

'Use mate link?' Thor asked, slipping past Oliver's control again. But as much as Amelia and Mitchel seemed to like each other, that didn't make them mates. His wolf huffed at him like he was being stupid.

Sam gave him a sharp look. 'You're sure they have one?'

Oliver rubbed his eyes, getting frustrated with his wolf. 'I'm sorry. My wolf doesn't understand how relationships work.'

'But your wolf thinks they're mates?' Sam said, touching Amelia's arm. There was no sense of disbelief in her.

Told you so, Thor said, thankfully inside his head this time.

When Oliver didn't answer, Sam smiled and gave him a look he couldn't quite decipher. 'I'm not saying some power that be, or fate, or anything like that brought me together with Hale. I really hope they didn't because what they put us through would definitely be considered cruel. But I do believe there's a link between us. Something more. Something that's part of our magic. How else could I use the pack magic?'

Sam paused to take a slow breath as she looked at Amelia. 'If I can connect to Amelia, I might be able to use the link to heal Mitchel. Hale was able to use our mate bond to heal me when I almost died the same day.'

Oliver's wolf snarled in his mind at the idea that someone had dared to hurt Sam, even though she was okay now. He remembered the scent of bleach in Sam's kitchen and on the grass outside. He'd thought it was strange that some stuff had been cleaned but not everything that night. But the feel of the pack lands had made it seem irrelevant.

Turns out that there were a lot of secrets the pair were keeping. Secrets that Amelia knew as well. All of them were going to have a long conversation later.

'I don't know if you're right about the bond between them,' Oliver said slowly, offering his hand to Sam, 'but I don't know we've any other choice but to try.'

Sam took his hand and shuffled closer. The ground was solid with no give, and his ribs twinged at the movement.

'If it works the same as it did with Hale, I think that once you're connected to her, you'll need to convince her to accept you in. And for her and Mitchel to accept each other,' Sam said.

Oliver nodded, but his chest felt tight as he took a breath. So much he didn't know. So much that could go wrong because of it. He wasn't even sure how exactly he'd made the small pack the first time.

I help. I good alpha, Thor said, pressing close.

Sam squeezed his hand when he didn't say anything. 'We've got this. We'll help them both. I promise.'

Oliver swallowed back the fear the best he could and let his grip on his wolf loosen. He reached for something, not the pack bonds, not exactly, but something else. Then he could feel Amelia. Feel her pain, feel her wolf.

The sense of Hale was all around him, wrapped through the magic, connecting them indirectly. His wolf pulled on it, pulled at a thread, and the world around him vibrated.

He felt Hale's surprise. But he didn't do anything to stop Oliver. If anything, Hale pulled back, giving Oliver space.

This wasn't a challenge. This was protecting the pack.

'Amelia,' Oliver said, pressing the power of the pack into his words. 'Let Sam in.'

'Amelia,' a voice said. It was distant. A man. Oliver. 'Let Sam in.'

Amelia struggled to focus on the words as the world spun around her. Her wolf huddled against her back. Where was Mitchel?

'Let her in,' Oliver said again. There was pressure there with the words. The insistence that she listen. She wanted to ignore it and continue her search for Mitchel, but she couldn't. 'Sam can help.'

Amelia froze, the fight leaving her as she turned towards the voice, letting the weight of it settle over her. Oliver's voice calmed her racing heart, soothing her. The reason she was afraid slipped away. Why was she here?

The lake flashed into view. Mitchel's memory, not Oliver's? Mitchel needed her.

'Let us help,' Oliver said, firmer this time. The pressure increased, and she could feel him. Feel the pack. The pack would help.

She reached out, touching Oliver, accepting him into her mind, but he didn't appear like she'd expected. Instead, she felt a bright warmth. It flooded through her as the spinning stopped.

'Let me in,' Sam said this time, travelling the same route as Oliver, voice coming all around. Sam was part of the pack. She had healed Hale. She could help Mitchel.

Amelia let the warmth settle into her and opened her eyes to see a large yew tree spread over a clearing. It was bright with colour, the woods hazy. This was clearly Sam's memory because the tree wasn't in this good a shape right now.

Sam knelt by the tree, head bowed. Something moved in the mist at the edge of the clearing. Black fur and gold eyes. Hale.

'Definitely need to work on how these images are chosen,' Sam said from behind Amelia. This version of Sam was wearing a long white jumper and black leggings, with her blond hair in curls loose around her face.

Amelia turned between the two versions of Sam. The one by the tree was silent and focused. The clothes were about the only difference between them.

'Where am I?' Amelia asked, struggling to rebalance herself. Something was wrong. Something important that she had to fix. She'd remembered a minute ago, but it had slipped away again.

'This was the day everything changed. When I nearly lost Hale,' Sam said. 'But that's not why we're here. I told you how I healed him. How I used our connection.'

Mates, Luna said, brushing against her leg as she moved to sit in front of Sam.

Sam smiled at Amelia's wolf. 'Yes. Now you've found your mate.'

Yes, Luna said, looking up at Amelia like she expected her to argue. She didn't. The pain in her chest was so bad she could barely breathe. Why would thinking about Mitchel hurt?

The memories of the icy lake came back in pieces. Spinning ice. Mitchel with blood on his side.

Mate hurt, Luna said.

Her breath caught as she realised her wolf was right. Mitchel was losing his fight. She could feel it.

'He is,' Sam said, offering her hand. 'Will you let me try to help him?'

Without hesitation, Amelia put her hand out. The warmth she'd felt before flared into a furnace as she let Sam in. Her magic felt like the pack lands. Like coming home.

The memories of the lake burst into focus again as Sam's magic gave her a boost of energy. Amelia hadn't realised how tired she'd been.

'You have to get him to accept your help,' Sam said. 'It won't work otherwise.'

Amelia nodded as the world in front of her shifted. Fracturing again. Amelia focused on Mitchel. Concentrating on finding him again. The warmth of Sam's magic followed her.

Amelia thought about the lake. The way that it had looked with Mitchel on the ice. She could feel him now that her thoughts were more focused. But he wasn't letting her back in, wasn't accepting her reaching hand.

Amelia's wolf rose in her mind, snarling in anger. Luna didn't reach out. She lunged, following the link between them. She knew Mitchel now; she had seen inside his head.

The lake came back into focus. But it wasn't the same as it was last time. The water was unnaturally still. There was no boy on the bank, no lights, no moonlight, though she could see the water clearly enough. This was no longer just a memory but something else.

Adult Mitchel lay on a patch of ice too small for him near the middle of the lake. His arm hung in the water, and he looked about ready to fall over the edge.

A narrow ice bridge connected the little island he was on to the bank.

'Mitchel!' Amelia shouted, moving to the edge of the bridge. It was barely half a metre wide.

Mitchel turned to her. 'You came back,' he said, voice cracking. Blood dripped over the edge of the little ice island. 'You shouldn't have. It's not safe.'

He wasn't wrong. Everything about this vision showed how close to falling he was. She could feel Sam's power under her skin, ready to help.

'You're going to be okay,' Amelia said, stepping onto the ice. The air changed the minute she did, freezing her chest as if the ice was trying to bury into her lungs. 'I just need you to give me your hand.'

'Don't,' he said. 'You'll fall.'

'I trust you. I won't fall,' she said, feeling the slick ice beneath her feet. Unlike him, she didn't have grip or grace. But she also trusted him. Her footing grew firmer as she stepped closer.

Mitchel pushed himself to his knees, shaking his head. 'You were safe. Why come back?' His voice shook as he watched her.

'It's my turn to protect you,' Amelia said, her voice breaking. Her wolf paced back and forth on the bank.

The ice was starting to crack under him. She was running out of time and never seemed to be getting any closer.

'I'm not safe,' Mitchel said as a piece of ice broke off and his foot slipped into the water. 'I hurt you. I hurt Oliver.'

'You didn't hurt us,' Amelia said, trying to think of how she could convince him of the truth. 'I'm fine. Oliver is fine.'

'You don't know that,' Mitchel said. He started to look away.

'You're my mate,' Amelia said, tears stinging her eyes as she took another step. A piece of the ice bridge broke away this time. 'I know who you are. I'd know if you hurt one of my pack.'

Mitchel turned back to her. But he still didn't look convinced. The magic inside her reached but didn't find anything to hold on to. He wasn't letting her in.

'Let me help you,' Amelia said, reaching out, though the distance still seemed endless. Blood had soaked through his shirt. The ice under him cracked further, threatening to break apart. 'Or do you think you can just abandon your mate?'

Surprise flashed over Mitchel's face. 'I'd never abandon you.'

'Then give me your hand.' Amelia's arm shook as the ice under them started to shake. 'Don't leave me alone.'

Mitchel reached out, fingers touching hers as the ice broke.

The magic exploded out of her into him the moment they touched. She felt herself fall into the icy cold water, the warmth of the magic battling to keep the cold at bay.

Mitchel wrapped his arms around her, holding her tightly, and she did the same to him. Her lungs burned as they sank, darkness pulling at her.

All the while, the heat filled them.

Then the darkness won, and they fell under.

CHAPTER FIFTEEN

Mitchel woke with a gasp. He felt like he was drowning, but he wasn't sure why. He wasn't in a lake. Except he could almost taste the lake water in his mouth.

'Mitchel?' Amelia said, drawing his head around. She sat on the ice next to him, looking as weary as he felt with her gold hair wild about her face.

'What happened?' Memories flickered like an old movie reel, fragmented. Amelia was there with him in each one.

Her wolf standing beside him, her pale gold fur warm against his fingers. Amelia kissing him. Less pleasant memories followed. Oliver being hit by the tail. The wyvern coming towards them.

But the locations didn't match. One was the lake, and the other was here. Amelia had never been in wolf form with him near a lake. Never been there at all.

'You saved us,' Amelia said, squeezing his hand. He hadn't even realised she was holding it. He let the warmth of it seep into him. The memories started to slip back into their correct places. The wyvern. Then, the dream and falling into the lake with Amelia's arms wrapped around him.

Mitchel looked over at the frozen wyvern. It was further away than he remembered but just as terrifying. The massive beast was encased in ice. Not the ragged block like what had happened with the car. No, this ice was a thin crystal-clear layer over the beast's skin, freezing it mid-swipe, claws out, wings spread wide, and lips peeled back to show blackened teeth. He'd done that. Killed it. He remembered the feel of it dying, its blood freezing even as it fought to keep moving.

He shuddered and looked away. The rest of the yard was a mess of rutted snow and trashed cars. His blood was splashed, melting into slush in places and frozen in others.

'How do you feel?' Oliver asked, crouching on the snow until he appeared in Mitchel's vision. He looked pale, eyes holding to amber with no sign of any other colour.

'He will be fine. Just give him a sec to remember where he is,' Sam said, her voice soft. 'I didn't want to take too much from the pack to heal him.'

'You healed me?' Mitchel asked, looking at Sam. She looked as pale as Oliver, leaning heavily on one leg as she watched him. 'I felt ...' He trailed off, trying to remember what had happened.

His side twinged, and pain like a burst of lightning flared out. He leaned around, touching the area. A thin scar crossed his skin. It hurt, but more like a bruise than a gash. He'd remembered the pain as Amelia had pulled him from the car. Then, in the dream, he tried to get her to leave so she'd be safe as he felt himself falling.

'I was dying,' he whispered, nausea rising at the memory. He'd nearly pulled Amelia with him as he tried to set her free before he fell over the edge.

Sam took a deep breath and huffed it out as she looked between Oliver and Amelia, then at Mitchel. 'Yes.'

Humans didn't have magic, but there was no magic he knew that could heal. 'How?'

'I'm an Earth Elemental,' she said, breath escaping in a rush of air as she looked away like she didn't want to see his reaction.

Shock rippled through Mitchel, and he scrambled for something—anything—he could say. Sam's magic was forbidden, and she'd trusted him with her life by telling him the truth and her freedom.

'I'm good at keeping secrets,' Mitchel said, picking his words carefully, feeling the weight of all their eyes. 'I'll not tell anyone the truth.'

His connection to Amelia flared brightly between them, a thrill of pure emotion moving so fast he couldn't pick up on anything except that she was happy. She and her wolf. Then her eyes went to the frozen wyvern. To Mitchel's secret.

'No one will reveal yours either,' Amelia said, turning back to him. Sam raised an eyebrow but didn't comment.

But hiding the frozen wyvern wasn't going to be easy. Most wouldn't know what it meant unless they were a Water Elemental. But even then, anyone local might not care about it if they did.

But unlike Sam's secret, Mitchel's coming out wouldn't cost him his freedom. Though it may make other people's lives slightly harder.

'I've been thinking it's time for me to stop pretending to be something I'm not,' Mitchel said as he took Amelia's hand. 'If I'd known how to use my power in the first place, a lot of this might not have happened.'

'None of this is your fault,' Amelia said, but Mitchel just tightened his grip on her hand.

'No, but it's past time I learned who I am,' Mitchel said. Saying it out loud felt like a weight had been lifted off his shoulders, and he was sure he could feel Oliver's surprise.

'I'm here whatever you decide,' Amelia said, tightening her grip on his hand.

Mitchel turned to Amelia, feeling the heat of her soak into him like a warm blanket.

'You were in my head too,' Mitchel said, touching the ice under him. It was solid but somehow bending to his body. His passive magic working overtime. He almost called it back, but he was too tired and sore to give up the small comfort it gave him.

Sam muttered something to Oliver as they got up and moved back to give him and Amelia privacy.

'I know things must be confusing. And I'd understand if you're mad at me,' Amelia said, looking down. 'But I didn't want to lose you.'

'I felt—' Mitchel broke off as the rest of her words caught up with him. 'Why would I be mad? I'm pretty sure you helped Sam save me.' Though he wasn't sure how he knew. But he was sure he was right.

'I strengthened our connection,' Amelia said, looking over at Oliver, then back at him. 'I bound you.'

Amelia's wolf rose in that link, and her eyes changed colour, the pale blue holding so much warmth that he squeezed Amelia's hand.

'My mate,' Amelia said, voice lower than normal. Because it wasn't Amelia, Mitchel realised, it was her wolf.

'Yes,' Mitchel said, smiling, remembering that part of the dream. 'Mates.'

Amelia blinked, the colour changing back as a flush covered her cheeks.

Oliver barked a laugh that choked off as Sam hit him on his arm.

Amelia gave Oliver a look, but the pair had gone back to pretending they weren't there. 'But that's not what I meant. When Sam healed you, I created a connection.'

Mitchel tugged on their connected hands, pulling her close enough that he could kiss her, letting her feel the answer. 'I'm pretty certain there was already a connection there.'

'This is something different. I made you part of the pack,' Amelia said breathlessly. Then she bit her lip as she looked at Sam, then back at him. 'I did it without asking.'

He raised an eyebrow at her. He wanted to crack another joke, but he could feel her fear and worry, and he didn't understand what it meant. Nothing felt different except for his link to Amelia.

'Does that mean that Hale can tell me what to do?' Mitchel asked, deciding to walk the line of humour. It felt safer. 'Coz if he can, I'm having words with him.'

Amelia huffed and shook her head. Either because she thought the idea of him having words with Hale was funny or because it was unlikely, he couldn't tell.

'No. You don't have a wolf for him to order around,' Sam said, looking at Oliver, who had lost his humour. 'I can feel Hale, and if he lets me, I can feel the rest of the pack.'

Which meant that whatever Amelia was saying had been done, had been done to Sam first. Or she wouldn't sound so confident.

'I can't feel Hale,' Mitchel said after a minute. He could feel Amelia but nothing else.

'That's because Hale didn't help bring you into the pack,' Oliver said, his eyes flickering to amber. 'I did.'

Mitchel felt something distant, like a half-formed thought in the back of his mind. It flickered, unsure of itself, and then it was gone again. Bringing someone into the pack was what had got Oliver sent north as a punishment in the first place.

'This better not mean you're my mate, too,' Mitchel said, offering him a smile to let him know he was joking and that he understood. 'I like you, but not that much.'

Oliver smiled. It didn't quite reach his eyes, but he nodded. 'I'm more into women, but I could do worse,' Oliver said, giving Mitchel a quick once-over. 'But you're not worth fighting Amelia over.'

Amelia let out a small growl that made Mitchel shiver as she pulled him for a kiss. He'd never been one for a show of possessiveness, but if it meant Amelia kissed him like this every time, he was all for it.

Amelia pulled back, lips a darker red than before and breath short. He doubted he was any better. 'Mine,' she whispered.

He couldn't help the thrill that rippled through him at the word.

'As cute as this is, can we go inside or something? I'm not cold exactly, but ...' Sam said, rubbing her arms as she looked over the yard, stopping at the wyvern.

No one disagreed with her. Amelia helped Mitchel stand, then wrapped an arm around him. He was so close to being burned out that he barely had the energy to help them keep their balance on the walk to the back door.

AMELIA SETTLED AGAINST THE worktop next to Mitchel in Tammy's tiny kitchen. It was a strange feeling being linked to him. She could feel his emotion even without skin contact, and no matter where she stood, she knew exactly where he was.

It should have worried her, being linked to anyone that closely. But all she wanted to do was bask in the warmth of the connection. Especially since Sam's healing had reduced her pain down to a twinge.

She had felt his acceptance of her actions as she'd told him the truth. His lack of concern. Though she suspected that was because he didn't understand it. She'd been so focused on saving him that it had never occurred to her to worry about the consequences of what that would mean. That Mitchel could become pack like Sam had.

Mitchel mine, Luna said, settling tiredly into the back of her mind.

Amelia didn't argue with Luna. Couldn't. She felt the same way.

'How are we going to get out of here?' Mitchel asked.

'Hale will be here soon,' Sam said, glancing towards the far wall.

Amelia searched for her link to Hale out of habit, but it wasn't there. Mitchel wasn't the only one Oliver had pulled into his new pack. It was strange to feel Oliver and his flickers of fear as he struggled to keep the walls between them up.

She wasn't sure how she felt about the switch yet, about how easy it had been for Oliver. She'd not even felt the change like she had when Shane had tried to bind her or when Hale had freed her.

Oliver good alpha, Luna said. *Hale let Oliver protect us.*

Amelia didn't understand the magic well enough to argue with Luna, but she hoped so. She didn't want to see Oliver and Hale fight.

'He should have got our messages by now, so he'll know where to come,' Oliver said, placing his rifle down on the worktop beside the door; hers had been damaged, and she'd not bothered collecting it. He was moving stiffly, pain obvious, though he was trying to hide it.

'Let me look at your side, Oliver,' Amelia said.

'I'm fine,' Oliver said, but their bonds flared with his pain. She also sensed how much he didn't want to share that pain with her. 'You can't do anything for broken ribs.'

Amelia wanted to push, but he wasn't wrong. There wasn't much she could do to help that. Frustrated, she turned to Mitchel. She'd already checked his wounds before he'd woken. He had a slash of pink, scarred flesh on his side that was about four inches long and one hell of a bruise.

Mitchel's lips twitched as his thoughts went in a different direction than hers. His desire slipped through the bond. If not for the others, she might have stepped closer.

'Let me look at your side, Mitchel,' Amelia said, hating how dry her throat had just got.

He flushed as if he, too, remembered they weren't alone and unzipped his thin winter jacket, stripping out of it.

She inhaled sharply as she saw what he had on underneath for the first time. Her T-shirt. Her heart did a stupid pitter-patter, and her wolf rumbled with pleasure in her mind. He could have worn any of his clothes after his shower, but he'd chosen to wear this. Her T-shirt that she'd given him that morning.

Mitchel flushed. 'I'm sorry I ruined it,' he said quietly, fingering the bloody edge of the hole where he'd been sliced.

Amelia shook her head, unable to find words. She wet a kitchen towel to wipe away the blood, being careful of the scar.

'It feels bruised,' Mitchel said as she cleaned the worst of the blood.

'I'm going to put a bandage on it so no one can see,' Amelia said, looking back to where Tammy might have stored a medical kit.

'I don't know that it's going to help much with all the blood outside,' Sam said, biting her lip.

'The ice is hiding the amount of blood loss,' Oliver said, watching Sam, his wolf still in his eyes. He had been in his eyes ever since Amelia had woken. 'No one here will tell your secret.'

'I'm not sure we'll have a choice for much longer,' Sam said, looking away like she was resigned to that future.

'Not with the Rift Scar changing and the prime alphas interfering to find out about the pack lands.'

'Your magic changed the Rift Scar?' Mitchel said, his excitement rising as he put together the pieces. Oliver didn't react, proving that he had probably already figured it out. 'That's why it's only on the border of the land you own?'

'Yes. And I know that keeping this secret isn't a fair ask,' Sam said, looking down at her hands. 'If I tell the IRS&D that it's changed because of my magic, it might give the scientists something to look at. Somewhere to start.'

'Don't even think about it,' Amelia said, giving Sam a long look. 'Hale will hit the roof if you do that.'

'I can't let the chance that we might have a way to fix the Scar slip away,' Sam said.

Mitchel's excitement that had flared at Sam's words dropped away. 'But not at the cost of your freedom.'

Good mate, good pack, Luna said, preening like she had something to do with Mitchel's words.

'So, we leave the land broken and let people like the farmer here and the woman yesterday die when I could stop it,' Sam said, wrapping her arms around herself. Amelia realised that this wasn't the first time Sam had thought about this.

'How likely do you think you can replicate this scenario?' Mitchel said, making everyone turn to him. 'An

Earth Elemental and Shifter who are mates?' He paused, waiting for Sam to nod. 'Then you have lived on your land next to the Rift Scar for what, twenty years?' Another nod. 'Those aren't factors we can replicate or study easily. Especially the first one. And the last one would take years.'

'But maybe the knowledge would help them narrow it down,' Sam said, scowling.

Mitchel sighed; this time, it was his turn to look away. 'Most scientists don't even believe that the Rift Scar is shrinking. The few I know who did believe volunteered to come, but not one of them made it except me. What makes you think that IRS&D is here to study the Rift at all?'

Sam cursed. 'Surely someone wants to know the truth?'

Mitchel turned back to Sam with a wan smile. 'I do.'

'Mitchel could help you study it?' Oliver said, the pack links trembling as he struggled to keep the need to protect the pack to himself.

A thrill went through Amelia at the idea of Mitchel staying. She felt the same sensation echo through Mitchel as he turned to her. Though, with the words came the reminder that his presence was only temporary. In the end, he was supposed to go home. The same as when her term finished.

Not leave mate, Luna said.

'I'd like that,' he said, hand twitching like he'd wanted to reach out and had stopped himself.

'I'd like that, too,' she said, feeling a little like she was back at her primary school disco, asking a boy to dance for the first time.

She wished they were alone as the heat spread between them, moving from simple joy into something more. Absolutely the wrong time and place. If the scent of Oliver's amusement was anything to go by, he'd also picked up on the change.

Turning away, her face heating, she went back to what she'd been planning on doing in the first place: finding a bandage. She searched the kitchen until she found a medical kit under the sink. It was old, but it had everything she needed.

Mitchel let her play nursemaid while they waited for Hale.

OLIVER COULD FEEL HALE getting closer. Feel his frustration and anger. His mate had been in danger, and Hale hadn't been here. One of his pack had been taken, and Hale had let it happen.

The depth of the awareness made Oliver's head hurt as he tried to mute the link. But it wasn't the same as it had been; now that he had Amelia under him, something in the link was stronger. Then there was Amelia and Mitchel. He tried to block them, but his focus kept slipping, and hints of their emotions slipped through.

He didn't know how Hale did this with thirty Shifters.

Will learn. Will be good alpha, Thor said.

No. We will give them to Hale, Oliver said. Hale was already going to be mad enough that Oliver had taken Sam into danger, and she'd ended up hurt. There was no way he would argue with Hale over returning Amelia.

Just as Oliver was about to tell the others Hale was there, Sam pushed away from the counter and headed outside. The others exchanged a look but followed without question.

Hale's car nearly skidded into what was left of Amelia's jeep. Almost before it had stopped, he jumped out and ran to Sam. He pulled her to him gently, his energy rising through the yard like a storm.

Amelia put her hand on Oliver's arm. He could feel her reassurance through the new bond. It didn't help ease the tightness in his gut. Not with Hale's anger so obvious.

Sam spoke quietly, and Oliver deliberately didn't listen to what she was saying, though he was close enough he'd have been able to hear if he tried. The scent of Hale's anger didn't lessen.

The rest of the patrol appeared, driving in more slowly, and a dozen rangers got out. None of them were scientists. A lot of eyes lingered on the frozen wyvern and dead imps.

'What the hell happened?' Hale asked, eyes on Oliver. Despite the energy rippling around him, his eyes were not the gold of his wolf. Usually, he would have taken that as a good sign, but not today.

'A whole clan attacked the farm,' Amelia said before Oliver could speak. She talked everyone through a clinical explanation of everything that had happened. She missed out anything to do with Sam's or Mitchel's magic, though it was obvious magic had been what finally stopped the wyvern.

'How many were left?' Hale asked, looking around, counting bodies. More than an average clan was already dead between the yard and the house.

'At least a dozen. They were climbing in the back of the house, so I couldn't see all their number,' Oliver said, glancing at the wyvern. 'That thing likely made them group together in a larger clan. Without it as a threat, and with no alpha, they may not stay together.'

The rangers muttered, looking at the wyvern.

'Ivan,' Hale said, looking over at a dark-haired Shifter. 'Take these four to the hospital.'

Oliver wanted to argue, but Hale's eyes flashed gold, warning him that this wasn't the time or the place. Oliver looked down, submitting. Even Sam didn't argue with Hale, which said a lot about how close to the edge he must have been. Oliver had never seen her let Hale get away with ordering her about.

After a moment, Hale shouted orders to the rest of the rangers. The snow would make it easy to track the imps.

Ivan looked happy to be given driving duty as they all piled into his car and headed to the hospital. No one spoke during the journey, though Ivan tried to press for more details.

Oliver checked his phone for updates every few minutes. Hale would be all right. He had an entire team with him. Oliver would have been a liability with his broken ribs. But even knowing that, he still wanted to be there. Still wanted to help.

After a wasted few hours in the hospital, Oliver finally escaped, leaving Sam, Amelia, and Mitchel in Pascal's capable hands. There wasn't an update from Hale on what had happened with the tracking, but Oliver could still feel him through their bond, so he wasn't hurt.

Oliver wasn't ready to go home. Even if he hadn't been in pain, his brain wouldn't stop turning. Hale might not have been willing to let him into the field, but there were other things Oliver could do. Other questions that needed answers, now more than ever.

With the patrol logs that Sam had taken from Madeline, it didn't take long to find who had picked up that patrol route. With the names in hand, he dug deeper, looking at where they had come from.

When he was finished, he leaned back, holding his broken rib as the pain flared. If Hale didn't kill him for putting Sam in danger and taking one of his pack away, this information might send him over the edge.

Just as he was about to text Hale, a message came through. The patrol had tracked the imps back to the Rift Scar. The area was safe again.

A small measure of relief filled Oliver, but it didn't last long as he sent his own text. He didn't expect an answer until late. But Hale replied almost immediately, asking him to come to Sam's in a few hours.

Good alpha, Thor said, pressing closer. *Saw us protect pack. Not be mad.*

Oliver didn't answer his wolf. He wasn't as convinced. The last time he'd stolen a wolf from his father, he'd been banished. How Hale, who was the most protective alpha Oliver knew, would react he didn't know.

But either way, he'd go.

THE EVENING HAD WELL and truly settled over Huntly as Oliver left, and it was fully dark by the time he parked outside Sam's two-storey sprawling house in the middle of the woods. Hale had paid to fix the damage from the attack last month, though Oliver couldn't see the repair from this side.

He remembered the arguments over making all the windows opaque. Oliver hadn't understood why it mattered at the time. Now he thought back to all that bleach and the bullet holes in the wall. There was only one reason Hale would have wanted that. If Sam had been shot rather than just bruised in the attack like they'd claimed.

It was all so obvious now, looking back.

Alpha protected us, protected mate, Thor said, clearly pleased with the strength and power of his alpha. He didn't care that the truth had been hidden. To be fair, neither did Oliver. Or at least he understood why it had been kept secret.

Shaking his head, he held his ribs as he exited the car and headed to the front door. Hale's energy surrounded the property, a casual spread, calm and relaxed rather than angry. A claim that this was his land. His home. Though neither had officially moved in together, they were rarely apart.

Hale met him at the door before he had a chance to knock.

'Sam's sleeping upstairs,' Hale said, looking over his shoulder as he motioned Oliver in. 'If we keep our voices down, we shouldn't wake her.'

Oliver winced at the words, unsure if Hale was reminding himself or Oliver. But he nodded and stepped inside to follow Hale through the house to Sam's kitchen. The faint scent of paint still lingered, but the rest of the room looked normal like the attack had never happened.

'Do you want tea?' Hale said, hands already moving to take out cups from the cupboard.

There was so much Oliver expected to be said, but being offered tea wasn't one of them. He didn't know how to answer. The lack of answer clearly equalled he wanted tea because Hale made two cups.

'I'm sorry for taking Sam to the house,' Oliver said.

Hale's shoulders grew tight. 'Sam explained what she did. It's not your fault,' he said.

His words had been strained, but his energy remained the same. Oliver didn't press, though he wanted to apologise again. There were still plenty of reasons for Hale to be mad at him.

'I can give Amelia back,' Oliver said, carefully suppressing his wolf as he jumped to the surface, realising what he was doing.

Amelia and Mitchel my pack. Not want to let go, Thor snarled. But he didn't let his energy out against Hale. *Fight with words. Keep pack.*

Oliver fought a smile at his wolf's suggestion that he argue with Hale. It wasn't something he thought he'd ever heard Thor suggest before.

'No,' Hale said, not looking up from the tea he was stirring.

'I took her into my pack without asking her. Or you.' Oliver stopped as Hale's energy stirred. The intent was hidden, as was Hale's scent, both carefully neutral, telling Oliver nothing. 'She should have been able to choose.'

'You're right. It's her choice. I've already spoken to her, and Mitchel,' Hale said, still with his back to Oliver as he poured milk into the cups, movements slow and precise. 'Both have decided what they wish to do.'

Not want to lose pack, Thor whispered in his mind, pain sharp.

It will be okay. Hale will keep them safe and protect them, Oliver said.

'They chose to stay,' Hale said, finally turning around, meeting Oliver's eyes. Though he knew he should look away, he didn't. Hale's wolf was there, bright and fierce. But it wasn't angry or challenging him. 'To stay with you.'

Oliver stared at Hale dumbly as he passed the teacup. His wolf howled in joy and triumph. 'I don't understand.'

'Sit,' Hale said, pulling his chair from under the new kitchen table. It had a solid wood top with a metal frame. It was the pack's present to Sam for letting them be able to shift here whenever they wanted. It was made from a fallen tree they'd found on her land.

Oliver lowered himself carefully into the chair opposite Hale, both from pain and shock. This wasn't how he'd expected this conversation to go at all.

'When you came here, you were an alpha with no pack. I thought you'd be trouble, but you were the singularly most controlled Shifter I've ever met. Until someone is in danger at least, but that is a curse of being an alpha,' Hale said, mouth twisting into a semi-smile. 'Why did your father send you here?'

Oliver took a breath, not wanting to relive that particular memory. Especially when Hale probably already knew what had happened. But who knew with Oliver's father?

'I stole two wolves from one of the alphas in my father's pack,' Oliver said, remembering that day: the knife, the frost, the anger and the betrayal—not only his.

'Why did you take them?'

'To protect Mitchel,' Oliver said, staring at his tea. 'Another alpha's son had challenged me to a duel, but his friend had tried to hurt Mitchel to distract me from the fight. I wasn't going to be fast enough to stop him, so I grabbed both of their wolves.' Oliver paused, looking up at Hale. 'The alpha suggested I be sent here as punishment. My father jumped at the chance, claiming it would teach me control.'

'Your father was wrong,' Hale said. 'You don't need to learn to control your wolf. You need to learn how to be an alpha, something your father should have already taught you.'

Oliver shuddered at the weight of Hale's wolf as he leaked out, filled with anger and frustration. It wasn't aimed at Oliver. He could feel it through the changed pack bonds in a way he'd not been able to feel before.

'We'll talk more on this later,' Hale said, pulling in the energy again as he looked up towards the ceiling like he was searching for Sam. Maybe he was. 'Tell me about what you found in the records.'

Oliver took a sip of the tea, barely tasting the hot liquid. 'I found out who was on patrol in that area.' He paused to pull out a piece of paper he'd printed before coming here. It had all the details he'd found. 'Three people had regularly picked up that shift for the last month, but that wasn't all I discovered.'

Over the next hour, Oliver walked Hale through all the connections and lies. By the end, they had a plan to deal with it. Providing they could get all the people in the right place tomorrow. Tired, angry, hurt, and his wolf writhing under his skin, Oliver got up to leave.

'Oliver, one more thing before you go,' Hale said once they were on the porch. A sliver of Hale's energy slipped out, wrapping around Oliver. 'Don't mistake my acceptance of what happened with Amelia as a carte blanche to do anything like this again.'

The unspoken threat was delivered in a mild tone that made Oliver shiver. He lowered his eyes and bared his throat to Hale, acknowledging that both Oliver and his wolf understood. More than a promise. A submission.

'Good,' Hale said, energy pulling back again. 'After this mess is resolved, we'll train together. Something, as I said already, your father should have done.' This time, the snap of anger wasn't aimed at Oliver.

Oliver nodded and stepped down from the veranda.

'If you want to shift to heal your ribs, you should do it tonight,' Hale said, pulling in a breath, then letting it go. 'Then go home, rest. Tomorrow will be a long day, I'm sure.'

Oliver hesitated, then nodded. He'd been so focused on everything else that he'd forgotten he could shift here. Shifting with a broken bone hurt like hell, but he'd rather have the sharp burst than the longer ache any day.

'Thank you,' Oliver said, still feeling slightly lost. Hale had let him keep his pack. Amelia had wanted to stay, and so had Mitchel.

Told you. Mitchel make good pack, Thor said, curling up in the back of his mind around the new links to their pack, satisfied. *Amelia make good pack. We good alpha.*

Oliver smiled, unable to help himself as a sense of peace filled him. Even with the drama coming tomorrow, he felt the best he'd felt in the six months since he'd left home. Probably longer. A lot longer.

But he'd been right about the shift. It hurt like hell. But it meant that tomorrow, he'd be ready for whatever happened.

CHAPTER SIXTEEN

Mitchel stood in Amelia's kitchen, hunting through her freezer for food, when a knock came. It was too early to be Oliver. Unlike the first time he was here, Amelia was with him, leaning against the door frame in a T-shirt and shorts. She stiffened as she drew in a breath, eyes going a brighter blue.

She didn't move to go answer it, but he could feel her curled rage and fury as strong as anything he'd ever felt from her before. He reached out, touching her arm carefully, and her eyes shot to his.

'My mate,' she said, touching Mitchel's face. Her wolf was a whisper of silk against his mind, and his heart skipped a beat at the claim. 'She can't have you.'

There was only one 'she' that made sense. 'I love it when you claim me,' Mitchel said, stepping closer to her so his body pressed against hers. 'My mate.'

The knock came again, harder this time. Amelia's eyes slowly faded back to their darker blue. 'What do we do about Clara?'

'I don't want her,' Mitchel said, letting Amelia feel his words, knowing they were true. He didn't want to leave this spot with her, but he also knew Clara wouldn't go away. 'I'll tell her to leave. Maybe she'll listen.'

Amelia didn't look like she believed him as the knock came harder this time. With a sigh, he pulled back and went to Amelia's front door.

Clara stood on the doorstep looking cold in her too-thin short jacket. Her nose flared as he probably scented Amelia on his skin and him on hers. Clara's eyes darkened.

'You can't have him,' Clara said. His earlier rage bubbled up to the surface, Amelia's echoing it.

'Mine,' Amelia snarled.

Clara's eyes flashed yellow, and he felt Amelia stiffen beside him. For the first time, he sensed what Clara's power looked like. The weakness and frailty that didn't match this woman at all spread around him. Amelia's wolf responded, moving closer to the surface, fighting the need to protect him versus Clara.

'You think you can take him from me?' Clara said, pressing the weakness further. It didn't match the body language or tone. It was toxic, just like her.

Mitchel moved so he stood in front of Amelia, straight through the toxic miasma. It felt like it should have had weight, but it didn't, parting like fog as he moved.

He'd been brought up being taught that women needed protecting. That he should one day be the man of the house, and he needed to act like it. His grandfather's way of thinking. Fighting was frowned upon—any violence was.

Going to Glasgow University after he'd abandoned all his family ties had taught him a very different way to think. All enemies were equal, women and men, and while he avoided fighting as much as possible, he'd learned not to discount any fighter.

Right now, Clara was attacking Amelia, but Clara wasn't using a weapon he could mimic. So, he didn't try. He shifted his weight and curled his fist, aiming for Clara's jaw. She didn't even try to block him as his punch connected. He'd not held back, not against a Shifter, and he felt the impact all the way up his arm.

She flew back from him, stumbling into the snow. Amelia's shock flitted through the link between them.

'Amelia is mine,' Mitchel said. 'You will not hurt her.'

Clara spun to him, scrambling to her feet, hand on her face. She'd heal quickly. He wasn't strong enough to do any real damage to her. Through Amelia, he could feel her wolf as she rose again, sharper and stronger this time, fear making his throat tight and stomach twist. Those gold eyes watched him, unblinking for a heartbeat. Then she lowered them, wolf submitting, backing away. The energy disappeared.

He could see Clara fighting her wolf, trying to bring the energy back so she could use it as a weapon against them. But until now, the Omega energy had meant no one could touch them. Now she knew better, knew there were consequences, and it was obvious she didn't want any part of Clara's games.

'This isn't over,' Clara said as she backed up another step, nearly sliding on the ice. 'I'll watch while Dylan rips you apart for touching his mate. Then he will take her back home where she belongs.'

Mitchel stepped towards Clara at the threat, but Amelia caught him, hand tightly wrapping around his waist.

'Leave,' Amelia growled. 'Before I let my mate loose.'

Clara didn't hang about this time, turning on her heel and jumping into a small Mini, wheels spinning as she left.

His and Amelia's hearts were beating too fast, pounding in sync. This wasn't how he'd imagined their morning would go.

'How bad is your hand?' Amelia asked, voice breathless in his ear. One of the many pleasures of dating someone his height.

He loosened his fist, letting out a low hiss as the pain reached him. 'I've had worse,' he said. His mouth had always got him into trouble more than not.

Amelia tugged him inside, closing the door. She went to the freezer, placing a bag of peas over his hand.

'Thank you,' Amelia said, not looking up at him. 'Her wolf is ...'

'Yeah, I felt it,' Mitchel said, making her head come up. 'Like a cloud, damned near visible.'

'It didn't stop you from hitting her?'

'I don't have a wolf for her to manipulate,' Mitchel said, watching her lips. 'But I don't think her wolf will be quite so helpful in the future.'

Amelia chuffed, eyes flaring to a brighter blue. 'Put her in place. Good mate.'

Mitchel took a slow breath, looking down at the peas, letting his heart steady, but some of Clara's words still lingered in his mind. Something that they had yet to discuss. A sliver of pain slid through him before he could help himself. He wasn't sure he could let Amelia go.

'Dylan was never my mate,' she said, lifting his chin so he was looking her in the eye, letting him feel the weight of the words. 'We never wanted him. We're never going back to him.'

The link between them was bright with her anger and pain at something that had happened that she was hiding from him. But he could sense that she wasn't ready to talk about that yet as she leaned into him, pinning him against the wall.

He could be patient, though. The peas fell to the floor, forgotten as she kissed him. The rest of their short hour before Oliver picked them up was well used.

AMELIA STOOD NEAR THE back of the council hall, leaning against the wall, watching the large crowd. All the rangers were present, including those who should have been off rotation.

The scientists were here too. They'd clustered together near the wall, Dylan and Clara both among them. The former stood with legs wide, arms crossed, and the latter hugged herself, looking like a victim. A yellowing bruise was already almost healed on the side of her face.

Pulling in a breath, Amelia let the mixed scents of the room settle into her nose: unease, fear, stale sweat, cigarettes, bacon. That and so much more that her brain didn't have time to process it. She couldn't make out anyone's scent in the mix.

Mitchel's fingers brushed hers, spreading warmth through her body and loosening a small knot in her chest. It was a shame they'd needed to shower before coming in; she wanted the world to smell her on him.

My mate, Luna said, sitting in the back of her mind, watching, waiting. *Kill traitor, then go back to den.*

She let a smile rise, brushing her fingers over Mitchel's, but didn't look away from the crowd, this time searching for faces rather than scents. Her wolf was right. They had work to do first before she could play. Though killing the traitor wasn't exactly what Hale had in mind.

Oliver had filled her in on the basics as they'd driven in. It was hard to believe that anyone had been so stupid that they'd put all the Rift Bloodlines at risk like this, but they had.

Someone had taken away the chairs and tables since she was last here, and instead, there was a small foot-high box at the far end of the room. Everyone had gathered in front of it.

Hale entered, dressed in black jeans and a T-shirt. Oliver walked to one side, wearing his rift gear, looking like a guard at Hale's back. Patrick, a Fire Elemental with multi-coloured eyes, walked on his other side, wearing the same gear. He'd become the de facto head of all Elementals in this area. He also dealt with the opposite shift to Hale, so she rarely saw the two of them together.

People moved out of their way quickly, even though Hale held his power tightly to his body. When they reached the small stage, all three climbed up, looking at the gathered group. The room grew quiet as Hale stepped forward.

'I know the last few days have been unusual,' Hale said, looking over everyone. 'Scorpions on our borders. Imps leaving the Rift. A wyvern.'

There was movement among those gathered, a shuffle, the scent of unease growing. Everyone had heard a version of yesterday's events by now.

'The patrols I sent out tracked the imps and confirmed they all returned to the Rift Scar. I also want to thank everyone who worked long, hard hours into last night and early this morning to ensure nothing else had broken past the border,' Hale said, nodding to a small group of rangers who still had wet hair and were probably the source of the fresh soap scent.

'We're safe now, and the Rift Scar is under control,' Hale said, looking around as his power rolled out of him, skimming over the room.

The pack energy stirred. It felt strange to Amelia. Like she was looking through misted glass, seeing shadows and shapes of what was on the other side. She could feel it, but it was separate. Disconnected. Mitchel shivered beside her, clearly sensing some part of what she did. This was the first time she'd been near Hale when he'd used the pack magic since she'd become part of Oliver's pack.

She caught Oliver's eye on the stage. A flicker of amber showed, and a flash of his power joined the flow. It was probably lost to the others under Hale's. Amelia could feel it, like Oliver was the rainbow and Hale was the rain, bringing it into focus.

They'd not spoken about their new pack when they'd driven in. She should have asked him first before talking to Hale, especially since Oliver had clearly not wanted to be an alpha before.

Oliver makes good alpha. Protected pack, Luna said. *We will help him learn.*

He did, Amelia said. *Though, I don't know what we can do to help him now. But Hale will.* At least, she hoped he would. Dominance was a strange thing in wolves, driven by instinct that was part human, part wolf.

We help him find mate, too, Luna said. *Find one strong, like Mitchel.*

Amelia turned away from Oliver, trying to smother a choking laugh. It was probably best that she didn't tell Oliver what her wolf wanted to do.

'The source of the problem has been laid at the wyvern's feet.' Hale continued. 'People are saying it was why the imps were driven out of the Rift Scar. That it was why the scorpions set up a nest at the border.' Hale paused again. The room was silent, but some of the energy was changing. A sense that something more was coming. 'I'm here to tell you they're wrong.'

The crowd rippled, sound and movement flowing as people reacted to Hale's comment. Hale didn't let them wait long for their answers.

'Some of the rangers in this group haven't been doing their job,' Hale said, voice going lower until it was almost a growl. 'Two people are dead, and one is critical in the hospital. They put the safety of other rangers and the public at risk. But not only that. They put all the Rift Bloodlines at risk.'

All Rift Bloodlines knew what would happen if the humans decided they were more of a risk than a help.

Hale let the rangers react, though the sounds all blended into a roar. Amelia searched for the faces Oliver had sent her this morning, picked out of the patrol logs, the ones who'd always picked those in that area. The ones who'd failed to do their jobs. They'd paled and were trying to edge away from the group.

'Quiet!' Hale said after a minute. The pack followed the order immediately, but the Elementals obeyed slightly slower. When silence had fallen again, Hale continued. 'Kenneth, Walter, Amos.'

As Hale said their names, the rangers parted, searching for the three men, then backing away from them. Amelia moved forward, Mitchel at her back, so she was at the front of the crowd. The three men tried to back up, but there was nowhere for them to go. They were in their mid-twenties, with hair ranging from brown to black and similar builds. Amos was a Water Elemental, but the other two were wolves. They were pack.

Kill traitor, Luna said, growling in her mind. She had not known what that word had meant yesterday.

Amelia didn't answer her wolf as Kenneth and Walter tried to step away, but Hale's energy wrapped around them, stopping them from moving. She shivered, remembering Shane doing the same to her. But this wasn't the same. He'd done it to hurt her. These two had got people killed.

Mitchel's hand wrapped tightly around hers. It helped ground her. These two men weren't victims. They'd made their choices.

'This is ridiculous. You all know me. We've worked to-gether for months. I wouldn't do this,' Amos said, backing up a step, unaffected by the pack magic.

Lance stepped forward into the open space, something in his hand, a flash of metal. Amos saw it, and Mitchel let out a low whistle of warning. He'd sensed magic. Lance moved forward so fast that she almost didn't see that flash of metal pierce the side of Amos's neck.

Amos screamed, cursing, taking a swing at Lance, but Amos had only ever used guns to attack at a distance. Lance had far better training and strength. In two moves, he disabled Amos, forcing the man to his knees, hands twisted painfully behind his back so he couldn't move.

'That was quick,' Mitchel whispered, smelling faintly uneasy. 'I didn't think it would block his magic that fast.'

Amelia didn't answer, but she squeezed his hand tighter. Knowing that the government had created a way to sta-bilise Rift venom and use it to suppress Elemental and Shifter Magic was one thing, but seeing it used was some-thing else.

Until now, she'd only heard of it being used in pris-ons. But Lance had moved like this hadn't been the first time he'd taken down an Elemental. It made her wonder why Lance—the only other Shifter to stay longer than a year—was still in the pack. His skills were clearly wasted here.

'You can't do this. This is illegal,' Amos said, head forward, body shaking as the venom took effect.

'You're being accused of murder,' Hale said, stepping off the small stage to approach the three men. The crowd opened again, letting Hale through. 'IRS&D will be dealing with you all from here.'

'What? No. We didn't kill anyone,' Kenneth said. There was deep fear pouring from all three men now. If not for Hale, the two wolves would have run. It was a surprise that Kenneth was even able to speak at all.

'You didn't do your job, and now two people are dead, and one may still die,' Hale said, voice carefully controlled.

'I did my job,' Kenneth snarled, but his face had paled even further.

'It would have taken weeks for the scorpions to build that nest. If you had been down there once—just once—in that time, you would have found it and prevented this from happening,' Hale shouted, then he stopped, a slow breath. The evidence that Oliver had found was even more damming, but that was something for the court to review, not an open forum here. 'The courts will decide what to do with you now.'

Three armoured men appeared at the door as if they had been waiting for those words. Amelia didn't recognise them, but they were dominant wolves capable of dealing with the traitors. They had an IRS&D logo but no name or rank on their right shoulders. Lance nodded at them as he handed over Amos, who was still pleading. The wolves nodded back like they recognised Lance.

There was a lot of muttering as the three men were cuffed. The Shifters were put in special ones, meaning they'd break their arms before breaking the metal.

'The rift warden is ultimately responsible for his team's actions, is he not?' Dylan asked, voice loud as he pushed through the rangers, standing opposite Amelia at the front of the crowd. 'Yet you dish out punishment and act like you're not at fault.'

Amelia snarled, stepping forward. Only Mitchel's hand in hers stopped her from going further. She let him. She was able to let him. The anger at seeing Dylan was just that—anger. Not rage. Not the twisting feeling that seemed to have its own power.

Have mate, Luna said, tightening their grip on Mitchel's hand. *Not need rage now.*

She couldn't answer her wolf, feeling lightheaded. The rage she'd been afraid of for so long had been tied to Dylan, linked to how she'd broken his hold on her. It wasn't the same rage as her father's. Maybe she wouldn't end up like him, out of control, and sent into the Rift, never to come back.

Mitchel's warmth threaded through her, wrapping her up in a cocoon that only they could feel. But now wasn't the time to deal with her emotions, not when Dylan was still very likely to cause problems. She squeezed Mitchel's hand one last time, then reluctantly let go. Let herself focus on the present.

The three armoured wolves paused to look at Hale, who nodded. They forced the three traitors towards the door and headed out. What happened here next wasn't their business.

Hale waited until they were gone to turn to Dylan. 'Do you take issue with my ability to do my job?'

'Yes,' Dylan said, a low growl vibrating through the silence.

'Then say it,' Hale said. A low pulse of energy flickered through the room.

Amelia braced for the challenge from Dylan. Because of what the three men had done, Dylan could do it. Though she doubted he'd be strong enough to win.

Dylan snarled once, giving Hale an up-and-down look, lip curling. 'You think you're untouchable because no one wants to be the Highland Rift Scar warden,' Dylan said, letting the words come out slow and measured, but still not a direct challenge. 'But some mistakes aren't forgivable.'

'If IRS&D wishes to investigate the source of the situation here, they're more than welcome. I've provided all the records,' Hale said, smiling wide, showing blunt teeth to Dylan. In their wolf forms, it would have been a threat. 'But until then, I'll continue to do my job.'

The prime alphas hadn't been careful in their planning, and more than enough threads pointed back to them. Whether the IRS&D would do anything about it was another matter.

'An investigation will not be necessary,' Madeline said, stepping forward for the first time. She'd been so silent with the other scientists that Amelia had missed her. 'The IRS&D is satisfied that the matter has been handled, and those at fault were held to account.'

Dylan stiffened like Madeline had hit him. He turned to stare at her, eyes flashing yellow, but Madeline didn't react to the glare. There was no way they could have investigated that quickly.

Amelia glanced at Oliver. This hadn't been what she'd expected to happen. They'd been certain Dylan would challenge Hale. But someone was yanking Dylan back.

Amelia hated pack politics. She couldn't help her relief that there wouldn't be a challenge.

'That's good to hear,' Hale said, eyes not leaving Dylan's.

'This isn't over,' Dylan growled, turning to Amelia, pulling a breath, scenting Mitchel on her despite the shower. Again, she expected that rage to rise, and it didn't. His eyes flickered colour, but he didn't speak to her as he turned to stalk away. The gathered rangers parted before he reached them.

'I wanted to take the time to thank you, Hale, and all your people, for protecting us while we worked,' Madeline said, continuing as if Dylan hadn't threatened Hale. 'It was unfortunate we were unsuccessful in our investigation, but should it be necessary to visit again, I'll be sure to reach out.'

Mitchel's frustration curled through their bond. The scent of the room shifted with it, uncertainty moving to surprise. The IRS&D were leaving? They hadn't done anything yet.

When Hale didn't reply, Madeline nodded and turned to leave. The rest of the scientists followed her closely. Clara stuck to the group's centre, giving Mitchel a wide berth, stinking of fear. Mitchel stayed with Amelia, and Madeline never even looked at him.

The gathered rangers muttered, exchanging glances.

'I know many of you have questions,' Hale said, taking a slow breath as he looked everyone over. 'I'll do my best to answer these over the next few days, but there's one thing that I wanted to address today.' Everyone grew quiet.

'Many of you are here as punishment,' Hale said, and the crowd shifted on nervous feet. 'People who don't want to be here are a risk I'm no longer willing to take. I'll be speaking to all the prime alphas over the next week, and any Shifter who doesn't want to be here and serve their year will be sent home. Patrick will be having the same conversations with the Elementals.'

There was silence in the announcement's wake. The scent of shock and uncertainty. Hope in some cases. Mitchel retook her hand as she considered what it would mean. How many would go?

'We'll meet again in a few days to discuss and answer questions, but for now, you're all dismissed to go about your day,' Hale said.

No one moved for a moment, and then slowly, the first person turned to leave. Then another. When the room had dwindled down to Oliver, Patrick, Mitchel, Lance and her, Hale drew in a breath.

'That was unexpected,' Hale said, giving a small smile. 'But probably just delays the inevitable.'

'Dylan doesn't deserve the right to challenge you,' Oliver said, voice a low rumble, amber shining in his eyes.

'Stupid way to resolve your differences,' Patrick said, shaking his head. But it was half-hearted and an argument he'd likely had before because he didn't wait for an answer. 'I'll make sure the patrols are on track and introduce the new varied schedules to keep people mixed.'

'Thank you. The mayor has set up a meeting tomorrow, and he will want the full details presented to the local council,' Hale said. 'Though I've updated him personally already.'

'I'll be there. I'm sure Joyce is going to have a field day with us,' Patrick said, emphasis on the last word and his next ones. 'I'll see you tomorrow.'

Hale nodded, a smile on his lips as he clearly recognised the word choice as well. This wasn't just pack business, this was ranger business, and Patrick stood with Hale. 'The rest of you go home, rest. Patrick has the patrols covered.'

Amelia wanted to argue, but she didn't know where to start. Or what to say. The prime alphas had backed off for now, but for how long? Offering to let the Shifters leave would only weaken the pack and make them more vulnerable.

She felt Oliver's discontent, too, his worry and fear. A challenge, though risky, would have put an end to the games. This was just going to drag it out.

Unable to do anything else, she went home with Mitchel, letting him distract her. Much later, Oliver brought food, pizza, enough that they had to shove leftovers in the fridge.

None of them spoke about the past few days. Or their new little pack. Those were things they'd deal with tomorrow. Today, they just let themselves be.

CHAPTER SEVENTEEN

Amelia let her mind wander as Oliver drove them both to Sam's house. It had been three days since the wyvern was killed, and Hale was having the Shifters gather to answer questions and allow people to leave as promised. Patrick was doing the same with the Elementals at the ranger headquarters.

The snow was starting to melt, turning it slushy. The weather warden was being careful not to let it melt too fast so it didn't cause floods.

'It's going to be okay,' Oliver said as she shuffled in her seat again, his pack energy spilling around her, offering comfort and easing some of her worries.

They still hadn't really spoken about the fact they were now their own little sub-pack, except for her to re-iterate that she wanted to stay with him. With Mitchel.

Like pack. But better when Oliver finds mate, Luna said, making her hide her smile. How her wolf thought she would find Oliver's mate when they were so rare, she didn't know, but she'd given up arguing with her wolf on the matter.

'Being okay and liking it aren't the same thing,' Amelia said, knowing she sounded sulky. But when Hale's entire pack could be leaving, it made her stomach knot. Even though she didn't have a direct connection to Hale anymore, she still hated it.

Oliver sighed and nodded. 'I wish he hadn't made the offer.'

'What happens if so many leave that we can't patrol the Rift Scar?' Amelia asked, stomach knotting again.

'They'll have to wait until new people arrive first, most likely,' Oliver said, adjusting his grip. 'If new people want to come of their own choice.'

Before she could answer, the road opened up into a wide yard. A dozen cars were already there, meaning they were probably among the last to arrive. Oliver parked with the rest of the vehicles, and she got out into the slushy mud. The scents of the pack surrounded her, all of them familiar.

The land brushed against her senses even with her thick boots on. The feeling of home and welcome was so strong she stopped to let it soak into her. It was like it could sense her worry and fear and was trying to make it better. Something that hadn't been there before Hale had brought Sam into the pack.

'I'm not sure I'll ever get used to this feeling,' Oliver said, pulling in a deep breath, eyes amber as he looked over the trees at the edge of the clearing. 'Or what I'm going to do when I have to leave at the end of my year.'

'Who says you have to leave?' Amelia said, pulling in another deep breath as her wolf damned near purred. Happy with Amelia's decision.

Not purr. Not cat. Am wolf, Luna said, disgusted with the comparison.

'I wish it was that easy,' Oliver asked, watching her. When she didn't answer, his eyes widened, energy sharp. 'You're serious?'

'It's not official yet. But Hale says he's going to sort it.' It wasn't an easy thing to negotiate. Her old family alpha had to agree, though, from the way Alaric had spoken when she'd left to come here, she didn't expect an argument from him. 'I can stay as long as I want. He's going to offer to everyone.'

To go home, to finish their term, or to stay. That was what he was going to offer.

'Would you have imagined three months ago that you'd have wanted to stay?' Oliver said, shaking his head. 'Could any of us? It's not an easy life working in any Rift Scar.'

'I like it here, and while the job isn't easy, it feels good. I feel good. I feel like I belong for the first time in a long time.'

'I envy you that,' Oliver said, but he smiled. 'I wish I had the same choice, but I doubt my father would allow it. He's already displeased with Hale allowing me to become alpha.'

Amelia winced. She'd never met his father, but the hints of pain she got from Oliver made her never want to. As much as she wanted to ask him to stay, too, it had to be his choice. A choice he clearly didn't feel like he had.

Protect alpha, Luna said, seemingly unworried. *Find him mate.*

A gust of wind caught her hair, twisting it, bringing the cold close.

'Come on, let's go inside and see what happens,' Oliver said as he headed towards Sam's house. 'All going well, you should be able to head off with Mitchel later today.'

Amelia fought a different kind of nervous flutter as she followed Oliver towards the front door of Sam's house. She was going to meet Mitchel's parents to help him tell them that he was going to train to use Frost Magic.

But first, pack business.

Hale answered the questions where he could, re-iterating his announcement about allowing those who didn't want to be there to leave, offering everyone the choice. He was tightly controlled, holding his wolf so close that she couldn't feel it at all. Oliver was doing the same.

'What about our bonds to our family pack?' Ivan asked from near the back. He slouched as the attention focused on him.

'If you choose to stay, your families will officially release you into this pack. If you wish to leave at any point or only serve the rest of the set term, I'll release you once you are ready,' Hale said, looking around at the wolves. 'We've been half a pack for too long. No matter how many choose to stay, there will be no half-measure links. We will be a pack, and this will be your home.'

That caused mixed reactions and more questions. How would it be managed and agreed upon? What if they wished to go home for a month and then come back at the end? Hale didn't have all the answers, but he promised to make the process clear.

By the end of the meeting, nearly a fifth had accepted Hale's offer to be released home. It slashed the pack down to twenty-odd strong. No one else but her committed to staying permanently except Lance, who had already gone past when he should have left.

It would take weeks, maybe even months, before all the decisions were made and they knew where they stood.

Potentially longer still before they knew if others would choose to come without it being a punishment. Not to mention how the prime alphas were going to react.

Overall, it was a long, tough day, and she was glad to slip into the warmth of Mitchel's rental to get away from it all. Even if it was only for the night.

MITCHEL TOOK THE CUP of tea offered to him and muttered a thank you. Amelia did the same, her thank you clearer.

He shifted uncomfortably in the kitchen chair, feeling like his skin wanted to walk off on its own. His family home didn't have many good memories but sitting at his dining room table with his father and mother opposite him and Amelia beside him felt strange.

'So, you're Mitchel's girlfriend?' his mum asked Amelia.

His mum had dyed her hair a light shade of blond. It looked nearly natural, but her grey roots were showing. The rest of her was just as he remembered. She was tall and thin, with a lifted chin as she looked down at the rest of the world. She kept moving nervously. His father, by comparison, was quiet and relaxed, with his grey hair slicked back and a newspaper folded at his side.

Amelia gave Mitchel a little nudge, and he realised he'd missed her answer. He thought back. Yes. She'd said yes. He smiled at her, wishing he was anywhere else so he could lean in and kiss her.

That she'd agreed to come with him to see his family—insisted, really—made him feel a warmth in his chest that he wasn't sure he'd ever felt. She reached down under the table and put her hand on his knee.

'So how did you two lovebirds meet?' his mum asked, playing with her own cup of tea.

'I'm going to learn how to use my Frost Magic,' Mitchel said bluntly, wincing as his mother inhaled sharply.

'I don't think this is the place to have this conversation,' she said as she stood, scraping the chair back behind her. 'It's family business.'

'I think this is the perfect place,' Mitchel's father said, remaining seated. 'In fact, it's long overdue.'

'Howard,' his mum said, voice cold.

'I almost died last week,' Mitchel said, throat tightening as he remembered everything that had happened. 'If I'd known how to use my power, I'd have been better placed to protect myself and those around me. Instead, I almost killed us.'

Amelia tightened her grip on his knee, offering support. They'd had this conversation more than once on the drive down to Glasgow. Now he was here, none of the words he'd rehearsed with Amelia came to him.

'There's no reason to exaggerate, Mitchel. I know how big your imagination has always been,' his mum said dismissively as she turned to Amelia. 'He was always making up stories as a boy.'

'With respect,' Amelia said, voice holding a touch of her wolf. It made Mitchel shiver as he felt the protective wave of it surround him. 'Your son isn't making up stories. Nor is he a boy.'

His mum narrowed her eyes as she lifted her chin just a fraction. She didn't like being talked back to.

'I've come to tell you I'm going to be looking for someone who can help train me to use my powers,' Mitchel said before his mum could argue again. 'I don't imagine it will take long before it reaches the gossip mills, so I wanted you to know first.'

'Tell him he can't do that, Howard,' his mum said, looking at his dad.

But his dad said nothing as he got up and left the room. Mitchel's stomach dropped. This is about how he'd expected this meeting to go. But it didn't make it hurt any less.

'See what you're doing to your father,' his mum continued. He could see her panic. Her fear. 'You've no respect for this family, what we have done for you. What we have given you.'

Mitchel stood, Amelia rising with him, taking his hand. When he'd initially decided to lie about what he was, his mum's fear had been what swayed his younger self. But he was done living his life for her.

Before he could take a step away, his father returned, putting away a set of reading glasses into his top pocket. Something else that had changed. He held a small white envelope with Mitchel's name written on it.

His dad handed the envelope to Mitchel. 'I may not know who your father is,' he said, looking at his mother coldly, 'but I was able to find a Frost Elemental. He's well regarded as one of the best with the ability in the UK, which I know doesn't say a lot. There aren't many of them here. But he's willing to train you.'

Mitchel's throat was too tight to risk speaking out loud, so instead, he nodded jerkily as he took the envelope. This wasn't something his dad could have done quickly. He'd have to have found someone and then talked to them. But he'd done it and had it ready for when Mitchel asked.

'Don't be ridiculous, Howard. He doesn't need a trainer. Think about how it will look to your father,' his mum said. The argument felt exactly the same as last time. The same desperation. The same manipulation.

'Quite frankly, I'm tired of worrying what my father thinks,' his dad said. 'I'm tired of it all.'

His mum stepped back like he'd slapped her. 'You're going to ruin everything.'

'I'm setting your son free,' his dad said, nodding at Mitchel. 'Something we should have done a long time ago.'

Amelia's hand tightened around his, and he looked at her. She tilted her head towards the door. She was right. It was time to leave. This wasn't something that his mother was going to accept.

Before he left, he turned back to his dad. 'Thank you,' Mitchel said, wishing that the years of distance between them meant it was impossible to do something as simple as hug him.

His dad nodded while his mother kept talking. Only Amelia's low growl stopped her from following them out. But the argument continued inside.

'You did good,' Amelia said.

'Then why do I feel like shit?'

'Because you're a good person,' Amelia said, giving him a smile. 'It's par for the course.'

Mitchel laughed, feeling some pressure loosen around his chest as he looked again at the envelope. Today hadn't gone how he'd expected.

'Thank you for coming with me,' Mitchel said, pulling Amelia in for a kiss.

He probably had a long way to go before he learned to understand his power, but at least he had a direction now.

AMELIA STOOD ON THE border between the pack lands and the Rift Scar. The snow had melted, leaving a grey muddied landscape as it struggled to handle the excess water.

It was barren except for the small patch of grass by her feet. It had been a week since Mitchel had been brought into the pack.

'Do we know how far it's moved yet?' Mitchel asked.

'Another mile,' Amelia said, moving to lean against him. 'Is Sam going to report it?'

'No,' Mitchel said, wrapping his arm around her slightly awkwardly with their body armour getting in the way. 'Madeline had officially marked the changes as weather-related, and due to old devices that have become inaccurate over time.'

There was bitterness in his words. Amelia could understand why. IRS&D had decided that the changes didn't need to be investigated. Scientists were supposed to push to find the truth, yet Madeline had let them cover it up.

'It's not like two miles of green grass could be a mistake on a machine,' Amelia said, shaking her head. Amelia felt a stirring of guilt. Part of why they'd decided not to investigate was because they didn't know all the facts.

'I'm going to keep studying it,' Mitchel said, nodding sharply.

Nervous energy made Amelia want to fidget. 'Does that mean you're staying?' It was the one thing that they hadn't really spoken about yet. After everything with his family, she wanted to give him time to figure it out.

Mitchel pulled back to look at her, giving her a smile. 'Like you can get rid of me that easily.' He hesitated, taking a slow breath. 'IRS&D has agreed to let me work remotely and specialise in this Rift Scar. If you want me to stay?'

Amelia pulled him down towards her for a kiss, ignoring the awkward feel of the body armour that stopped her from pressing herself fully against him. 'Yes.'

'Though I really hope we can decorate your living room, that white is a lot,' Mitchel said as he pulled back, a smile wide on his mouth.

'I'll think about it,' Amelia said, looking behind them. There were still patches of grey on the ground, but the green was mixing with it.

There was a lot to still figure out. The other prime alphas. The IRS&D. But seeing the grass made her hope that maybe, with Mitchel's help, they could figure out why the pack lands were affecting the Rift Scar.

TO BE CONTINUED IN BOOK THREE OF THE HIGHLAND RIFT PACK SERIES

PREQUEL SHORT STORY

In "Those Who Break Us Down," readers will join Mitchel on a journey of self-discovery as he searches for his magic and confronts the harsh realities of a life he never imagined.

In "Those Who Hope We Break," Amelia longs for freedom and faces a shocking revelation that threatens to upend everything she's ever known.

If that isn't enough to entice you over, you will also find other free short stories, including the prequel stories for book 1.

HIGHLAND RIFT PACK SERIES

Battered by Storms

Book 3 of the Highland Rift Pack Series

Staci's storm magic has always set her apart from the rest of the town, but she's always had her mum. Until now. With her mother's mind and health in decline, Staci faces the prospect of a life of isolation.

Oliver's family has always told him that he'll never amount to anything, but now he's an Alpha with a pack of his own. But not for long. At the end of his year at the Highland Rift Scar, he must give them both up, even if he has more than one reason to stay.

When a dangerous storm hits the town, Staci's magic fails her, and only Oliver can protect her from the destructive force trying to drain her magic. As the storm finally dissipates, Staci is blamed for the storm's creation, and Oliver is faced with an impossible choice that could put everyone he loves in danger.

Can Oliver find a way to keep Staci safe and protect his pack, or will forces beyond their control tear them apart?

Join Staci and Oliver in this thrilling paranormal romance novel as they weather the storm and find a way to be together. Will they be able to withstand the storm and find a way to be together, or will they be torn apart forever? Find out in the third book of the Highland Rift Pack Paranormal Romance Series.

https://jemmaweir.com/books/highland-rift-pack/battered-by-storms/

WISHING FOR TRUTHS

Contemporary Fantasy Short Story

Vanessa considers her mother's drinking and crazy schemes her biggest problem. Until she meets the Genie.

When Vanessa finds a bottle on her doorstep, the last thing she expects is a wish-granting Genie. What could go wrong with a wish for her two friends and herself? Everything.

On top of that, her mothers' newest scheme is starting to unravel, and the only help Vanessa can think of is the Genie. But he's refusing to come out of his bottle. Now Vanessa must use nothing but the truth to help her friends before her mother ruins everything.

This is a story about wishes gone wrong and a Genie who isn't telling the whole truth, served with a dash of Romance.

Buy this Short Story now and join Vanessa as she learns what it means to 'be careful what you wish for.'

https://jemmaweir.com/books/standalone/wishing-for-truths/

THE LIFE AND CHAOS OF A RETIRED OLD GOD

Humour, Magic and Old Gods who should know better: A Collection of Ernie Smith Short Stories

Being retired was supposed to be easy. No drama, no family, no problems. Considering Ernie is a god, he should've known better.

In this collection of short stories, Ernie struggles to live a quiet life as Death loses his scythe, a genie wants a holiday, and Ernie's family keeps dropping in.

Then there's Ragnarok. Because who doesn't need an end-of-the-world event to keep things calm and quiet?

But it doesn't stop there. This collection contains a brand new bonus short story where Ernie is asked to mediate a feud between Dragons. With tensions running high, maybe the poker game wasn't the best idea.

Also included in this collection is a series of flash fiction originally published on my blog. Follow Ernie as he deals with Cupid shooting the wrong person, Wererabbits for April Fools, Santa stuck in the chimney, and what happens to snowmen when the weather changes.

The Life and Chaos of a Retired Old God is a collection of humorous short stories where Ernie learns that quiet is the last thing he's going to get.

https://jemmaweir.com/books/the-life-and-chaos-of-a - retired-old-god/

ABOUT AUTHOR

Too many Ideas - Never enough time

How many jobs let you build your own world? Create strange magic? Develop a diverse cast of people who will live on in the minds of others?

As an author, Jemma Weir gets to do all these things and more, as her cats chase unicorns across the breakfast table, and werewolves dig holes in the garden to torment her chihuahua, it is always an interesting day.

Fantasy books have always been her first love, from dragons to werewolves, and vampires to elves. Now, as she writes her own stories, she pulls together myths and legends, and all the crazy worlds that are her own to create stories she loves.

Working from her Scottish home, she writes fantasy, with a dash of humour, and a pinch of sass.

Want to keep up to date on new releases and get some free stories? Check out my social media or join my newsletter by clicking on the link below.

https://www.jemmaweir.com/newsletter

https://www.jemmaweir.com/blog

https://www.facebook.com/JemmaWeirAuthor

https://www.instagram.com/jemmaweir

www.ingramcontent.com/pod-product-compliance
Lightning Source LLC
Chambersburg PA
CBHW050958180726
48291CB00006B/1890